BARRY SADLER

Barry Sadler was a legend among fighting men everywhere. A Special forces and Vietnam combat veteran, he rose to fame with his hit song, "The Ballad of the Green Berets," and his phenomenally successful adventure series, *Casca*. He is also the author of numerous military thrillers including *Razor* and *Rescue*. In addition to his careers in the armed forces, the recording business, and writing, Mr. Sadler fought in various armed conflicts as a mercenary.

His sudden tragic death in 1989 shocked the world. But the legend of Barry Sadler will live forever through his dramatic and authentic novels. . . .

CASCA
The Eternal Mercenary

The unforgettable saga of a soldier cursed by Christ and doomed to fight forever, the *Casca* series is Barry Sadler's most exciting creation. In his never-ending adventures, Casca is plunged into battles across the world . . . and across time. The Vietnam War, the Middle East, the Mongol Rebellion, the Spanish conquest of the Aztecs, World War I, World War II—these are just a few of the wars Casca must fight . . . for all eternity!

Over Two Million Casca Books in Print!

D1293288

CASCA
THE DEFIANT

Paul Dengelegi

JOVE BOOKS, NEW YORK

CASCA: THE DEFIANT

A Jove Book / published by arrangement with
the author

PRINTING HISTORY
Jove edition / November 2001

Visit our website at
www.penguinputnam.com

ISBN: 0-515-12954-2

A JOVE BOOK®
Jove Books are published by The Berkley Publishing Group,
a division of Penguin Putnam Inc.,
375 Hudson Street, New York, New York 10014.
JOVE and the "J" design
are trademarks belonging to Penguin Putnam Inc.

PRINTED IN THE UNITED STATES OF AMERICA

10 9 8 7 6 5 4 3 2 1

ONE

" *aus aus dem zug!*" The unpleasant throaty sound awakened Dr. Goldman from his slumber.

"*Nächste Halt Strassburg!*" He heard as he tried to focus. The setting sun made Dr. Goldman's eyes water as he looked through the opened train door. He reached toward his neck to find it covered with sweat and grime.

He inhaled deeply, shaking the ugly memories the rough language had reawakened. Looking at his watch, he noted he had been asleep for nearly an hour. Recollecting his dreams he figured it was better to stay awake from now on than return to his nightmares.

Dr. Goldman stretched out and placed his feet up onto the opposite seat. Rubbing his knees he realized how stiff they had gotten over the long train ride. He winced while his hands ran over the anterior cruciate ligament of his right knee. It had not been a sports or war injury, just the remaining soreness from the old method of repairing ligaments and tendons. He grimaced in pain as he recalled slipping on the ice while handling the quarter keg of beer. At the time carrying the fraternity elixir had seemed important, but now he would have gladly traded it for a sound knee.

A few more minutes and he would be in Strassburg. A warm and hearty meal was not far away, along with a good night's sleep. There was nothing like your own bed, but staying with his cousin was still much better than an impersonal hotel room and—

"*. . . nimm die Füsse runter . . .*" Goldman did not understand completely what had been said so quickly, but the tone of it made the message fairly clear. He rapidly pulled his feet off the seat and drew them underneath his own. A painfully overweight woman sat down across from him, her orange rat-dog jumping right next to her. She sat, but her body refused to stop gyrating for a few seconds longer. It was unlikely she had turned down too many meals or adhered to strict portion control in recent years.

Definitely not a prime member of the herrenvolk, Goldman thought. Gasping for air, she attempted to adjust her harness-like brassiere. Her hands dug in underneath the wire mesh, bringing ever-quickening beads of sweat from her brows down to her face and neck. The aroma that hovered around her did not endear her either as it was only quenched by the wet fur smell of her little prize that drooled loudly. It was not a pretty sight and Dr. Goldman considered closing his eyes. Only the voice of the stone-faced *schaffner*, the ticket taker, again raking against his ears, prevented him from doing so.

"The bench is not for your dirty shoes. Are you American?" The broken English words of the *schaffner* scratched at Goldman's ears.

"Yes, American," he responded.

"Have a good day." The sour words and unmeant feeling of the ticket taker remained in Goldman's ears and eyes for a while.

He looked across to see the small terrier sitting up, tongue wagging, dripping sticky drool onto the floor and the edge of the bench.

Definitely a male, no question about it, Goldman thought while closing his eyes, trying to erase the image from his mind. Apparently the dog's four paws and privates were less of a cleanliness concern than Goldman's new Bruno Maglis.

Strassburg could not come fast enough. Grabbing his briefcase and suitcase Dr. Goldman left the train, anxious to end this long day of travel. A ten-minute cab ride brought him to his cousin Peter's house. It was a pleasant night with good food and conversation, revisiting old times and childhood pranks. An oversized Robusto hung from Goldman's fingers for nearly an hour until the powerful flavor of the tobacco demanded a break. It had been an embargo treat Goldman only enjoyed overseas.

The eagerly welcomed bed creaked under his stiff back, but one could not complain as it was a two-hundred-year-old bed, supposedly worth thousands. Creaky as it was, it would have been considered an antique of great value in the States, while here it was something people slept on when tired.

The following day was Dr. Goldman's to spend as he wished. The conference was not until the day after, ten hours of interminable lectures were at the waiting. Professor Helmut Dieter was "a brilliant man," as Dr. Goldman was constantly reminded, but Dieter was also a man that demanded super-human feats from his audience. Dieter refused to change tone for the five-hour morning and afternoon sessions, sounding not unlike white noise designed to help infants sleep. The proverbial watching paint dry would have been more desirable. Dr. Goldman remembered one of his colleagues joking about how a slow root canal, preferably performed without anesthesia, would have been more welcome and still less monotonous.

Dieter's subject matter was dry and arduous, although very important, still the effort it took to follow along demanded a day off all on its own. Using silk sutures, so thin that light refused to bounce off of, to train on was challenging enough. The philanthropic rats that had donated their femoral nerves for the workshop exercises were also something Dr. Goldman did not look forward to. Working on dead rats, unlike the previous year, did not make it any less miserable. He looked at the map and realized Mainz was only about ten minutes by train. This was an opportunity not to be missed.

Mainz was a German town as any. Clean, proper, and filled with stiff, hygienic people. Once in a while a smile came to his eyes, but not too often. A few disturbingly overweight people waddled by, most of them yammering on in a very familiar east-coast accent. No bratwurst kiosk had been left undisturbed by the tourists on this day. It was a hot day for early June, almost soggy and heavy, unfortunately adding to the unwelcome ripe aroma of the overseas visitors. Goldman turned his head and held his breath for a few seconds. It was time to pick up the pace. Not wanting to be overly pampered by civilization, he decided to walk to his destination.

It was not long before he reached a small plaza, just adjacent to the museum. Dozens of merchants filled every square foot of the opening, placing tables covered with goods wherever there was open space. Shopkeepers and traders lauded their items with the same enthusiasm as it had been done for thousands of years in all corners of the world. This day and place was no different. Spargel was the item of the day, dominating the plaza, hanging, bunching, or piling on everyone's display. Its taste was fair, making good soup or stew, but definitely not worth all the attention.

Walking through the cobblestone plaza, Dr. Goldman found his way to his destination. "Johannes Gutenberg Museum," the sign read.

"This is it." An American voice caught his ears. "This is it Lori; isn't this exciting?"

"Remind me to hose you down later, Jill; it is only a museum. Just a place to store old stuff!" Her friend responded with angst as she shook her head and rolled her eyes.

Goldman watched the girls run up the few stairs and disappear inside the museum. His eyes widened as he watched the shapely blonde weave her way up the stairs. With metronomelike precision her perfect hips swayed underneath a slender waist, hypnotizing his weary eyes. Her thin tanned legs carried her out of his sight, for an instant angering him for missing the opportunity to admire them longer. Apparently he was not as tired as he had thought. Following them in, Goldman paid his four marks while he watched the girls giggle their way into the first room.

"Stop teasing your hair; these poor locals will just have to be disappointed with a bad coif; the gods of hair will not condemn you to purgatory just for one day's failure." The blonde laughed at her friend.

"Enough! You know how important my hair is to me," the brunette demanded, unable to stop picking at her mane even for a minute.

"I do, that's why it is impossible not to tease you. You will just have to wait until we return home so you can see your personal hairdresser. . . . I am sure she misses you, too . . . you baby," the blonde jabbed as she ran ahead.

The two laughed their way into another room, not the type of behavior one would have expected in a museum, especially in Germany, but the two were on their vacation, definitely not rehearsing for ambassadorial duty.

It was pleasantly cool inside the museum, which Dr. Goldman welcomed eagerly. The long walk from the train station had made him break into a sweat, but now he felt refreshed and cool. He had read and heard of the Gutenberg Museum ever since he could remember. Curious how such an important man in the history of the world was not well known by most, he thought. After all, many historians credited him with helping bring much of Europe out of the dark ages. And a long and harrowing journey it had been.

With the ability to produce a mass quantity of the written word, religious or secular, information could easily be available to most, if not to everyone. The arduous task of penning every copy by hand was to be in the past. Sadly, he had been a man vastly underappreciated.

With a bounce in his step, Dr. Goldman made his way up the stairs to the second floor and the famous vault room. It was smaller and darker than he had imagined it, but it held one of the nearly perfectly preserved copies of the Bible and a few other books and manuscripts. Other than the one in the National Library of Congress in Washington, D.C., this was the best-preserved copy. The room was cooler than the rest of the museum, walls heavily reinforced with all that a bank walk-in safe would offer, including a painfully stiff, armed guard. Goldman eyed the young man who gazed out into infinity with his gray-blue eyes.

"Good morning," Goldman attempted, for a moment forgetting where he was. This guard would have made the guards at Buckingham Palace look like hyperactive children, he thought to himself. The man continued looking deep into the far wall, perhaps hypnotizing himself to be able to get through the mind-numbing job.

"Hey, do you think he could fog up a mirror?" Lori, the brunette whispered to her friend while pulling at her hair.

"I dare you. On second thought, forget it, I just remembered what you did to that vicar in Rome. Maybe we can leave out this country. We don't have to embarrass ourselves in all of Europe," the blonde responded, dragging her friend out of the room.

Dr. Goldman stood alone in the vault room, pleased to have the solitude in which to take in all that this place offered. With history lying a few inches from his hands behind the thick protective plastic, he smiled. The middle of the room held one of the Gutenberg Bibles, opened halfway through, beneath the nearly impenetrable layer of wired plastic. The thin wiring was certainly hooked up to a sophisticated and sensitive security system. For a moment a dim light flickered in the room, causing Dr. Goldman to squint and refocus.

There it was, the majestic Gothic type, almost romantic in its feel, more rounded, with smoother lines than the later works of Gutenberg. As if the gentle letters had been reserved for the holy scriptures.

Dr. Goldman's fingers caressed the letters from behind the protective glass, his hands longing to touch the work of the great master. Unfulfilled by the frustrating experience, he turned away from the Latin script. On the walls, a few more books were displayed in reinforced frames behind the same type of protective plastic. Dr. Goldman looked at them curiously, wondering what else Johannes Gutenberg had chosen to print. He read on, but it was difficult to determine what the books were. Probably not of as great importance as Goldman figured it was.

Suddenly, his eyes became glued to the top of one of the pages. The dark, nearly pointed, and obtrusive type grabbed Dr. Goldman's attention as he tried to read the words behind the poorly lit plastic protective layer. A sentence was ending followed by half a page of empty space and an apparently unrelated paragraph.

In the cool air-conditioned room Dr. Goldman became drenched in sweat. ". . . the one calling himself Longinus." The words burned themselves into Dr. Goldman's soul. He read the line over and over, hoping that he had missed something of possible significance. Angrily he mouthed the words, clearly displeased at how the following chapter appeared to be unrelated to the previous.

Unable to help himself, he grabbed the plastic lid and foolishly attempted to open it. It was obvious he would not succeed, but the significance of what was hidden behind it overtook his actions.

"Verboten, American!" The strident words froze Goldman in his tracks. It was as if he were back on the train again. The guard had walked up behind him, giving him an eye of disapproval and annoyance. The man slapped at his side arm, the ring on his finger clicking against the clip of the Mauser. No doubt a full clip, the firing pin anxiously at the ready.

Skewing his eyes at Goldman, he walked out and repositioned himself adjacent to the doorway.

Dr. Goldman stepped back, startled by the man's actions and the words of admonishment that still rang in his ears.

"Is it possible for me to look at this book?" he found himself asking the guard in German.

"Verboten!" was the only reply.

"Are there any more of Johannes Gutenberg's works that can be looked at? Perhaps things that are not on display?" he inquired, accentuating the words *"on display,"* while he reached for his wallet.

The guard glared at him and squinted his eyes. He watched Goldman's pleading face.

"Verboten!" He again answered with a sour smile on his face, yet he signaled for Goldman to follow him. A few feet away from the vault a large metal doorway stopped their advance.

"Six tonight," the guard whispered into his right hand while his evidently well-practiced left hand took the wad of money Goldman had offered him. Goldman was apprehensive, nearly like a prisoner in a Turkish jail offering the cross-eyed warden a bribe, yet he could not help himself.

Six in the evening came excruciatingly slow. Goldman had sat at a *bierstube* next to the museum, nearly drowning in half-a-dozen iced teas while the afternoon dragged on. A few locals had gazed at him, wondering why the fragile American did not partake in the unlimited supply of cold beer. By five thirty he made his way back to the second floor and the vault, unable to wait any longer.

The guard was no longer there, making Goldman's heart sink. Another had taken his place, somehow looking even stiffer and more distant than the previous one had been. Goldman looked around, but could not find the other guard. A few people milled in the area, one of them taking flashless pictures, while others eagerly discussed the significance of Gutenberg's accomplishments.

There was nothing that he could do and no one to complain to. He bit his lip, reinjuring a paper cut that had been stinging his lip since earlier that day. He walked toward the guard who, just as the one earlier, looked toward the far wall without any apparent purpose.

Imperceptible at first, he noted the guard tighten the lid around his left eye, as if attempting to point. Following the line of sight, Goldman found his way to the large metal door he had been walked to a few hours before. He looked at his Longines. It was just a few seconds before six.

"Ten seconds before I have to reset the alarm." A clear voice from the now-opened door came to his ears. The guard from earlier in the day stood in the darkness of the hallway leading into a lower room. Without a moment's thought, Goldman followed the man down the concrete stairs. It was cold and nearly dark, only the glow of a red security system light leading him to his destination.

"One hour, after that you must be gone. That is all," the guard's unyielding Bavarian-flavored voice ordered him.

Dr. Goldman stood at the entrance to a relatively small room. It was poorly lit, yet he could discern boxes of books, some old printing equipment, and reams of apparently unused paper. The coldness of a flashlight found its way into his shaking left hand as the guard handed it to him and then left the room. He was not certain what he was searching for, yet he found himself in a possible gold mine.

Holding the flashlight over his head like a dagger in battle, he feverishly searched. Boxes upon boxes crowded the dark and mildewy room, the heaviness of the air smothering his lungs. The sweat from his brow unceasingly ran down his forehead, burning his eyes and face, his glasses constantly slipping down his nose from the sweat and grime. The slightest ray of light had found its way through a crack in the foundation, aiding him in his search. The yellow light fanned over his body, lighting the swirling dust his feet had kicked up. Ankle-deep in debris and filth, he searched knowing his time was running out. At times he stopped, bewildered at how it had all been allowed to deteriorate, allowing pieces of history to be buried in this disorder and ignorance.

Exhausted and filthy he held a thick parchment in his trembling hands. His face was blacker than night from all the dust and grime the basement had held all these years. He had taken no care in keeping clean. The madness of the search had almost distorted his mind, his hands frantically opening any container time had allowed. But now he stood with his prize in his hands.

Holding the parchment on his knees, he crouched against the door and opened the drawstrings that held the stack of papers together. The string ripped and sheets of paper crumbled from the force of his hands as his eyes found the words of Johannes Gutenberg. This was not a printed document, but a manuscript in Gutenberg's own handwriting. He had seen enough of the man's penmanship to have no doubt about its authenticity. The page was filthy and blackened by time, but the words came to Dr. Goldman's mind with clarity.

I met a mad man today!

Goldman shook his head and rubbed his eyes. The combination of burning eyes and the intensity of the moment pounded in his brain. Inhaling deeply he tried controlling his anxiety to gather himself. He forced his eyes to focus and his mind to sharpen in order to decipher the document written in old German. He needed to know.

> *It was not the first time I have met such, but he truly was. Words of the damned or insane came from him. Or, so I first thought. Only the fire in his eyes made me doubt my certainty about his madness. He came to me one night, clearly a man with a twisted past. I first thought injuries of battle had so distorted his mind. No man should know of things he carried buried in his soul. Who knows how many had perished by his hands? Heaven and hell must have been burdened by his doings. I prayed for the Lord to keep me safe and out of harm's way as this creature—*

The metal door creaked open, awakening Goldman from a near delirious state. He stood with the pile of blackened papers firmly against his chest, heaving from the excitement and nerves.

"Follow me!" The guard nodded his head and led him up the stairs. Without questioning or awaiting any requests he happily filled the guard's hand with another wad of money as he stepped through the doorway into a narrow alley.

• • •

Dr. Goldman could not remember the return to his cousin's house. Something about a taxi and a loud Turkish driver that smelled of cheese and olives was all that he could recall. He could not even remember why he had decided to take a car instead of returning by train. The last hour shifted in his mind, nothing pertinent coming into focus except for the stack of paper he held with a death grip. The shower he took in an attempt to wash off some of the grime and soot he could not recall either. It could have been hot or cold, he could not remember and it hardly mattered on this day.

Huddled underneath a worn yellow robe he sat in his bed, shifting his feet while trying to find some comfort. His hands and face were still covered with filth, the shower having been brief and ineffective. Shaking with anticipation, he attempted to find his place in the document that lay spread out over his bed.

Dr. Goldman read on.

> *This creature was what the good Lord warns of hell. He seemed uncomfortable in the clothes he wore, albeit they were the best and most expensive our modern times could offer. It seemed he would have felt more comfortable wearing a robe or perhaps nothing more than a loincloth. He was a man not in his time.*

Goldman reread the last sentence, wondering if his knowledge of the language was failing him or if the words had really said such. "He was a man not in his time," Goldman read once more, questioning if he had missed some nuance of this convoluted language. Scraping dark grime off the bottom of the page, he continued.

"His face and hands held many scars. Not of the pox that had scared most of our land, but scars of injury and battle. He was a man burdened with memories. This mad man was unlike anyone I had ever met or have ever heard of. His words reached me from the past, frightening me as I traveled along with him."

Dr. Goldman struggled between the dirt that covered the pages and the continued difficulty he had with the verbiage. Anxiously he turned the page.

TWO

*A*n uncertain shadow slipped across the dark walls running down the alleyway leading to the western canal. From time to time the moon reappeared from behind wispy clouds, brightening an unsavory waterfront. A few moored gondolas floated on the dark waters, at times breaking the silence as they bounced against each other and the wharf. They creaked and moaned from the movement of the water, their worn and dilapidated hulls just sturdy enough to stay afloat in the fetid, thick water. Filth, dead fish, and unidentifiable remains slithered between the wretched boats, further poisoning air and water alike.

The filthy walkway paralleling the canal offended the senses with its endless debris, defiled humanity hidden in any hole that could protect from the elements and the animal remains that were only out-massed by the feces the present human dwellers had left behind. It was difficult to believe this place could have ever been any different from the way it was now, at one time having been described with words such as the "Jewel of the Adriatic." The western winds coming in from the open sea could not quench the decay of the air on this day.

The shadow moved along, stopping suddenly when a muffled yell broke the silence. Hunched-over shoulders and the filthy cape that covered them did not hide his size well. He stood and faced the alleyway that had yielded the cry. His large hands flexed as he moved once again, the palm of his right hand reaching under his dark robe, finding cold steel.

"I don't suppose you need any more help with that bundle?" he inquired, stopping the three from their evil task.

The men turned and faced the interloper. Sizing him up, they continued their mission. "Keep barking you filthy beast, soon you will be drinking down the sludge of the gutter . . . that should shut you up," one of them hissed at the armload, laughing at his own words while the three of them tried to control their burden as they walked toward the water. A sack that at one time might have held wheat or barley now held someone captive, whose life was nearing its end.

They hurried their pace, trying to pass the unwanted stranger that had blocked their path.

"Move it, unless you want to join him in the water," one of them threatened, spitting at the stranger's feet.

The cloaked figure took one step to his left, blocking their passage, and pulled the hood off of his head and onto his shoulders, exposing his face. Cold eyes pierced the heart of the three would-be assassins. The moon brightened the arena for an instant, allowing the three one last moment to decide on their immediate future.

A flash of red amber appeared from within a mountain of garbage. It held its brightness for a moment as a reluctant witness lit his pipe. The bearded figure quickly retreated behind a broken wooden crate, realizing that he might be beholding something that, if found out, could lead to his demise. Many other unseen eyes hid within the safety of the refuse, watching the confrontation unfold.

"We have no quarrel with you stranger," the smallest of the three coughed from bloody lips, softening the tone, trying to get by and not raise the wrath of the man.

"This does not concern you, out of the way!" The apparent leader tried standing his ground, hoping their number would drive the stranger away. Foolishly he let go of the bundle and attempted to draw his sword.

Steel glittered in the night sky as the capped man unsheathed his sword and backhanded his opponent with the hilt of the weapon. The other two did not fare much better. They were too foolish to realize the strength of their adversary. Throwing the bundle over the edge of the wharf they attempted to better the effort of their failed leader. Within moments they both lay on the ground, bleeding and broken, trying to hold on to consciousness and possibly their lives.

Knowing there was little time to spare, the cloaked man approached the water. Splashing about in the dark waters someone was nearing death. Thousands he had seen lose their lives. How much difference would one more make? The night sky lit the edge of the water as a hand reached into the wet darkness pulling the drowning man ashore. His life would continue for now. Perhaps the world would change for it.

"My Sofia, where is she?" He blabbered, forcing the words through a makeshift muzzle that tore at the corners of his mouth. Filthy slime escaped from his ripped and bleeding mouth, drooling down toward his neck, making him sound as if he were still talking under water. His lungs heaved from the labor of purging itself from the inhaled canal water, but he continued, almost oblivious of the three downed men and how close he had come to death. "Thank you, the Lord has sent you on this night, thank you," he cried, nearly delirious as his hand bindings were removed and he was helped up to his feet. "Who are you? Jesus Christ has answered my prayers. He has sent you to my aid. The Lord does hear our prayers . . . blessed be He, tell me that is so—"

"Enough!" interrupted the words of the cloaked man, repelled by the endless chatter, and fed up by the mention of Christ at every turn of life and death. There was no escaping His name.

"Who are you?" The young man continued undaunted, caught up in the moment that had nearly ended his life, yet now had given him further faith. "I must know. . . . I will pray for you, Jesus will answer your prayers, too. . . ."

The young man continued aimlessly, at times demanding an answer, at other times offering himself in servitude, but always returning to questions about Sofia, his beloved.

"You must come to my house, I beg of you," the boy continued, in some way wanting to repay the man that had saved his hide.

The two of them left the filthy docks, leaving behind the men that had regained their senses, finally able to stand and move with purpose. They had failed, perhaps their fate would lead them back to the same waters in the not-so-distant future.

"Do you need shelter for the night? My house will provide a warm bed for you." The young man persisted, knowing that returning home would not do away with all his problems.

The two walked in the near darkness, only an occasional oil lantern and the now-clear night sky lighting their way. Without an apparent need for a response the young man continued talking. At times asking random questions with answers it seemed only he could hold while at other times offering thanks and words of praise to the man who had saved

him from certain death. Only the arrival at his home forced
him to return to reality and truly address his guest.

"It is late, but I doubt anyone has been sleeping, not with
my disappearance. . . . I wonder if my friend Vittorio is here
tonight?" He once again rambled on, more disconnected
thoughts than a conversation one would have with someone
present.

"My poor Sofie, she probably thinks I am dead . . . they are
being completely unfair . . . stupid is more like it . . . don't
they understand that—" His words suddenly stopped the instant a light appeared behind the worn gray curtains.

"Get in here, where have you been? It is her again, isn't
it? Get in here!" a filthy and fidgety man greeted them at the
doorway. He scratched at his greasy beard with his right arm
while his foot kicked the door open. "Who have you brought
home with you this time?" he demanded.

His drunken words went unanswered as a woman's voice
split the night with her shriek of anger and concern. "Is it
him? . . . Get in here!" her words echoing his, "you had us
worried to death. Can you think of nothing but yourself? I
bet that little trollop has something to do with this."

"She is not a trollop and I love her," the young man protested. "Aren't you at least happy that I am alive?" He
searched their eyes for a response, trying to find some acceptance, but found little comfort.

The four of them stood in the doorway, all at once realizing
that it was probably best to close the door and retreat into the
safety of the secured home. While still scratching his beard,
the old man rotated the revolving bolt between two door handles, the spindle fastening and tightening the oak door against
the wooden beams that also held up the front of the home.
Other than knocking the door off its hinges, this door was
locked for the night.

For a moment the four of them searched each other's eyes
and possible intentions. "Please sit, everyone," the woman
offered, more out of habit than pure hospitality. She watched
the cloaked stranger, for the moment uncertain if locking the
door had been prudent.

The four of them sat in silence for a few seconds before
the young man again questioned relentlessly. "Have you heard

from Sofie? Is she all right? Where is Vittorio?" he anxiously inquired.

"That is enough Marco! Your uncle and I have been worried sick about you," she declared unconvincingly, "and all you care about is her."

"I love her, I plan to marry her," Marco interrupted, refusing to allow for anyone to soil her name. "Don't you want to know what happened?"

"Thank you, sir, if it is indeed you who have preserved our Marco. The boy's father is dead and—"

"He is not dead, stop saying that! Please stop saying that," he begged with an angry but heavy heart. "He will return, soon, I know he will," Marco snapped back, for the moment angered even more than the talk about Sophie, his beloved. "I have prayed for his return." He suddenly turned toward his savior, his youthful face went pale and flaccid. "Are you my father?" he asked, wondering if his prayers had finally been answered.

"Don't be foolish," his aunt snapped. "Your father, may his soul rest in peace, is probably dead and, if fortunate, buried with a cross over his chest and a headstone to keep him company. His grave will probably never be visited by anyone that follows the word of Christ. Your father has long given up his faith dealing with the savages of the east—"

"They are not savages," Marco interrupted, not certain why he had chosen that part of her argument to challenge. "My father is alive and will return. He did not have me never to know me. He will return." Marco sat back, surprised at his own conviction and choice in words.

All attention turned toward the strange man sharing their table. Through all this arguing they had forgotten that whoever this man was, he had probably saved young Marco's life. "Do you need food or water perhaps?" the woman inquired, realizing they had offered nothing.

They all looked at this very unusual man. He was large and thick. His dirty and worn face betrayed of age, yet his blue-gray eyes were clear and youthful. A deep scar from probably many years past ran from the corner of his mouth to his left eye.

"Thank you for returning Marco to us." She tried her best

at sounding genuine. "He has caused endless trouble for us, especially with his Sophie."

Marco was ready to protest but a quick stern look from his aunt quieted him for the moment. Having Sophie spoken of as being his surprised him, almost making him grin.

"Girls, that is all that you have on your mind." She returned to scolding the boy some more. "This man probably risked his life for nothing but—"

Marco gritted his teeth, his jaw crackling from the anger at his aunt, ready to respond.

"The boy needed help," the man interrupted, almost pleased at embarrassing the woman for speaking so lightly of her own flesh. "I happened to be there, that is all," he concluded.

"He will get himself killed off some other way," the old man yelled, spilling dark red wine from his quivering lips. Coughing from the wine that had probably found its way into his lungs he offered the flask to their guest. "Here, this is not horrible. I'm sure you have had worse."

"I must be going." The stranger deflected the offer of wine, realizing that it was best to depart for now.

"Please stay, forgive my husband," the woman almost begged, realizing how foolish her husband had been, possibly angering the stranger. That in itself was dangerous enough these days. With all its wealth and splendor, Venice was also the home of thieves and murderers, not unlike any other major port. "After all, you are a guest in our house," she continued. "Allow me to offer you a warm bed, please," she pleaded, ashamed at their words and her spouse's behavior.

"Please stay," Marco also implored the man.

"I am called Casca," the man finally spoke. Marco smiled. Perhaps he had found an ally.

THREE

"I have brought you fresh bread." Casca inhaled the intoxicating aroma of the offering. Marco stood at the entrance to Casca's room, holding a tray with two loafs of still-warm bread upon it. A fine mist swirled away from the bread, as if by design finding its way to Casca's anxious nostrils.

"Please have some. I also have some honeyed milk for you. It is my favorite. I figure if I get through life without it rotting my teeth to the bone, it will be worth it. It is more than just my favorite, I can't help myself," Marco added, trying to hide his nervousness. "It is best when still warm."

The honeyed milk Marco offered in a large copper goblet that he delicately held in his left hand. "Please, have some of both," he offered with both hands.

Casca sat up in his bed, surprised how well he had slept in a stranger's house. It was an hour or two past dawn and he could hear the sounds of everyday life outside the home. Venice was a busy town after all. It had been many years since he had roamed this land with the savage Huns. Memories of Attila returned.

Casca stood and followed Marco through the doorway to the same table they had all sat at the previous night. Nervously Marco led the way, unable to help himself from staring at his new guest.

"I am good with horses," a short, fat youngster called out as he stood by the table, scratching his chin with anxious fingers.

"His name is Vittorio; he is my best friend," Marco helped out. "He just gets nervous around people, and says the first thing that comes to his mind. Usually it is something about his father's horses. Or his never-ending appetite," Marco added, seeing Vittorio stare at the loaves of bread.

Casca sat at the table and happily devoured the first loaf. The sweet nectar of milk and honey easily washed down the warm and savory bread. A large cup of unusually cold water washed away the remains, cleansing his palate. He eyed the second loaf, then looked at Marco's friend Vittorio. Vittorio's eyes widened then smiled as Casca tore the bread in two and offered a half to him. They all sat for a moment, Casca watching the two young men stare at him, Vittorio trying to form some words, fighting the half loaf of bread on the way down, while Marco was struggling to organize the thousands of questions he had for this unusual man.

"You know they will search you out," Vittorio mumbled to Marco, again scraping at his hairless jowls. "You were lucky, but they will come back for you. You gave them no choice. Her parents cannot let you live *now*. Had they succeeded, no one would have known about it. But now, even if it is your word against theirs, it is still trouble. I am afraid for you," Vittorio finally whispered, frightened and concerned for his friend.

"I love her," Marco insisted. "My Sophie loves me and I do not care if her parents do not think I am worthy of their daughter. I do not need their acceptance, their approval, or a dowry. Just her love. Only death will separate us. I will marry her," Marco asserted.

"Don't be foolish," Vittorio whispered, for the moment forgetting that this strange creature who had saved his friend's life sat right across from them at the small rectangular table. "You can love her all you want, but her family will not have you. You must flee. We must. Her family is strong and merciless. The Donatellos have always been so. They have hated your family even before you were born. Now it gives the perfect opportunity to exact revenge."

Marco sat quietly, quite displeased with the turns in his life, for the moment forgetting that this stranger that called himself Casca had given him a new life. Perhaps it was a sign from above to let Sophie go, possibly to miss her his whole life, but at least he would be alive.

"I do not care," he blurted out, continuing his thoughts out loud. "I will marry her whether it is here or if I need to take her away with me. Vittorio, how long before our boat is seaworthy?"

"Marco, please, our boat will not make it far past the port. You know that. You cannot be serious. We must flee before her family catches up with us. All we have is maybe a few days before they will look for you again. If that. We cannot dare take her with us. If they do not get us, the sea is certain to do so." Vittorio attempted to reason with his heartbroken friend.

"I see you are still alive." Marco's drunken uncle slithered into the room, holding a bottle of wine close to his chest, holding it with more reverence than anything else he had likely ever held. He wiped his mouth clean, probably for no reason other than to be able to get a good grip on the bottle with it. "I wish you would take your friends outside, I do not want blood spilled in my home when the Donatellos catch up with you."

"It is my home, it belongs to my father!" Marco insisted. "I will leave when I please."

"You little rat! How dare you!" his uncle screamed. "Your damned father is dead. Dead! Dead! Get it through your thick skull. He is dead and . . ."

The man stopped talking seeing the rage in Marco's eyes. His mind might have been floating in a barrel of wine, but there was no doubting Marco's anger and intensity. He was nearly twice the size of his nephew, yet he knew he had gone beyond what Marco would tolerate. Marco stood gritting his teeth, tears of anger running down his face. His thin slight frame bent, nearly crippled in anger, his belabored lungs fighting, gasping for air.

"Don't you ever say that about my father again! Ever! You only wish him dead. This is my house. This is my father's house. I do not care if I am only seventeen years old. It is still my house! You are lucky I allow you and my aunt to stay here. Know that!" Marco shook from the rage his uncle had brought out in him. "It is my house and will be so until my father returns or I decide otherwise." Marco boiled in fury, almost wishing his drunken uncle would try to hurt him. This was a fight he was not about to lose.

Marco's aunt stood in the doorway, realizing this was not the boy that had left the previous night. Marco would not be pushed around again. Seeing it was for the best, even if only for now, she dragged the drunken fool through the hallway, away from what was not going to turn out to be a savory confrontation.

Casca, Marco, and Vittorio sat quietly at the table. The shock of what he had witnessed actually caused Vittorio to stop eating for the moment.

"I did not recognize you for a moment," Vittorio was finally able to get out, flabbergasted by his friend's anger and reaction. "I think your uncle was lucky your aunt was here. I have never seen you such."

"My father will return, he will return," Marco mumbled to himself over and over, nearly oblivious of anything around him. He pounded his fist against the wooden table, spilling the water and overturning the dish that had held the honeyed milk. Standing up, he neared the curtained window and looked out toward the harbor. Another ship was about to dock. Perhaps his father was on this one.

The creaky merchant ship was returning from Acre in Palestine. Its hull, broken just above the waterline, patched haphazardly by unskilled seamen, told the tale of a ship fortunate to be still afloat. Half a dozen men with missing arms and legs were brought off the deck, the stench of decaying flesh keeping them company. They might have made it home but it was doubtful any of them were going to enjoy life for long. If nothing else, they would die in their own beds.

Four fishermen also came ashore, laughing and yelling, telling tales that even they were not likely to believe. Marco stood on the quays, as he had done hundreds of times before, every time a ship had docked. The same news. No one had heard of his father and uncle, two brave merchants who had left for the mysterious world of the land of Chin nearly eighteen years ago.

Head down, talking more to himself than anyone that got in his way, Marco returned to his home, once again disappointed, but not yet ready to give up. "No news, again. No one has seen or heard of them," he sadly reported to Vittorio.

The two of them sat at the table, Vittorio trying to wipe his hand clean from the honey that was still stuck to the wood. He opened and closed his mouth, ready to offer comfort, trying to choose the words that would not hurt his friend. "Maybe you should search for him, not just wait for him," Vittorio suggested to Marco. "Maybe if you . . . well, if *we* travel to places overseas, perhaps to Acre or Alexandria we can speak to other people, we can send messages, leave messages behind. Someone must have heard of them." Vittorio attempted to cheer up Marco with new ideas.

"I just don't know anymore. At times I hate to admit it but I wonder if he really ever will return. Maybe he has found a new place to live, maybe a new family. . . ." Saddened by his own words, Marco rested his sun-weary head against the palms of his hands and rubbed his eyes. "No, I refuse to believe it, he will return. I know he will." Marco stood and walked toward the door. Pushing it open with his left hand he covered his eyes with his right hand, squinting from the afternoon sun. He stared out into the sun's burning rays, shaking his head, oblivious of all else.

"Please sit down, Messer Casca, please," Vittorio anxiously offered. Casca sat with a large pitcher of cold water in one hand and a bowl of olives and goat cheese in the other. He pushed it toward Vittorio seeing the boy's eyes glisten with envy. "Thank you Messer Casca."

The two of them sat eating, watching Marco look out toward the harbor, preoccupied with his own thoughts.

"He has been on this vigil for as long as I have known him." Vittorio broke the silence, unnerved by what was taking place and somewhat fearful of this strange creature that had joined him for this meal. He again handled his chin and neck, nearly peeling the reddened skin with his anxious hand. "Marco's father, Niccolo, and Uncle Maffeo left this home almost eighteen years ago. Before Marco was born. Marco does not even know if his father was aware that his wife was going to have a child. For a few years Marco's mother received letters and once in a while gifts that Niccolo had sent. There hasn't been anything for nearly fourteen years. I myself doubt if he really is alive—"

"He is alive, I know it," Marco interrupted, surprising both Casca and Vittorio who had thought Marco was not listening.

"I am sorry Marco, I really am. I do want to believe you, but it has been so long. . . ."

"I do not care, the last letter my mother received before she died promised that he would return," Marco insisted. "My father, although I have never met him, is an honorable man. He planned to travel to the court of the Great Khan in China. He promised to bring back silk for my mother and spices from the farthest corners of the empire. My mother has told me many things about him. He may have his faults, God forgive him, but he is a good man. He is my father. You will both see."

"I have met many merchants who have traveled the Silk Road, the road that leads to the land of Chin." Casca surprised both with his first words of the day.

"You have? Please tell me more," Marco implored his savior, suddenly feeling like he had gotten a new life. "Vittorio told you that my father is with my Uncle Maffeo. I have never met either of them, but I was told they are great businessmen, honorable, and God fearing."

"I have never heard of the two of them, but it is not impossible that they are both alive. The road to China is filled with peril but I have traveled it before. Men who travel the road are probably safer than ones walking the dark alleys of this city," Casca added.

"Thank you, Messer Casca, for your words and your actions. You have given me hope . . . and saved my life. The Donatellos were going to kill me. I . . ." Marco's face suddenly darkened again. "My Sophie, she must think I am dead or have abandoned her. I was supposed to meet her at St. Paul's Cathedral this morning."

"You can't see her again. They will kill you, Marco, you have to give her up," Vittorio begged with conviction in his voice.

"It is just too much, I need help . . ." Once again Marco was unable to finish his pained words, shaking his head and leaning over the table.

"Marco, are you listening?" His aunt's shrieky voice jarred him out of his thoughts, making him stand up as if at detention. "You need to pick up the cloth. I told you about it; it came in yesterday from Genoa. I just don't understand it— we continuously war with Genoa, yet trade flows freely. I wonder. Anyway, Messer Giancarlo's wife will give you the bundle, but don't drag it on the ground like you did last time. Are you listening to me?"

"I will pick it up," Vittorio volunteered, "I know Messer Giancarlo's wife and their son Paolo. I will be glad to pick it up for you."

"Fine, I don't care as long as I have it by the afternoon. Don't you forget it either, and do not drag it. My lord, what kind of seamstress am I, counting on such help?" she mumbled to herself as she left the room.

"Thank you Vittorio, I just was in no mood to go anyway. I think I will reread the last letter my mother got from my father. Yeah, I want to do that," Marco concluded, happy not to have to see the cursed harbor again, and pleased to hear his father's thoughts once more.

"I will go with you." Casca stood and left the room. Behind him Vittorio stood up and looked at Marco, shrugging his shoulders, wondering about the giant of a man who would keep him company and the nerves he would have to have in any possible conversation.

The harbor was crowded and noisy. Ships from throughout the Mediterranean swarmed the foremost trading port of the western world. Small insignificant boats, able to carry perhaps a few fisherman and their catch, bobbed furiously between much larger ships that had returned from Egypt; many others had made the long journey from as far away as the Black Sea or even Old Carthage from the northern coast of Africa. No patch of water was left unoccupied for more than an instant. Loud, aggressive seamen furiously pushing their way in, trying to find the best access to dock. From time to time, anxious frightened voices won out over the steady murmur of all the sounds the harbor made. Men and women screaming, eventually to be drowned out by the screams of others or the sounds of boats crashing against each other. For all its madness, a certain order remained, as if a higher power maintained people and ships from certain chaos. Hundreds, perhaps thousands, of people crowded the wharves, fisherman carrying their salty equipment and foul catch and traders handling any item that would fetch a good price. It was probably the only type of place that Casca could go unnoticed. A place where men wore strange clothes and spoke even stranger languages was the only place he would not stand out.

"Right here, Messer Casca, over here," Vittorio tried to help. "Paolo, I am picking up the package that was left for Marco; your mother knows about it."

"I am fine, and how are you?" Paolo sarcastically answered. "Who is that mountain that is following you?" Paolo inquired, nodding toward Casca with inquisitive eyes. "I think he just got off one of the merchantmen last week, the one returning with soldiers from Caesarea."

"I don't know, but I doubt he likes to be referred to as a mountain. Mountains can crash and pulverize little pebbles like you very easily," Vittorio whispered, again nervously clawing at his chin and neck.

"The black velvet is here, take it Vittorio. I take my words back signore, I am sorry," an ashen Paolo whimpered realizing his foolishness. "Were you returning from Acre and the holy wars? I am certain you have sent many of Allah's heathens to hell and turned back their advances," Paolo added trying to find his way into the man's graces. He nervously looked at Casca, hoping that even if his guess was off the mark, his words of praise had a chance at making Casca forget about his previously poorly chosen words. Casca was in no mood to talk, which Paolo found comforting for the moment.

Casca and Vittorio left the landing, the smell of salt water and fish staying with them for quite a while. Vittorio struggled with the heavy bundle, the black velvet wrapped tightly, teetering over his left shoulder, its ends and corners turned in around the edges to hold it from unrolling. The whole burden seemed to be moments from finding its way onto the dusty walkway. The lack of handles and rope that usually encircled such an item made Vittorio struggle, within minutes making him gasp for air and constantly try to dry his sweating hands to be able to get a better grip. From time to time he groaned and whimpered, but was definitely not about to ask for help. His round frame, hunched over and nearly beaten down, moved on slowly along the dirt road, words of prayer intermixing with curses escaping from his pursed lips as the task at hand exhausted him to his limits.

"I am . . ." Vittorio's words ended as he probably figured it was not necessary to state the obvious since Marco could tell he was back. Also, it was quite possible he had no energy left to complete his words.

"Sit down, I'll get you some water." Marco smiled at Vittorio, thankful to his friend for the task completed, and also amused at how much it had taken out of him to carry this load.

Vittorio sat, placed both hands on his quivering thighs, then moved in closer to the table and rested both elbows and forearms on the edge of the table. He breathed slowly, his lungs probably needing more air, but for the moment he was too exhausted even to take deep breaths. Vittorio closed his eyes and brought the cup of water to his lips.

"I will go to St. Paul's Cathedral tomorrow. My Sophie will be there, I am sure. The Donatellos will not dare do anything in broad daylight. I have to speak to her," Marco stated firmly.

Invigorated by the short rest and cold water, or more likely by his friend's brave words, Vittorio once again tried to discourage Marco. "You cannot go Marco. If they do not get you, then they will surely do it later. You, *we,* must leave Venice, now!"

"I have not seen St. Paul's Cathedral in years," Casca interjected, making his offer to go along and possibly protect quite obvious.

Casca spent the remains of the day recounting tales of the world where he had traveled. Marco and Vittorio sat as if dumbfounded hearing of places and people no one man could know of. Sometimes they glanced at each other unbelievingly of how any one man could have traveled and lived so many adventures. They heard of the land of the ancient Egyptians and the pharaohs who had lived thousands of years ago, of the holy wars that still incinerated Palestine, of islands far off in the endless oceans where strange men carved giant statues to gods unseen, to the Silk Road that traversed half the world and the wonders of China. They listened attentively, Marco almost refusing to blink, fearful that he might miss the slightest facet or minuscule nuance of the descriptions. Casca soon came to realize he would need to backtrack in his stories and retell even the smallest of detail as Marco wanted to absorb everything there was to know about the world. At the beginning, Vittorio or Marco interrupted, unbelieving or not understanding how one man could know of so many places and people, but they soon came to realize it was probably best not knowing as this stranger was beyond anything they had ever met or dared to imagine.

FOUR

Casca could not remember when sleep had come, but he awakened before dawn, the crackle of the fireplace the only sound disturbing the night. Marco and Vittorio still slept leaning sideways against each other, Vittorio with a goblet of milk in his hand, most of which had spilled onto the floor, and Marco with his eyebrows furrowed as if he had struggled to stay awake and absorb every word Casca had said. The air was clean and fresh coming in from the waters, a slight twinge of brine lapping at Casca's nostrils. He inhaled the morning air and listened to the silence. It was cold and lonely in this world; soon the world would wake. Perhaps the company of these young men would make it more tolerable for a while.

"Good morning, Messer Casca." Marco broke Casca's musing. "At first, last night gave me hope listening to your words,"—his own face suddenly disheartened—"the world is too large, I will never find my father," Marco sadly stated, the dreams he may have had having been rudely interrupted by the reality of waking.

"I am hungry," Vittorio groggily moaned, smacking his lips. He looked at the half-filled goblet of milk but even with his appetite he figured the milk had likely curdled. He was not about to ruin his stomach and miss the chance to eat for the remainder of the day.

"Good morning all. I bet you never expected to see me again." A familiar voice stirred Marco and Vittorio's attention.

"Who is that? Sounds like Umberto, doesn't it?" Marco questioned a still stretching Vittorio. Marco snapped to his feet and approached the heavily bolted door. Struggling to open it, he came face to face with a short, fairly muscular man.

Marco stared at the short bald man with one hand on the door ready to slam it shut and the other hand by his temple, trying to rub sleep out of his eyes and sense into his still resting mind.

"Come on, Marco," the voice teased, "has it been so long? Of course it is me."

"It is Umberto," Vittorio yelled from inside the house. "Out of the way Marco, let him in," Vittorio continued yelling, pushing Marco out of his way as he neared the door. "What happened to you?" Vittorio inquired, not seeing what he had expected.

"It is only my hair, fat boy. I see you have not missed too many meals. I'll bet Marco has nothing left in his aunt's pantry." Vittorio, Marco, and the new arrival embraced, laughing at the situation and their familiar mockery. Casca watched the three of them clasp their fingers in a strange manner, almost like a secret hold or sign language.

"The hair was not my choice," laughed Umberto, realizing

that, of all that Vittorio or Marco needed to know, this was the most urgent for them, no matter how trivial it was.

Umberto finally walked into the home, his steps slowed by a stiff left hip, and evenly paced walk. His tunic sported the cross of the crusaders. He rubbed at the cross as he entered, realizing they all eyed his clothes. Stains, green, red, and black, crisscrossed his clothing, the obvious remains of conflict and death.

"I came face to face with death too many times. Vittorio, you always speak of cats having many lives—well I must have more than one myself."

"Maybe God has a special purpose for you, my friend," Vittorio generously and warmly offered. However, he was unable to complete his thoughts as Marco, as usual, jumped in on the subject.

"God has a special purpose for all of us," Marco quickly interrupted. "Umberto was doing God's work. You don't think He made us just to wander aimlessly?" Realizing this was not the time to debate the argument, Marco decided to let it go for now.

Vittorio again embraced Umberto, gently tapping him on the shoulder and back, not wanting to aggravate some injury he may not have been aware of.

"I am not going to break, you know, but thank you anyway. Oh, yeah, the hair," Umberto returned to the mystery.

"That's right, Umberto, let's hear it. You told me you would never cut your hair. That old nonsense about strength in your hair," Marco kidded his old friend, glad that the conversation had shifted back to that of a few moments ago.

"It was lice in my hair, everywhere. On the way back from Caesarea everyone on board got it. I had all my hair cut off, more like shaved off. All of it," Umberto added seeing Marco's eyes widen. "I was fortunate to have a sharp blade, I am still pretty as ever." He tried joking his way out, his voice again quieting down, a somber look returning to him. "Some of the men jumped in the water and let themselves be dragged for hours, hanging on to ropes, hoping the little horrors would let go. We lost a few of the men that way. What a useless way to die after surviving the hell . . ." Umberto's voice trailed off even more, obviously the memory he was reliving paining him.

"I am sorry," Vittorio and Marco's words ran over each other.

"I am all right," Umberto snapped back. "I have returned and look forward to doing everything I had ever complained about in the past. Everything I have ever said was boring."

"Sit down my friend," Marco invited Umberto toward the table. "I will get you something to eat. When did you get back?"

Umberto sat carefully, stretching his left leg out with the use of his left arm, easing himself down so as not to irritate an obviously recent injury. He was squarely built, with strong dark features. Maybe far enough back in time his relatives might have had some doings with Hannibal and his invading troops. His dark eyes sat beneath a wrinkled forehead, battered by the sun and the darkness of war. Casca watched this man, perhaps ten years older than Marco and Vittorio, looking twenty years older. His time in the Holy Land had drained him of much of his youth. Being a soldier of Christ aged men in many ways.

"His name is Casca." Marco introduced his recent savior to his friend of many years past. "Casca saved me from certain death, he . . ."

"Let me guess, a girl—what was her name again? Oh yeah, Sophie? Same girl, right?" Umberto continued not needing an answer, entertained at how little Marco had changed over the last few years. "I knew the Donatellos were thrilled with you," Umberto chided his friend.

"They had had it in for your family even before your father was born," he continued. "Thank you for preserving my lovestruck friend, I am grateful to you." Umberto extended a steady hand to Casca. Casca shook the steel-hard hand of Umberto, their eyes meeting for a moment, their thoughts melding and drifting to the ravages of the holy wars. Casca had seen thousands of men like Umberto perish, drenching the Holy Land with their blood.

"It is Sophie; I have loved her ever since I met her," Marco insisted defensively, Umberto's mention of his father making his response even more feverish. "I cannot even remember not loving her, almost as if she had always been—"

"Easy Marco, you worry me," Umberto jumped in. "You

kept this a secret from her family for almost two years? Unbelievable."

"I love her, that is all I know," Marco insisted. "She is for me and I am for her, that is all. I am going to see her today!"

"No, you are not! You are going down to the docks to pick up a package for me. Mr. Giancarlo's wife has more of the velvet for me," Marco's aunt cut in, destroying the morning conversation.

"Umberto, you are looking old, but it is good to see you. Just don't put any crazy thoughts into Marco's head about traveling to the Holy Land and saving Christianity. The Jew's blind followers will have to wait for another savior. What happened to your hair? Tell me it is not some new religious idiocy. This war of yours, it is damned, just as are the followers of Allah and the Jews."

"How can you say all that," Marco yelled at her, infuriated at how, within a matter of seconds, she had insulted his friend and trampled on everything else that got in her way.

"Be quiet boy, I gave you a break yesterday, but don't get any ideas." She nervously shifted her eyes toward a pensive Casca. Seeing no reaction from him she continued barking. "Go get my package."

"I will get it again," Vittorio offered, remembering with pain how difficult it had been the previous day, but also wanting to direct some of her anger away.

"Same as yesterday, I don't care who gets the package. Just get it here by noon, and don't drag it or I will have you dragged face down along the same road," she snapped back in her usual loathsome way to anyone who would listen. Staring at Casca with contempt, she stormed out. She had handled all of them before and was not about to be bullied. Casca was another matter. Hopefully he was to be gone soon.

"Thank you, Vittorio, I promise you fresh bread, just the way you like it, with honey and milk, by the time you return," Marco thankfully offered, worried the reward did not match the task, but also having nothing else to offer for now. He knew their friendship was a bond that forgave all.

"I will return as soon as I can," Vittorio promised. "If Umberto tells you anything about the last two years you better remember it all. I do not want to miss the smallest detail."

"I promise," Marco guaranteed.

"And that you won't go to the St. Paul's Cathedral?"

"I promise that, too," Marco reluctantly agreed.

Using his better judgment, something that usually did not win over his desires, Marco remained at home, awaiting Vittorio's return.

The rest of the morning he spent deflecting his uncle and his aunt's usual unpleasantries that did not seem any less harsh even with Casca and Umberto present. Without having to ask even once, Umberto flooded him with the events of the last two years.

As the hours passed, perhaps slower at the beginning, Umberto's words disillusioned and demoralized Marco's idealistic views on the wars in the east. Could it be all true? Marco wondered. It was not supposed to be a war anyway! The Christian forces were present to prevent the desecration of the holy land and of the religious landmarks. Force was only supposed to be used in a defensive manner.

"You must be exaggerating," Marco kept insisting at the onset.

"I am sorry Marco, but it is true," Umberto answered. "Sure, we tried reasoning with them, but that did not last at all. It has been years since a truce had been called or peace even discussed. It is now simply a war. An ugly war between them and us where thousands die daily. The Saracens are the devil's work. Without end they flood the land with their unchristian ways, filled with demons and ugliness. They are soldiers of—"

"But we are soldiers of Christ," Marco interrupted. "The followers of the cross would do no such things."

"They are soldiers, Marco, and so are we. Once blood is drawn most things are forgotten."

"Don't they remember Pope Urban's words, the words of the scriptures? How can they not remember?" Marco hopelessly tried to find sanity in Umberto's words.

"I'm sorry, Marco," were Umberto's only words of consolation. "I do not believe many of the men wanted to remember why they were there. Greed and their own weaknesses often took their charge. At one time our hearts might have been pure, but that is in the distant past. For the last hundred years there has been nothing but war and destruction."

"But Umberto . . ." Marco's voice trailed off, for now beaten down by what his heart did not want to believe.

By the time noon came about, Marco sat at the table, holding his forehead in his hands, again shaking his head left and right, his mind and soul ravaged by what could and should not be. His simple view of the soldiers of the cross freeing the holy land, defending the holy city, the cleansing of pagans and infidels from the birthplace of Christ as God had intended it to be, was no longer a reality he could hang on to.

They sat in silence, Umberto with a look of concern for his disillusioned and aggrieved friend. Casca's mind had raced through the last hundred years as he listened to Umberto's remembrances, reliving a time when he had hoped Christ would return to the holy land and he would receive peace and an end to all his suffering. He had hoped the conflict bringing all mankind together would have compelled Christ to return. It was not to be the last time he would be disappointed.

For now only the everyday sounds coming from the outside broke the silence that had overtaken them.

"Marco!" Vittorio said only this, and it was not necessary for him to say more. Marco knew instantly that something he had dreamed of as long as he could remember had finally happened. His head jolted upward. The tone of Vittorio's voice told all there was to know. With tears in his eyes Marco ran out of the house to face his future.

Vittorio approached flanked by two well-dressed merchants and a large man carrying endless baggage pushing a wheelbarrow. The two men walked with a certain sense of confidence and purpose in their step. They attempted to hide their emotions and thoughts but today it appeared a difficult task. For now they were home.

"Marco!" Vittorio yelled once more, exhausted by the events of the day.

Marco stood in the shadow of the archway looking out, welcoming home his father and uncle.

"So, you are young Marco." The shorter of the two men smiled at him. His bronzed face hid the wear and pain of many long roads traveled. "We have come back from near around the world. Surprises await us in all corners of world, don't you think brother?"

Marco shifted his gaze back and forth, between the tall quiet one who walked with a tall stick in his right hand and the smiling man who had addressed him. The tall one was sleek and muscular with large hands. His hands and fingers squeezed the thick shaft of wood, almost strangling it. Unusually handsome, he walked with the strong confidence of a man hardened by untold experiences. *Which one is my father?* Marco wondered. He waited anxiously, not knowing what to say, or how to say it. The shorter of the two was friendly, not unlike himself, but, then again, that is not how he had imagined his father.

"Come here, give your uncle a hug. A nephew, well that's something new. Not too bad looking either. Must have gotten his looks from his mother, don't you think Niccolo? Get over here." The smaller of the two men smilingly offered both arms to embrace Marco.

Marco leapt from the doorway and embraced his uncle while looking higher up toward his father.

"I am Marco," the boy blubbered through quivering lips and tear-filled eyes. "I always knew you would return."

Marco unclasped himself from his uncle's bearlike embrace and stepped into his father's path. He reached out to be greeted by a strong and firm handshake. "So you are." Niccolo shook his son's hand. "We have traveled long."

Marco stood as if frozen in time, grasping his father's hand, afraid to try and embrace him and even more afraid to let go and perhaps not get a chance to do so again.

"Let's go inside Marco," Maffeo suggested. "It will be nice to climb the steps of our own home, sleep in our own beds."

"You are right Maffeo, let's do so," Niccolo agreed stepping to the side, allowing their baggage carrier to get a better grip on the handles of the wheelbarrow and push it toward the door.

Marco stood facing his house, watching his father and uncle go inside. It had finally happened. His father had come home.

" up Marco, let's go. Let's go inside," Vittorio Marco, watching his friend gripped in emotion and g what to do.

k a deep breath, trying to cleanse his thoughts is emotions. His life would never be the same

"Welcome home Niccolo," Aunt Francesca greeted the two, nearly straining her face in a smile. "Maffeo, it has been a long time. My gosh, I almost do not recognize you. Come on in, both of you. Move it Marco, help you father!"

Marco awoke from his momentary daydream, his aunt's strident voice still pierced his ears, but her obvious attempt at being sweet was not unwelcome for the moment. Finally she could not wallow in her own self-righteousness. Niccolo and Maffeo were home. Running up toward his father he attempted to help in some way but Niccolo was carrying nothing but a walking stick and did not seem to need any assistance. For once he did not mind being pushed around by his aunt. She could no longer deny the existence of his father.

They all stood inside the house, for the moment no one speaking, just eyeing each other, looking for someone to take the lead.

"Welcome home, Maffeo," Maffeo yelled out, trying to break the sudden moment of tension. "You are looking great, great I say," he continued, with a sense of humor Marco did not realize would be the staple of his uncle's personality.

"Welcome home, Uncle Maffeo, father." Marco squeezed out the words he had been looking forward to saying for as far back as he could remember. "I knew you would return."

"Had I known, I would not have stopped off so often trying to find myself," Maffeo kidded.

"You mean you did not . . . you did not know that I was expecting you back?" Marco inquired with a worried look in his eyes.

The moment of silence was brief but was more than enough to tell the truth. "You did not know that I existed?" Marco forced out through straining lips.

"I surely did not," Maffeo answered reluctantly, realizing that this casual discussion was tearing at Marco's heart.

Marco looked at his father and in an instant realized neither one of them had known. "My mother's letters, didn't they tell you of me?" Marco inquired, well knowing of the answer.

"Well, we are back. For now, that is. It has been long coming from the court of the Great Khan, and it is good to be back. But we must go soon," Niccolo finally spoke.

"But, you just got here. I have waited my whole life, please . . ." His words trailed off, realizing that he was not nearly as important in the world, or, sadly, to his father and uncle, as he had always imagined.

"Marco," said Uncle Maffeo, taking a serious but friendly approach, "the Great Khan of the Mongols and now most of China has sent us on a mission. It has taken us nearly two years to return to Venice, but now we must return to him with a message from the blessed pope. We have stopped here on the way to Rome. The pontiff does not even know of our mission yet. We are the ambassadors of the Great Khan. Khubilai Khan has sent a letter entrusted with us that must be delivered to his Holiness, the pope. All of this is of great importance."

Marco stood as if struck by a bolt of lightning. The pope, the Khan, returning to China, the words swirled in Marco's head, not knowing which one to hold on to, which he was going to argue over. None of it sounded right to him. How could anything be of greater importance than what he had waited for all of his life?

"Rome does not have a pope," Vittorio attempted to help, "I believe there is no holy father at this time. I don't believe there has been one in years, not since Pope Clement has passed on."

Niccolo eyed Vittorio and looked back at his brother. "Now what, brother?" Niccolo shook his head toward Maffeo.

"They must be selecting a new pope, they always do. The conclave of cardinals must be anxious to find a successor. Things could not have changed that much since we have been gone. Without the Holy One how could the church operate? Hold together?" Maffeo argued out loud. "When the new one is chosen, we will take the Khan's letter to him. The Khan does not know or even care who the pope is," Maffeo tried to reason, answering his own concerns.

"I believe," Umberto interjected, "there is a papal representative in the Holy Land. He has gone there following the pope's last consitory with his cardinals. The Saracens are growing in number and strength," he continued with fear in his voice. "It was thought best that an emissary of the pope be present to support the cause. Teobaldo of Piacenza, legate of the Church of Rome, has been in the Holy Land for nearly two years. It was believed that with his presence and support the soldiers of Christ would be invincible." Umberto finished his words, shaking his head, doubting much of what he was to believe the truth had been in the Holy Land.

"We must leave at once Niccolo," Maffeo jumped in. "We will find the emissary and take his response to the Great Khan. Palestine is going to be difficult to traverse if it is true about the Saracens, but we have no other option."

"It is true," Umberto insisted. "It will be very difficult, there are more of them every day and they are getting bolder by the moment. You will have it very hard. Anything outside of Acre is trouble, it is the only city the Saracens have been unable to take. There has not been any major offensive against them in years. The powers of Europe do nothing but bicker, more concerned about who will lead them than what their mission is. They are greedy and more anxious to plunder and gather wealth. I have seen thousands die from lack of leadership. I myself . . ." His words trailed off as he touched his left leg and hip.

Marco's shallow breathing further slowed. He could not believe it. Tears started flowing down his cheeks wetting his hands that covered his face. Everything was falling apart. Was his life just one big joke God was playing on him? For an instant his anger raged against everything he had ever believed in. Moments ago he had found his father and now his father was ready to leave to perhaps not return for many years, if ever. This was more cruel than never having found him at all.

"I am coming with you," Marco heard himself yell out. He held his breath and anxiously shifted his eyes between his father and uncle.

"Octavio," Niccolo turned to the man that had carried their belongings, "take this and grace us with the use of your ship once again. We will be off for Acre within days. I need provisions, livestock, grain, salt, same as before." Niccolo in one smooth motion removed a pouch from within his clothes and tossed it to Octavio. Without breaking his stride Octavio turned, caught the pouch of coins, and left. No one spoke for a while and no noise broke the silence in this tense moment, they were left with nothing but Octavio's dry cough ringing in their ears.

"I am coming with you," once again Marco stated, even

with more conviction than before, angered that he had been
ignored.

"You will stay here, you are but a boy!" Niccolo stepped
on Marco's words, refusing to listen to his wishes. "I doubt
if we will make it out alive ourselves," he added, trying to
soften his words, realizing he had been overly harsh. It was
too late. Marco had been wounded in a way he had never
before felt in his whole life.

"I am coming with you," Marco tried once more, almost
whispering, likely no one hearing his words any longer.

Marco opened his eyes. He alone sat on his bed, his door
closed, only his father's letter of nearly sixteen years past
keeping him company. He did not remember having left the
rest of them, but now he sat alone, perhaps more alone than
ever before. There was no need to read the letter again. He
knew every word it contained, yet he still held it. Its content
had been without any great significance, telling Marco's
mother of the people he had met and places he had been. It
had allowed Marco to imagine himself along with his father
and uncle, discovering the world.

Marco had always imagined traveling along with his father,
filling the chasm his absence had caused. This letter and his
mother's stories of his father had added hope to a seventeen-
year-old dream. Hope, the one thing he had refused to give
up his whole life, was now fading.

From the adjacent room he could hear voices but his mind
was too tired and distracted to be able to decipher any of it.
It didn't matter much for now. His father had returned, yet
he felt more alone than ever before. Marco's mind swirled in
pain and uncertainty. His heart was breaking.

"Marco, Sophie's father, Carvo Donatello, is here." Vittorio's
voice made Marco jump off his bed. Marco had never met
Messer Donatello, no one ever saw him other than the closest
of family and trusted business acquaintances. Trouble was not
far. Marco shook his head and looked around trying to find
an escape route; however, there was nowhere to go other than
to face the wrath of signore Donatello. Life could not have
turned against him any more than the disappointment of his
meeting with his father.

Marco faced the standoff. It was not his father, but his Uncle Maffeo who stood face-to-face with Carvo Donatello and two of his henchmen. The men stood in the archway of his home, eyeing each other, waiting for the other to make a move. Carvo Donatello was small of stature; only his width and richly thick clothing making him noticeable at all. The way he had been described, Marco had expected a man ten feet tall that shot lightning from his eyes and thunder from his words. Carvo stood with his hands clenched, not yet ready to reach for the short sword by his waist, but anxious to be satisfied. His venomous eyes glared toward Maffeo. Beside him two huge men stood, dwarfing both Maffeo and Carvo himself.

"Your son escaped me once, but no more. He will rot in the darkest of jails or swing from the rope," Carvo hissed, eyeing both Maffeo and Niccolo who now stood by his brother.

"He will do neither," Niccollo quietly answered. "You will leave now. This is my house. Take your men with you."

"How dare you?" Carvo barked back. "Are you foolish enough to stand in my way? Marco desecrated my only Sophie. Your filthy kind touched my daughter."

"Once again: Leave now," Maffeo calmly and quietly echoed his brother's words. "We are allowing you to leave; do it while you can."

All noise in the alleyway had ceased. Everyone stood watching, listening to the standoff unfold. Two young girls carrying water pots over their heads stopped out of fear to walk in front of the house. They looked at each other, regretting their decision to take this route to their own home. A mother held her infant son to her bosom, cringing away from the conflict, with small steps trying to get out of harm's way. Others just witnessed, speculating if bloodshed was just moments away.

Casca stepped out into the street and eyed Carvo. Carvo Donatello, patriarch of the most powerful family in Venice, had been told to go home not unlike a dog that bothered a street vendor, and, not unlike a mad dog, Carvo foamed at the mouth, spitting his drool at Maffeo's feet. Carvo was not about to be pushed around.

"All of you will regret this day. You, your filthy boy, and

anyone else who bears your peasant name." Carvo stood his ground, made much easier by the two mountains that acted as his bodyguards and henchmen. He grunted toward one of his men who took a step toward Casca.

"Back off! This does not concern you." The larger of the two men tried sounding tough, raising his fist, wielding it toward Casca. "Aren't you . . . ?" The same instant Casca and the behemoth locked eyes, memories of a few days past returned. They had met along the canals when Casca had saved Marco. "It is him." He turned toward Carvo at the same time sweeping horizontally with his extended right arm as he tried taking Casca down to the ground.

In an instant he found himself groveling on the ground, gasping for breath, clutching his crushed right knee. Casca had deflected the swinging arm with his left forearm while at the same time had turned and forced his knee sideways along the giant's own knee. Ligaments and tendons ripping from the bone was followed by the man's screams of pain and the sound of him crashing violently. It was not a particularly honorable way to disable someone, but Casca was not displeased for the moment.

The other henchman did not fare much better. Seeing this shocking turn of events, he wasted an instant of precious time deciding between drawing his sword or attacking Casca with his bare hands. The moment of indecision cost him a broken nose, a mouthful of bloody teeth, and the ability to swallow or speak without pain for the next month. Casca had brought his elbow against the man's unprotected chin, crushing and dislocating it from the rest of his skull, causing it to grotesquely swing sideways on a mangled hinge. Blood rushed from his body, spilling out from newly formed holes in his face, flooding what used to be the white part of his eyes. Like a tree cracking in the winter from ice splintering within its trunk, the man's jawbone shattered. The short sword that had been meant for Casca now lay on the ground as useless as the two men.

Carvo stood all alone, his two men at his feet trying to gather their broken body parts, attempting to find an escape. "Stand and fight," Carvo demanded, clearly unaware of what it felt like to be assaulted in such a manner.

"Go home, Carvo, it is a gift from me, courtesy of Marco's

friend. Cherish the gift of life." Maffeo grinned with pleasure. "Leave now!" he further ordered his enraged opponent with the same quiet and calm voice he had used before.

"You will pay dearly, that I guarantee!" Carvo tried posturing as he turned, kicking at his fallen protectors. The two broken men limped away, leaning against each other, cursing Casca and the cobblestones that hampered their flight. The three of them fled, leaving a bloody trail behind them as they escaped to safety.

"I am sorry, father, Uncle Maffeo. It is all my fault; forgive me," Marco implored, realizing what danger he had brought upon himself and his whole family.

"What is her name . . . a Donatello? Weren't any other girls to your liking?" Maffeo tried to gather the whole story.

"Sophie, her name is Sophie, and I love her," Marco repeated his words from the day before. "I am sorry, I should have known better. After all, she is—"

Marco was unable to finish as his father jumped all over what he was about to say. "Yes, a Donatello; they have got you saying it now. What? You believe she is too good for us? Well, we are too good for them. I wouldn't want his bloodline spoiling ours," Niccolo yelled at his son, angered not by what had transpired, but by what Marco had actually come to believe.

Marco was not displeased, even if having been yelled at; at least his father had spoken to him, and defended him. Peculiar as it was, his father had taken the first step in accepting him. Marco smiled into his hands and rubbed his face as he turned toward Casca.

"Thank you again. How many times will I have to repay you now?" he asked, realizing he could never even begin to repay, and Casca likely did not desire payment. "I am sorry—"

Marco's words were drowned out by his father's voice. "Enough sorries already! Signore Casca, within all this I have forgotten to offer my appreciation." Niccolo thankfully extended his hand.

Casca reached out and accepted Niccolo's firm and brief handshake.

"Apparently you have been lucky enough for the last few days. Do not tempt fate. Just as fast, your good fortune may run out," Maffeo added, admonishing Marco. "Thank you, signore, thank you for preserving my love-struck nephew." Maffeo bowed his head toward Casca.

Casca nodded his head accepting Maffeo's gratitude. He looked down the alleyway catching the last glimpse of Carvo Donatello and his two men as they disappeared around a distant corner. Carvo may have been beaten but he would return. It was not the first time Casca had been involved with a family quarrel. Over the years he had found his way into more feuds than he could remember. This was just another. Men fought and died for reasons they could not recount. Over the years the families had likely forgotten the reason and source of their animosity; only the hate itself remaining clear and undisturbed.

With his head bowed Marco entered his father's home, realizing the trouble he had brought onto himself and his family.

"Marco, we have but one choice." Vittorio's voice broke him from his thoughts.

"You are right, we must get away," Marco agreed. "Our boat is almost ready, we can be out of here by tomorrow and sail down the coast. I have shamed my father and caused too much trouble . . ." Marco's words trailed off, for the first time the seriousness of the situation settling in.

"No, Marco, not our boat; you must ask your father, it is the only way." Vittorio shook Marco's shoulders, trying to make his plans obvious.

"Ask your father what?" Maffeo inquired, well knowing what the intent was. "It won't be easy," he casually added, his tone giving Marco hope, for the first time since his father refused even to listen to his wishes.

"Father? You won't leave me?" Marco's begging tone, pitiful as it was, was not about to change Niccolo's mind. "I am sorry about Signore Donatello."

"He will rot in hell; that is the only thing I am certain of for now," Niccolo calmly stated. "Carvo has not changed in nearly twenty years. Maybe he has gotten fatter and more bitter, but I expected nothing different from him."

"Father?" It was all Marco could still muster to say, the effort to ask his father again to take him along almost too painful to revisit. Marco watched his father and Uncle Maffeo stand in the doorway weighing their options. Niccolo did not seem angered by what had happened with Carvo Donatello or what the repercussions may be. He almost appeared to be pleased to have had a conflict with Carvo and his men.

"Niccolo, what about Octavio? He could help us," Maffeo suggested.

"We will see." Niccolo abruptly ended the conversation and left the house.

"Uncle Maffeo?" Marco questioned, confused by the mention of Octavio.

"Wait for your father," were the only words of response Maffeo offered to Marco.

Wait for your father, the words echoed repeatedly in Marco's mind, bringing the essence of the last seventeen years into focus.

The rest of the day felt like an eternity. Marco and Vittorio huddled in a corner of the house, eventually to be joined by Umberto who had gone to his own home until early afternoon. Maffeo spent the remainder of the day recounting events of the last years to Aunt Francesca, eventually quieting her protestations of misery and poverty with a pouch of noisy coins. Aunt Francesca had nothing but a frozen smile on her face following that exchange. For that Marco was to be eternally grateful.

Marco's day was filled with misery and fear. He tried talking to Vittorio about it, but that did not seem to help. For now, Vittorio's mind appeared to be focused on his own self-preservation. He endlessly raked at his chin and neck with his worn-down nails, almost threatening to rip his throat open.

Marco kept wondering what had happened to his father. When would Carvo Donatello return with more men or perhaps the local magistrate? He was sure to do so. The defiance could not be ignored. Half of the city's officials worked for him, or had family members working for him, while the other half feared him just from having heard about his quick temper and brutal henchmen. Marco pounded his temples realizing he and his family were possibly moments away from jail, or worse. He had forever hoped and prayed for his father to return, and now his actions could have possibly endangered all their lives.

Marco had stayed up nearly all night, only the chill of the morning finally drifting him off into restless sleep. His father had not returned, giving Marco thoughts of death. Could Carvo Donatello have caught up with his father? Perhaps his father had searched out Carvo to settle their disagreement and had run afoul? Only thoughts of death and despair found their place into Marco's troubled mind.

Casca had slept comfortably again. It was going to take more than an angry father, rich patriarch or not, to unsettle him. Maffeo had proven to be quite a storyteller and Casca had found it entertaining to once again hear tales of the Silk Road and the land of the Chin. It had been many years— Casca was uncertain how many—since he had traveled east to the farthest corners of the world, riding along with Temujin, who was to become Genghis Khan, the Khan of all Khans. Maybe it was time for Casca to return beyond the Great Wall and see what seeds had sown of the Great Khan.

"Wake up, Marco! There is much to be done in the next two days." Marco stumbled out of bed, nearly falling over his own feet as his tired and distressed mind held poor control over his legs.

"We are leaving for Acre in two days, do you hear me?" Maffeo's mention of Acre instantly cleared Marco's slumberous mind.

"What of Carvo Donatello?" Marco inquired.

"To hell with him; didn't you hear your father? We are off for Acre while Carvo will be off for Hades, that is what is important," Maffeo abruptly added, trying to get a smile out of his nephew.

Marco stood in the middle of the room looking across at Maffeo and Vittorio who had entered his room within the last few moments. "You are going to Acre, leaving Venice so soon?" he inquired.

"How many times do I have to tell you? *We* are leaving. You are coming along . . . to Acre that is," Maffeo added.

Marco's eyes widened with happiness and anticipation. His mind had refused to hear or believe what Maffeo had said a few times. This was it, he was finally going to leave this cursed town to be with his father.

"What about me? I must come along!" Vittorio stated with uncertainty. "Marco and I are brothers . . . well, almost brothers. I must come along," he repeated, wanting to have no chance for a misunderstanding. Without Marco he could not imagine existing. The two had been inseparable since before he could remember.

Marco, Maffeo, and Vittorio left Marco's room and entered the eating area. At the other entrance to the room Aunt Francesca stood, her eyes furrowed, wondering when she had lost all control over her house. She moved her head back and forth between the map-covered table and her husband, who was more concerned with mastering the first bottle of the day. He licked at the pungent red wine and sucked at his teeth making his wife snarl at him in disgust.

Niccolo and Casca sat at the table. Ignoring everyone else, they hovered over two maps: one, the waters between Venice and Palestine, the other, lands farther east. Behind them Umberto and Octavio stood watching and listening intently.

"We should be in Acre in a few weeks. Once we meet with the papal representative it should not take too long." Niccolo sat back, replaying his own words, wondering if traveling to Acre and beyond was not going to be much less difficult than gaining audience with the emissary of the pope.

"I believe he will listen." Umberto attempted to help. "Our forces are frail and unsupported in and around Acre, actually throughout the area. I believe any support, no matter how distant or what shape it would take, the church would welcome. The emissary is sure to know that."

"I have never had much faith in such men. Their own agendas too often get in the way of their true mission. I fear we may fail the Great Khan," Niccolo added with clear concern in his voice.

"It has been many years since we have had any control in Palestine," Umberto continued, "I am certain you and your letter from the Khan will be welcome."

"The *Saladino* will be ready. I am proud to sail with you again, my friend. It could use a few more days in dry dock, but we will be all right. Some of the men have already been rehired, and getting the provisions has been easy," Octavio added, proud of his ability to provide transportation on such short notice.

"I have seen the *Saladino*, it was moored on the most southern part of the harbor." Niccolo nodded with disquiet in his manner. "It looked like it needs a lot."

"It is fast and the repairs should not take too long," Octavio jumped in, trying to quell any concerns. "I will take charge of the sails. It has been long since I had been home myself, the faster we get to Acre, the sooner I can make my way back to Alexandria."

"Marco, make quick friends with Octavio. The two of you will be spending a lot of time together," Niccolo urged Marco, noticing him enter the room.

"Maybe he will let you meet one of his sisters," Maffeo added smiling at Marco.

Marco stood listening, doubting there was any need for him to respond. He had caused a lot of distress and near disaster in recent days, and was not about to protest. Niccolo and Octavio looked over to him and, for now, that was enough to settle his questions.

"So it is set," Maffeo continued. "In two days we sail at dawn. Two or three weeks and we will be in Acre. If all is well, we should be on our way to China a few days later. Heaven help us if what Umberto says is true about the Saracens. Time may be running out for the Holy Land . . ." His words trailed off, his thoughts made heavy by concern for their mission and future of the sacred land of Palestine and holy city of Jerusalem. Would the emissary of the pope have time to concern himself with the message of a nonbeliever? Maffeo wondered. After all, the Great Khan was not a Christian and had subdued half the world, making nations grovel at his feet out of fear. Why would this barbarous nomad that commanded countless armies be more trustworthy than the Muslims who were on a mission to conquer Palestine and push their way to Byzantium and the western empire? Maffeo shook his head trying to make sense of it all. He knew it was going to be a great task convincing the pope or his emissary that the Great Khan was a man of reason who could be trusted and counted on.

"The *Saladino* has a small crew, so for now we will need some recruits." Octavio eyed Umberto and Casca. "We will need some strong hands and brave souls."

"I am ready to go," Vittorio yelled out, aware that he had not been thought of for this mission.

"We need men of experience," Niccolo interrupted, not ready to carry a burden along. "We need men who have sailed before, who will not ride the rail the moment a wave hits."

"I have good sea legs and can tend to horses, tell them so Marco," Vittorio implored his friend while feverishly rubbing his knuckles against his chin. "I am also a great cook," Vittorio added realizing there was not much need for anyone to tend to horses.

"He is." Marco's unassertive voice did not bring much confidence to any of them, but apparently it was sufficient to warrant a question.

"You are a good cook?" Maffeo inquired.

"Guaranteed," Vittorio firmly stated, instantly trying to remember everything his aunt had ever taught him about cooking. He nervously glanced toward Marco and Umberto, hoping he would not be given away for his obvious lie.

Casca sat back with his hands on the map, with one ear listening to Niccolo and Maffeo's plans while the other ear hearing his own thoughts of concern for their mission and the ragtag group that was about to attempt it. Under the palm of his right hand the map was coming alive, returning his travels along the Silk Road.

By the following evening the *Saladino* had been loaded, leaving nothing but a few hours until morning when Marco's new life was about to start. It was a cold, rainy day when they set sail, not the type one wishes for when heading out to sea, but Marco probably saw nothing but sunshine. The world and the company of his father and uncle were ahead. That was not about to change, while the sun was sure to return. Aunt Francesca had wished him good luck, working her way through the words, nearly finishing the last of them before her true sour self returned. Even Niccolo's generosity of handing over his house to her and the wealth of his past journey could not break her of who she had become over the years. It made leaving much easier. Marco smiled as he, Vittorio, and Umberto joined his father, uncle, Octavio, and Casca on board.

Casca had stood on the docks, watching the boat rock lightly from the tide the full moon always seemed to bring about. The boat swayed and gurgled like a large man trying to settle into a hot bath, bringing worry to Casca's mind. A few rounded boards patched the belly of the ship just above the waterline causing Casca to instantly survey the rest of the ship. It's mainmast was charred from a recent fire, yet appeared strong. A wide band of steel held it to the deck, the rivets that fastened it also blackened by the same recent flames. The rigging appeared to be new, along with the sails themselves. Octavio had been quite confident about it's overall sturdiness and reliance. For now, it had to do.

Carrying his bundle of belongings, including his long sword and dagger, Casca stepped on board. The moment the motion of the sea took his legs, memories of a hundred sea voyages returned.

FIVE

"Release the ropes!" Octavio's booming voice rang out over the water, frightening half a dozen seagulls that had found the *Saladino* as their new home over the recent days. With a flutter of filthy feathered wings they took flight, leaving behind the echo of their noisy beaks and a day's worth of refuse Marco was sure to be responsible to clean.

Anxious and full of excitement, Marco and Vittorio ran from bow to stern, and back again, following any orders Octavio, or anyone else for that matter, gave. Vittorio carried his weight well, trying to keep a step ahead of all other help, realizing that he needed to earn his keep quickly, before it became obvious his cooking skills rivaled few. Marco gritted his teeth trying to hide a smile that told of his exhilaration for sailing away from home. After all, Venetians were merchants. *Venice is a place to leave, only to return when family or war demands it.* Marco thought back at the words of many elder Venetians, wondering if those words had cursed all of his short life. Not unlike his father, he would travel the seas, trading and discovering the world.

Only thoughts of Sophie kept Marco from true happiness at this point. He had given up his love, yet he had found his father. It was a choice not easily made, and one that would haunt him for years.

The first two weeks passed uneventfully, from time to time

a distant sail bringing concern to the crew and passengers of the *Saladino*. Some of the ships passed far off in the distance, while others that approached tended to their own affairs, at times flying their flags of recognition, quelling Marco's worries. It was a route well traveled and relatively free of trouble. Secretly, Marco had hoped to encounter pirate ships, but a few well-told stories of their cruelty and brutality rapidly adjusted his desires. Quickly he came to learn that tales of pirates were best when it involved others.

Even though they were Venetians, Marco and Vittorio had difficulty getting their sea legs. At times there was no comfort; looking at the water, looking at the deck or sky, or closing their eyes did not much ease their misery. The boat bobbed like a toy in a rainwater-filled barrel, and there was nothing that was about to change that. "The water is like glass." The voice of Octavio often angered them as there seemed to be no comparing. The open sea was heartless, breaking the weak, however, allowing the strong at times to tame it and forever gain an affinity toward it.

They traveled south along the coast, then eastward within sight of the many Grecian islands, passing along the western border, past the cloudy coast of Dalmatia, stories of sea monsters and pirates that hid in the fog, frightening and exhilarating Marco at every step.

"Is that Ulysses' island?" Vittorio beamed with the widest of smiles, half expecting the songs of sirens to echo from the mention of the great one's name. Marco returned the smile, remembering the story of the famed warrior, Ulysses, who had returned after twenty years of war to find his son and beloved wife Penelope.

"I myself have been to Ithaca." Octavio grinned with a gleam in his eye. "It is a beautiful place. Ulysses must have been drawn back by the island just as much as by his love for his wife. The wine is sweet and so is the bread. And so are the women." Octavio was unable to keep that last portion of the story to himself, bringing a wry face to all who stood and listened.

Their journey continued, leaving Crete along the south then heading into the open sea, heading toward Cyprus where a well-planned stop furnished them with fresh water and food. Acre was not far off, yet eating dried and salted pork or equally salty fish was a taste not easily acquired. Anxiously they pulled into a well-sheltered port to bargain for fruit and warm bread.

A small gem that Maffeo kept sown within his clothes was able to pay for all their supplies. It may have appeared to the untrained eye that Maffeo and Niccolo had returned with not much wealth from China; however, the truth was far from that. Only the clothes they wore and their restrained demeanor likened them to merchants who had done poorly over the years. They had likely parlayed all their wealth into diamonds and other precious stones, items more valuable than gold, and much easier to carry and conceal.

Off in the distance the sandy beaches of Palestine interrupted the horizon. The walled city of Acre appeared slowly from the mist as they finally approached the coast. From so far away it seemed peaceful, a few dozen ships anchored just off the seacoast giving the impression of a quiet port ready to welcome merchants and travelers. That, however, was far from the truth.

Acre had been the last stronghold in all of Palestine, all other ports and reinforced cities falling one at a time, pilfered and destroyed by the Saracens. The soldiers of Christ had done little over the last few years, and now, nearly two hundred years since the prophetic words of Pope Urban II, the future of the holy land seemed ever more bleak.

It was midday before the *Saladino* pulled into the busy port. A huge stone gateway dominated the walled city, forcing their eyes to marvel at the size of the approach. The fortified gate seemed to look down toward the harbor, threatening anyone who might have dared consider overtaking it. Massive towers flanked the thick portal, the shadow of dozens of archers crowding the openings along the parapet. High above the tower, the crest of the crusader wavered in the western breeze marking the last outpost. Not much had been left to chance in defending the last city the crusaders still held.

The passengers of the *Saladino* stood on deck, awaiting that time when their journey would truly start. "Down with the remaining sails, let's move it, drop the anchor," Octavio commanded, endlessly ordering his men about, his commands only interrupted by his cough that always seemed to return when land was near.

Marco's chest heaved for the excitement of finally traveling and seeing the world. He had nearly cried out once the shore of the Holy Land had come into clear focus. The homeland of Christ and Christianity, Marco thought. In just a few weeks he had done and seen more than most could have ever dared dream of.

Casca and Marco stood side by side, with their hands on the wet and salty rail, wrestling with their own hopes and fears as the full view of the coastline entered their eyes. Marco leaned over the rail, grinning from ear to ear, trying to hasten their arrival into the Holy Land. Until now he had only dreamed of this, seeing the birthplace of Christ, the cradle of religion. This was where Christ had walked among men and had died by their hand. Marco crossed himself and lowered his head. The heart and soul of Christ flowed in Marco's chest as he breathed in the salty air.

Casca's eyes shifted farther north, his eyes searching for the city of Caesarea. The ancient port of Palestine originally built by Herod the Great all those years ago, before the world had even heard of Jesus of Nazareth, lay hidden from his eyes. Now the city named for the patron of King Herod, Caesar Augustus, served as a port for the dreaded Saracens. The city built by Herod had had many masters.

His eyes drifted over this land recalling events of the past, events that likely had caused more bitterness and conflict than any other place in the world. He shuddered at the memory of the two years spent defending the city atop the mountain— Masada, the Jews had called it. In the middle of the desert, along the sea too bitter and salty to sustain any life, thousands had fought and died to defend, and others to capture, a pile of rocks. There were no victors in that cursed conflict.

The bitter memory of the Jewish revolt against Rome, with the eventual destruction of Jerusalem and the Temple, returned to Casca's mind. During the Bar Kokhba revolt the Romans had tortured and killed the ten greatest leaders and philosophers of the Jewish people, including Rabbi Akiba. Casca had tried to prevent the killings, knowing full well the memory of their greatest being killed would not be forgotten or forgiven by the Jews. He had been right. The death of the Ten Martyrs had never been lost from memory, the holy Day of Atonement forever reminding of the unforgivable. The thousand years that had passed had never eased the emotion of that day.

Caesarea had gone on, serving as a haven for traders for hundreds of years. Eventually the harbor and part of the citadel had been rebuilt by the crusaders, serving as the major landing site for the never-ending ships carrying men on their journey to free Jerusalem and the holy land. Ultimately, Caesarea met an unfortunate fate as Baybars the First, the Malmuk sultan, strong-armed his way and forever wrested the city from the soldiers of Christ.

Casca had fought along with the English and French, had been in the service of Richard the Lionhearted, and had even served time in prison with the great leader, to eventually lead a breakout and escape. During the dark nights spent in the bowels of filthy prisons, Casca had wondered if fighting the Saracens had been wise. Perhaps Christ would have been compelled to return seeing His land and people enslaved. It did not turn out so. It was going to take more than just the action of men for His return.

Once more Casca had returned to the Holy Land, the place that had caused him misery and pain. Over a thousand years had passed since that fateful day on Golgotha, and, every time he returned, Christ mocked him by allowing the pain and suffering to continue in a purgatory worse than death. "Soldier, you are content with what you are. Then that you shall remain until we meet again." Perhaps it would take another thousand years for Judgment Day.

SIX

"Long live Pope Gregory!" The first words that met them rang in their ears. An apparently delirious horseman thundered by, raising dust in his wake. He bounced in the saddle, nearly falling off in his frenzied ride. "Pope Gregory will lead us against the infidels. The soldiers of the cross will turn back the followers of Satan." His voice echoed and drifted away as he rode off, his contorted body jolting from side to side as he whipped the horse with his left hand and gesticulated with his right at anyone who would listen to him. The sentiment of his words would be heard often during their stay in Acre.

Vittorio and Marco stood by, watching the horseman ride off into a cloud of dust, soon to be followed by a dozen others who repeated his words while they twirled their swords and banged their shields against the blade or hilt of their weapons. Within moments they disappeared as the road led them north, away from the walled city.

Casca unloaded the last of his gear, his mind preoccupied by memories of this land. Another pope was about to take his turn, nothing more than that. He had seen dozens of popes, each imparting their own rhetoric while interpreting the message of the Lord, wording their well-thought-out diatribe to serve the church and possibly their own needs. It was not the first Pope Gregory that Casca had heard of. The last one had died in quite questionable circumstances. If history repeated itself this one was presumably not unlike him.

It did not take long for all of them to make their way into the city, a few guards wearing the emblem of Christ's soldiers only detaining them long enough for Maffeo to exchange some coins for their unhindered passage. "Move along, inside!" The voice of a gruff soldier pushed them through the gateway, hastening them along, trying to prevent anyone who had not made their forced donation from entering with them.

Thousands milled about in the overcrowded and narrow streets, most unaware or uninterested in anything but the success of their trade. Hundreds of men and women displayed their merchandise, presenting it all as if the gods had parted with their best food and drink. It was all the same, an endless variety of goods, some of it presented tastefully to catch the eye, while some of it was thrown haphazardly, possibly catching one's attention for other reasons. Likely not much had changed along these streets for the last thousand years, no matter who ruled the land.

Fish that still twitched, hung from perforated tails along drawn-out ropes, while the singed stench of chickens and geese also permeated the cramped alleyways. Overburdened camels and donkeys carried baskets of dates and olives, bundles of cloth or wood, further crowding the already limited openings and alcoves. The beasts' sweaty, pungent bodies added to the maelstrom of the day, further swirling the dust and grime their feet churned up.

Ripped chain mail and broken weapons were displayed on makeshift tables or piled into wooden barrels adjacent to crucifixes of different styles and sizes, at times all of it placed next to food or drink. Anything that could serve as sustenance or could bring a price was available at a moment's notice. The smell of people, dozens of different foods, the gutters filled with sewage, garbage, and excrement intermixed, challenging the mind and nauseating all the senses. All the world and its people seemed to have been thrown into this one small city, suffocating the air and its occupants.

Marco's tearing eyes and cloth-covered nose, however, did not keep him from his usual exuberance. Nothing would pass him by without his scrutiny of the item or interrogation of the person involved. He ran back and forth, from alleyway to alleyway, only returning when his own common sense or the voice of his father beckoned him. Vittorio, also excited by all of it, kept close to Casca, feeling safer walking alongside a man who seemed unfazed—almost oblivious to all that was going on around him. "Marco, where are you?" Vittorio called, his concerned voice trying to penetrate the thunder of all the adjacent activities.

Not unlike anyplace else, pickpockets thrived in the great crowds, at times to be chased when found out, usually without success. It was an unforgiving place, as Casca noted many of the thieves still practicing their trade with severed hands or scar-crossed faces. Loss of a hand was not a deterrent, until they were without both right and left. At such times they were fortunate if starvation did not take them, in turn becoming beggars that crowded the intersections of any major avenues, hoping that someone would take pity on them and perhaps ease their misery with a generous moment.

"We will find rooms for tonight . . . let's stay together." Niccolo's orders and admonitions kept Vittorio and Marco close to the rest. "Move it boy," he yelled at Marco, sometime almost seeming to direct unnecessary wrath toward his son, unquestionably more than toward anybody else. "We will need to be at our best tomorrow if we hope to be granted audience with the most Holy One. Maffeo, we might need to further lighten our resources." Niccolo nodded, obviously hinting at the need to continue buying their way in closer through the never-ending entrances secured by greedy-handed guards.

The night did not bring much rest to them. Marco sat up in his bed pulling straw out from the ripped mattress that cushioned his back from the hard ground. From time to time he shifted about, trying to find comfort, eventually succumbing to the fact that it was the day to come that kept him from a restful night.

A small window allowed the moonlight to enter and keep him company, while the sounds of the street below with its endless diversity of tongues kept him entertained. The accommodations were fair enough and the food and drink had been to his liking, yet the excitement of what the new day would bring prevented Marco from falling asleep until early in the morning. Vittorio and Umberto twisted and turned in their sleep, perhaps trying to find peace in their dreams, possibly fighting their own demons that sleep had brought.

Casca had been unable to sleep at all. It had been a long time since he had had company of his liking. Down the street from their place of respite he revisited a drinking hole from many years before. The proprietor, an old Syrian with a missing left hand that he had lost early in his life as punishment for stealing a loaf of bread, had allowed Casca in. He looked at the scar-covered man and searched his memories, struggling to recall the reason for his familiarity with the stranger.

It had been nearly forty years and Casca did not feel like reacquainting himself with the old man. For now it was easier to take his drink and head for a dark area of the enclosure. The old man would have to find his own explanation for his questions. Before long, company of the long-haired and even longer-legged variety found its way to Casca. Loneliness had many faces over the years. Especially for Casca.

The legate's mansion was impressive and foreboding. It had stood for hundreds of years serving Jews, Muslims, and now the holy pontiff of the church of Rome. A large, nearly impassable iron gate and fence made even more impassable by stubborn and greedy guards thwarted all who had planned to see the newly elected pope.

Anxiously, Niccolo, Maffeo, Marco, and Casca stood in a

cramped room, waiting for their chance to enter the audience chamber, which also housed an altar. Eventually they were led into a larger room filled with representatives of the city administrators, priests, emissaries of foreign courts, dignitaries, and delegates of anyone and everyone, all of whom were fervent to meet with the new pope.

Perhaps hundreds crowded the audience chamber, shoulder to shoulder, pushing and sharply elbowing each other, attempting to gain better position, to be as near to the Holy One as possible, more likely attempting to find a place from where they would be recognized and hopefully be heard.

Marco continually wiped the sweat from his brows, wondering how anyone could be calm moments before meeting the leader of all Christendom. He looked at Casca and was surprised to see more of a look of boredom and annoyance than that of awe and subservience. "Have you met the pontiff before?" Marco found himself foolishly whispering into Casca's ear, quickly realizing Casca had not since the pope had only just been selected.

"He is a man, nothing more. A few days ago he was but a foot soldier," Casca answered matter of factly.

"He is not a man!" Marco hissed indignantly, shocked at how Casca dared speak such of the representative of God and surprised at himself for his defiant response. He could not know and was better off not knowing much of Casca's past. It was enough to witness his near superhuman strength, sharp mind, and endless supply of knowledge spanning centuries. The man had saved his life twice already, that would have to do for now.

"Quiet boy, or I'll feed you to the guards!" Niccolo snapped at Marco. "It was a mistake bringing him along," he continued, nudging Maffeo in the side.

"He is just young, can't help it." Maffeo attempted to diminish his brother's anger. "I seem to remember . . ." his words trailed off.

Nervously Maffeo eyed his brother, the two of them watching the hundreds of men and women who had assembled, each hoping to hear and possibly be heard by the pope. Who else would they need to pay to gain private audience with the pope? What if they could not relay the Khan's message and would fail a lifetime's promise? The world could change. Niccolo shook his head with clear concern on his face, their silent communication ending for the moment as the appearance of the pope was imminent.

Two cardinals stood at the foot of the steps leading up to the altar where amongst a crowd of bishops and acolytes Pope Gregory was likely hidden from the crowd. A dozen monks to the left of the altar softly sang an old hymn honoring the newly elected pope. Eventually their voices fell, quieting the crowd. An altar boy was moved to the side by one of the bishops as the boy had lost strength from the intensity of the moment. He kneeled with his face buried in the floor, still holding a vigil light in his trembling hands, humming along while he tried to find strength. Five other altar boys held thin tapers in their left hands, wincing as the hot drippings ran down their forearms. Marco eyed one of the bishops who allowed a smile to escape his parted lips, watching the young boys cringe from the hot wax. The monk pushed them to the side, forcing them to stand hunched over against the wall as complete silence overtook the audience chamber.

Facing the crowd of anxious faces stood Pope Gregory, supreme pontiff of the church of Rome. Of average build and stature, he appeared uncomfortable wearing the single crown tiara, nearly writhing in the loose papal vestments. A heavy papal ring turned on his right index finger. He was a man obviously not yet accustomed to his newly found position as head of the church, his scared hands more used to the feel of the crusader's blade than the holding of sacraments.

Behind him a larger-than-life-sized cross dominated the wall. It leaned forward, nearly threatening from above with its size and positioning. Beams of light escaped through the cracked framing that held up the wall, eerily lighting the face of the figure that stood in the mist of dust coming off the wooden rafters. Marco continually looked up at the wounded face of Christ and crossed himself as words of prayer appeared upon his lips. "He died for all of us," he ceaselessly whispered.

Pope Gregory turned slowly, first only his head moving, then the rest of his body turning to make contact with all who were present. He was clad in an ordinary white cassock covered by an overflowing, wide-sleeved loose surplice. A gold cross, hung from the surplice, brushing against his chest as he moved. Pope Gregory reached for the cross, brought it to his lips, and kissed it while looking out at the crowd.

"Until recently I had been Teobaldo of Piacenza, Legate of Palestine. I welcome this undeserved obeisance; no pope has ever received such grateful tribute. I thank you." He paused for a few seconds that felt like an eternity. "Now I stand before you humbly as Pope Gregory," he continued. "I have chosen the name to honor Pope Gregory the Seventh, he who had brought back so much hope and strength to the church. I stand here to serve Jesus Christ, our savior."

Shouts of agreement and cheer rose from the crowd as men shook their fists, pounding the air, echoing Pope Gregory's words. Marco nearly fell to his knees, only Casca's left arm steadying him, helping him maintain his place and composure.

Casca closed his eyes, wondering if it had been wise to come along. He could recall no pleasant memories. The taste of Christ's blood returned to his lips as he looked up at the crucifix and he heard the pontiff's words.

"Who is that?" Marco sheepishly whispered into Casca's ears, breaking his reflection, as a smallish round man made his appearance from behind the altar and approached the pope. The man walked slowly and repeatedly pulled at the red surplice covering his head, in the process hiding his face and eyes.

"It is Benedicto of Aquilonia, son. How could you not know of him?" a monk next to Marco who had apparently overheard the question inquired.

"I have heard of him, but I thought he had died long ago. Was he not the emissary of Rome about ten years ago?" Marco whispered to the monk.

"He was. Until recently, that is. When Teobaldo of Piacenza, now the blessed Pope Gregory, came to the Holy Land, Benedicto was demoted to serve as co-council. Not surprisingly, he has been quite bitter ever since. He had expected to be next in line for the papacy."

"Why wasn't he?" Marco asked, ignoring the continuing ceremony and shouts of praise.

"Benedicto had no interest in making peace, just in ridding the land of all nonbelievers, you will—" The monk's words were cut off as Niccolo grabbed at his son.

"What is wrong with you, boy? Is it just too much to ask

for you to listen? One moment you are frozen in silence and awe, and the next moment you disrespect the holy Father. Be silent, for once!"

"Forgive the young man, my son." The monk smiled at Niccolo. "It is my fault for stepping in."

Niccolo attempted to return the smile while he pulled Marco closer to himself. "Listen to Pope Gregory, you might just learn something about faith."

Marco lowered his eyes, ashamed for embarrassing his father, yet unable to have his curiosity so easily quelled.

You might just learn something about faith. Niccolo's last words rang in Casca's ears, somehow stirring something distant from his past. He shook his head, clearing his thoughts.

"Long live Pope Gregory, praise be our Father." The cheers continued as Pope Gregory stood by, holding his hands out toward the crowd.

"We are blessed to have Benedicto of Aquilonia at our side," Pope Gregory continued, pulling Benedicto next to him, presenting him to the eager audience. "He has been in the Holy Land longer than most of us. Without him, all would have been lost years ago. For years he has served along with me, teaching me of this land and its people. He has sacrificed more than any one man has even been asked to in this holiest of pilgrimages."

Benedicto bowed slightly and exposed his face to the crowd, solemnly accepting the praise, yet unable to show anything but darkness in his eyes.

"Pope Gregory is the chosen one. I will be honored to serve by his side." Benedicto nodded toward Pope Gregory and dropped to his knees, kissing the papal ring. His words of acceptance were gravely spoken, yet to Casca they obviously lacked true veracity in their delivery. Casca's eyes narrowed while watching the man speak.

"Rise my son, rise. You have labored for years in this cruel world; together we will overcome our fears and our enemies."

Heartened by Pope Gregory's words of praise, Benedicto rose and addressed the crowd. "It is so, we will overcome our enemies, the enemies of our blessed father and Holy Land."

Cheers again rose from the crowd, making Benedicto continue with new-found vigor. "The enemies of Christ have for too long occupied this land. Palestine must be for true believers only. Jerusalem must be returned to us." His voice and venomous words began to flow freely as the crowd reached a fever pitch spurned by his speech, hanging on every one of his words, repeating them in unison. Chants of *Benedicto will free the land of Christ* erupted from the masses as near chaos broke out. Suddenly, all attention turned away from Pope Gregory as the intensity of Benedicto's voice and message sounded a collective agreement amongst the hundreds.

Maffeo and Niccolo looked at each other in fear, realizing all may be lost. For a moment Maffeo wondered if their lives were in danger if they attempted to carry through with their mission. With terror in his eyes, Marco pulled himself between his father and Casca, frightened by the turn of events.

Pope Gregory stepped back and held the golden cross to his chest with his left hand while with his right he continuously crossed himself. For the first time his eyes showed concern, near panic for the emotion he felt from the men assembled. In a matter of minutes madness had taken them.

"Pope Gregory will lead us against the infidels. Before long we will be rid of all nonbelievers. It is my last mission in this world to cleanse the land of all heretics, all that do not have the blood of the lamb coursing through their veins. Only the followers of Christ will step on the soil He drenched with His blood . . . for all future generations." Benedicto stood in front of Pope Gregory and raised both of his hands above his head.

"Our enemies are within us and all around us," he continued. "We can trust no one. The ones unwilling to admit it themselves will need to be so coerced. They will be found and dealt with." Benedicto's voice rose and the intensity grabbed at the crowd. People pounded their feet and bellowed Benedicto's voice in unison. "Invaders of this land, Jew, Muslim, or Mongol will be turned back, away from our holy city. Jesus Christ did not die for them, they must not soil the land with their presence."

The crowd feverishly continued chanting Benedicto's name, repeating his words of single-minded loathing and his mission of death. A cold wave of hatred spread through the crowd, further frightening Marco. It was like a cloak of darkness that clouds a bright day, bringing shivers to unsuspecting ones. He looked at his father, then at Casca, his eyes begging for an explanation and assurance. Pope Gregory's words of hope and compassion had suddenly been lost to all as the darkest mission of the crusades instantly returned to everyone's hearts.

This was not what Pope Gregory had had in mind. It was supposed to be a moment of strength and reaffirmation of their belief in the Lord, not a renewed crusade to exterminate all who stood in their way and challenged their beliefs.

"Let those who oppose us know their ways will not be tolerated. They will be banished from this land. The soldiers of Christ will be victorious," Benedicto concluded, wiping beads of sweat from his now uncovered face.

"Let all not born of His blood perish in His presence. It is His will. Is there anyone out there who defies us?" Benedicto demanded, eager to receive continued words of support and praise. Ever-louder shouts of support and affirmation rose from the crowd, filling the audience hall, stirring the walls from the noise and mass of pounding feet. Pope Gregory took a step back, shocked by the rage that had overtaken the hundreds who stood present.

"The infidels, the worshipers of the devil, we will annihilate. Our lord has ordered us to be off with them. They are the spawn of hell, to hell they will return," he continued, not expecting a challenge to his oratory.

"Let the Lord judge them, the one without sin shall set them apart," a clear voice sounded, shocking Benedicto with its brazenness. A murmur spread through the crowd as no one had expected a challenge to Benedicto's diatribe. Instantly Benedicto's eyes lowered, finding the man who had spoken in the sacred old language.

"We are obliged to be done with them," he continued, trying to dismiss what he had heard. "They are the messengers of hell, the servants of the devil. Hell had overflown with their kind, it is our duty to return them to hell. Jesus Christ will reward us in the afterlife, for we are doing His work. I can hear the angels calling—"

Once again, the man interrupted Benedicto, his words echoing in Pope Gregory's ears. "Do not judge the ignorant, for they know not what they do."

"Do not let the devil's words poison your ears!" he screamed at the man who refused to be silent. "His twisted words are weak and without meaning." Casca finally stepped forward, clear for all to see, as the man who had challenged Benedicto of Aquilonia. He raised his eyes toward Benedicto, penetrating him with a cold stare, all the while catching Pope Gregory bringing his hand to his mouth. Niccolo and Maffeo stepped back, exposing Casca to the wrath of Benedicto and the anxious crowd. Nervously Marco also stepped back, dumbfounded by the actions of the man who had twice saved his life.

"Who are you?" Benedicto demanded. "How dare you speak such things in the old sacred language!"

In an instant not a word could be heard as all eyes set upon Benedicto and this strange scarred man who challenged him. Pope Gregory looked down toward Casca with bewilderment. *Who could know of such things,* he wondered.

"You must be the devil's messenger or the devil himself to challenge me and the mission of the church. Your words are those of an infidel who will die by the will of Jesus Christ," Benedicto barked at Casca.

"They are not my words," Casca simply replied shifting toward Pope Gregory. Their eyes met as they both understood. Pope Gregory nervously smiled, pleased by what he had heard from Casca, yet wondering how anyone could know the passages. Marco watched one of the bishops point toward the monks, who whispered to each other.

"How dare you!" Benedicto screamed at Casca. "You will die at the pontiff's feet for your insolence. He is the devil your Holiness, that is who he is!"

Ten armed guards with lances pointing at Casca stepped in front of the podium, threatening to impale him if he made even the smallest attempt to escape. "Take him now. You will say no more, the rope will make certain of that." Benedicto laughed. Casca, within all that was happening around him, smiled toward Pope Gregory and the monks who had huddled in a protective manner around the pontiff. They all knew.

"You do not remember the words of your countryman," Casca hissed softly at Benedicto, knowing his voice would carry more than just a simple message.

"You will hang and then you will die, that is all." Benedicto laughed.

"He will not," Pope Gregory finally spoke, bringing a collective gasp from the crowd. "The man does not speak for the devil. He speaks the words of the great one, Pope Urban the Second. He who has led us on this crusade nearly two hundred years ago."

Nothing more came from Benedicto's mouth. The message of Pope Urban returned, flooding his mind as his whole world collapsed around him. He had defiled the words of a prophet. In near panic he cringed away and stepped back, away from the altar. Within minutes he had gone from nearly leading hundreds on a new crusade to virtually excommunicating himself from the holy church. Shaking uncontrollably, he finally collapsed at Pope Gregory's feet, his hands reaching out, pleading for forgiveness.

"Join me in my chambers," was the last the audience would hear for now as Pope Gregory, surrounded by a dozen members of the clergy, escorted him out. The hundreds of men who had assembled would have to wait for an explanation of the previous events.

Casca along with Marco, Niccolo, and Maffeo were led into a small room lit by dozens of candles. Two broad swords crossing over an oversized oval shield hanging from the wall betrayed Pope Gregory's soldierly background. Adjacent to the shield, half a dozen lances rested against a wooden beam adding to the small armory in the pope's chambers. It was a small enclosure made of carefully arranged stone blocks and thick long beams that supported the walls along with an overhead stone slab that served as the canopy. In a few places cracks allowed the midday sun to break through, the sunshine intermixing with the light the candles gave off. A chamber clearly not fit for a pope, yet Pope Gregory had chosen it as his personal audience chamber. The four of them stood by a worn, thick wooden table as Pope Gregory sat and addressed them.

"How can you know this?" he finally asked of Casca. "You could not be of the clergy. Are you? I have never heard those words spoken by anyone. They are in the sacred texts, from many generations ago." Without giving much time for a response he continued, "Why have you come to the Holy Land of Christ?"

"We are on a mission of great importance," Marco interrupted, dropping to his knees, reaching out toward Pope Gregory's ringed hand.

"Quiet down, boy. How dare you speak without being addressed," Niccolo yelled at his son in a low, threatening voice.

"You are a brave, and brazen, young man. Forgive the boy, his heart seems to be in the right place." Pope Gregory smiled at the four of them, waving at Marco to rise from his knees. Marco gasped for air, shocked at his own impudence and foolish actions, yet he rose and made his way next to Casca, a few feet away from the table.

"Please forgive him, my lord. He is young and too often acts without thought. It is my fault, I have failed . . . ," Niccolo pleaded, as his voice softened and drifted off.

"What is this great mission of which you speak? Who has sent you to me?" Pope Gregory inquired.

Casca watched the man trying to act in a manner befitting his newly found position. Pope Gregory sat on his high-backed oak chair, digging his fingers into the arm rests, striving to appear comfortable, yet showing the obvious significance of his position in the church.

"We have traveled many years to bring a message from the Great Khan of the Mongols," Maffeo finally spoke.

"Genghis Khan? I thought he had returned east, far from here, to the land of his people."

"He has, your holiness, and since has passed away," Maffeo answered, surprised that it was not well known, as it had been many years since. "It is Khubilai Khan who now rules," Maffeo added, not wanting to embarrass Pope Gregory with the fact that Khubilai Khan was Genghis Khan's grandson.

"What is it that he wants of me? His world is far from mine, it is the Saracens who are of concern in the land of Christ," Pope Gregory queried.

"Khubilai Khan rules most of the land east of here. He has become emperor of China and now governs many people and many lands, from Persia to the endless ocean beyond China, from the frozen northern seas to the southern jungles of Burma and Champa. His armies are in the hundreds of thousands, while his subjects are in the tens of millions."

Pope Gregory sat back, trying to take it all in. *Hundreds of thousands? Millions?* The enormity of it all shocked him. Was Khubilai Khan friend or foe? A man who commanded such armies could rule the world. No force the church could assemble would ever be able to rival the numbers the Khan's messengers spoke of. Was this letter a strangely delivered message to demand surrender? What was he to do? Compared to the Khan, the Saracens were insignificant, if what he was told was the truth.

"He does not desire what you fear the most," Maffeo offered seeing Pope Gregory cringe and pull back in his seat. "The years have changed the Great Khan."

"How can you speak of him as being great? You honor and respect this man? That should not be! He is not a follower of Christ!" Pope Gregory found himself questioning Maffeo's beliefs, and acting in a manner befitting the leader of all Christianity.

"The world is immense, my lord. Most of the world has not heard of Jesus Christ, our savior. Some may consider them pagans and infidels, but that is not the truth. They have followed others in their beliefs," Niccolo concluded, well aware that his brave words were likely to be considered sacrilegious. "Perhaps they need saving," he added.

"Perhaps they do." Pope Gregory smiled at Niccolo, showing he understood the effort it must have taken Niccolo to speak of Jesus Christ in such a manner.

Pope Gregory walked back and forth in the small enclosure, reading the message sent by Khubilai Khan. He nervously paced, his boots clicking against the stone floors, as he reread the letter, at times looking at his four guests, at other times looking up toward the unseen heavens. Eventually he returned to the head of the table and sat back down.

"This Khan of yours, he is a man that can be believed?" he inquired. "He wishes to open communication and trade with us? It does not sound like the words of a man who has conquered half the world."

"He is, as I said, a man much changed by the years, your Holiness. Life has schooled and hardened him well. He understands the world has changed around him faster than he has been able to change. His son, Chen-Chin, an intelligent and able young man, has spent all of his life learning of different peoples, religions, customs, languages, and philosophies. The Great Khan plans for the next ruler of China to be a man who is educated and able to lead the empire. Khubilai Khan has sent us to help him connect our two worlds together. He wants to learn about us and for us to learn about him."

"Why should we learn about him?" Pope Gregory inquired, listening to Maffeo's words.

"Because not knowing would be ignorance," Marco interjected. "That is not what the Lord wishes of us."

Niccolo glared at his son for again speaking without being spoken to. He looked at Pope Gregory to see the reaction to his son's brazen interruption.

"You are right young man, it would be ignorance. That is not what the new church is about. We have been closed in for too many dark years, but I will make it different. Christ our savior wants us to be men, not puppets that sway in the bluster of time." Pope Gregory stood tall and raised his head up proudly. "I will send a message to the Khan, with you as my special envoys," he continued. "Your way will be safe and clear and your travel aided as long as you are within our territory; from then on, it is God's speed to you. I believe our Lord Jesus Christ will be your protector in this holy crusade. Return to me tomorrow for my reply."

SEVEN

The rest of the day they all spent preparing for their departure. Octavio had returned to the harbor completing his trade with some local masons and artisans. He watched as four of his men checked and rechecked the sail and the rigging, making certain nothing was left to chance. It had been years since he had seen his home in Alexandria and his many sisters of whom he often spoke. He was not about to allow any mistakes so close to home. Octavio looked forward to returning to the sea, which unfailingly relieved the endless cough that always seemed to punish him whenever land was near. Had it been up to him, the ocean would have been his home forever. Nonetheless, duty and family called.

"I will be on my way in a few days," he gleefully reported to Maffeo and Niccolo. "It has been too long. I wonder how my sisters have changed. Time can hurt so much. Well, half the boat is filled with gifts and trinkets for them. I must have cleaned out all the shops along the wharf," Octavio added, laughing, trying to mend his own aching heart.

Maffeo, Niccolo, and Casca sat at a table in a tavern downstairs from their sleeping area, for the hundredth time going over maps, trying to decide which way was most secure for their return trip to the court of Khubilai Khan.

"I will be ready to leave," Octavio repeated his words, trying to get someone's attention.

"Forgive us, Octavio. I have been too preoccupied with this. Our map shows us the land, not the people who are occupying it. It is a difficult decision which way to take." Niccolo sighed. "The land route to Hormuz, then off to India then China by sea appears most promising, for now, that is. Things change so much. What do you think, Octavio?"

Octavio lowered his head trying to get his bearings on the poorly drawn map on which they were hanging their lives. Coughing into his rope-burned hands he shook his head. "Will I ever see you again, Niccolo? What about you Maffeo, how long before you make it back to Alexandria?"

"It will take at least five or six years, anyway we have to, unless Marco decides to make his way back to Venice before we return," Maffeo conceded.

Casca watched Marco cower in horror, Marco suddenly realizing what his father was saying. It had caught him completely by surprise. Marco grabbed at the sides of the chair he was sitting on, trying to control himself, or at least not fall over.

"What are you saying? You can't be serious; I have come so far. You are sending me off for safekeeping? This is more horrible than having stayed in Venice and dealing with Carvo Donatello's henchmen," Marco protested with anger in his voice.

"Did you not understand?" Niccolo inquired, surprised by his son's reaction. "Was it not clear that you will be going to Alexandria with Octavio? We cannot take you with us, not knowing what awaits us. The Saracens are everywhere. You will like Alexandria, I have spent many wonderful years there."

Marco could not hear and did not care what else his father had to say, even his father's concern for his life could not improve on how he felt. He had traveled this far, having thought his father had grown to accept him, and now it was all gone. He would not see his father for years, maybe forever. The pain of shattered dreams was worse than of dreams never realized. He slumped down in his chair, drained of energy, not even enough anger or disappointment left in him to protest.

"Well, there it is." Maffeo attempted to break the tension. "Marco, I told you to make friends with Octavio, don't you remember that? You will like Alexandria, and no doubt you will not be displeased to meet his sisters," Maffeo added, hoping that his words would help Marco, and hopefully not unduly anger an overprotective brother.

"It is time to return to the legate's mansion, if you can call it that." Niccolo tried changing the subject at hand. "A blessed day this is. The pope has thankfully decided to riposte to the Great Khan's message, and we have been so honored to be chosen as Pope Gregory's emissaries. We have been blessed by Jesus Christ, praised be His name."

Casca had decided to remain at their lodgings and not accompany Maffeo and Niccolo on their trip to the pope's dwellings. Seeing Marco suffer with Vittorio at his side, hopelessly trying to bring a smile to his face, soon made him question his decision and curse at himself. Seeing other people's pain, no matter how much time had hardened him, had become a burden that at times was as difficult as dealing with his own cursed life.

Umberto sat with Vittorio and Marco, the three of them with their heads bowed, at times recalling some event of the past that brought smiles onto Umberto and Vittorio's lips. However, most of the time the moments of silence brought only sadness.

Casca watched the three of them hold each other's hands in the peculiar way he had seen a few times earlier. With their arms extended and elbows bent, the three formed a circle, only their forefingers, middle fingers, and thumbs making rings that they clasped onto each other.

"It is the ring of eternal friendship." Octavio whispered into Casca's ear as the two observed this unusual joining. "They used to call it *the four corners of the circle,* but that was before Vittorio's older brother died. Umberto told me of this while we journeyed to Acre. It has something to do with being blood brothers, and the interlocked fingers is their sign of all being well. I am not certain. Umberto started telling me about it, but it seemed too personal for me to ask more questions."

Casca nodded and turned away. He was going to miss Marco and the others while heading to China. Hopefully Marco's thirst for knowledge would be quenched elsewhere. His father was not going to be part of it and Marco needed to accept that. Once more Marco was about to lose his father. Life had a way of scattering people over time.

Casca struggled to think back and remember his own father, yet he could not. He could not picture his father's face or recall even if his father had cared for him. Angrily he bit his lip, saddened by how time had raped his mind of so much, yet memories of horror, pain, and death refused to leave. He anxiously yet unsuccessfully attempted to turn his mind away from further torturous reminiscence.

Niccolo and Maffeo returned later in the day cheering loudly, congratulating each other, pleased by their success. Pope Gregory as promised had written and handed them a message to be delivered to the Great Khan of China. As important as their accomplishment was, Casca could tell even in their exuberance the clear knowledge of the task still at hand. Possibly years would pass and endless obstacles would need to be overcome before the message could be delivered.

Casca awoke before dawn. He sat up and tasted the air. A moment later he was on his feet pulling on his tunic and unsheathing his sword. His heart pounded and blood started to boil as the cold steel of his sword reawakened memories of death. It had been long since his hands had taken a life; however, it was only moments away. The eternal soldier had reawakened. *Soldier, you are content with what you are. Then that you shall remain until we meet again.* The cursed words returned, punishing him from over a thousand years. Casca shook his head, trying to clear and ready his thoughts. Was it possible? After all, he had returned to the land of Christ. Was this the day he had been waiting for?

Next to him, Octavio snored mercilessly, nearly rattling the cloth that hung flatly against the opening in the wall that allowed the night air in, oblivious to how his life had changed while he had slept. The salty taste of the western breeze could not hide the truth of the night. The harbor was on fire.

"Get up, we need to get everyone!" Casca yelled at Octavio, knocking him out of his bed. Tightening the belt around his waist Casca kicked down the door leading into the hallway, splintering the wood, sending it tumbling down the stone steps.

"What is going on?" Octavio blabbered incoherently, painfully coughing at Casca. "What is that stench?"

Ignoring Octavio's cries, Casca ran into the hallway. The curved steel of the invaders met him. As they had slept, the enemy had been hard at work. With the cover of darkness, dozens of Saracen ships had drifted into the harbor and had burned down any ships that were laying anchor. Hundreds of vessels burned in the night, trapping all who were aboard, sending them into the death of fire and water. Meanwhile, on land, thousands had broken into the city from north and south, overwhelming the sentries and bursting through the protective gates. Now it was just a matter of time and fortune before Acre, the last bastion of crusader stronghold, would fall.

Casca ran down one of the stairwells slashing side to side with his own heavy sword, the tip of his blade sending sparks as it met shields, swords, and the stone bricks that formed the walls.

"Marco, where is he?" Maffeo's concerned voice overcame the noise of battle. "Is he still upstairs?" A half-dressed Maffeo ran down the hallway, pulling on his pants with one hand while wielding a short sword with the other. He caught Casca's eyes and pleaded for an answer. A dozen Saracens had broken into their lodging, trying to take best advantage over all who slept.

The street was noisy as many ran for cover and filled with the shriek and battle cry of the invaders and the cries of the soon to be dead. Horses thundered by, seemingly by the thousands, bringing reinforcements to back up the unrelenting attack, the soldiers of Allah taking down any who did not wear their colors.

"He is still upstairs!" Niccolo yelled at his brother. "Marco is trapped on the other side." Standing back-to-back, Maffeo and Niccolo fought valiantly, outnumbered, desperately trying not to be separated and outflanked. The followers of Allah, although in great numbers and well armed, struggled as Niccolo and Maffeo proved themselves to be more than just merchants.

Ending a Saracen's life with a horizontal slash of his sword, Casca kicked the huge man in the chest, hastening his fall to the ground, allowing himself to run past the man, and cutting short the man's last praise to Allah. Not much was more annoying than hearing the endless chants that permeated every waking moment in joy or despair. It was doubtful Allah reveled in the death of any. Casca's ears were glad to be spared.

At the end of the small alcove Casca pushed a drunken patron out of the way and made his way up the stairs. The poor fool would never feel the blade of death that was sure to follow on this night. For once, a night of drinking would serve him well.

Taking three steps with each leap he quickly reached the hallway leading to Marco's room. Six robed men had already made their way up before him and were crashing down the two doors leading to the sleeping quarters. Casca ran as fast as his legs could carry him and met the blade of two henchmen. The struggle was brief, one of them dropping his sword the first time it met Casca's blade while the other lasted a few seconds more. The fury of Casca's assault and the weight of his sword cut the men down to their knees as they collapsed, their lives ending by the time their limp bodies were sprawled on the wooden beams.

"Take up your sword, help me!" Umberto's pleading voice reached Casca's ears. Casca pushed his way by a man and made his way down the poorly lit hallway. He stumbled over the contorted body of another man still twitching in the throes of death. Steadying himself with his left hand, Casca continued his frenzied pace and came face-to-face with another picture of death. Time nearly stood still watching Umberto fall to the ground holding his bleeding belly, his eyes still pleading for Marco to help him out.

The three invaders had made their way into Marco, Vittorio, and Umberto's room, surprising them in their sleep. Umberto had been the first to wake and take to arms; however, he did not last very long. Vittorio had been backhanded by a shield, landing him in a bleeding and whimpering mass all his own. He lay there, cowering with his knees drawn up underneath his chin, hiding his bleeding face from the table that had collapsed on him.

Marco had not fared as well. Unharmed, he came face-to-face with a one-eyed would-be servant of Allah. Frozen in terror he watched the man slash at Umberto and beat him back with quick and powerful strokes of his scimitar. "Help me, Marco." The pleading words pierced Marco's soul, begging him with their urgency. The sound of horror reverberated in his mind, yet he was unable to move and come to Umberto's aid. Marco could not help his lifelong friend.

He watched as the man knocked the sword out of Umberto's hand. Umberto fell to one knee, pleading for Marco to intervene. The one-eyed man laughed, watching Marco stand like a statue, with his hand on his sword, yet unable to help. Pushing him out of the way the man pierced Umberto's belly, giving him the final blow that would take minutes of agony to cause death.

Laughing, the Saracen watched Umberto slowly bleed to death, then turned his attention to Marco. Marco could not look up and face his adversary. His eyes were transfixed on Umberto slowly drifting away from life; however, his inaction forced Umberto's executioner to hold his assault for a moment, just long enough for Casca to intervene. The Saracean smiled, pleased at how he was fortunate enough to receive more pleasure than he had expected.

Casca's blade struck, a shower of sparks flying from the meeting of swords. They battled evenly, each man taking turns pushing the other back with his thrusts. The man stepped toward the table Vittorio was cowering under, interrupting his assault, and kicked a fallen-over chair toward Casca's feet. Anticipating this, Casca stepped to the side and struck the flying chair with his sword, sending splinters of wood toward his opponent. "Die, you ugly beast," he hissed at Casca in Arabic, not knowing if his words would be understood, but needing to spew his venom at this creature who was proving such a challenge.

Stepping toward a still motionless Marco he at first tried using the boy as a shield, then pushed him toward Casca in an attempt to gain advantage. All the while Vittorio whimpered and feverishly prayed for his life, yet refused or was unable to help. He watched from behind the shattered table and gasped for breath, stunned by the proximity of death.

Needing to end this soon, Casca struck down with all his might against the small round shield his opponent was parrying with and also pushed Marco out of the way, knocking him against the wall. The force of the blow initially drove the man's hand down then caused him to stumble, knocking his yellow turban to the dusty floor. It was more than enough as Casca came at him with fire in his eyes. The man's life ended moments later as his body was impaled against the wooden beam in the corner of the room. Casca had no time for delicate swordplay. They all needed to flee this house of death and the city of Acre. The sun would rise upon new flags the coming dawn.

The dark veil of battle continued enveloping Casca, watching Marco kneel by his dying friend. The fever of the kill was not about to leave him soon. More were about to die by his hand this night. Breathing deeply, his eyes searched the room and the opening that led into the street below. Hundreds clashed in the streets as men, women, and children tried to stay alive, their cries rising toward the sky.

"Forgive me, Umberto," Marco pleaded. In his last conscious moments Umberto tried a faint smile. Blood came from the corners of his mouth and the cough of near death. "I am cold," he whispered with the realization that the end was near. "Hold my hands," he begged weakly. Marco looked up at Casca. Casca shook his head; there was no helping Umberto any more. The convulsions of death settled quickly as Umberto's hands unclenched. Marco's head slumped toward his chest as he sobbed, listening to Umberto's life drift away.

"We must leave now." Casca's orders finally forced Vittorio to stand. Casca's chest heaved with the effort of battle still fresh and the knowledge of what lay ahead. With the tip of the sword he pointed to the door, hastening Vittorio's steps. There was no time to be wasted.

"I have to leave you," Marco whispered to Umberto's lifeless body. He kneeled for a few seconds longer, crossing Umberto's arms over his chest, laying him to rest. Marco traced the silver cross on Umberto's tunic with the fingers on his right hand and closed his unseeing eyes with his left. "Forgive me; may you rest in peace . . ." Marco's voice drifted off in a quick prayer.

The three of them reached the bottom of the stairs moments later. Marco and Vittorio stood side by side, their heads down, cursing themselves and their inaction, knowing that they would never be able to change what had happened. It was punishment that would last a lifetime. "Where is Umberto?" Maffeo inquired and was quick to understand seeing their demeanor.

"The city is crawling with them, we must flee immediately," Octavio interjected, trying to get everyone to pay attention.

The streets were a picture of doom. Men and women, young and old, littered the ground, the bodies of horses and camels twisting amongst the dead and dying debris. Cries were heard from the piles of flesh and from the ones still able to flee. The massacre was to continue throughout the night. It was doubtful any gods reveled by the death in their name.

"This way, move it!" Casca ordered seeing that the shock of what they were seeing nearly froze everyone in their steps. Time was short and only good fortune and the likely pillaging would keep the invaders occupied and distracted from causing more death. This was their time to attempt an escape.

Casca regretted going back to retrieve Umberto's fallen body, yet he had felt driven to do so. It was a foolish thing to do, knowing how brutal the Saracens could be and how much they delighted in imprisoning and torturing their enemies. Casca had spent many dark and miserable nights in the bowels of prisons in the Holy Land, wondering if he would ever see daylight. At such times the idea of having the Mongol horde overrun all of the world just to give him a chance for freedom had seemed like a reasonable idea. Empires came and went, except for Casca who had been cursed to outlive the ages.

Even taking that into consideration, Casca had been unable to help himself. There was something about this young man Marco that compelled him to help, just as he had done before and, unbeknownst to him, would do so in the future. Seeing Marco and Vittorio and expecting them to fall into a deeper and deeper depression had persuaded him to act. They needed to see their friend laid to rest. Casca had seen more men fall than he cared to remember, yet he knew he was unlike any of them.

Ducking into a dark alleyway they fled on foot carrying Umberto's body along with them. The chaos of the attack and the dark veil of the night kept them hidden as they made their way along the narrow streets of Acre. There was no going back toward the harbor to flee by boat. The *Saladino*, Octavio's pride and joy had probably burned down with the rest of the ships. Their only escape was south, away from the city, into the desert, straight into the heart of Saracean territory. It would be the place where, for now, their number would be the fewest. To the west and around Acre any escape would have been impossible.

Not much was said over the next few hours. Remembering the old streets, Casca led them south, away from the major avenues that were likely to be traveled by the invaders, into the narrow and unlit passages that cloaked their escape. At times they stopped and hid in darkened alleyways, avoiding the rush of Saracean horsemen. Possibly it was the end of the crusaders in the land of Christ. By dawn, they had distanced themselves from the field of battle, away from the city, onto a less-than-well-traveled road.

Here, on the outskirts of Acre, in a field next to a thin, nearly-dried-out stream, they laid Umberto's savaged body to rest. Marco and Vittorio dug the hole with the blade of their swords, in the end cleaning the area of rocks and dried roots with their bare hands. It was a shallow grave, but it would have to do. It seemed the earth did not want to receive Umberto's broken body in this place, sharp and jagged rocks hindering their work. Eventually Umberto was allowed to rest with his arms crossed and his eyelids covered with cloth.

Kneeling by the grave, Vittorio and Marco covered up the last of their friend's body with large rocks and dusty soil. With their heads down they watched the gray soil trickle amongst the stones to settle over Umberto's cold body. What sorrow it had been to water this land so wastefully with his blood. He was just another one who had come so far on a mission in the name of God, Marco thought. Or had he? Was this what God had intended for Umberto, or had they prevented him from fulfilling his calling? They would never know. He had become one of thousands to litter the landscape in the Holy Land. The insignificance of Umberto's existence shook Marco's thoughts, again making him question his faith and man's destiny.

Using two roots Vittorio had ripped out of the ground, Marco managed to fashion a cross to place by Umberto's grave. A strand of cloth torn from his tattered shirt held the dried pieces together, the tears Marco shed wetting the cross and the grave.

Marco and Vittorio once again clasped their fingers and thumbs together, attempting to form the four corners of the circle. *What was the use?* they both pondered simultaneously. All was not well. The ring of friendship had not served Umberto. They had failed their friend in the most horrible way. Time would soothe, but never forgive them.

They traveled toward Tabriz, eventually onto Persian soil. News of Bibars, fourth of the Mameluke sultans, did not deter them from pushing on. Meeting his forces or of others, they would just have to contend and reason with them. They did not appear a threat on their own, as long as they kept their mission a secret. Casca figured the great grandson of Bibars the First was not any more gentle to people not of his kind than he had been while wresting Caesarea from the Christians years before. Memory of bloody years came back, rushing into Casca's mind. He reached to his right thigh, feeling for the thick scar that had refused to heal any other way than as a knot the size of his thumb. Casca's debt to pay to the Mamelukes would have to wait for another day. Eventually one of the Mameluke descendants would need to make amends for their actions, of that Casca was certain. For now it seemed a near death wish or a suicide run to traverse this area, yet there was no other choice.

They moved on, Niccolo and Maffeo following Casca closely, realizing this stranger was a blessing with all his knowledge of the area and its people. Casca seemed to walk the hills and valleys as if his eyes expected every turn of the road without any surprises while his feet were revisiting old grounds. When encountering villages where strange tongues were spoken, Casca was easily able to get by. Other times, when water became scarce, Casca quickly found hidden water beds, unseen rock-sheltered springs, or plants rich in moisture.

Maffeo unhappily handled the four mules they had been

fortunate enough to acquire on the outskirts of Acre. For some reason the stubborn mules would not allow anyone else to lead them, feed them, or water them. It was an honor Maffeo could have easily done without. Unfortunately, they had been unable to purchase or barter for horses. For now, they would have to be content with the mules; only their feet were available to carry them.

Even with their wealth of precious stones, there had been not much else to purchase. A few sacks of food and flasks of water was all they had been able to barter for, along with the mules. In this land, a bladder of water or pouch of salt was life itself, while gold or diamonds held little value. Casca had tried to acquire sheets of white cloth as protection from the elements; however, he had been unsuccessful. There was nothing they could barter for as most of this land had been drained by poverty. The rest of their supplies they hoped to acquire on their way.

"How long to the next village?" Octavio often inquired, not unlike an anxious child, trying to hasten their arrival. Octavio seemed to suffer the most from the travel, endlessly coughing dryly into his hand or his shoulder, at times getting a mouthful of sand when the winds picked up.

Vittorio and Marco had been quiet ever since that unforgettable night in Acre. They had both cowered and allowed their friend of a lifetime to die at the hands of the dreaded Saracean. At times they spoke to each other, but not often. If addressed they answered, keeping the conversation at the barest minimum. Mostly they traveled with their heads down, hoping that time would soften the nightmare of their inaction.

They had both lost much weight over the last few weeks. Marco had not much weight to lose since he had always been thin and wiry. However, the hard road had a way of finding and ridding the body of all excess. His chest had become sunken and his ribs nearly showed through his torn white shirt. Vittorio still carried a lot of excess weight, but that was not to last much longer. The intensity of the road and his nerves were sure to strip him of every last bit of fat. For weeks he kept retying his belt, tightening it as his thickness vanished. His cheeks eventually also deflated, showing a surprisingly rugged jaw and a highborn look.

"How much longer before we reach this town Narheez that

you spoke of?" Octavio inquired of Casca on a painfully hot afternoon. They had been traveling for weeks and Tabriz still seemed as far off as it had ever been, while Narheez was supposedly not even halfway to Tabriz.

"It shouldn't be too many more days. We will be able to get fresh water and food there."

"How can you be so sure?" Octavio asked, nearly defying Casca's words. "Can we not go directly to Hormuz? The sooner we get to the sea the sooner I can sail home and the rest of you can head off for India and China," Octavio continued, coughing painfully into his stained left sleeve.

"We must travel north toward Tabriz, my friend," Maffeo attempted to help Octavio, trying to deflect his anxious words. "It will not be much longer. In Tabriz, just a few of these stones will provide us with horses and supplies. We cannot expect these poor pathetic village dwellers to have what we need."

They continued along the barren landscape, the land turning more difficult and drier as every hour passed. Southern winds picked up at times, bringing the furnace of the sun against their backs, burning their feet at every step. The summer months must have been particularly hot and dry this year as even the Euphrates, the river that had given life to civilization, had nearly run dry.

Nothing more than thick stagnant water awaited them. The bodies of hundreds of creatures littered the riverbank, many of them having traveled for days and weeks, only to be disappointed by the murky darkened water that poisoned them. The ones leary of drinking it perished by the sun, having chosen one type of death over the other. Disease and death hovered over them. Casca's shaking head was enough to tell the tale as they came to the banks of the river. Marco had been anxious to see the legendary river and admire its history and grandeur. There was nothing but death here. They would need to push on and hope.

The village of Narheez, which they had expected to pass through, was never found. Perhaps they had been near and had just not seen it. Sand dunes and mounds of rock and debris were all that met them for days. Possibly Narheez lay beneath, and the desert had laid claim upon it. It was not the first time the unforgiving sand rewrote history in this part of the world.

Eventually the land became more merciful, the sand turning into soil, and the incline of the plain taking them toward the mountains. Finally, thin grasses and plants showed signs of life. On a plain, they reached the outskirts of the city of Tabriz. It was not what Marco had expected. Just another city of the desert world, still a world of traders, brimming with human and animal wares and the never-ending winds that lashed man and beast alike. Venice seemed so far away with its canals and endless waterways.

The main marketplace was also not unlike the one in Acre. Anxious merchants displaying their goods, ready to make a sale or a trade. Huge camels waddled by, packed as high and wide as the beasts could take, threatening to topple over and crush any bystanders.

"Salaam aleikum!" The eager greeting of merchants offering their goods rang out from everywhere they went.

"Neharkum sa'id, aleikum salaam." Casca often answered when prodded by overly zealous traders and shopkeepers, "May your day be prosperous." Some responded with more fervent advances; others returned a smile still hoping to make a trade with this curious assembly of men.

They rested for a week, allowing their bodies to recover from the cruel road and scorching sun. It was a difficult repose, knowing the hard road ahead; yet, Niccolo and Maffeo insisted, because other than Casca it was a delicate group that could easily become overwhelmed by the intensity of the road.

Over the next few days they learned of their good fortune. Apparently large forces of Said Khan, a nephew of one of Genghis Khan's half brothers, patrolled the area, constantly attempting to push the Saracen forces farther south or keep them toward the west. Said Khan had been born into the Khanate and been brought up to serve the Khan of all Mongols, Khubilai Khan. He was a man with his own land and people, yet he served the Great Khan just like a dozen other Khans did in this part of the world.

Thousands of miles from each other, Said Khan performed his duties to the empire, keeping the western borders strong and resistant to any possible invaders, while at the same time at the ready should Khubilai Khan decide to extend his empire farther to the west. Casca knew that they would have likely had no difficulty dealing with Said Khan, possibly they would have been welcome. However, it was never undesirable to avoid the clash of huge armies where loyalties are often not observed until all the dust had settled. For now it had been preferable to slip through, and continue on their trek.

A few well-bartered hours allowed Maffeo to purchase eight horses and all the supplies they needed. His never-ending stash of precious stones had been gladly received in this town. Possibly a hand in marriage or the beginning of a journey would turn on this exchange, a journey not unlike their own. Casca sometimes wondered where the stones would end up and how many owners they would have over the years. For now, these gems had given them survival in the manner of food, water, and horses.

The road to Hormuz was long and difficult, but much easier traveled at the offset. They headed south, following along the path of caravans that had snaked along this terrain for perhaps thousands of years. The road turned southeast, through Persia, legends of which exhilarated Marco and Vittorio while bringing the most horrifying reminiscences of pain and suffering to Casca. His body had been nearly consumed by fire at the hands of the Persians. The pain he had endured would never leave his body and soul.

The desert world brought new lessons to Marco and Vittorio. Even Octavio, who had traveled through these lands, could not get used to the endless snakes, flies, and mosquitoes whose existence he often questioned, wondering why God had decided to curse the deserts with their presence. As if God had constantly sent plagues upon these lands since the beginning of time. Never did Octavio's wounds caused by plant or insect ever heal, forever irritating his skin, forcing him to scratch helplessly at sores, reopening them for the creatures of the desert to again torture him.

At times, small mounds of dirt and rock formations reminded them of the casualties the desert insisted upon. Often human and animal remains just lay bare, broken over rocks or intertwined in death throes, wastefully littering the land, no one having had the desire to bury them. Marco shook his head, realizing how far from home he had come. It was an existence less glamorous than he had expected. Wonders of life and the world awaited him.

"In three days we should reach Ablah-sin, *the four brothers of the crest*," Casca remarked, startling his fellow travelers. No one had spoken much in recent days, all of them trying to save their energy. It had been weeks since they had been through any village for supplies or fresh water. Without speaking about it, they all cursed themselves for not having brought camels along on this trip, foolishly having believed that this usually well-traveled road would be easy and better supplied along the way. It had been a much drier season than they would have believed, and not surprisingly no one had alerted them to it. Maffeo thought back on the man who had so anxiously sold him the horses, complimenting his reserve of fine animals, without a mention of what he likely knew.

The last of the water dribbled meagerly at the bottom of a collapsed bladder. No one dared touch it, symbolically, if not foolishly, trying to hang on to the last elixir of life. Most of them had not had any water in days, allowing all there was to be drunk by the horses. Now even that was nearly gone. Without the precious liquid the great beasts were as useless as the mounds of rock and sand they endlessly passed.

"How do you know that?" Marco started asking, then realized his question was without substance. Obviously it was not the first time Casca had traveled these lands, and questioning him was unnecessary. Wearily, he covered his eyes from the blazing sun, regretting that he had challenged Casca and expended the energy in doing so.

"Ablah-sin has been around forever, the fires marking this land even before I ever walked this . . . We should be able to get as much fresh water as we need, also sugar dates, bread, and cheese," Casca continued, realizing there was no point in speaking of his strange existence or explaining the fires. Marco and the rest would certainly remember nothing but the black fires. It was a sight to be branded in their minds.

In three days they reached the outskirts of Ablah-sin, or what had been left of it. Most of them were delirious, the heat and the sun having sapped them of strength and thought. They had not had anything to drink in too long. A few times Casca had dug deep into the dirt with his dagger, looking for wet

soil or roots that held perhaps a few drops of water. Eagerly
Marco and Vittorio had attempted to do the same, but with
no success. Eventually they abandoned the search when the
success of their work was outweighed by the effort involved.

Four of the horses had made it this far by some good fortune, though they had not had anything to drink in almost two
days. Even the foam that had bubbled through their strained
lips and nostrils had ended, possibly nothing but the blood in
their bodies still flowing, with no other moisture still present.

The other four had died along the dusty trail, leaving their
bodies to become the feast of vultures and other creatures of
the desert. Casca had ended their lives, terminating their painful existence, making certain they were not to be feasted on
by predators while life still beat in their broken bodies. In a
matter of days their skeletons were likely to be the only thing
marking the road, indicating the passing of their small caravan, and the direction they had taken in their last steps. The
desert would claim victory over them as it had over previous
thousands.

For the last day they had watched a dark cloud rise toward
the horizon, staining the setting sun with its murky veil. During daytime the earth endlessly belched the blackest of smoke
and ash into the air, eventually the winds carrying it higher
into the heavens, poisoning the clear blue skies. At dusk, the
dark red fires lapped into the darkness of the coming night,
darkening the blanket that eventually overtook heaven and
earth.

Nearing the village Casca brought his hands to his eyes,
trying to shield from the glare, hoping that his memories of
this place were true. He saw life. Holding Marco's shoulder
he pointed to the outskirts of the village where a young girl
was watering an Arabian baby camel. Even with Casca's
coaxing, Marco and Vittorio could not look at her, their eyes
nearly transfixed by the black cloud that drifted upward.

"Who dares send that black smoke of death toward the
heavens? It must be the devil's work!" Vittorio spoke for the
first time in weeks. He whiffed at the air, trying to find something in memory that had smelled as foul as this poison of
the sky. "It comes from the belly of the earth, does it not,
Messer Casca?"

"It does come from the ground, from deep below," Casca

responded, wetting his lips as best as he could, for the moment amused at how all that was dark or evil was the devil's work.

Within minutes they reached the well, which the girl had been using to water the camel. By then, eight armed men had formed a semicircle around the well, shielding it with their bodies and drawn swords. The girl had retreated and hidden within the safety of a hut. Peering through an opening, she watched the six strangers approach.

"Salaam aleikum," Casca whispered through cracked lips and a painfully dry throat. Casca knew well he was in Persian territory, yet the men seemed to be of Arabian stock.

There was no response from the armed men. They were nothing but shepherds, trying to act as soldiers, protecting their land and precious source of life. Poorly dressed, their tattered clothing clung to their bodies from the filth and oil. All of them were covered with a black pasty film and the sand that had adhered to it. Their faces thin and worn spoke of a life not much more pleasant than death. One of them grunted to the others in a manner of speech difficult even to acknowledge as spoken words. The apparent leader, larger and better fed than the rest, turned and gave orders to one of the younger men who turned and ran to the huts.

"Moya," Casca again attempted in Arabic, "Water, please." He saw no recognition from any of them for the word he used.

The leader again grunted something to one of his men, this time his words more clear and understandable to Casca. It was a rough form of Persian, broken by lack of contact with others who spoke the traditional form. Casca smiled to the man and spoke to him again, this time in the man's tongue.

"We have come a long way. What has happened to the rest of Ablah-sin?"

The leader furrowed his brows, surprised that this stranger knew to speak his language and of his knowledge of this part of the world. Marco and the rest stood and watched in amazement as once again Casca surprised them with his knowledge of people and languages.

"What happened here? Does Masrah the Proud still live?" Casca once again inquired, bowing his head with reverence while mentioning the name.

Stepping back, the leader of the defenders sheathed his

sword and ordered the rest of them to do so also. Hearing the name of Masrah was more than enough for him. He was about to share the well with his new guests.

Casca and the leader of these men spoke for a few minutes; meanwhile, Marco and the rest were led to the well and offered water. With their bellies filled to the limit the five of them joined their hosts by the huts. The enclosures were made of nothing but straw, pieces of wood, and dirt, covered with black soot and filth, as was everything else in this land. Nothing much seemed to be holding the walls together other than the thickness of the grime that glazed the roofs of the decrepit huts.

Marco and Vittorio crossed themselves and looked at each other. Fire and smoke billowed in the background, burning and poisoning the sky. Down by the foot of this inferno the little village of Ablah-sin went on. Marco measured the short distance between the village and the wells of burning oil with his eyes. *Only the River Styx seemed to be missing in this inferno,* Marco thought.

Sitting on the ground by one of the huts, Casca spoke for hours with the leader of the village. Casca knew Masrah, the round little man who refused to smile, so as not to show weakness, the man who had been the leader of all Ablah-sin for dozens of years, could not still be alive. Masrah had been a beloved leader who was likely the source of song and folklore to his descendants. Casca had taken a well-weighed chance in mentioning his name.

Quietly they exchanged words, at times the leader becoming animated, gesticulating frantically, pointing to all four corners of the world. Casca mostly nodded his head and looked toward the west. The little girl who had earlier watered the camel, approached and brought a tray of fruit. There was not much there, but her eyes joyfully offered them to Casca. With a look of quiet desperation she tried to steal a glance from Casca, then quickly retreated and disappeared inside the hut.

Night came quickly and Casca was led to one of the blackened straw and clay-brick huts where Marco and the rest anxiously awaited his return, hoping for an explanation of the day's events and this strange place in which they found themselves. They all sat cross-legged on the dirt floor, almost like students awaiting their teacher to inform them of the day's subject. Again crossing themselves, Marco and Vittorio begged for an explanation.

"I have visited here a few years ago," Casca began, not wanting to share the truth about his return to this village nearly fifty years since he had last traveled through. "Much has changed since. Thousands of people used to live here; now only a few remain."

"What happened to them? What of these infernal fires? How can they burn without being consumed?" Vittorio questioned, his words running into each other, clearly not patient enough to hear Casca's story.

"The fires have been around for as long as anyone remembers," Casca continued. His thoughts drifted into the past, to Callinicus, his friend from the land of the pharaohs. The little Egyptian, a mannerly youngster, more concerned with designing buildings and writing poetry than anything that would upset anyone's sensibilities, had inadvertently also created an unquenchable fire the Greeks had used against the Muslims during the Byzantine invasion. Callinicus' intentions had been to create an oil that would burn clean and bright, allowing him to work during the night by the light of the fire, not to decimate thousands, burn down ships, or decide the fate of empires. Had he known, he would have been shamed in horror and wished for his own death. This oil of the earth burned the same, insatiable even when water flowed over it. "The burning wells have been salvation and purgatory for these people," Casca said, finally completing his thoughts after a moment of recollection.

"How could that be?" Marco questioned. "These fires could not be of earthly origin, only the devil could fan the flames that burn on forever."

"Not all is heaven and hell, Marco," Maffeo insisted. "What would these people think if they saw the canals and waterways of Venice? Or the endless oceans? It is a different world, son."

"But why do they stay in this infernal place?" Vittorio wondered, adding his puzzlement to it all. In anticipation of the answer, he roughly scratched at his chin, raising welts.

"They are trapped," Casca continued. "Years ago there was a great battle fought on the crest of the valley, on the outskirts of Ablah-sin. Tolui Khan, one of Genghis Khan's sons, was at war with Jamshyd the Bare, a Mameluke sultan of the Bentren-Ran Caliphate. Eventually Ablah-sin became the battleground. Thousands died on both sides, with most of Ablah-sin destroyed in the meanwhile. Following that—"

"What of these fires?" Marco interrupted.

"The fires have been around forever," Casca patiently continued. "With this great battle fought, the fires became the symbol of their war. To the sultan and his people, these fires are what preserve them, as the Mongol horde will not advance beyond them. The Mongol people believe the fires will rage on throughout eternity, poisoning the Eternal Blue Sky, yet symbolizing the beginning of the end for the Muslim world—"

"What is the Eternal Blue Sky," Marco interrupted once more, bringing another look of anger from his father and Maffeo who have been carefully listening.

"It is the Mongol's heaven. They believe that all warriors who are lost in battle will eventually end up in heaven, well . . . in the Eternal Blue Sky. These flames that burn forever poison and desecrate the heavens. The Mongols believe it will bring an end to the Muslim threat. Eventually the Muslims will be beaten and banished from this world. At such time, the flames that burn will be extinguished . . . or so they believe."

They sat for a while, Marco and Vittorio trying to understand what Casca had said. Less concerned, Niccolo and Maffeo's thoughts drifted to the hard road ahead. Ablah-sin was soon to be in their past as their road led south toward Hormuz and the open sea.

"Why do they not leave this miserable place? The air is thick and foul. Their death here will be no better than anyplace else," Octavio finally spoke, fighting the cough that always kept him company.

"They believe they are trapped, forever to be the sentinel, holding balance between the two powers. The people of Ablah-sin have accepted their role in this world to—"

"They have accepted death for themselves and their children?" Marco yelled out, aghast at the sacrifice these people were willing to make.

It was a situation better left for others to ponder, they all supposed, as no more was spoken of this for days to come.

They all watched the oil from the belly of the earth spout out of the fire wells, burning day and night, soiling the land and air. At times the flames reached up into the heavens, roaring upward from the splintered earth, shaking the ground and making all creatures of the earth cower. The road ahead was to test them further. Hormuz still lay weeks toward the south, through unfriendly land and people.

They traveled on toward Tabriz, eager and pleased to distance themselves from the burning inferno. *Hell on earth,* is what Marco had named it, the name not inappropriate. It was not the last time he was to use those words, as the world held more of hell's fury than he could have imagined.

Their pace had slowed with only three horses left to carry the supplies and sometimes give an exhausted one a reprieve, the rest of the horses having perished two days after they had arrived in Ablah-sin. The water and food had not been enough to bring the beasts back from the edge of death.

The road eased for the next few weeks, food and water becoming more plentiful and the weather becoming less oppressive. Two days spent in the old city of Kashan allowed them to renew their spirits with the purchase of six well-rested horses. Their own three horses they left behind, not wanting to drag them on, worn as they were, and slowing their pace. The three beasts had come a long way and tolerated much; they had earned their release.

With less effort spent searching for supplies, they had almost become able to enjoy the long trip. For the first time, not every waking moment demanded the search for sustenance and a constant struggle for survival. For the time being, their senses were able to enjoy the wonder of this world. Marco and Vittorio marveled at the village of Eshafan, walking through the ruins of temples believed to be three thousand years old.

"This was placed here thirty centuries ago," Marco remarked, embracing a man-sized stone pillar that still held up the side of a wall. He ran his hand along the rough edge, his fingers tracing indentations obviously made by hands wielding carving tools. Pensively, his fingers touched the marks.

"And it will be there thirty centuries from now, most likely," Casca answered, causing Marco to further widen his

eyes in bewilderment. *Thirty centuries?* Marco tried to grasp
the generations that spoke of. The time was without meaning
to someone who had lived less than twenty years. Maffeo
smiled watching Marco observe and note everything they saw,
the young man almost refusing to blink in the fear that he
might miss something worth remembering. At times Marco
would stare, his eyes wide open, taking it all in, detail by
detail, trying to absorb every nuance of all they encountered.

Five days after passing through the ancient Moslem city of
Yazd the incline of the land took them to higher elevation.
Water had become quite plentiful, allowing them for the first
time not to have to consume days-old water that tasted of
rancid leather. The city of Kerman soon came to follow, allowing them two more days of rest and fresh food. They rode
along the well-traveled trails through the mountains, retracing
the steps that thousands had taken over many centuries. A
few days later a thick layer of snow slowed their travel, forcing them to find shelter and rest for a few more days. It was
not unwelcome or badly timed as the saddle sores had made
their travel quite painful in recent days.

EIGHT

"**I** can smell it, I can almost taste it!" Octavio's delighted
voice and unusual choice of words made them all smile
and listen up.

"We should see it by tomorrow," Casca agreed. The sight
of the Strait of Hormuz and the city itself brought all of them
to a near gallop the following day. The sea seemed to go on
forever, touching the horizon at its bluish-green edges. They
had come far, probably the most difficult portion of their
travel already behind them, or so they hoped.

"We should reach the outskirts of the city by sundown. I
know a place where the food is good and the rats are few and
small. I can promise no more."

They all looked at Casca, shaking their heads, wondering
if there was any place he had not yet been. Cheering on, they

led the small caravan of horses down the slopes of the mountain toward the edge of the quiet city of Hormuz.

"It is the first day of the holy month of Ramadan. We need to be quiet and respectful if we want food and shelter," Casca advised.

"I have heard of this Rama-something, praying and not eating, from what I remember," Vittorio added, amused at how the thought of deliberately not eating went against everything he had been about.

"Slightly more to it than that," Niccolo cut in, displeased at the disrespect Vittorio had shown. "We must honor their beliefs, even if we think different. This is their world and we are the foreigners."

"I suppose—"

"You must! We must show proper respect or we will never make it through here," Niccolo insisted.

Embarrassed by his words and foolish thoughts, Vittorio slowed the pace of his horse, pulling back, away from Niccolo's displeased glare.

"Moslems celebrate the revelation of the Holy Bible during Ramadan. According to them, Mohamed brought the last words of God; he was the final prophet who completed God's message to the world. Mohamed is the prophet, bringing the words of Allah to his people." Niccolo found himself repeating his thoughts, trying to find a proper way of explaining to the Muslims how Jesus Christ was one of the prophets, yet not the one who exposed the final truth of God.

"But that is blasphemy. Jesus Christ died for our sins. There is no other truth but His truth, the word of God," Marco insisted, unable to help himself, the lessons of the church unstoppably flowing from him.

"It is Ramadan in this part of the world. That is the way it is!" Niccolo concluded, tired of the argument and angered by his son's insolence.

"Octavio, you must find us two ships promptly." Niccolo angrily spurred his horse along, pulling ahead of the rest of them.

Marco and Vittorio cringed in their saddles, having suddenly remembered Maffeo and Niccolo's plans. Their journey to the east was about to end. Soon they, and Octovio, would be on their way back toward Alexandria by sea, while Niccolo, Maffeo and Casca would travel on toward China and the court of Khubilai Khan. Marco had not forgotten their deal, yet he had hoped that all the time spent together with his father and uncle would have changed their minds. He was never to see the summer palace of Shang-Tu.

It was dusk by the time they all reached the first homes. There was a heavy stillness in the air, warm, nearly overbearing, not unusual for this time of the year. Casca raised in the saddle, trying to get a better look, his instincts awakening something distant in his mind. The water so near usually brought in the scent of brine and the fresh catch of the day. No matter where he had traveled previously, the smell of the sea was unmistakable and unforgettable. Somehow today was different. Nearby and off in the distance the sound of bells reminded the followers of Mohamed of time for prayer to Allah, the vibrations the air carried sending a chill throughout his body.

Hormuz was not what Marco had expected. Its streets were dark and dingy, filth and decay staining the crisscrossing avenues, at times only the different color refuse delineating the twists and turns of the roads. Most houses were broken down and decrepit, with many of them looking abandoned or overrun by barnyard animals. The lack of people in the streets did not surprise them, yet it appeared a town nearly dead. This was not what they had heard of Hormuz for the last few months. It was a city that rivaled Venice, from what many had said.

A strange aroma came to their senses as they passed the first houses, one of burning wood, refuse, and perhaps anything else that burned.

"Is that you, Kasah of Acre? It has been so long." A short, stout man, smoking a hashish pipe startled the six travelers. "I have not had any guests in months, I had not expected visitors . . ." He reluctantly stopped his words and smiled. He looked at Casca, his eyes suddenly realizing the man he called Kasah looked not much different from the last time they had seen each other, possibly thirty years ago.

"You have not changed much my young friend, this couldn't be one of Allah's mirages, could it?" The man continued speaking without a response, while also taking a careful look at his pipe.

"Yes, Mahmud, it is me. Years have been kind to you, too," Casca offered, trying to bring Mahmud out of his confusion.

"Not quite the same as you, but thank you," Mahmud agreed, pleased at Casca's exaggerated compliment. "Come in; you must be hungry and stiff after a long day's ride."

Tapping the pipe against the back of his left hand, Mahmud took the reigns of Casca's horse. Marco watched the dark smoke that still swirled from the extinguished pipe and wondered what could give off the unusual smell emanating from it. Mahmud was a man of sixty, rounded and shortened by time. Still with vigor in his step, he happily assisted Casca off his horse. "Omar, help my guests, hurry." Mahmud pointed to a young man who quickly took Niccolo and Maffeo's horses.

"Come in; my house is safe and clean. The magistrate will not bother us here," Mahmud continued.

The inn was poorly lit and smelled of sweat and burned food. Hardened by use and slippery from cooking oils, the floor was cool and felt good to their feet after long days spent in the hot desert. A few mice scurried in the corners and overhead in the rafters, frightened by the light that came through the opened door. Ducking his head, Casca walked toward the main table and leaned his sword against it. The six of them watched Omar, and another who looked much the same as he, bring everyone's gear into the dingy room. "It is all here," Omar insisted.

"Fresh water from my own well. It is clean . . . like the tears of Allah. Everything is clean here," Mahmud added, pointing the rest of them to the table Casca already sat at.

The six of them happily devoured the offerings, washing it down with Mahmud's cool well water. It had been long since they had feasted such, sitting at a table, the road usually only allowing for eating while riding in the saddle or hunkered on the hard ground. Dining on reasonably fresh and well-prepared food was also welcome, having suffered endless meals prepared by Vittorio. Curiously, none had challenged his near complete lack of knowledge in the art of cooking, something Vittorio was quite pleased by. It had not taken long for them to realize that unless Vittorio had salt, greasy meat, and some sort of spicy plants, the meals did not taste unlike sweat-soaked stirrups.

"Eat, my friends, there is plenty more. You honor me with your presence," Mahmud insisted, looking as pleased as he had stated. "You will have any rooms you want, I have not had many customers recently . . ." his voice trailed off.

"The plague has returned," Casca stated matter-of-factly while he swallowed a handful of olives, his words nearly stopping everyone's breath.

"You are safe here, my friends, honest," Mahmud nervously jumped in, realizing he had taken too long to answer.

"How long has it been?"

They all sat, Casca's words ringing in their ears, awaiting an unwelcome response. Vittorio started crying and humming something that sounded like a child's song. He nervously rubbed at his chin and pinched his neck, hoping he would wake from this nightmarish moment. Marco looked at Casca, his face frozen, suddenly recollecting everything that he had heard about the black death. Octavio coughed heavily into his greasy hands trying to get his breath, the terrible revelation causing his chest to spasm in the agony of his affliction.

"It is far from here, only around the harbor. It clings to the ships," Mahmud tried to assure them.

"We must leave now," Niccolo jumped in. "This curse moves without boundaries. One day it is elsewhere, the next day you are burying your loved ones."

"We have seen it in the land of the Khan years ago; nearly all perished in the city of Hangzhou. A thousand people were buried each day for weeks, until there was no one left to bury them," Maffeo whispered with his eyes closed.

"You are safe here, I swear," Mahmud maintained. "Only homes that are suspected of harboring the plague are boarded up."

"Boarded up? Why? Does that stop its spread?" Marco innocently asked.

He was barely able to finish his words when the sound of hooves pounding on dried dirt roads and approaching voices interrupted their conversation. "By the order of the magistrate, the honorable Alfas el-Hayoun, your house is condemned." The man's booming voice shook the walls. "You will remain inside for the duration of one moon. If you do not perish by the blight, your travelers will need to leave this city. You, Mahmud, will pay either way."

The voice had not spoken more than two words when Casca was on his feet, the long sword that had been resting against the table now primed and ready in his pulsating hand. Casca had dealt with such men before. *Only following orders* was as old as time itself.

Mahmud's son Omar ran to the door, trying to open it, to be instantly cut down by the lance of one of the soldiers. "Do not try to flee, Mahmud, any of you, your punishment will only be worse," the same voice threatened from the outside. "It is me, Khayaam; listen to me Mahmud. No more need to die by the sword." The sound of possibly a dozen men approaching the entrance of the inn was clear to everyone inside it. "Advance, side by side," orders from the outside continued. The smell of burning oil slithered through the doorway.

Nothing could be heard other than Mahmud's cry of horror. In an instant he had lost his son, bleeding, fading from life as fast as his blood left him. Mahmud lay in a pool of red, holding the now lifeless body of his son, shaking him, trying to bring him back. "Do not take him Allah, he is the last one I have. I offer myself, I plead with you, do not take him. I have no one left." The grieving words of a father, likely spoken thousands of times before, again went unanswered. Omar was no more, while his father would never be the same, his smile forever to break whenever the memory of his son was to return.

For a moment they stood paralyzed, staggered by the sight of a father holding his son, only the pounding of soldiers against doors and windows breaking them from their numbness.

"Help me! Push at the same time!" Casca ordered, realizing time was short if they hoped for an escape. Grabbing the thick wooden table from both sides and behind, they crashed it against the doorway of the inn. Breaking and splintering, the door collapsed, knocking back three soldiers who were about to nail planks against the outside in their attempt to board up the doorway, preventing anyone's immediate escape.

A shower of arrows rained upon the six of them as they reached the alleyway. The sun had already set, the light of a few street torches and the moon brightening their struggle for life and escape. Casca ducked an instant too late, taking the sharp edge of an arrow in his right shoulder. He grunted from the pain and the grating sound the metal tip had made against the bone of his upper arm.

Reaching across with his left hand he broke the shaft of the arrow and threw it against the ground. The rest he would have to contend with later. For now there were other matters. His eyes searched the surroundings, watching half a dozen archers standing behind the ten robed men holding lances. In an instant the archers had all restrung their long bows, ready and anxious to fire again.

Niccolo buckled from the prodding of a spear, dropping to his knees from the impact. Still holding the shaft of the spear, Khayaam, the leader of the armed contingency, tried holding Niccolo at spear's length in an attempt to prevent any physical contact. The shaft of the spear soon shattered, the blow against it knocking to the ground both the wielder of the weapon and Niccolo, who held the broken shaft against his left shoulder. Shifting the blade the moment it had cut through the spear, Casca redirected it, leveling Khayaam and pushing him against the other men who also held spears. Khayaam's falling body was quickly impaled as he broke through the line of the defenders. The carefully arranged line of attack had been collapsed, sending each man to fend for himself.

"Shoot, shoot them down!" One of the subcommanders ordered his archers, trying to hold back Casca, Maffeo, and Octavio. Behind them, Marco and Vittorio had also taken to weapons, reluctantly and fearfully trying to hold their position.

Arrows whistled through the air, harmlessly landing against the side of the inn. The manner of confrontation the magistrate's men had clearly hoped for had now disappeared as the alleyway was drowned in a pool of bleeding men, men whose fear of the plague was replaced by something much more immediate. The sound and feel of steel biting into swords, shields, and the flesh of men.

"Hold them back, do not let any of them touch you—" The voice of one of the soldiers ended abruptly, his mouth filling with blood from his bursting lungs. Still mouthing the words, no more sound came from him, only the heavy thud from his forehead crashing against the stone slab that met up with one of the walls of the inn.

With Maffeo on his left side Casca continued breaking any

formations the magistrate's men were attempting to form. Using their long spears they had thought Casca would be easy prey. Their confidence became their undoing with every moment that passed, Casca wielding a quick and heavy blade, finding sheaths of flesh. Bodies crashed on either side of him as Casca made his way through the overconfident soldiers. Many of them, wild eyed, fearful of the black death that had taken so many, fought on, finding the devil in the form of this scarred wild man, possessed by the strength of a dozen.

Rapidly recovering from the shock, Niccolo had found his way to his feet, courageously wielding his own sword, holding back one of the soldiers. Maffeo, exhibiting the moves of a seasoned warrior, knocked one of the men back, the stumbling body pulling one of the other soldiers off his feet. The two having lost their spears cried in horror and quickly ran, abandoning the rest.

Within a minute most of the soldiers had run away, equally fearful of the plague and the men flailing away with steel, while the rest lay dead or dying at the feet of Casca and Maffeo. Niccolo sat on the edge of a water trough, while Octavio's helpful hands bandaged his left arm and shoulder.

"This should hold." He nodded to Niccolo, tying the last of the cloth in a knot by the elbow. Regaining his breath, Octavio rinsed the blood from his hands, for the moment sitting down next to Niccolo. Reaching into the trough he washed his face and refilled his flask. Handling a wooden ladle he poured water over his head, trying to quench the fever of battle.

"Are you all right, father?" Marco anxiously looked at the blackened redness of the bandage, helping his father up to his feet. "Help him up, Vittorio," he insisted to his friend. "We must flee, I hear the clatter of hooves and dozens of voices."

The sound of approaching men was unmistakable. There was not much time to waste. In a matter of minutes, or possibly even seconds, they were likely to be surrounded by more men sent as reinforcements. In the moments they could afford themselves, they reached for their gear and made flight from this terrible place of death.

As they turned away, the memory of what they left behind burned into their minds forever. In a pool of thickening blood lay Omar, the first to have died by the hand of the local justice on this night. Still holding and cradling him, Mahmud also lay lifeless, a spear having grotesquely impaled him through the back. In death they remained together forever. Mahmud had decided not to spend another moment here in this world, allowing the curse of time to drain him of life and happiness while he mourned his son, the last of his sons. Perhaps life was precious, yet burying one's son would have proven too painful to Mahmud. Omar left this world the same way that he had entered it, cradled in his father's arms.

NINE

They fled into the night. Unable to retrieve their horses in their hasty escape, the six of them had to rely on road weary legs to carry them to safety. Running from the voices of men and the bark of dogs, they made their way into the hills on the outskirts of Hormuz.

Before long their legs burned in the agony of the forced escape while their lungs gasped in the effort of taking a breath. Falling over each other and the rocks that seemed to hinder every step, they tackled the incline of the land.

"Run father, please," Marco urged, seeing Niccolo falter, the injury and loss of blood slowing him down more than the others. Hearing Marco's plea, Niccolo attacked the mountain with renewed vigor. Casca looked back toward Hormuz, another city to be soon laid to waste. The plague would make certain of that.

The pursuing voices had softened, only the bark of dogs was still carried by the southern breeze. They had been allowed to escape. The followers would return to a land of death. Eventually, most of Hormuz would be a giant burial ground, littered with thousands, while the rest would hopelessly question the will of the gods.

"It is all right." Casca finally gave the word, allowing the rest of them to collapse unceremoniously. They had been running for nearly an hour, time that had felt like an eternity, singeing every fiber of their bodies as fiery blood coursed through their veins.

He watched the five of them sprawled on the cool wet ground, trying to find the energy to take a deep breath. The torture of the escape had drained them of life, their bodies unwilling to obey and continue farther. Octavio reached for his flask of water; however, he was unable to open it. Giving up, his face lost in the dew-covered grass he gasped for air, waiting for his breath to return.

Taking a few steps toward the edge of the grassy plateau, Casca looked down toward the path they had taken and the dark horizon leading south where the city of death lay. He could just about make out men carrying torches, presumably their former pursuers, making their way back toward the outskirts of Hormuz.

Uneasily, Casca reached for his right shoulder and found the wound had already closed up, growing around the shaft of the arrow that had found its mark. He squeezed at the flesh around the wooden shaft giving himself a horrid preview of what it was going to be like to remove it. No blood came from the area, only pain, the skin already sealing off his wound, preventing the blood from flowing out.

It was not until the next day that he would be able to retrieve the tip of the arrow. Not wanting to make a fire during the night and give away their position, he waited and rested. The pain would just be postponed.

Casca watched the five of them, lost in their shallow breathing, for the following hours embraced in the sweet escape, if the demons of the night allowed them. It was much like the doorway to death that they had experienced that night, their bodies pushed to the limit, their hearts nearly bursting in the effort. Within moments, all of them were unconscious, Octavio the last one to be so, in his last seconds having taken water from his flask, which now lay open, its contents draining into the ground.

Standing watch over them until early morning once again forced Casca to relive times past. The cold and impersonal night enveloped him, empty loneliness keeping him company as he stood high on the mountaintop, looking out over the city of Hormuz. It was a quiet night, only the rhythmic sound of crickets and the howl of wild dogs far off in the distance

disturbing the silence. He crouched against the cool ground
and pulled a blanket over his shoulders. A smooth boulder,
evened by the eternity of time, wear, and rain acted as his
backrest. Moving against it, his shoulder blades rolled, finding
comfort and rest. The midnight sky was clear, each star shining brightly, trying to outdo the others. His eyes drifted into
the endless expanse of the heavens, the blanket of stars laid
out in front of him, tempting him with its mystery. . . .

"Get some rest, I will stand guard." Maffeo's offer interrupted
Casca's contemplation an hour or two before dawn.

Casca stood and straightened his cramped legs. The hours
had passed by swiftly. Nearly half the night he had acted as
sentinel on this ledge, almost becoming one with the mountainside. He welcomed the few hours of sleep to follow. The
days to come would not be without strife.

Casca opened his eyes from the sun's early light and the
aroma that grabbed at his nose. Something unusual, nearly
pleasant, stewed in a pot hanging over a small fire. Vittorio
crouched by the simmering pot, with one hand fanning the
smoke from his eyes while the other brought a wooden spoon
to his lips. "I think it is ready," he called out. "The early
bird—" His words ended abruptly, realizing this was likely
the best meal he had prepared and was probably not the right
time to test everyone else's patience.

Maffeo ignored him while changing Niccolo's dressing.
The wound was swollen and angry-looking but did not appear
to be life threatening. Eventually, with proper care, it would
heal. If he was fortunate he would not lose much use of his
left arm. "Looks good, Niccolo. I think you got lucky this
time," Maffeo happily reported. Niccolo sipped from a cup
and nodded, the fresh spring water cooling his recently feverish mind.

They all sat by the fire, each tending to his own affairs,
straightening gear, or caring to bruises and wounds. With his
legs crossed, Casca pulled his short dagger from his belt and
brought its tip into the edge of the fire. It quickly turned red,
bringing everyone's attention to it.

Tightening his chest Casca ripped the shirt over his right
arm and shoulder, instantly quieting all. It was a sight not for

the squeamish, no matter how time might have tempered their nerves. Marco and Vittorio's eyes narrowed, nauseated by the self-infliction of pain. Using his left hand, Casca reached for the arrow embedded in his right arm. It had not gotten very far into his arm, the tip of it likely bent by its meeting with bone.

His fingers searched around the shaft of the arrow, trying to get a good grip. Turning it slowly, Casca attempted to free and discard the cursed thing; however, it refused to budge, almost appearing as if it had grown roots.

"How can he do that to himself?" Octavio whispered to Niccolo, beads of sweat forming on his own forehead from what he was witnessing. "Should we offer help?" he inquired, without directing the question to anyone, while he softly coughed into the palm of his left hand.

Ignoring him, they all sat mesmerized by the act, repulsive in itself, but even more incomprehensible watching a man perform this most difficult and painful of tasks on his own wounded body. Casca took a deep breath and refocused his efforts. He dried his thumb and forefinger on his shirt then again attempted to retrieve the arrow.

A dull, almost inaudible sound sent shivers through them as Casca turned the shaft and tip of the arrow, the steel edge of the arrowhead finally letting go of Casca's bone. He clenched his teeth and tightened every muscle in his body, slowly pulling the barbed arrow from his arm. Blood spurted out, pulsating over his arm with every beat of his heart, draining down the side of his forearm and hand, finally dripping onto the grass. Hungrily, the earth took the crimson rain to feed the devil's soul.

Breathing out at last, Casca discarded the arrow by his side, unable to relax, knowing the pain to follow was to be worse than the pain just experienced. As fast as Casca had been drained of blood, his lacerated arm began to close up, stopping the surge of red. With their eyes unwilling to blink, they watched in horror as the man burned and singed his own flesh. The short blade had been prepared, reddened by the heat of the flame. "Should we help him?" Octavio again whispered as he coughed into his hand.

A response, or even the horrid sound of the glowing blade meeting Casca's flesh, was lost on them as they all, including

Casca, suddenly stared at Octavio. "I just thought we should help," Octavio's defensive posture and answer suddenly becoming unimportant. "What is it?" he again questioned, confused by everyone's eyes on him.

Once again he coughed into his hand, suddenly realizing that he had truly become the focus of attention. Marco, Niccolo, and Casca looked at him with concern. Vittorio's chest heaved from the sight and eyes welled up in tears. He could not look at Octavio for the moment, realizing what it all meant.

For nearly a year they had heard him cough incessantly, by now the sound of it having become commonplace. But this was different. The dry cough had changed. Octavio's left hand was covered with a frothy red matter, not unlike what a horse has around its bit, or a mad dogs has hanging from its jowls.

He wiped his hand on his tunic and took water into his mouth. "It is just my cough, that death run from yesterday has made me cough harder, that is all," Octavio tried explaining through tearing eyes. He knew what they were all saying without words.

Fever took his body by midday, shaking him in its devilish grasp, further torturing him with the severity of the cough that seemed to come more often and with greater intensity. Maffeo tried lessening the fever with a wet cloth that he repeatedly placed over Octavio's face and neck. His hands shook as his fingers felt knotted swellings along Octavio's neck.

The intensity of Octavio's cough increased into the night, the slimy sputter eventually turning bright red and free flowing. His lungs were being torn apart.

By nightfall his fever had lessened, giving them false hope. Octavio finally rested, for the first time able to sleep for hours without the rattling of his cough awakening him. There was not much that they could do for him now other than wait. Marco and Vittorio prayed endlessly, hoping Christ had perhaps time to hear their pleas and offer another miracle.

By morning all hope had been lost. Octavio awoke at dawn, unable to stop himself from coughing until lack of air in his lungs finally caused him to lose consciousness. He lay covered with the red spray of impending death, his eyes open and barren. It was only a matter of time before it would all end, and he knew it. A few sips of water that Maffeo had nearly forced down his throat gave Octavio a sudden burst of energy in the early afternoon.

"Help me." Octavio's pleading eyes searched them for understanding. Holding him by the shoulder and waist, Casca walked Octavio to the ledge of the mountainside, overlooking the open sea far off in the distance. It was not home, but it would have to do. Crumbling to the ground, Octavio pulled the short dagger from Casca's waist and started digging. His lungs heaved from the effort, forcing his cough to intensify.

He speared the earth continually, only stopping when his cough stole his breath; otherwise, he dug into the ground, fashioning his final resting place. A long way from home, and from the sea that he loved just as much, Octavio was approaching death in the most horrific of ways. He would face it with bravery. Kneeling by him, Marco and Vittorio took to the task Octavio had started. Watching their friend toil with every last bit of life left in him, they labored on while holding back their tears.

Eventually Octavio lost consciousness in the grasp of pain and lack of air. His face had turned purple and his hands trembled from the agony of the dark destroyer and lack of strength. "Rest, my friend," Maffeo whispered while pulling a blanked over Octavio's fading body. "May the angel of death take you while you sleep."

Octavio never coughed again. The exhaustion of his effort had given him his final reward as death took him just as Maffeo and the rest had hoped. They awoke at the first light of day to witness Octavio's last act. He had reached toward the blue ocean with his right hand while his left hand held a talisman on a necklace he had worn, unbeknownst to them all. It contained a message Octavio had held sacred, which had kept him strong all these years away from his loved ones. "Return to us," the burned inscription said in large block lettering, blackened into the leather patch by the sweat of his neck and chest. "We love you." The words ended on the other side, followed by the names of his seven sisters.

They spoke little the following day. Octavio had to be buried and left behind while the rest of them continued on their trek. In less than a year this ragtag group had lost another one, to be buried in a foreign land. They covered up his lifeless body and face with his blanket, forming a shroud, then placed five stones in the shape of the cross over his chest. More soil followed on top of the cross. In this land where the followers of Christ were few and unwelcome, his body would lie undisturbed.

Heading north, the road again became treacherous. It took four days until they were able to find the path they had taken while heading toward Hormuz. Now they were about to retrace their steps for a few more weeks, until the road led them once more toward Kerman. Without horses the travel was long and difficult. The small villages along the way they encountered were unable to provide them with any transportation other than one old decrepit mule that at least was able to carry some of their supplies. Other than that, the weight of their gear slowed and burdened them.

Not much was spoken the first days following the death of Octavio. Umberto had fallen in Acre a few months before, and now they had lost another one. Not to the gluttonous gleaming edge of steel, but to the black executioner that harvested the dead without prejudice, ripping men, women, and children apart from the inside. Some had thought it was God's way of thinning the herd, to cleanse the earth of the weak; others suggested the impatience of the devil. Regardless, it spread like the fires of hell, knowing no boundaries or mercy. Like the waves of the ocean it traveled, banishing all that stood in its wake.

"We must find another way," Niccolo muttered while battling the road that seemed to travel against his feet. Hoping someone would hear his complaint and offer a solution he continued, "What about farther east along the coast?"

"There are no major ports." Maffeo shook his head. "We probably couldn't get anything big enough to brave the ocean."

"There must be something south of the Makran Range; there has to be a way to travel by sea," Niccolo insisted. "What about in Solui or Rajesh?"

"I fear we will find the same: more rats and the plague. Solui is nothing but a village of thieves and murderers, from what I have heard, and Rajesh is too poor even to feed itself. Anyways, it would be death to us all if the plague has spread all along the coast."

"What about Karachi? Is it not a busy port?" Niccolo stubbornly insisted while looking at Casca, hoping this stranger that had known every patch of land they had visited might know also of a way out.

"I have been to Karachi. It is northwest of the Indus delta, along the Arabian Sea, probably five to six weeks travel, but it is nothing but a fishing and trading village. They have nothing we need," Casca disappointed Niccolo.

"I know, I know," Niccolo grunted, knowing well that to be caught on the open sea on a boat carrying the blight would guarantee their deaths, even if they were fortunate enough to find a vessel along the Arabian coast. "I had hoped not to have to walk the length of the world again. Once is enough for a lifetime."

"I would travel north of the Afghan mountains, over the Pamir range. Once we cross the mountains, the northern range of China will be within our sights. From there we will be in the land of the Mongols where your imperial paiza should give us free range to travel. Three to four months after that we will reach Shang-tu."

They looked at Casca, trying to follow all he had suggested, considering the option of traveling by land. Niccolo smiled for an instant at the mention of the summer palace of Shang-tu. He turned toward Maffeo who reached toward his waist where hidden within a pouch lay the paiza, the golden tablet Khubilai Khan had given them. Maffeo traced the edges of the plaque with his fingers.

"The Pamir range may be our only way." He nodded. "What do you think, brother?"

They had all stopped at the edge of a stream, weighing their options. For once Marco had decided not to interfere and sat on a large boulder, refilling his water flask. He drank deeply from his cupped hands and washed his filthy and dusty face. Looking at his hands he realized the swirling winds had battered him, digging grooves and pits into his face, hiding the waste of the road.

Vittorio sat down alongside, watching Maffeo, Niccolo, and Casca look east toward the Afghan range. Unsheathing his sword Casca attempted to draw a map of their way. "In two months we will reach the Kasar, a branch of the Oxus. All we need to do is—"

"Legend has it that the Pamir peaks reach the sky and of men who dwell with demons of the netherworld." Marco found himself speaking, without being addressed, something he had tried to refrain from.

"What do you know of legends, or of Pamir?" Niccolo yelled at his son. "Must you always interrupt?"

"I am sorry, father." It was the last words Niccolo would hear from his son for a while. Marco cowered away, fearful of his father and angry at himself for not being able to keep quiet.

"I have taken this road a few years past," Casca continued. "We can travel along the Oxus River, following it until we reach the foot of the mountains." He traced the bank of the Oxus on his makeshift map, ending it at the edge of a large boulder, where the blade of his sword sounded off against the side of the rock. "We will need to wait until spring, most likely, but that is a loss well worth taking. The winters come quickly and are long."

"It will take an additional year if we go by land, but I see no other way." Niccolo nodded, accepting their fate. "Then off we are, toward the Pamir," Maffeo enthusiastically agreed. "Let's get a few more hours today before we turn in."

Quietly, Marco and Vittorio assumed their place behind the rest of them. Marco smiled at Vittorio with a pleased grin. Angry as he had made his father, it was the first time ever there had been no talk about them returning to Alexandria or Venice. They were all headed toward China and the court of Khubilai Khan.

TEN

"Those mountains do not seem so tall," Marco whispered to Vittorio. The two of them stood on the northern banks of the Oxus looking east. Off in the distance, behind swirling white clouds, the peaks of the Pamir range confronted them. To one that had never scaled such heights, the size of the mountain was difficult to grasp; to others, it threatened with its immensity. Marco and Vittorio faced the mountain un-knowingly.

Casca shielded his eyes from the glare coming off the Oxus and allowed the memories of crossing the gateway to the east to flood his mind. There were few mountains of the world that Casca had found any more difficult.

Niccolo gritted his teeth, more from the pain his left shoulder still punished him with than his disagreement with his son's opinion. He knew what they were about to challenge. The wound the spear had made did not appear more than a simple white scar, circling upward from his chest to his left shoulder, fading eventually into reddish knots at the tip of his shoulder. However, the scars ran deep. Facing east he rubbed at his shoulder and arm trying to loosen the knotted skin that clung and pulled at his neck. He had been fortunate, and he knew it. The water that Octavio had used to cleanse his wound did not bring the black death. Octavio had not been so lucky.

"That is where we are headed." Casca pointed to a turn of the river. "We will find food and shelter. Perhaps we have something to barter with. The villagers take pride in the strength and stubbornness of their mountain mules."

"Why mules? Why don't we trade for horses?" Vittorio whispered to Marco. "It would be nice not to have to walk all day," he hissed through clenched teeth, while he nervously scratched his chin.

"Could be there are no horses in this part of the world." Marco tried finding an answer.

"Stop talking and start moving," Niccolo snapped at his son. Niccolo's patience with his son had grown short over the last few months. Time had been on their side, allowing for Marco to try to discover his father, and his father to learn about his son. However, they had grown more distant in re-cent months. More and more it had become a burden for Niccolo not to show his displeasure in having taken Marco along. It did not seem to Casca that Marco had deserved it, but every turn of the way, anytime there had been something that was debatable, Niccolo had found a reason to doubt or step on anything that his son did or said. At times, Maffeo shook his head, wondering if Marco would ever be allowed to find his father.

Picking up the pace they headed toward Khorough. It was a small village of perhaps fifty people at the base of the mountain that led to the Pamir range. A group of children ran up the slope of a small hill chasing butterflies, while two women, likely their mothers, looked on, amused at the exuberance of the youngsters. Whistling after them, an older man unsuccessfully tried to herd them back toward the houses. His puckered lips broke into smiles interrupting his attempt at catching their attention with his high-pitched whistle. Undaunted and ignoring all, the children ran up the crest of the hill. In this tranquil valley, life went on as it had for hundreds of years.

The five of them approached the village, only the bleating of a dozen broadtail acknowledging them in their approach. A huge gray and filthy dog started barking, trying to protect the wooly sheep from the strangers. Baring its teeth, the dog awaited a command. The shepherd raised his head and continued carving his walking stick with the use of a short curved knife.

"May your winter be without anger," Casca addressed the first man that met up with them at the edge of the village. The short stocky man continued chewing at his mustache as he took in the five strangers and the words of the scarred man who had addressed him in an old Afghan dialect. He scratched the ball of his left foot against the instep of his right and stared at Casca. His dark eyes, hidden behind long scraggly hair and folds of flesh that protected him from the winter winds penetrated and held everyone's attention. He nodded with a small bounce of his head and watched the five outsiders.

"What did he say?" Marco whispered into his uncle's ear.

"No doubt a greeting," Maffeo mumbled, once again surprised at Casca's knowledge of the language.

"And your woman patient," the short man answered, waiting to see the response in Casca's eyes.

"That is true in all seasons." Casca's words brought a smile onto the villager's face. "We seek shelter and guidance," Casca continued. "The passage is not very forgiving and we seek your wisdom." Casca finally completed the pleasantries the moment required. Casca had met with men of these parts.

They were sheepherds and guides of the mountains, proud people, seemingly as they believed, entrusted with the portal between east and west.

The five of them left behind the village of Khorough two days later. It had been a pleasant respite, sleeping under a roof and the luxury of warm and plentiful meals. Winter was still two months away, and as they had made good time the decision to brave the mountains had been if not eagerly, at least reluctantly made. The locals had been pleasant, Casca and the rest not having been the first people to pass through their peaceful town.

They bartered for five horses, two mules, and a thick water-buffalo-hide tent, leaving behind two well-edged curved swords Casca had acquired a few weeks previously. Along with it, Maffeo had parted with a thumb-sized sapphire, well worth more than they received, yet necessary for the trade. The men of Khorough may have been shepherds, but they were no fools; they were well aware of the value of the precious stone and its possible worth in continued bartering. Casca mumbled to himself about the trade, not at all happy about the horses, knowing the fate that awaited them.

They continued into the Pamir range, slowly challenging the edge of the mountain following the lead of Pak, a surefooted guide they had been fortunate enough to hire. Pak was a short, muscular man, with wide feet and powerful legs. His flattened feet grabbed at the trail, his curved and elongated toes reaching and neatly holding every turn the path seemed to take. Mumbling to himself, he led them up the torturous trails. He along with the rest were covered in the furs of broadtail sheep, the like they had seen back in Khorough, thick and heavy, probably the only covering that was going to keep them warm.

They traveled for days, the size and grandeur of the mountain range refusing to diminish as they neared the first summit. Breathing heavily their lungs struggled in the attempt to take in more air. Slowly, almost imperceptible at first, the air thinned, making each day's journey more exhausting than the previous. Fatigued by the last two days of climbing, they enjoyed the rest the plateau offered while their eyes raised off into the distance measuring the cloud-covered peaks.

"It seemed much closer a few days ago," Vittorio admitted to Marco while tightening the furs around his back. Vittorio nodded while also pulling the hood over his head. They squinted from the cold blast coming off the mountain. The icy wind had picked up the last two days, surprising them with its edge and intensity. Pulling a heavy wool hat over his reddened ears, Casca turned to face Khorough, wondering if they should retreat. Winter was impatient this year.

The weather improved the following days giving them hope. Feeling better, and less stiffened by the penetrating wind, the horses had also picked up the pace, allowing the six of them to rest for a while.

"A few more days and we should reach the pass." Vittorio's words resembled more a question than a statement. Marco smiled back at him and dug his feet into the side of his horse, hoping to spur everyone else along, too. Overhearing him, Casca raised his head and caught Pak's concerned gaze. For days Pak had appeared unsettled, not unlike a man anticipating the worst to come. He had traveled along and over these mountains too many times to be fooled.

Their concerns were not unfounded as they awoke the following day to the angry shriek of winter's premature fury, Casca nearly falling backward the moment he had opened the flap to their tent. Rebundling and hiding his hands within his sleeves he exited the wind-blown enclosure. Pak had already been up and was tending to the horses. He pounded his hands against his sides trying to warm them long enough for his fingers to work.

"What is going on?" Niccolo nervously inquired, seeing Pak.

"We must let them go, they will never make it," Casca answered, knowing the fate of the horses if they were forced to move along.

"We can't let them go, we paid for them. I don't plan to walk over these mountains and the rest of China on foot."

Casca turned toward Niccolo and tried to explain. "We must. The mules will be enough. In a day or two the horses will die if we do not let them go. Their instinct will take them back."

"Damn!" Niccolo teamed with anger, furious at losing the

horses they had just purchased and at the thought of continuing this increasingly difficult trek on foot.

They all soon came to accept the truth. Wet snow followed by icy snow had fallen during the night turning their way into a treacherous ice-shard-filled impediment. No horses would have survived the barrier the sudden change in weather had thrown up against them. Vittorio and Marco kicked at the tent from the outside, knocking large sheets of ice off the stretched buffalo skin, eventually clearing it of enough ice to bundle and pack it on one of the mules. Overnight winter had taken its place on this mountain.

Slowly leading the mules along the icy plateau, battling the winds that seemed to ignore the coverings they all wore, the six of them braved what winter's fury had brought. Shivering and cowering from the wind that intensified on the flattened area, their eyes longed for the side of the mountain that potentially offered refuge from the elements. Eventually they reached the escarpment of the mountain, finding shelter underneath a rocky overhang. The temperature had dropped, but at least the piercing winds could not find them in the alcove they all huddled in.

At times, large boulders threatened them from overhead, creaking underneath the fury of the winds and the weight of the newly fallen snow; at other times, loosened rocks showered them, eventually chasing them into open ground. This place only offered to entomb them forever underneath snow and the side of the mountain.

Walking in front of them, Pak turned and motioned ahead. "Not long . . ." His voice suffocated by the wind and creaking of ice disappeared in the cold. "Watch for the warm ice . . ." was all Casca could make out before Pak had turned his head, his warning disappearing in the wind. They all looked up and ahead from the sound of Pak's voice and saw what he was likely pointing to.

In front of them, beyond snowdrifts that were growing like the waves of the ocean during a storm, the mountain split in two, offering the pass they needed to take. Farther ahead, the road presumably would lead toward China.

Even this short distance took all day for them to traverse, the winter and mountain itself impeding them at every step. The ground creaked and groaned strangely in the grasp of winter beneath their feet. At other times, pockets of snow piled on by the winds buried them waist deep.

Battering them repeatedly, the winds changed direction, pushing the group back and forth, making their desperate journey even more arduous. Hours that seemed like days held them prisoner, time itself nearly standing still in their wretched and miserable journey. Tortured and exhausted they reached the base of the mountain.

"We will make camp here, stay together." Casca's words were likely lost in the wind, but his intentions were clear and welcome. Pulling closer to the northern face of the mountain, underneath a wall of rocks that seemed to reach up into heaven, they set up the tent. With the heal of his axe, Pak pounded stakes into the ground, fastening the tent against the soon-to-be-frozen earth, attaching it to boulders for additional strength. He was not about to allow the tent to roll over them from the winds or the weight of the snow, possibly to suffocate them underneath.

Vittorio was the first one into the tent the moment it was raised. Rolling into it, he set up his blanket and gear, quickly hiding underneath every piece of cloth that was available. Niccolo was not far behind, pained by the cold that had spread through all the clothing he wore. He pulled his knees against his chest and placed the fingers of his left hand into his mouth, trying to have the blood return to his numb fingers.

"Where is Marco?" Maffeo's concerned yell tried breaking through the sound of winter's fury. No one was able to hear his question, but the urgency in his voice instantly warned all of them. Casca looked around in a haze of swirling snow, trying to allow his senses to detect where Marco was. Pak quickly jumped onto a boulder at the entrance to the tent, hoping his higher vantage point would help him spot Marco. Looking into his eyes Casca saw nothing but despair.

Pak half jumped, half tumbled off the slippery boulder and ran to the back of the tent, feeling his way around in the blindness the white blast of the snow had created. In a moment he was also gone.

"This way, quick!" Casca's yell urged Maffeo. Following the direction Pak had run, they both fell to the ground from the strength of the wind. Casca struggled to his feet and was the first to reach where Pak, and presumably Marco, had disappeared. He stood with his hand on a boulder while with the other hand he tried blocking the snow that was blinding him. He felt Maffeo's hand on his shoulder. "They are gone."

Looking into the white nothingness they stood incredulous of the whole situation. They blinked repeatedly from the wind and the white fire that the endless snow blanket had created.

"Watch for the warm ice." Pak's warning returned to Casca. He fell to the ground disappearing into the icy hell an instant later.

The cold water enveloped Casca shocking his senses. His feet kicked against the water and ice, quickly bringing him to the surface. Casca reached out and grabbed for anything that would prevent him from going under again. He coughed the frigid water from his lungs, shards of ice and a curse spewing from his wounded throat.

His soon-to-be-frozen hand pounded against the snow and ice it encountered, eventually grabbing one of the wooden stakes Pak had driven into the ground. Casca searched the watery grave he feared he would soon be a part of. Within seconds, numbness started overtaking his whole body as every fiber of his being was being drained of warmth.

Frantically he searched the icy depth while trying to keep his head above the closing water. A sheet of ice pushed against his face and tore a mass of flesh from his neck. The coldness of the water numbed his neck, for the moment withholding the pain that was sure to come. His toes stumbled against something. Casca tried to get his footing but there was nothing but the strength of his left hand holding the wooden stake keeping him from sinking farther into the water.

Casca's thoughts drifted back to the canals of Venice where he had given life to Marco. His hand reached out. Within the snow that was falling faster than the water could melt it, Casca found Marco struggling for life. Pulling the young boy toward him, Casca also tried nearing the edge of the water.

"Give me your hand!" Maffeo yelled into the blizzard that was trying to cover them. Snow lashed at his face, cutting into his already reddened cheeks. He wiped the heavy snow from his face and beard, struggling to see what the storm had tried to keep from him.

Using every last bit of himself, Casca pushed Marco's nearly frozen body out of the water, away from the thin ice.

Maffeo grabbed at both of them, desperately pulling them away from the edge of the water. Casca stood, his wet clothing beginning to stiffen as he tried to find their brave guide, Pak, who had been the first to search for Marco. He yelled into the storm that blasted snow and icy water into his face. Pak was gone. He was never to be seen again.

Fighting the elements that had demanded more victims in this winter that had come too early, Casca and Maffeo carried Marco's shivering body into the tent. "Close it, quick!" Maffeo did not have to finish before Vittorio closed the flap to the tent.

"Strip him quickly." Casca struggled taking his own clothes off while Maffeo and Niccolo pulled and cut Marco's clothes away from his cold body as fast as they could, realizing there was nearly no time to waste.

"I don't know what happened," Marco finally spoke through trembling lips, the words themselves a burden. His hands and fingers bent by the icy water had been drained of warmth. What had been toes now resembled ugly dark roots one would find buried deep within the ground. Underneath the blanket Vittorio had thrown over him, Marco pulled his knees up close to his belly and hugged his legs. "I am so cold," he moaned. "I cannot stop shaking." Not knowing how to help, Vittorio reached out toward Marco in an attempt to comfort him. He extended his forefinger and thumb toward Marco's hands, hopelessly trying to form their ring of friendship. All was not well. Their fortune had turned dark on this day when a glimmer of hope of finding the passage had turned into a nightmare. At one time they had been four, but now, with Marco on the edge of death, Vittorio's fear of becoming the last one of them shook him. All was definitely not well. Vittorio sobbed watching his friend suffer.

Marco's hands and face had turned blue and purple, nearly white by the lack of life. He tried raising his arm toward Vittorio, however his body would not cooperate. His whole body shook underneath the blanket while he whimpered and cried. "Help me," he begged.

Casca had finally been able to remove his own clothes and now awaited the pain of winter's curse. His fingers and toes were nearly completely numb while his face felt as if it had been burned by fire. The cut he had received just moments earlier by the jagged sheet of ice had already stopped bleeding. The scar would add to Casca's collection. Memories of frozen winters returned, yet none seemed as painful as the moments he knew were just ahead.

"Help me, I am so cold." Marco's cries filled the tent. He trembled, unable to stop himself while his body struggled for life.

They all sat powerless, looking around, hoping someone would take charge. There was no way to make a fire and, other than their gear, there was nothing to burn. "Help me father." Marco's plea jolted Niccolo. It was the first time it all hit him. Marco's life was drifting away. His son needed him.

All anger Niccolo had ever held toward his son disappeared in that moment. "Help me father," Marco again cried, shaking uncontrollably from the cold that was draining him of life. Niccolo gasped for breath from the pain his heart was feeling and the horror of helplessness.

Niccolo kneeled and placed his blanket over Marco's contorted body. He removed his own heavy winter covering and wool tunic, baring his chest, placing on his son all that was available as cover.

"Help me father," Marco softly whimpered while turning his head, trying to roll up and disappear underneath the two blankets.

Niccolo looked down at his son. Marco was not going to survive. Within moments Marco's cries for help became fainter and fainter. The winter that had come too early was about to claim one more victim. Niccolo's chest heaved and his trembling voice broke in desperation. He was not about to allow the death of winter another offering.

Placing his bare chest against Marco's shivering back, Niccolo encircled his son's body with his own, sharing his warmth and his life. Tears ran down Niccolo's face, wetting his son's cold cheek, tears of fear. Marco moaned from the agony of the cold that held him and cried within his father's embrace. In this hellish winter, in this valley of death in the middle of nowhere, Niccolo had found his son, once more giving him life.

ELEVEN

The blizzard had raged on for five days. Every few hours they had taken turns clearing the path from the entrance of the tent to where the mules had been placed in an alcove at the side of the cliff. That became unnecessary after the first day when even the mules, hearty and accustomed to the type of weather the winters of Pamir brought, had died. There was nothing to be done but wait and attempt to survive this winter that promised to be long and brutal.

Just as abruptly as it had started, they awoke the sixth day to the silence of the storm having passed. The tent was fairly warm from the heat of their bodies and the insulation the chest-high snow had created. Upon exiting the tent their eyes teared from the endless white blanket the storm had deposited. Moving stiffly, his feet and legs weakened by the cold that refused to leave his body, Casca turned east toward the mountain pass they had failed to reach. It stood defiant, threatening anyone who would dare challenge it.

"We will never be able to make it through, will we?" Vittorio whispered into Marco's ear. Marco stood by his father, holding Niccolo's shoulder and arm, steadying himself, for the first time in his life feeling comfortable to seek help and find comfort being by his father. Casca had saved his life once again, but that was far from his thoughts. Marco knew Casca did not need any more words of thanks or praise. How many times over could a man owe his life to someone else? Something much more important had happened. He had found his father.

A quiet winter held the mountain range in its grasp on this day. As far as they could see the cover of white reached to the horizon where it met the sky. High above them and farther east a few peaks pierced the sky climbing into the clouds.

Casca dug the heals of his hands into his teary eyes, trying to get accustomed to the brightness. The rest of them also shielded their faces, nearly blinded by the sun's rays and the reflection from the snow.

Using a small shovel from his gear Casca cleared the snow adjacent to the tent and proceeded to make a fire. He cut a small piece of the leather saddle and burned it in the smoky flame. Curious at what he was about to do Vittorio turned toward Maffeo. "Is he going to eat that?" Maffeo shook his head, doubtful if Casca would attempt to do so, yet unsure of what use the burned leather could possibly have.

Casca slowly rubbed the darkened leather under his eyes, staining his cheeks with the soot the burnt leather had left behind. In a semicircle underneath his eyes he applied the dark stain until both cheekbones were covered. Casca used both hands, trying to control the shaking that had not left him over the last few days. He extended the marks along his eyes until the leather stain reached his eyebrows. They looked at him strangely, but in a few days they all followed his lead, realizing their eyes would better tolerate the whiteness of the snow and the bright rays it reflected into their eyes.

Maffeo gathered a few rocks and placed them around the flames, temporarily safeguarding the fire from the snow that melted adjacent to it. There was not much to burn, other than a few twigs and dried moss Casca had scraped off the side of one of the boulders next to the tent.

"I will look for firewood." They watched Maffeo cautiously walk away from the tent, taking care at every step, trying to avoid any more possible warm ice. Pak had warned them of the danger, yet he had been the only victim to fall in nature's trap. Marco had likely caused yet another man's death, something he was not soon to get over.

They had eaten nearly nothing during the last few days while the storm had held them prisoner and the sight of the fire quickly reminded them of recent feasts. Casca roasted the flank and leg of one of the mules, ignoring Marco and Vittorio's queasy look. The mules would be of further use even if their meat was not much dissimilar from the saddles they had held on their backs.

The following days were calm with a slight rise in temperature. Still, winter held its grip, the true winter months not quite present. Before long this whole mountain range was to become a deep freeze not suitable for anything but mountain goats and gray wolves.

"Should we dare the pass, brother?" Maffeo asked of Niccolo on a clear morning. The warmth of the sun had started to melt some of the snow, causing small streams to find their way downhill.

"It does not look very far but I fear that if winter returns we might get caught in a place worse than this." Niccolo's unsure words caused Maffeo to nod, satisfying his own doubts about their crossing.

Marco and Vittorio crouched by the fire, playfully poking the embers with a jagged stick. They rubbed their hands over the crackling flames, for the first time in many days enjoying the comfort of a warm fire. Youthful outlook allowed them to enjoy the moment, a temporary respite from the reality of dangers that awaited them. Their bellies were full and even if the choice of the available meals was questionable, it had satisfied their hunger. The two of them had come a long way from the comfort of honeyed milk washing down three meals a day.

"What are you looking at, Messer Casca?" Vittorio inquired watching Casca gaze upward toward the face of the cliff. He tried following Casca's line of sight but he saw nothing. A few clouds swirled amongst the peaks, chased away by the winds.

Up on the side of the mountain something manmade caught Casca's eyes. "There!" He pointed. Vittorio shielded his eyes from the yellow glare coming off the mountain with his right hand while, with the left, he wiped the tears from his squinting eyes. "I still do not see anything."

"Smoke, I see it now," Marco gleefully jumped in. Pointing with the stick with which he had been teasing the fire, Marco excitedly ran toward the side of the cliff. "Stop!" Casca yelled at him, angered by Marco's foolish actions.

Walking through ankle deep puddles and rapid runoff streams, Casca pushed his way ahead of Marco and Vittorio, protecting them. His feet were nearly frozen, never having quite recovered from falling into the icy water. Casca had nearly given up on trying to keep his feet dry, or even warm. It was usually morning by the time his footwear would dry while the numbing cold never left his feet. *The warmth that heals your body and soul comes from deep within oneself.* The words of his long gone friend, Shiu Lao-tze, returned to Casca's thoughts. On this day they meant nothing. Nothing could replace dry land, a warm fire, and a change of footwear.

Trying to keep up, Vittorio bumped his shoulders against Casca's. "You think someone actually lives there?" He turned toward the man who had served as their guide and protector. "Cave dwellers," Marco chided him. "Maybe the snow creature the shepherds have told us about live there."

Casca ignored the usual banter that always went on between them and approached the mountainside. Smoke escaped from an opening hundreds of feet up from the base of the cliff, adjacent to large boulders that appeared to rest on a small plateau.

"What is it, what is going on?" Niccolo's concerned voice approached the three as he and Maffeo also neared the area.

Casca had seen these before, but never so high up in the mountains. Many such places were scattered along the Silk Road.

"I must know what it is," Marco insisted, the blood of the explorer flowing through his veins, sparking his never-ending quest for knowledge.

Within moments they stood at the base of a nearly vertical rock wall, their heads thrown back, trying to see where the smoke was coming from. "I don't see the smoke anymore. Maybe it was just a mirage," Vittorio warily suggested, suddenly fearful of what they might encounter.

Casca's eyes followed from the base of the cliff upward toward the area where he had seen the smoke. The sun's rays and the shadows played tricks on his senses, hiding much of what he searched with his eyes. Casca kicked at a sheet of ice by the base of the wall, exposing a stone step. It was clearly there by design. One step of many led upward, spiraling along the face of the mountain, disappearing within an alcove in the rock face. Some of the snow had melted along the path, exposing the crude stairway, while the rest they would have to contend with.

Maffeo and Niccolo shook their heads in unison, clearly displeased by the idea of scaling the side of the mountain.

"We must know what it is," Marco protested, while begging with his eyes.

"There is no reason, Marco," Niccolo tried reasoning. "It is dangerous; who knows what or who awaits you in there. You cannot go alone . . . or with Vittorio."

Niccolo regretted his words, realizing he had given Marco an out. Marco looked beggingly toward Casca who was already measuring the side of the cliff with his eyes. Niccolo shook his head. Marco had just escaped certain death and now he was willing, foolish as it was, to challenge life again. Perhaps Niccolo was no longer ready to risk losing Marco.

Casca had made no attempt to discourage Marco and Vittorio from following him. It would have been a long and drawn-out affair.

The three of them made their way up the side of the mountain, sometimes taking long minutes for each step leading them along the torturous path, while other times easily knocking sheets of ice or piles of snow off the stone steps. It was a path not designed to be taken in the winter, yet at the onset it was quite easily accessible once the snow was removed. Casca did not mind the time it took, the monotonous effort giving him the time to think of what awaited them. Their effort was soon to be challenged by winter's early arrival.

An icy wind blew in from the south, shredding their hands and faces. Vittorio tried hiding his face in a cleft the mountain offered, to escape even if only momentarily from the cruel wind. "I am freezing, I can't feel my hands. . . . We must go back," he cried out in pain.

"Quiet!" Casca cut off any more words. He had seen mountains move from even the sound of a whisper. The blanket of snow caressing the mountain trembled from the sound of Vittorio's voice. It had been a close escape. Casca did not again wish to challenge winter's vengeance. Seconds later the wind died down, allowing the sun a moment to warm the three weary, nearly frozen climbers. However, winter's edge would not allow it for long; the warmth the sun gave was immediately stolen by the frozen face of the mountain.

At times Marco tried warming his hands by pounding them against his chest and side. He soon learned the pain his stiff cold hands felt while being hit, as well as the danger of placing his frozen fingertips into his mouth. He left much of himself on the ascent, his frozen skin ripping and remaining on the frigid gray surface of the mountain's edge.

Slowly and carefully they made their way up, far beneath them Niccolo and Maffeo disappearing amongst the snow and boulders. At times chunks of ice broke off the steps they crossed, or broke off overhanging rocks, to plummet seemingly forever into the never-ending abyss. As if hypnotized, Marco watched the ice and snow shed off the side of the mountain to disappear below. Every step became more of a burden, soon changing into nothing but prolonged torture. Casca struggled in his own private hell, his hands and feet never having recovered from the icy water. His fingers were unable to grip and hold, soon turning into distorted claws. Memories of the Hold came back to haunt him.

Halfway up the side of the mountain Vittorio had stopped looking back as the experience and feel of leaning over the side of the world unnerved and eventually nauseated him. He inhaled deeply, trying to settle his nerves. Seeing him tire, they rested for a moment, unfortunately long enough for winter's tentacles again to hasten their ascent. Nothing was heard for a moment but their pained lungs trying to gather enough air. They pushed on.

The air grew thinner with every step they conquered. Breathing became more labored, the effort of inhaling less rewarding. Marco started rolling his head, his mind slowly drifting into unconsciousness. Viciously the wind battered the mountainside and the three irrelevant victims who had dared challenge winter's fury. There was no returning.

"There!" Vittorio yelled out, quickly to have his mouth covered up by Casca's frozen hand. A sheet of white rumbled from overhead, burying them momentarily. Casca held Vittorio with one hand, while with the other he grasped the edge of an overhang. Marco had fallen to his knees, for an instant disappearing beneath the snow. Casca shook his head, his eyes focusing on what had made Vittorio yell out. They had made it. A few steps above them yielded a plateau. Marco stood leaning over the edge of the mountain, wavering in the wind, watching the snow tumble downward toward the valley, eventually burying all there was in a cloud of white.

Pulling with all his might, Casca managed to drag both

Marco and Vittorio onto the ledge overlooking the rock face. They lay there, gasping for breath, waiting until their lungs could recover in the thin air.

"Here, I welcome you. Wondered we have if you would come to us. I believed you would, that you have scaled toward the heavens to our humble place; I am pleased," a soft voice greeted them. He had spoken to them gently, his words only understandable to Casca, yet his delivery soothing Marco and Vittorio's concerns for the moment. Casca was not certain what language the man had spoken in. However, he had understood enough.

The three of them looked up at the man who had welcomed them. With a hand extended, the robed man turned his eyes upon them. "Follow me, if so far you have come." The little man had a thick red robe covering his slight body. His bald head was exposed in the wind as were his hands that he held clasped against each other. Bowing slightly from his waist, he smiled.

Vittorio held Marco's shoulder and arm, trying to steady his exhausted legs. It had taken great effort for them finally to stand. Marco was not in much better shape, the thin air and the climb having drained him nearly as much as Vittorio. They turned and looked out into the infinite panorama their position allowed.

Snow-covered mountain peaks seemed to go on forever in all directions. A dark winter threatened with a storm in the west, chasing the thin wispy clouds that had allowed the sun to shine through earlier during their ascent. Soon all but winter would be a distant memory.

They looked at each other, then dared look down. Far below, Niccolo and Maffeo were likely covered by the snow that had fallen off the face of the mountain, or, if not buried themselves, mourning the fate that had surely become of Marco, Vittorio, and Casca.

Laboring for breath more out of exhaustion than shock of what they had found, Marco fell to his knees at the entrance to the small corridor leading from the small plateau.

"Follow me," they heard again, as Vittorio stepped in behind Casca. The two of them held Marco by his shoulders, helping him along, step by step.

Within moments the frozen hands of winter disappeared. With every step they took, a new world of sight and thought awaited them. "What is that?" Vittorio cringed away, pulling back at Marco. They cowered from the sight, trying to hide behind Casca.

Hollow eyes looked down at the three of them from above. The creature was monstrous.

"It is alive!" Vittorio cried out, pulling back away from Casca, letting Marco hang off of Casca's shoulder.

"Our guardian, he has been, for long now. Of ones that lived in the mountain before us," the robed man answered, unable to understand Vittorio's foreign tongue.

Casca looked up at the guardian who greeted them in the darkened passage. A huge jaw and skull, easily three times the size of the largest Burmese tiger he had ever seen, stood as sentinel. Its empty eye sockets, larger than Casca's fists, did not diminish much of the ferocity it must have once held. Teeth not unlike Turkish sabers extruded from its jaws, pointy and yellowed by time. The skull almost seemed imbedded in the rock over the walkway, as if it had been captured, the mountain itself not allowing it to break free into the world. Casca's eyes followed the length of its teeth. Larger creatures than he had ever seen must have warred with this beast and ended up as its prey. It hung from overhead in the narrow passage, a creature out of its time, not unlike Casca.

Holding Marco and prodding a still-frightened Vittorio, Casca followed the small robed man. Vittorio mumbled a prayer, wondering if such creatures still inhabited the area. "It is the devil itself." He found enough energy to cross himself repeatedly while he passed underneath the beast's remains.

The mountain chamber was huge. From a narrow entryway it spread sideways and upward, taking up the side of the mountain. Small passages branched from the main chamber, disappearing in the darkness. In the middle of the huge enclosure a statue stood surrounded by four men who were also dressed in robes.

"Is this heaven or hell?" Marco whispered to no one. His eyes followed the hooded man who stopped by a central pit.

"Come, warm yourselves in the heart of the mountain," the man offered in an old Mongol dialect. "Come sit," he indicated, using words that sounded more like the rustling of leaves in the wind than actual speech.

A kettle hanging from thin white strands stirred noisily over a hole in the ground. Mounted on four curved rods overlaying the pit, the ropelike strands tied the rods together and also held the kettle. The fire pit glowed from underneath, sending crackling noises, steam, and gusts of hot air from within. No flames escaped from the opening, yet the stewpot was clearly hot and something not unsavory boiled inside it. "Have some, eat," the man offered, yet in another language Casca could not identify.

The three of them crouched on the ground and took the man's offering. It was a soup of sorts, strange green and brown objects floating within it. Vittorio tasted it and quickly made its contents disappear. He smiled and extended the bowl back at the man. The second bowl did not take longer to be empty.

Casca sat, waiting for the bowl to warm his hands. He looked at Marco following Vittorio's example. Drinking the soup did not seem to warm them no matter how hot it was. It was going to take more than that to bring warmth back into their frozen, near lifeless bodies. They all shivered, still covered in their thick furs, waiting for the unseen fire to warm them. Marco placed his hand against the stone floor, and was surprised to find it nearly hot. He reached with both hands, feeling the rock; however, he was unable to find pleasure in its warmth.

"It is the devil's work," he whispered to Vittorio. Buried in the third bowl of concoction, Vittorio ignored him.

"Your blood will soon warm," the robed man extended his hands toward his new guests. He had spoken in Afghan, finally making it easier for Casca to communicate with him. "Tazrack, many call me, yet I am known by other names also. The Seer of the Mountain and Caretaker . . . these names have brought me pleasure. Some call me the Father of Dolhan. . . ." His words trailed of.

"We have traveled from around the world," Marco attempted, using the Afghan words he had learned recently in the village of Khorough and from their fallen guide, Pak. "My name is Marco. And this is Messer Casca; he has saved me." Marco struggled with his delivery watching Tazrack and

Casca look into each other's eyes, almost with a sense of recognition or reverence. "This is Vittorio, my friend of many years," he added, concluding the introductions.

The little man smiled pleasantly. He had a thin, bony face, with features coming to life from his dark, penetrating eyes. His heavy lids pulled at his brows, drooping downward, giving him a foreboding look despite what his smiling face offered. Tazrack, as he called himself, pulled his hands out of his robe and pointed to the surroundings with pride.

"Your journey will not be without reward young one," Tazrack continued, looking straight at Marco. "Much there is here for you."

Marco gazed at Tazrack and then at Casca. He thought he could understand little more than simple greetings, yet he had been spoken to in such a way, personal and nearly hypnotic, that it brought a certain calmness to the young Venetian. He looked at Tazrack and found himself understanding more than just what the mere words had to offer.

He sat back and smiled at their host. In this strange new world there was much to be learned. He was no longer afraid. Marco rubbed his hands together and tried warming them next to the opening in the ground. Less hesitant, he returned his hands to the smooth rock floor, which seemed to offer more warmth than the area closer to the open pit.

A golden statue cast a shadow over them. From within the opening in the ground a yellow light escaped, caressing their faces and the faint smile upon the mysterious icon. "You are in the Lamasery of Dolhan. Your karma has brought you all here. No demons have followed." The man stopped talking, realizing his guests still shook from the cold that refused to leave their bodies. "Budha understands your journey to us; he welcomes all."

Marco bit his lip, catching himself from saying what was on his mind. *Budha . . . some called him the Enlightened One. Could not be, he was just another false prophet. One for the weak. Budha had done nothing but contemplate and preach.*

Vittorio looked at Marco, fearful of his friend's tendency to speak without thinking. Marco started mouthing something until Vittorio's glare stopped him. *Budha did not suffer and die to save mankind. He was truly a false prophet. Christ did not die in vain on the cross. . . .* His thoughts drifted off.

"Budha lives within us. Much he has taught us." Tazrack's words brought Marco out of his private contemplation, preventing him from speaking foolishly.

"I thought we would all die," Marco finally spoke.

"Old and gray you will be, young one. Your karma is unfulfilled."

"My karma?" Marco questioned, trying to recall what he had learned of Budha over the last few months.

"Your destiny. It is not here. Today is just a step."

Marco shook his head, trying to understand. He reached toward his head and rubbed his eyes with the palm of his left hand. His icy hands held his feverish head, attempting to make sense of it all. Tazrack smiled.

"I will give a gift to you, young doubter. You, too!" Tazrack suddenly turned his head toward Casca. "You, too, have been burdened by much, for too long. Long you have suffered. What you seek is within you." Tazrack's face stiffened as if touched by something unseen. It was not the first time Casca had met such men. He was no stranger to the followers of Guatama Buddha. The Sage of the Sakyas had many disciples. Casca's breath slowed as his eyes met those of Tazrack.

"There is more to the world than you dare believe, young one, much more," Tazrack continued, deliberately looking away from Casca. The words, *young one,* that had been meant for Marco seemed to jolt Casca's thoughts.

"Many things that you dare not imagine or imagine you can not. There are things beyond here and now and the thereafter. Today is not always now. It may be a long time past." Tazrack turned toward Casca with the last remark he had made.

Marco struggled to keep pace with what he was hearing. He had nearly given up. Was that mere doubletalk or did he just lack the wisdom or understanding? Perhaps the words he understood, yet the meaning of this strange and twisted language escaped him. What did he mean by today is not always now? Today could not be in the past or definitely not be into tomorrow. Only the sudden quiet brought Marco back to reality as Tazrack had apparently stopped talking. His words rang in Marco's head, but other than echoing hollow in his mind they did not bring any more understanding. Marco turned toward Vittorio who had apparently not even looked up from his bowl, as if time itself had held its breath and halted. Only Casca's pensive demeanor assured him he had not imagined it all.

Quietly, a young man approached carrying a long, thin pipe. Not unlike Tazrack, he was dressed in a simple dark red robe with a drawstring encircling his waist. Betraying his curiosity toward the three guests for a moment, he forgot his mission. His eyes reached Marco's while he stood next to Tazrack. Suddenly remembering his duties, he handed the pipe to Tazrack, bowed slightly, and disappeared as quickly as he had come.

Tazrack reached toward two small copper bowls by his feet that had escaped his new guests' attention. Onto each finger he placed a small amount of the contents. One bowl held a red powder while the other a white powder. Snapping his fingers, Tazrack rubbed the two powders, causing smoke and fire to come from his fingertips. In an instant the contents of the pipe were on fire, moments later giving off a swirling gray smoke of their own. Tazrack drew on the pipe while a subtle smile found its way onto his lips.

Marco and Vittorio sat paralyzed by the witchery they had experienced. "Almighty father, protect us from the devil's hold," Marco mumbled while he quickly crossed himself. Vittorio just sat, stunned, his eyes following the trail of smoke. The two of them cringed away from Tazrack, anxious to escape, yet powerless to move. They watched as once more Tazrack rubbed against each other the fingers he had used to create fire. A few sparks caressed his fingertips, disappearing within the cradle of his palm. Unable to blink, Marco and Vittorio stared at his hands, marveling at how he had been left unharmed by the fire.

"Warmth it will bring from within." Tazrack smiled while he offered the pipe to Casca, somehow momentarily reassuring Marco and Vittorio that the devil had not taken hold of them.

"The fire of life is rekindled," Casca answered in Afghan, ignoring Tazrack's show of bewitchment. He had seen men perform illusions with the powders that burned spontaneously while the smoke that had been created shielded the true focus of their magic. For now, Tazrack had shared this unusual ceremonial offering, if nothing else, while Casca's answer was a response of friendship, of men who searched and followed a similar path, according to an ancient Chinese teaching. Tazrack nodded and smiled, recognizing the words of Shiu Lao-tze. He watched Casca inhale deeply from the pipe.

Casca bit down on the edge of the pipe. It was the only way he could prevent his teeth from chattering. He moistened his lips in an attempt to create a seal around the pipe and be able to draw in the smoke. The bitter-sweet smoke traveled down into his lungs. He inhaled once more and handed it over to Marco. Still shivering from the cold, he watched Marco and Vittorio cough dreadfully while they also took part in Tazrack's ceremonial offering. Vittorio returned the pipe and placed his hands back on the warm stone floor. With all the fear Tazrack's show of magic had created, the two of them could not refuse to take part in the offer. Frightening as it had all been, they could not deny the affinity and reverence they suddenly held for the man. Humbled by all they could not understand, the three shook within the cold that was long to leave their bodies.

Another young apprentice approached carrying a small kettle. Marco's head wavered watching the kettle swing side to side, hanging from the same type of thin white strands he had seen previously. Cautiously, the young man placed the copper pot by Tazrack, settling it over a small, round, smooth-edged stone slab. They all watched the youngster bow and disappear quickly into one of the passageways.

Marco and Vittorio looked at the strands that still clung onto the copper bowl. They were not made of cloth or leather, but of some unusual material that resembled simple thread, yet it could not be. The strands were gray and white, some were just long threads that looped around the handles of the bowl, while others were interwoven like the mane of a horse or cloth spun like wool.

The short strands served as the handles to the copper bowl, while the longer interlaced ones allowed the bowl to hang freely over the open pit. Suddenly Marco reached out, unable to help himself. He held the handle to the bowl and closed his eyes. Marco mumbled to himself, questioning his reason for such foolhardiness. Slowly opening his eyes, Marco looked at his hands. His hands lay unharmed, as if the heat had disappeared magically. He sat back dumbfounded. It was a world where fire came from nowhere, and left without warning. He looked at Vittorio and then up at Casca. Venice was very far away. It was time to learn of all there was in a strange new land.

"Best it is when hot," Tazrack offered, taking a sip from one of the small copper bowls. He looked at his guests and smiled, guessing all their questions at once. "Some flavor it with salt and butter. I myself prefer it without," he added.

Marco leaned forward and took the offering. The hot liquid was dark and had a peculiar tart aroma. Unable to help himself, he raised his eyes inquisitively.

"It is called tea. It will soothe your throat and warm your body." Tazrack smiled at his three guests.

Casca took a long gulp, allowing the smooth, warm liquid to splash down his throat. He had had the concoction many times previous. *How long had it been?* He tried to recollect. Temujin, the young boy to become Genghis Khan all those years ago, had favored this drink of the steppes. Even after many years, Genghis Khan still drank it with the unsavory ripeness of old yak butter, to remember when the days had been hard and the empire nothing but a dream. Nodding with the remembrance, Casca smiled and finished his cup. Following his lead, Vittorio and Marco also finished theirs, for the moment holding back their displeasure.

"Rest you must for now." Tazrack stood and waived the young man who had brought the pipe moments before.

Casca, Vittorio, and Marco stood and left the main chamber, directed toward a small passageway. The young man led them into an adjoining hallway, following a well-lit corridor. Unable to help himself, he constantly turned and eyed the newcomers. Still shaking from the blistering cold that had not left their bodies, they followed closely hoping for warmth and rest. Many paintings adorned the walls and ceiling of the passageways. Over the smooth surfaces the walls allowed, beautiful images kept them company. Uneven places the mountain had provided, the walls had been plastered in straw and mud to create a canvas for men long gone. Mirrors must have been used, Casca figured, as no smoke could be seen staining the highly ornate drawing of the Budha and his followers. Casca shook his head wondering how long before some greedy and narrow-minded European nobleman would pillage this monastery in the sky to adorn their own dark and repressed castle. Crusades throughout time in the name of God had cursed many people and lands that had been previously hidden from greedy and savage hands.

Moments later, they all stood within a chamber lit by the flame of elongated and twisted yellow candles that cast uncertain shadows over three beds. Thick blankets covered the straw-filled beds adjacent to the walls of the enclosure. Backing out, their guide left while mumbling something unintelligible. Shaking his head Marco ignored the man as he left. "Three beds, how did they know there were three of us?" Marco whispered to no one in particular.

Exhaustion overtook them almost instantly. The excitement of what they had witnessed had aroused them, yet now there was nothing but sleep and rest on their minds. Discarding their still nearly frozen and wet clothes they allowed the warmth of the stone floor and the comfort of thick blankets to satisfy them.

Casca drew his feet under the blanket, waiting for the pain to come. It was not the first time he had experienced the thawing of frostbitten toes or hands. His feet had been without any feeling for days now, working more like lifeless stumps attached to his legs. Sinking into the straw-filled bed he waited and clasped his hands to each other and against his chest. Soon, blood would return to his crippled hands and feet with a surge of fire like thousands of daggers torturing every fiber of his body. The memory of being burned at the stake returned to punish him.

Reaching next to the bed he pulled the sheathed sword closer to himself. He turned his head watching the candlelight throw shadows against the walls. Bathed in the light of the candles, a smiling image of the Enlightened One looked down on him. A mysterious offering from above reached out toward Casca, drawing him toward the red eyes within the bluish-green image. Casca's eyes softened and closed slightly from exhaustion and the nearly hypnotic stare from above. For a moment Tazrack's smiling face overlaid that of the Budha, further clouding Casca's senses. Out of the corner of his eyes he caught Vittorio and Marco also mesmerized by the dance of the lights upon the ceiling. He blinked.

The pain he was certain would overtake his body and torture him never came. A warm wave spread from his lungs into his chest and then toward his heart. His eyes clouded up, remembering the pipe smoke that had burned his lungs. Casca felt his heart warm and pound gently against the walls of his chest cavity. Slowly, the warmth he had felt in his lungs spread into the blood rushing from his heart to the rest of his body. "The warmth that comes from within." He remembered the words of Tazrack and his friend Shiu Lao-tze. He blinked again.

"Wake up son," a soft voice tried to raise him. Casca inhaled, well rested, surprised at how he had not heard anyone approach. It had been a long and restful sleep. He was no longer cold and his feet and hands were not numb anymore. The warmth of the bed enveloped him, nearly cradling him in its embrace. He felt content and refreshed. Perhaps he had slept for half a day, his sleep deep enough to shelter his body from the agony of the dissipating cold.

"Come, son, please wake up." The voice now much more familiar, instantly brought him back to consciousness. The same moment he reached for his sword. It had been moved.

"I knew he would be all right. He is too stubborn to die." Another familiar voice roused him.

"How are you feeling? You had me scared to death."

Casca sat up and looked into the eyes of his mother. "What?" he mumbled, no other words coming to his lips.

"Well, the snake didn't make it." The man's voice again rang in his ears. "I've got it here for you." Casca squinted, trying to focus his eyes at the hazy face of the man who had spoken to him and the item that dangled in front of him.

"Aren't you too old to still play that game with me?" the man inquired.

"Uncle Aro?" Casca heard himself say.

"Your favorite uncle, that is. You know how much I like to hear that." The man laughed.

"It is time to go, son. Your unit will be off in a few hours." The woman's voice burned in his mind. "You are a proud citizen of the Republic, aren't you?"

"Mother?"

"I hate that game. Can't you just keep that one with your uncle?" she inquired.

Casca sat in a straw-filled bed rubbing at his eyes. The room he had shared with his older brother all his childhood years looked smaller and darker than he remembered. A small window, half covered by broken wooden planks, allowed the morning sunlight to brighten his room. What a peculiar dream, he thought. It had been so long, perhaps over a thousand years . . . but it was so real. He looked at his mother's smiling face staring down at him and Uncle Aro's round grin.

"Come on, Ufio," his uncle teased him.

Casca reached for his neck and cringed from the pain. A large gash underneath his ear throbbed from his touch. Something bitter came to his lips.

"I took the dressing off last night to let it dry. It has been five days already. You were very lucky." She sighed.

"Here it is, I promised you." The man handed Casca the dried pelt of an asp. "Should make a handsome belt, I think you deserve it," Aro continued. Casca held it and suddenly remembered.

He had been rummaging for hours in his father's wooden locker, at times playing with a small ivory sphere that held smaller and smaller ivory spheres within it, other times with the broken blade of a bronze dagger that still held a reddish-brown mark his father had insisted belonged to one of the Great Caesar's assassins. Casca had often shuffled through his father's belongings, trying to get to know the man who had given him life. His father was a loyal citizen of the Republic, serving the emperor to the best of his abilities, offering his sword wherever and whenever it was needed. In all the years, the chance to be a father had been few for Tiberius Lazarus Longinus.

It had been completely unexpected. The asp had come out of nowhere, striking right at Casca's unprotected face. In the instant that it took for Casca to try to move, the deadly serpent had struck, embedding its poisoned fangs into the side of Casca's neck. Casca could remember little else other than trying to reach for it, then crashing against the stone doorway . . . and now he was awake, apparently five days later, having survived days and nights of unrelenting fever, delusions, and near death. In those five days he had lived a lifetime.

"Yes, you crushed the little beast's head against the wall. There is nothing much harder than marble—other than your head, that is." Aro laughed.

"Stop that," she interrupted glaring at her brother. "Are you all right? You want to eat or drink anything?" She again smiled at Casca.

Never having refused a meal in his short life, Casca nodded, trying to find a shred of sanity in the events he had recalled and the reality of what he was experiencing.

He quickly emptied a bowl of cold water and looked up into his mother's eyes. The water was refreshing, yet somehow could not rid the bitter taste that refused to leave his mouth.

"You must be exhausted," she continued, trying to comfort him, seeing confusion and fear in his face. "No one expected you to survive," she sobbed. "The bite was deep and very close to . . ." She reached out and hugged Casca.

Casca closed his eyes and enjoyed the moment. His eyes trembled while his face broke into a smile. The smell of her hair and the aroma of freshly baked bread brought back memories time had hidden, yet had been unable to erase.

"On your feet soldier!" Uncle Aro's voice vanquished the sensation of comfort and warmth. Casca's right hand quivered from his uncle's words as he awoke from his momentary daze. "I suggest you move it before they send for you. You must report on time or they'll have you scrub the decks the whole trip over to Judea."

"You must go, my son," she sobbed, trying to hold back tears. "It is time. The last seventeen years surely have passed quickly," she whispered while shaking her head.

Casca sat dumbfounded. He looked down at his thin, unscarred boyish body. His ribs stuck out toward his stomach, further accentuating the fallen shape of his chest. He sat up and dropped his chin as the room had started to spin around him. His belly heaved, constricting his emaciated torso and punishing his lungs that searched for air. Smacking his lips, he tried ridding himself of the bitter taste. His eyes teared and burned from the pain within, and something unseen.

"Judea? Why there?" he whispered between spasms.

"That is where Emperor Tiberius has ordered his armies," Aro responded with surprise in his voice. "We have never had peace there. The Jews call to their god to bring plagues upon us. . . . Many fear a messiah, one like Moses, to rise—"

"To hell? That is where our gods have chosen for me? To spend years marching around in a sea of sand?" Casca questioned angrily.

"Do not challenge the gods, my son. It is their will for you," she said, trying to soothe.

"Blasted gods! Which one has so decided, I wonder," Casca defied without fear in his voice.

"You sure are feisty all of a sudden." Uncle Aro laughed. "Then again, you are right. There are so many gods to choose from, aren't there?" he continued, amused at his own observation. "I still don't think you are well enough yet to challenge any of them."

"Quiet, the both of you. Sometime I don't even believe you are my son to have such little faith."

Embarrassed and perhaps frightened by his own challenging manner, Casca sat back down. "I do not believe our gods want me to perish so wastefully so far from home. I do not believe in them," Casca quietly concluded, nervously waiting to see if his protestations would bring the wrath of powers unseen.

Surprised by his nephew's sudden defiance, Aro looked at his sister while he also sat. Casca cringed in his bed, still shivering from the spasms that traveled throughout his body. He drew his arms around his chest trying to stop himself from shaking. "I do not believe I was meant to die in a foreign land, quieting another revolt. I do not want to be a soldier, not now, not ever!" he insisted.

"My son, I fear for you. You must have faith in the will of the gods. It is the only way, you must . . ." Her words trailed off.

Casca sat, shaking his head, angered by these unseen gods that ruled his life. He looked at his mother's saddened face. Casca regretted his angered words. Why bring such sorrow to her, he mused.

"Talk to him, Aro, help him . . . help me," she begged through tears.

Momentarily taking a serious voice, Aro stood. His eyes turned down and forehead darkened from the furrows in his brow. "Some say he is a madman. A man who acts from voices and visions within his own self. Almost a world all his own. Some believe his visions are a sickness cursed by the underworld, while others think different."

"This is a man our emperor fears? A man with delusions?" Casca ridiculed. "He sounds more of a madman than a leader."

"Many believe him to be a messiah, a savior of men. Do not tempt things you do not understand, my son. For years it has been prophesized—"

Cutting her off, Casca yelled out, "Blasted they all be." He sat cringing from the pain that his sudden actions and exertion had brought on, yet he held unflinching from his beliefs. "I do not believe in them, any of them," he stubbornly continued. "How could there be so much concern over just one such man?"

"You must have faith in our gods; they know what is right for us. They have spared you, maybe they have a special purpose for you in this world," she insisted.

"I do not have faith in any of them. Who could believe such foolishness?" Casca insisted, unable to believe he had been spared from death for any particular reason. "The gods are just stories for children and the weak. They are imaginary beings for adults who cannot deal with the world on their own. I do not need any imaginary friends. . . . I will make my own decisions, not follow empty and elusive wishes of gods I do not believe in," Casca insisted.

"Many believe he is a great man. Maybe you will meet him someday and learn something about faith. They call him Jesus of Nazareth. Perhaps he will teach you a thing about faith and God," Aro somberly chimed in.

Casca tightened his brows and upturned his lip. *Perhaps he will teach you a thing about faith and God.* The words unreasonably rang in his ears, repeating endlessly. He sat shaking his head and pounded his feet against the dirt floor. His mind hurt from the news he had dreaded and from the poison the deadly snake had left in his body.

"Judea is a worthless wasteland fit for scorpions and thieves," he angrily insisted. "I may never see you again." The words momentarily drained him. Casca suddenly looked at his mother while a single tear started to run down his face.

She smiled and extended her hands toward him. "I may never return to you, mother," he lamented.

"A man will seek you out when you reach Acre," she continued.

Casca raised an eyebrow. "Who will?"

"He will be pleased to see you. It has been far too long. I know he has missed you greatly. Your father has requested to be reassigned to Acre for months now." She smiled. "Your ship should be arriving there in a few weeks."

Casca's somber face lit up as he extended his hands toward his mother's warm embrace.

"Some warm tea to soothe your throat and worries? The bitter taste you must hate."

Casca blinked and received the goblet of tea. His hands quickly warmed from the hot brew.

"Some tea to wash away the bitter taste?"

"How could you know of tea?" Casca suddenly questioned his mother as he raised his head to meet her eyes.

Propping himself up on his elbows Casca watched Tazrack's warm smile and offering awaken him. His mother and uncle Aro were gone.

Casca sat up and allowed his head to fall once again toward his chest. Time as it was had returned. This frozen hell in the heart of the mountain had imprisoned both his body and soul, playing ruthless games with his mind. The wound of over a thousand years ago pounded against his neck, nearly oozing the poison that had refused to leave his body and clear his senses.

Casca reached toward his face and rubbed at the reawakened wound. He cringed from the pain. His fingers drifted and brought to his lips a tear that had run down his cheek. The aroma of fresh bread returned. His mother was impossibly lost in the recesses of his mind, yet she was still with him, within his soul. The warmth and strength of his father's hand also reached through time and held him. Casca smiled. He sat in the shadow of the undulating light, only Tazrack's reassuring smile keeping him company.

They did not speak. There was nothing that could explain what had happened, and there was no need for any explanation. Casca's face softened while the nodding of his head spoke more to Tazrack than any words of acknowledgment or thanks would have done. Tazrack's gift to Casca, the re-membrance from the beginning of time, would stay with Casca forever.

Eventually Tazrack was also gone, leaving Casca to muse over his reminiscence. Casca's thoughts returned to the time of his youth spent in Acre, the years that had followed and eventually imprisoned him, his impossible journey into the past having reawakened joyous memories of his long gone father. Ever since, his life had been filled with more sorrow than any man deserved. Strange how the wheel of time turned, destiny playing cruel games. . . .

TWELVE

Not much was said by any of them the following days. Casca, Marco, and Vittorio went about their ways, pon-dering their own dreams, wondering if it had all been a mi-rage, or if perhaps the time they were experiencing now was the true reality. Tazrack did nothing to lead them either way. He just smiled and allowed the three to attempt to answer their own questions. They soon learned it was Tazrack's way, not to overburden one with explanations, but to allow one's thoughts to reach and find the truth itself. At least their own truth, one that would satisfy. The night spent in the dream of shadows was something none of them spoke of to each other. Perhaps the joys and sorrows they had experienced were not to be shared.

The weeks to follow passed uneventfully, Casca watching Marco become lost in the world of Tazrack's teachings. Re-sistant at first, Vittorio also soon came to value Tazrack's wisdom. "It is not all heaven and hell." Vittorio sometimes remembered Maffeo's words. He would still cross himself when in fear of losing faith in all that he had learned as a child about Christ and his sacrifices, but, before too long, both he and Marco began to understand there was more to the words of Tazrack than learning about divinity.

Within days Vittorio and Marco spent every waking moment learning of Budha, the Enlightened One, and of the many who had followed. The days were not of endless prayers and joyless readings of scriptures, as they had feared and expected. Tazrack spent much time teaching of the life and times of the Enlightened One and how he had come to his revelations, allowing Marco and Vittorio also to ponder humanity and the truths that had mystified men since the beginning of time.

The ways of the Budha may have been contemplative and nonviolent, yet Casca stayed clear of all such involvement. He knew of the Sage of the Sakyas, having met his followers numerous times over the years. At least the followers of Budha had been peaceful, not having attempted to enlist or burden potential newcomers with interminable genuflection at the altar of their icon, or days learning and suffering from the wrath that would be unleashed if they did otherwise. The students of the Enlightened One were unlike disciples of other gods who used the fine edge of steel as their instruments of persuasion.

"What do you mean, oneness with god? Surely one such as I could not," Marco interrupted one of Tazrack's teachings.

"Your god could not be much different from what you tell of Him," Tazrack calmly responded.

"Heaven is what we aspire for, eternal bliss in the kingdom of God." Marco tried finding the words that could explain his lack of understanding.

Tazrack smiled at the thought of eternal bliss, as Marco had stated it. "Oneness with God, becoming part of Him is what awaits us. Slowly, if we follow the right path, our soul is purified. Eventually, after many lives and lifetimes, we can achieve Nirvana, oneness with God."

"Nirvana," Marco whispered, trying to recall where he had heard the word before.

"Your personal salvation awaits you, if you follow the ways of the Budha. Self-denial and rejection of superstition will all lead to the purification of your soul. One must meditate and reflect on that which is common to all humanity." Tazrack paused, allowing Marco and Vittorio a moment to ponder.

"Suffering, that is what binds all of us together," Tazrack continued, with a sigh in his delivery. "The demons that find us in our sleep, demons we cannot hide from. Life, with all

its glory, can be arduous if one resists the truths about man."
Tazrack calmly looked at Marco and Vittorio, somehow
knowing that the dream of shadows they had experienced
days earlier had demanded much from both of them.

"Forsaking oneself, family, wealth, and power is our way,
it leads us on our quest for the final truth. Without obstacles,
the journey it is not. Stubbornness and narrow-mindedness is
one's undoing, only leading to foolish actions and lies about
what is around us," Tazrack continued. "I do not ask all this
of you, my young friends. Yet it is the path many of us have
chosen. The Enlightened One has shown us the way to personal salvation. Oneness with the almighty awaits all who
follow. Your soul must be cleansed, from all the poisons of
a decadent humanity." Tazrack bit his lip and shook his head,
as if disgusted or perhaps disappointed with mankind and its
never-ending failures. "If not," he continued gravely, "with
each lifetime your soul will be born into a lesser form of life,
a heartless beast, even a vermin that lives underground and
exists as nothing but the patron of what dead flesh has to
offer."

Marco cringed from Tazrack's frightening description, the
thought of his being becoming nothing but a thoughtless
beast, or worse, shaking him to his very essence. Was this the
netherworld that Tazrack spoke of? Could Tazrack be right?
He warily questioned his own reason and sanity. Vittorio just
sat by, at times still crossing himself as a way to ward off
evil spirits, shaking his head, unable to offer any words of
encouragement to his friend or of disbelief of the possibilities
of which Tazrack spoke.

"I may never see my father again, not even in heaven."
Marco suddenly realized he had not thought of his father in
days, and now the possibility, if Tazrack was right, that he
never would. "My father . . ." His voice disappeared as he
looked at Tazrack, begging for words of encouragement.

"What does your heart tell you?"

Marco allowed his head to fall into the palm of his hands,
afraid of what possibly awaited him. He shook his head, his
mind unable to deal with all that had assaulted his senses
within the last few moments. Tazrack's beliefs, if true, might
never allow his finding his father again. An eternity could
pass before their souls would ever cross paths again. Was his

father alive? And, if so, did he agonize wondering if Marco had died? How much more pain could his father endure, the loss of his son having, once again, become a possibility. Marco's eyes filled with tears as he sobbed uncontrollably, the caress of Vittorio unable to soothe him.

The following days brought false hope to a desperate Marco. For weeks they had found comfort in the warm caves of Pamir's highest mountain, perhaps physical comfort, yet the torture Marco was feeling was worse than the cold he had suffered from for days. "Stubbornness is your undoing." Tazrack's advice repeated endlessly in his mind, and he wondered what it referred to. The calmness and insight Tazrack's meditation and pensiveness eventually provided was unable to overcome the worry Marco had for his father and uncle's probable concern for him. Even the thought of not reaching heaven was not as important as the way he felt about his father. Just as he had found his father after all these years, the two might have been separated again. Forever.

As days passed, Tazrack's soothing voice had revealed much to Marco and Vittorio about their own selves, eventually creating a certain peace and reflection. Tazrack had felt and understood Marco's suffering and pain. It was time for him to try to comfort Marco's soul. A task not easily met, as Tazrack soon found out.

During the fourth week of their mountain exile, the southern winds brought a surge of warm air, melting the snow and thick ice that had blanketed the mountain and the small plateau overlooking the valley. "My prayers have been answered," Marco exclaimed, seeing the snow quickly melt at his feet and the gusts of wind warm his face. He opened his robe and removed the thick scarf that had been wrapped around his neck, for the moment allowing the pleasant breeze to exhilarate his soul.

Grinning to each other, Marco and Vittorio walked to the edge of the cliff and joyfully kicked at the thinning ice. Slow at first, the snow melted and washed down the steep incline of the mountain top, exposing the stone steps they had taken on their ascent to the world of Budha four weeks ago. Nervously, Vittorio stepped to the edge of the cliff and attempted to take the first step down the mountainside.

No longer bundled in the thick furs Tazrack had provided

them, Marco's smiling face caught Casca's eye.

"Let's not waste time, I am certain my father and uncle await us below. We should say our good-byes now, and go." Casca stood by them and shook his head, realizing he would need to disappoint Marco and Vittorio. "What are you trying to say? I am sure they expect us. I know they are safe, probably not as warm and comfortable as we have been, but all right," Marco insisted.

"We cannot go." Casca's words angered Marco.

"Why not? We will get our gear and make our way down. Should not take more than a day or two, maybe less." Eventually Marco stopped talking, watching Casca's demeanor. "Why not?" he protested.

"By nightfall it will be impassable. It has been an unusual winter, yet it is still winter. By morning it will be nothing but ice," Casca explained.

Marco stormed away, sobbing, unwilling to believe God would be so cruel. "Help me, father!" Marco demanded while looking up in the sky. Tears soon found their way down Marco's weary face. Cursing at the powers that had failed him, Marco entered the corridor leading to the inner chamber of the mountain lamasery. Vittorio crossed himself repeatedly, not knowing if Marco's words had been a plea or demand, and who they had been meant for.

The following morning came, winter having returned with a vengeance. A thick, smooth sheath of ice covered all but the highest peaks of the mountain. Glare coming from all around teared Marco's and Vittorio's eyes, further angering Marco.

"Blasted winter," he yelled out into the nothingness, his words echoing and returning as the sound bounced from peak to peak and valley to valley. The wind again battered his face, ripping at his skin, the icy claws of winter trying to find another victim to subdue. Marco fell to his knees and tried to cover his face. The cold blast of air had singed his throat, ripping the breath from his chest, momentarily quieting him. Finally crying out, he rose to his feet and struggled as he leaned into the wind, eventually working his way to the edge of the plateau.

Slipping at every step, Vittorio followed his suffering friend all the way to the near vertical drop the mountain was offering. A few jagged rocks peaked through the ice, creating a more hazardous and foreboding terrain. Vittorio's trembling hands reached for each sharp edge, aiding him on his painfully slow struggle to the first rock step leading down the mountainside. Quietly Casca followed along, curious to see how this unusual winter had entombed this whole world of theirs.

"It is hopeless," Marco finally admitted as he craned his neck, trying to look down into the valley. His voice almost immediately trailed off, becoming lost in the screaming wind.

Down below, a thick mist covered the valley making it seem as if an ocean engulfed all but the highest of peaks. The winter winds cut at their faces, pushing Casca, Marco, and Vittorio away from the edge of the plateau. Struggling from an even more intense gust of wind that had suddenly picked up, Marco and Vittorio fell to the ground amongst the hundreds of shards of ice the winter had created. They hung on to each other, the sudden blast of air threatening to sweep them off the mountainside.

"It is colder than before," Marco whimpered while he attempted to hide beneath his winter covering. The thin air quieted him down quickly, ravaging his lungs in the process. Vittorio managed a nervous smile and tried to console him. He also gasped for breath as the colder air demanded more of an effort as time went along.

Unable to help himself Casca stood and stepped to the edge of the precipice and looked over the edge. An alien world the vengeful winter had created, exiling them upon this misty mountaintop. It would be long before this winter's grasp was going to allow them an escape.

Marco and Vittorio sat huddling on the icy plateau, trying to shelter each other from nature's fury. Next to them, Casca stood looking down into the endless valley, his left hand shielding his eyes from the icy glare while his right hand held a part of his winter clothes over his mouth, in an attempt to warm the air. The wind shrieked as it bounced between the giant sheets of ice. Up in the sky, the sun's rays were powerless, unable to offer comfort. The scorching blast of the desert sun was a distant memory to the three of them.

"I wish they knew we were all right." Marco turned toward his childhood friend.

"I am sure . . ." Vittorio returned a smile, for the moment not even able to imagine how they themselves would survive this winter's curse.

Crumpled to the ground, Vittorio and Marco sat by each other, their quivering thumbs and forefingers interlocked, forming the ring of friendship, their heads bowed, wondering if Niccolo and Maffeo were alive. All was not well, they knew quite well. The last vestige of their symbol was wasted on each other. Their own survival was not much more certain than the ones they held concern for. There was no one left to offer the ring of friendship anymore. By their own hands they had exiled themselves. "I wish they knew . . ." Once again, Casca thought he could hear Marco's desperate wishes. Casca turned around in this icy wasteland, his eyes scanning the horizon, looking to find anything but this frozen world. It was hard to believe this was a place that life could or would ever return to. Casca had spent many years frozen into winter, yet this place appeared more desolate and lost.

"We must get to cover!" Casca yelled to them, hoping his voice would pierce the deafening wall of sound the winds were creating. The two looked up and quickly shielded their eyes from the icy wind and the sun's blinding rays. They both reached up, hoping that Casca would lead them toward safety, away from winter's punishing grasp.

Casca dug his feet in and grabbed both Marco and Vittorio. His hands slipped and struggled trying to pull firmly, while at the same time keeping his own balance. Exhausted and shaking from nature's wrath, they made their way back to the cave's entrance. Casca turned and took one last look into winter's demon eye.

Unrelentingly, the cold hand of winter's revenge took hold over the mountain and likely the whole region over the next three days. At times gusts of wind shrieked against the passageways leading into the inner chambers of the mountain escape, disquieting even the many who had lived there for years. This was to be a winter not soon to be forgotten.

"Follow me." Casca startled Marco and Vittorio on the first night after the winds had died down. Casca had seen Marco more despondent than ever before, sulking about, eating nearly nothing, even becoming testy and impatient with Vittorio who just stood by trying to make his friend feel better.

Vittorio had his own concerns but for now had veiled his thoughts, spending all his energy in an attempt to console Marco, his friend of earliest childhood.

"Where are we going, Messer Casca?" Vittorio inquired, clearly startled by Casca's actions.

"Come, Vittorio, I need your help. Put on all your winter ware."

Vittorio and Marco followed along, covering themselves with all they had. They walked behind Casca, eyeing the large bundle Casca held underneath his left arm. Within moments they were walking down the passageway that led to the outside plateau. Not nearly to the opening of the cave, the sharp air grabbed them, reconfirming winter's presence.

The night sky was without clouds and the air still as darkness ruled in its domain. There was no sound on the icy plateau, as if winter had held its breath for the moment. The air was cold, yet not as biting ever since the wind had died down. From time to time the crackling of ice beneath their feet broke the silence, eventually the sound to be swallowed by the emptiness of the night.

The moon had not shown itself on this night, only the blanket of stars lighting the night sky. The cloudy star beneath Orion's belt twinkled into Casca's eye. It held the same as always, as far back as Casca could remember. The followers of Quetza of the Teotec people, that had called Casca the Quetza himself, messenger of God, all those years ago in the new world had named it Quatelequa, *The smoking star*. Shuddering from the thought within this wretched cold, Casca tried shaking the memories of the horrible sacrifice the people of Teotah had demanded of him, eventually ripping his heart out on the altar. Not unlike the light in the sky, the memory of that day had not dimmed.

Casca's eyes shifted upward, finally resting on the Seven Sisters. Foolish men had tried steering by it, believing it held the arm of the Little Dipper that pointed to the North Star. The bodies of such men littered the coasts along with the broken hulls of their vessels, while other perhaps even less fortunate had drifted aimlessly, forever to be lost in foreign lands.

Cassiopeia still pointed toward another cloudy region, as she had always done. Twisting in its own path, Cassiopeia's sad eyes looked upon her daughter Andromeda as she struggled in the chains on the great rocks along the wave-beaten shore. Casca smiled at the stories of the old Greeks, told through the generations for hundreds of years even before he was born. For now, Cassiopeia forever watched from above, awaiting Perseus to rescue her daughter. Farther east, the red star that traveled along the horizon winked at Casca, the god of war reminding Casca of his destiny.

"I will need both of your help." Casca's voice broke the silence.

The three of them stood just a few feet away from the edge of the precipice. The eerie silence and solitude slowed their breathing while they stood on top of the world. Far off in the distance, a few peaks glistened in the night sky while the endless veil of stars enveloped all around. Marco put his arms out, trying to hold onto handles unseen as the endless expanse of the universe rotated around him. There was more sky than earth on top of this mountain, for a moment allowing Marco to consider his closeness to heaven. He sighed at thoughts of his insignificance. Closing his eyes, he pondered why fate had stranded him in this place of solitude.

Marco and Vittorio watched curiously as Casca opened up the bundle he had carried under his arm. Casca breathed in slowly, allowing his mouth and throat to slowly warm the cold air that still cut at his lungs. The sound of Marco's beating heart reminded Casca of the last words he had heard the young man utter. Casca continued working, revealing the mystery of his actions.

He had fashioned something unlike either Marco and Vittorio, or even Casca himself for that matter, had ever witnessed. He had collected dozens of the long, white spiny fibers the three of them had seen Tazrack and many of his disciples use. The strands that had held up under the intense heat of the fire cave and burning wood had been intertwined and braided, eventually shaped into spheres the size of a man's head. Within the fibers that locked onto each other Casca had tightly packed pieces of cloth and straw.

Marco and Vittorio looked at each other wondering whether Casca had lost his mind.

Understanding their confusion, Casca looked up and smiled. "I have made two of these." He pointed at the rest of the bag's contents. "Hold this one, Marco, carefully."

Marco held the strange contraption with both hands, wondering what thoughts must have been passing through Casca's mind. Vittorio just stepped back shaking his head, while holding his chin.

"Closer, Marco, toward the edge, walk slowly." Frightened by the proximity to an endless fall, Marco gasped for breath as he followed Casca's orders. "Turn sideways and hold the sphere by the strap. Right there. Now, let it hang down toward your ankles."

Casca walked to the side of the mountain face and held the strap of the other sphere in the same manner. Marco and Vittorio's eyes widened, watching flames overtake the sphere Casca held. Blue and green sparks flew from the burning straw and cloth, glowing with the flames they had all witnessed within the cave at Tazrack's hands. Within an instant this strangest of contraptions was on fire, brightening the whole plateau. Casca took one more step. His right foot stood firmly planted on the outermost craggy step the mountain offered.

Casca smiled at Marco, waiting to see the realization in his eyes. "Step back a few feet and face me." Marco stood within ten feet of Casca with his left foot on the edge of the mountainside.

"Vittorio"—Casca shook his head toward Marco's wide-eyed friend—"help light the sphere Marco holds." Vittorio flashed a smile as he finally understood. Within moments the contents of both spheres burned equally, fed by the fire of the red and white powder. Flames shot out from within the straw and cloth, encircling the white strands with their yellow glare.

"Follow my lead," were Casca's last words as it all became clear. Slowly at first, Marco started spinning the flaming orb by his side, mirroring Casca's actions, allowing more and more of the leather strap to lengthen from his grip. In seconds the burning sphere had created a nearly ten-foot-diameter ring of fire that broke the night sky. Steadily Marco spun the flaming circle with the exuberance of a child wielding a toy, yet with the understanding of what they were about to do.

Casca also started spinning the fiery orb he held while he approached Marco. Marco held out his arm over the edge of the mountain and continued spinning his arm. Casca slowly turned the angle of his wheel of fire until the two rings almost met. Faster and faster they spun the burning orbs over their heads, allowing the two rings nearly to interlock and become one. The burning wheels of fire circled in their ever-quickening path, whistling, crackling as they whipped through the frigid air, splintering the night sky. Eventually the circles of fire melded into each other, lighting the edge of the plateau, giving anyone who witnessed, legend for generations, tales of the fires that came from heaven. Had the gods from above looked down upon their children, they would have marveled at the lights that danced beneath them.

Far below, in the emptiness where the two sides of the mountain met, two men sat at the entrance to a buffalo hide tent. Into the depth of the abyss the height of the mountain had created, a message of hope had found its way down. They looked up at the interlocking rings of fire and smiled. For now, all was well.

THIRTEEN

Spring came in a few months to the dwellers of the Cave of Dolhan. Winter had finally loosened its grasp, giving a temporary respite to the mountain and its people where winter was certain to return with a vengeance. The words of the Budha had been shared with the two young men for months now, adding wisdom beyond their few years in this world. "Destiny awaits you in a land far from here," Tazrack smilingly encouraged Marco and Vittorio while he looked longingly toward the east. With grateful yet heavy hearts, Marco and Vittorio parted from their recently found home and teacher.

"I will see my father soon!" were the last words Marco spoke to Tazrack. There was no need to offer endless words of thanks. Tazrack did not need to hear what he knew quite well.

It took less than one day for Casca, Marco, and Vittorio to descend along the face of the mountain. Many of the rocks that had served as their steps on the way up had splintered or vanished during the brutal winter; however, there was more than enough to allow for their descent. There was little in the world that would have prevented Marco from making his way down into the valley where his father and uncle awaited.

For days Marco and Niccolo traveled side by side, ignoring everyone else, talking from sunrise to sunset. Their reunion had been long overdue, Marco having missed his father more over the last few uncertain months than the previous nineteen years. Maffeo and Niccolo had not had it easy either over the long winter months, most of their time spent rationing their food and fighting the ravages of winter. The fiery rings that had lit up the sky two months previously had kept them away from despair. Once more Casca's actions had preserved both father and son.

Vittorio walked beside Maffeo, hoping to remember all there was to tell. In those few months they had all lived a lifetime. At times Niccolo made eye contact with Casca who mostly walked alone, ahead of all of them. A father once again offered silent and heartfelt thanks to a man who had likely saved and preserved his son.

The mountain range disappeared behind them within a few days. Vittorio looked back, his eyes searching the highest of peaks that they had looked down from. He found it hard to believe the endless mountain that reached the sky could be so distant as to vanish behind the horizon. Just like traveling over the open seas, where the ships themselves disappeared before the highest of sails, so did the mountain range escape from Vittorio's sight, only the lonely peaks still barely visible at the horizon.

Marco had looked back just once and had tightly closed his eyes. Much had happened over the past months, the exhausting effort it had taken to cross the mountain range, the terribly unfortunate loss of their guide, Pak, the days spent in the world of Tazrack and his Budhist teachings, and finally the reunion with his father once again when all had seemed to be lost. The rings of fire had been right; all was well once again.

As he had done countless times before, Maffeo was able to barter for horses using his endless supply of precious stones. A small village at the base of the Pamir range offered horses and supplies they desperately needed. The way through the great desert, the Gobi, could not be challenged foolishly. The Silk Road was littered with such men, the path through northern territories frequented by Tartar marauders and Mongol nomads who challenged all that dared trespass. Longingly, Vittorio looked at the beautiful jade ring and necklace Maffeo had parted with.

"I want them, father, they are beautiful," Anka, the daughter of a local Urgich chieftain exclaimed while her father had put on his most unshakable of faces. He frowned hearing her exuberance, figuring it had likely cost him one extra horse. "Thank you, father," she continued, while she held the polished green jade necklace to her chest before the deal had even been struck.

Marco watched her thin fingers lay the necklace over her delicate neck, the small round pieces rattling against each other as they nessled in against her bosom. He smiled at her, embarrassed at having lowered his eyes so bravely. She returned the pleased grin and blushed. In an hour the five of them departed, her beautiful smile eventually to be lost in the recesses of Marco's memories.

The terrain quickly changed from green valleys covered with flowering fruit trees and knee-high grass to dryer, dead soil, to scarred, desolate crushed rock and sand. The cool air that had refreshed and invigorated them also disappeared, the dry and dusty winds of the desert taking their place. Water became more and more difficult to find, eventually forcing them to ration even the foulest and warmest of what there was left. The nights did not offer much comfort either, the sand keeping the heat the sun had imparted on it during the day. At times when the eastern breeze picked up, it brought the sounds of the shifting sands to their ears, sounds that were not much unlike those of a thousand snakes trailing through the sand.

Their fresh and muscular horses soon became haggard, creatures that lived on just enough dead grass, roots, and water to continue moving. The desert sun had returned with a vengeance, humbling and breaking their spirit. Even Marco, with his unflappable exuberance, walked with his horse's reins in his hands wondering if they would make it to the next watering hole. Exhausted and depleted, they rested in the shade of a long-dead tree. Its splintered limbs offered little comfort.

"It won't be long now." Marco and Vittorio listened to Casca, trying to figure what he had meant. Realizing the effort it would take to question him, they huddled against each other, trying to block the scarring sand from torturing them. Opening their mouths just meant allowing the desert to suck the life and moisture out of their already enfeebled bodies. Whatever there was that was soon to follow would just be. Casca sat, scanning the uncertain horizon to the east. It was not long before they all saw what his eyes had picked up.

A large figure moved as if floating over the sand, eventually the image separating, the outline of six horses coming into view. The hot air moved unevenly over the sand, confounding their minds, distorting their sight and thought. Drained and approaching near exhaustion, they all stood to meet their destiny. The pounding of hooves approached them, rhythmically announcing the arrival of the desert warriors. Out of the corner of his eye Niccolo watched Casca's lips upturn, appearing pleased at the approach of the riders.

The ragtag team came to a halt, possibly eyeing their prey, perhaps puzzled by the lack of response from them. A short beastlike creature with his bearded face looking more like something that only comes out on the darkest of nights acted as their leader.

"How dare you trespass without offering bounty?" the man angrily demanded. "I am Tangut, oldest son of Khaidu, Khan of the mountains, great nephew of the Genghis. No one may pass through the gateway without payment. With life or blood," he continued while raising a light, curved sword over his head. "The Great Khan does not have time for this insignificance. You are wasting his precious time with—" The man was about to continue his obviously rehearsed diatribe until his eyes rested on Casca.

"You, can . . ." He was unable to form any more words as apparently his whole mission had become undone. Wide-eyed, he looked at his men and grumbled something under his breath. The man shook his head, trying to clear the drunken veil that still clouded his mind. He belched sourly into the wind, regretting the previous night's thirst.

"We are ambassadors of the Great Khan. We have journeyed for over five years to return." Maffeo stepped forward holding the golden paiza with both hands.

The six bowed in their saddles at the sight of the golden tablet. It was the p'ai-tzu, the metal tablet that served as a guarantee of safe passage. This they had not expected. It was the seal of Khubilai Khan, the Supreme Khan of all Mongols. They had all heard of such, yet none had ever seen one. It held the power of the Khan himself. Everyone and everything were at its disposal. Still troubled by what he had witnessed, Tangut tried raising his eyes to get a better look at Casca. He shook his head and smiled. It could not have been. His thoughts must have betrayed him.

Not unlike the rest, Tangut wore a cuirass, a leather and brass garment that protected them from arrows and at times even deflected poorly aimed swords or lances. On his head, a helmet also made of leather and brass lined with sheepskin almost came down over his bloodshot eyes, covering his filthy and greasy hair. He scratched at his face, leaving tracks where his gnarled nails displaced the filth. They all stood in silence, shocked at the sight of the golden paiza, yet displeased.

"We will take you to our Khan," was all Casca and the rest heard for a while.

Taking huge gulps, the five of them quickly emptied the two sheepskin bladders they were offered. The contents of the containers were unmatched. Clear and cool water. Ambrosia would have paled by comparison on this day. Truly the nectar of the gods.

The terrain worsened for the next day, bringing misery to the horses that had already been on the edge of death. Marco and Vittorio walked side by side, gently holding the reigns of their mounts, trying not to overly burden them, yet at the same time attempting to keep their own balance over this miserably treacherous ground. Marco looked up at the relentless sun that drained them of strength and cringed from the rays that scorched his eyes. A breeze picked up from the east, swirling the dust, nearly suffocating all of them with the blast of hot air. Hell could not have been much hotter, Vittorio thought, mouthing the words in his exhausted, delirious state. Casca continued calmly, relieved that rest and comfort were not far away. Tangut and his advance guard never traveled more than a few days off.

"Beyond that range," the Mongol leader yelled into the wind as he turned his head to the five he continued leading. Tangut turned forward and laughed, amused at how men not of this land could be so frail. After all, summer had not yet arrived. The curse of the desert was still weeks away.

They trekked through a narrow valley where a small, nearly dried out stream provided their horses much needed water. Anxiously they lapped at the thick water, ignoring the filth and refuse that floated on top. The ground had softened somewhat over the last few hours as they had entered the incline of a small mountain range. Following a rocky path, they advanced slowly, more often finding shrubbery and leafy plants the horses were able to eat. By midday they had reached a plateau where, to the surprise of them all, they could see wild horses grazing in the open. Tangut looked toward the horses and pounded one of his men on the back while laughing. The rest of his men returned the laughter and continued riding. From farther east, the barking of dogs and the bleating of sheep traveled along the wind. Smoke rose into the sky from fires not far off. A new world awaited Marco and Vittorio.

Wide-eyed, Marco and Vittorio stood at the eastern edge of the plateau looking at the immense tent city that awaited them. "Follow along!" Tangut pointed to a small path that led down into the main area.

Hundreds, perhaps thousands of leather yurts lay spread out over the whole expanse as far as the eye could follow. Curiously, all the tents had been arranged to have their entrances face south. Dozens of young boys rode toward them, whipping their horses in the excitement of the visitors. Only covered from the waist down, they looked like a pack of wild animals that had taken off in a maddened escape. Riders and horses becoming one creature, as if centaurs had returned to earth. Using no saddles or stirrups, the young boys clung to the back of the horses with no more effort than one would sitting on a comfortable seat. They continued riding around them, cheering loudly. Born in this world, they had likely learned to ride long before having taken their first steps.

Tangut, ignoring the joyous and acrobatic charge, led the five of them down a wide path into the heart of the tent city.

"Why don't they cover up?" Marco pointed at two young girls, no more than fourteen or fifteen years of age. The girls ran after each other, playing with red and white ribbons, giggling while they watched the strips trail behind them as they ran. At times the wind caught the flickering strands, amusing the girls that ran with them and others who just watched and cheered. Not much more than a small piece of cloth covered their waists, clearly exposing to all their impending beauty.

"Have they no shame?" Marco leaned toward Casca this time, having had no response from Vittorio who just stared.

"These are not Muslim women, Marco. There is no shame in what they do here," Casca responded.

"Do they not know what they do?" Marco insisted.

Casca smiled. "They certainly do."

The girls continued running, eventually disappearing behind one of the larger sheepskin tents. Their voices also soon trailed off, quickly to be replaced by that of barking dogs and the yell of boys bickering.

Two boys stood face-to-face, with their shirts off, ready to test each other's mettle. Within seconds they were both covered with dust and grime as their arena sullied them. A dozen other children cheered and whistled at them as they stood in a circle, watching the two boys get the better of each other. Gasping for breath, the two continued wrestling, unwilling to admit weakness or lack of heart. They did not have long before their training was over. Once they reached fourteen years of age, they were Mongol warriors, ready to be led into battle, eager and able to fight for their Khan.

"This way for now." Tangut showed Maffeo and Niccolo to one of the tents. "You will be brought food and drink. Marja, bring our guests some water, ayrag, and meat. It will suffice until tonight." He indicated to a young woman by the side of the tent.

Vittorio and Marco were also pointed to a small tent, while Casca was led to a larger and much better kept tent. Removing his pack and sword, Casca entered the enclosure. Unlike the yurts he had been in before, this one did not have the dusty dirt floor under his feet, but the covering of fine Persian rugs. The rug was clean of filth and stain. Casca had seen enough bloodied rugs in such tents that served as reminders of what a not-well-settled discussion could bring. This was no ordinary tent or reception for Casca. What he had sensed was becoming a reality. The Old Young One had returned to the land of the Khans.

It was a day of celebration. Feasts, music, dancing, feats of strength and endurance were just some of the activities planned around a hedonistic schedule of food and drink. The barrage of entertainment would continue until morning or until the drink lasted. Somehow the available supply could never outdo the thirst and hunger these men and women of the steppes were used to wielding.

Khaidu Khan had had many recent victories in the north, fighting off invaders of the empire. Foolish Anjuks had attempted to overtake this more fertile land Khaidu Khan and his people presently occupied. Or so they had said. Conflict did not need many reasons. When men were strong and armed, metal clashed and arrows flew easily. Just as much as Mongols cherished life, bloodletting was quick and without remorse if it reserved an honorable place in the Eternal Blue Sky.

"Is this all for us?" Marco whispered into Casca's ear.

Casca stood by Marco and Niccolo, a feast the size of which was usually reserved for kings was within their sights. Approaching them, Vittorio rubbed at his belly, smacking his lips without the slightest attempt to control his nauseating slobbering.

"Someone will need to roll me back to my tent by the time I am finished." He laughed, putting his anxious hand on Marco's shoulder.

Hundreds of sheep, lambs, calves, chickens, and goats had been slaughtered and prepared over dozens of open fires. Throughout the afternoon and into the early evening many had worked feverishly to prepare the feast. The charred carcasses, dripping with oil and covered with burned and spiced leaves were racked one on top of another and end to end around a huge cleared opening. Around it, hundreds of Khaidu Khan's warriors noisily sat, awaiting their Khan to commence the indulgences.

"This way, honored guests. You will be sitting on the Khan's right tonight." A small and muscular man extended his hand, pointing to a narrow opening through which he led them. "My name is Angor. I am here to help in any way. Any way." He repeated the last words while his eyes pointed toward a small yurt. "They will be available, if you please," he added in case the offer for women was not obvious enough by his first actions.

Niccolo, Marco, and Vittorio followed Casca through the opening in the noisy crowd. Most had started the festivities early on this night, as their wavering and loud voices obviously betrayed them.

"This way." Angor pointed to a small open space by the edge of the clearing.

The four of them stood side by side, awaiting the Khan's arrival. "Where is Uncle Maffeo?" Marco inquired, raising concern in all of them as they realized none of them had seen him since early in the afternoon.

"Do not despair." Maffeo's pleased voice eased them. "I have made good use of the time. The young man was quite generous." He pushed his way between two drunken behemoths, shielding his head from swinging elbows.

Niccolo looked back at his brother. "He cannot help himself, it is in his blood." Niccolo cut in. "A Venetian that does not barter is no longer a Venetian," Maffeo and Niccolo together recited the old adage while facing each other.

Casca looked around at the multitude of faces. Clearly of distinct races and tribes, thousands had gathered for the Challenge. From the Buryats of the northern great lake to the Ando of western Chin, to Tartars and Uighurs, Mentok and the dark Atavi of the frozen northern land, men who could not get along for longer than it took to restring a bow, except for the day of the Challenge, when Khaidu Khan's patience was not to be tested. Casca had witnessed and taken part in such events, many having taken days of celebration, games, and feasts. Dull it had never been, the events of today promising no less.

Groups of men huddled side by side, telling unbelievable stories between gulps of ayrag and throat stretching chunks of flesh they devoured endlessly. Horses were the only flesh that would survive the feasting of today. A Mongol would gladly starve to death before even considering killing and eating the sacred beast. It would have been unthinkable and inexcusable. Mongol warriors had been put to death for lesser offenses.

Most men had come, pleased at being part of the Khan's empire, eager to add their swords and arrows in the ever expanding land Khaidu oversaw, others more concerned with gaining the protection that an alliance the Khan and his armies could offer.

"It is the Khan!" A roar spread through the crowd with the arrival of Khaidu Khan, grandson of Genghis, the Supreme Khan. Men all around bellowed, howling into the night sky, shaking the mountainside, the voice of the thousands echoing and reverberating in the valley below. The sun had set already over the horizon, reddening the edge of the mountain. By the light of the stars and dozens of campfires the feast and celebration would continue.

Khaidu Khan entered the circle, his right hand holding a sword raised over his head. He turned, eagerly accepting the howls of the crowd, pausing momentarily as he neared his new guests. "So, you have returned after all these years."

"By the order of Khubilai Khan, we have traveled far with his message. We are honored to be in the land of the Great Khaidu Khan. You offer the hospitality worthy of a king." Maffeo bowed while gracefully addressing Khaidu Khan. For a moment there was silence, allowing Niccolo and Maffeo to wonder who Khaidu Khan was welcoming back. They watched as Khaidu almost nervously—if that were even possible for this man—looked at Casca. Casca returned the look, nodding unemotionally to the Khan.

"Forgive our insignificant gift. It is not worthy of the Khan's eyes. The Great Khan should not even waste his time gazing upon it," Maffeo attempted.

With their mouths agape, Marco and Vittorio stared at the diamond and sapphire necklace Maffeo had handed to one of the Khan's men. Imbedded into the yellowest gold they had ever seen, almond-sized diamonds and sapphires adorned this most intricate of neckwear. The ornament was huge, making Marco and Vittorio wonder where Maffeo could have possibly kept it hidden all this time. It was a dowry worthy of a queen, or a king's ransom.

"Sit, all. The time has come to celebrate your return." Khaidu Khan watched one of his men place the golden offering next to him. "Your offering is not unworthy of my eyes, for now," were the only words he offered in acceptance of the gift. "I welcome your return." Once again Maffeo and Niccolo eyed each other, wondering whose return Khaidu Khan was referring to, and what the Khan had meant by "for now."

Khaidu Khan sat, pulling his feet underneath himself. He rested his elbows on his knees, clasped his thick and knotted hands together, and peered out into the endless anxious faces. On his right, two of his sons took their place, nodding their heads, acknowledging their position of importance by their father, the Khan. The two of them were both larger than their father, hulkish men raised on meat and war. Tangut, the one who had led the advance guard had not joined in the celebration on this day.

A large plate of food was immediately placed in front of the Khan by two young women. Another plate, covered with mounds of rice, loaves of bread, and an assortment of fruit was also placed by his feet. He looked at the steaming heap of roasted meat and at the two girls with the same hunger and anticipation. They would each have their time.

A soft beating of drums sounded with the beginning of the feast. Rhythmically it reverberated in the valley, echoing far off in the distance, sending the sounds of celebration toward the skies.

In a frightful way Khaidu Khan began to devour the meat put in front of him, clearly ignoring the bread and the rice. Perhaps as much as sixty years of age, he was a strong and powerful man. Time had passed slowly for him, allowing for his strength and intensity to remain. Long and knotted hair covered his head and flowed freely by his sides. His beard, like his hair, was ragged and laced with gray. Dark and foreboding eyes were hidden behind thick eyebrows. A tattered cuirass covered his muscular and hardened body; in a few places the cloth was shredded, exposing old wounds. He did not wear clothing befitting a Khan, not even one worthy of someone of high rank. The cuirass clearly showed the wear of time and battle. Perhaps more.

Marco cringed behind a cup of ayrag as he watched Khaidu Khan devour slab after slab of meat. The Khan's teeth and sharpened nails ripped at the roasted flesh, at times obscenely laughing at the blood that had spurted from the barely cooked meat. He grinned, feeling the juices flow down his face and neck. His swordlike teeth tore the meat off of oversized bones, at times crushing the brittle bone in an attempt to suck out the still red marrow, his teeth only taking breaks when he inhaled impossibly large chunks, the size of a man's fist. Belching noisily, he wiped his bloody and greasy hands into his beard and filthy cuirass, attempting to rid his hands of the slippery grease that slowed and hindered his eating. Only a few minutes had passed, yet he had devoured more flesh than a pack of wolves in winter.

Khaidu rose to the cheer of thousands. His insatiable ways would no doubt continue shortly. He slowly turned, allowing the voices to intensify as he faced them. His name thundered on the lips of thousands in this valley, their voices pounding along with the beating of drums. He was Khan. The one they would follow to their deaths without remorse, if it served the empire. Today was a day of duty and celebration.

Casca stood alongside Angor looking at the Khan and his followers. A few dark-eyed men stood next to the Khan, clearly enjoying their position. One of them, standing slightly behind the Khan, watched with sober eyes the events of the night unfold. His right hand held the hilt of his sword, the nail of his right thumb almost in a nervous twitch, scraping the handle of the blade. Pulling on the leather cuirass, he scratched at an ugly war wound by his chest. He had likely had good fortune surviving the impact of a spear.

"His name is Nomukh," Angor whispered into Casca's ear, having followed Casca's line of sight. "He never takes part in the celebration. His duties lie elsewhere."

Casca's eyes shifted toward Angor, wondering why the man had offered the information. "You might meet him soon enough," Angor continued, just as Casca was about to inquire. Casca's eyes returned to the one called Nomukh who had just moved up next to the Khan. Nomukh stood by, as if guarding the Khan, something that did not appear to be necessary. Most would have given their lives for the Khan, or taken endless pleasure in punishing any who disobeyed or threatened their leader.

"Who is that?" Marco's question startled Casca as he had been focusing all his attention on the Khan and Nomukh.

"It is Khutulun," Angor responded with a heavy sigh in his voice.

A moment of silence was followed by the roar of thousands having seen the princess enter the circle. The sound of men was deafening, outdoing what they had offered their own Khan.

"She is ready for the challenge," Angor added with trepidation and excitement in his voice. He ran his thumb by his lower lip, moistening his finger in the process.

A woman unlike any Marco and Vittorio had ever seen stood by her father, the Khan. She was nearly as tall as he, larger, more ferocious, yet more beautiful than anyone Marco and Vittorio had ever met or imagined. Her hair was blacker than night, darker than the cover of a raven at midnight. It hung loosely by her sides, overflowing her otherwise unclad shoulders. Little cloth and leather had been used to cover her body. Her shoulders were broad, yet not overly muscular, thinning down to a waist that Casca figured he would eagerly encircle with his hands. Endless legs anchored her to the ground, smooth and covered with oils. She looked at the men around her, dismissing the frail women that sat or stood cowering by the sides of men. Khutulun was a woman unlike any other. She turned, allowing her hair to be caught in the night wind, to have it flutter against the starry backdrop.

"She is a goddess," Vittorio spoke out loud, not caring if anyone was to hear, perhaps unable to hold back.

"It is why men conquer worlds." Angor smiled at Casca for an instant, then returned his gaze upon Khutulun. Maffeo nodded, overhearing Angor and his reasoning, realizing that in one statement Angor had told much of the world's history. Helen of Troy would have cowered at her feet.

"Time has come once again for my daughter to offer herself. Who believes himself to be worthy?" Khaidu Khan called into the night, challenging any and all who dared deem themselves deserving of the princess. The steady rhythm of drums ceased, allowing for complete silence to welcome the challenger.

"I will have her. Much time she will spend on her knees by my feet, giving me pleasure, earning her keep." The challenge had been met with defiance and foolhardiness. For seconds that seemed to last an eternity no one spoke. No one dared be first to break the silence.

"She will do fine. I trust she is well broken in by now,"

the same voice challenged the princess and the Khan. "If not, I will take the pleasure in making her yield," the man continued. "I am Altar of the Bitrix-hun. My people have lived in this land since time has been worthy of reckoning." He stood tall and brave.

Khaidu Khan nodded slowly and pursed his lips. He stroked his beard, wiping the last of the grease off his hands. Khutulun looked on unemotionally as if she had not heard the challenge met.

"So you say, young Altar; it is your first time within my land, I trust," Khaidu addressed the man, dismissing Altar's insistence on his claim. "It is a bold way you have decided to let yourself be known. I hear your father has departed us. May he be joyous for eternity in the Eternal Blue Sky."

Unconcerned with Khaidu Khan's response and nearly kind words, Altar continued. "A thousand horses I have brought to offer in the Challenge. They are the best the steppes have to offer, only their offspring will outdo them. They will feed and be watered in your land. I will then return them to the north, victorious, and with my prize. Perhaps one day I will return to further my claim," he again challenged the Khan, while pointing toward Khutulun.

Khaidu Khan stood and faced the man that had spoken so bravely, yet foolishly. Altar was nearly a head taller than all the men around him, men who defiantly stood by their leader, realizing that on this day their boldness was a life-and-death gamble. He flexed his huge arms. The robe he had been wearing to conceal his body fell by his feet.

He was a monstrosity of a man, fleshy and muscular, his arms nearly straight out by his sides, the size of his chest and arms not allowing his limbs to fall by his hips. He had spared no time or effort in gaining strength and size, perhaps even experience. However, his advisors were no doubt going to be met with anger upon return to the north. Breathing noisily, he stepped in front of his men.

Stiffly he walked into the circle, quieting all that could see him. The sound of drums softened and faded. Altar raised his hands toward the dark skies, embracing the quiet of the night. He stood defiantly and faced the Khan. Wetting his oversized middle finger he pointed toward the princess.

"The challenge is mine." He repeated his brave words. Khutulun adjusted her belt, clearly making every attempt to ignore Altar and his boasting.

"What madman will protect her and take his challenge," Marco whispered while he tried catching his breath. "The Khan is too old to deal with Altar."

Casca shook his head at Marco. "It is not their challenge to take. She will defend herself. It is her life to give."

Marco and Vittorio smiled, amused at Casca's response. "It is impossible—" Marco was about to say when his words were cut off by the princess's entry into the circle.

Even the creatures of the desert and the winds became quiet, awaiting the princess's challenge. Unemotionally, she found a place in the sand and stood her ground. Using a leather strap, she tied her long and flowing hair together, keeping it out of harm's way, making certain it could not become a hindrance during the contest.

"Yes, you will do fine," Altar repeated, pleased with himself. He again licked at his finger, gesticulating at her.

The two of them stood ten paces apart. Huge mounds of flesh moved over his body as he flexed all his muscles, trying to hypnotize Khutulun and intimidate anyone that might have considered coming to her rescue.

"He looks like he could crush boulders with his bare hands and snap tree trunks with the strength of his legs," Vittorio whispered into Marco's ear.

Casca smiled overhearing Vittorio. "Rocks and trees rarely hit back."

Altar pushed his own long hair back over his shoulder, snapping his head backward in mock gesture imitating Khutulun. His eyes measured her wrists as he approached. He strode forward and swung his long arm in her direction. She was nowhere to be found, at least five steps from where she had been by the time his long arm concluded its arch. He smiled and took a few steps forward, trying to cut off her escape and crowd her against the wall of men who stood all around the opening. Even Altar had not expected for her to fall too easily.

Casca watched Khaidu Khan smile at the two contestants. He had trained his daughter well. Next to Khaidu, Nomukh stood, his right hand on his sword, anxiously scratching it with his thumb. His emotions toward her betrayed him. It was easily understood.

Marco and Vittorio cringed from this most obscene of challenges. Never before had they seen or imagined a woman fighting for her life and freedom in such an unsavory way. Thousands of voices rang out, many from the intensity of what they were witnessing, while the rest farther behind the crowd, as a response to what they were hearing. The mountainside shook beneath their feet. It was a long way from Venice.

Accelerating his pace, Altar continued swinging his arms at Khutulun, feinting with his legs and body, hoping to get his hands on her. He figured once within his grasp the contest would be over. Their awkward dance continued for a while, Altar making more and more abrupt rushes at her, driving his arms violently and at times even sweeping sideways with his long legs, trying to knock her down or at least off balance.

"Stand your ground," he hissed at her, clearly becoming aware that even with all his efforts he was not about to catch up to her.

She smiled and ran the palms of her hands over her chest, pausing momentarily when her fingertips reached the drawstring that held her clothing together. With a devilish grin, she reached with her fingers toward her lips, flicking with her tongue, wetting the tip of her middle finger.

"Damn you!" Altar gritted his teeth between ever quickening struggles for air. Blood rushed to his face as he foolishly doomed his future. Digging into the sandy dirt with his flat feet he kicked at the direction of Khutulun, trying to momentarily blind her and disorient her. Khutulun stepped to her left, not allowing even a grain of sand to find its mark. Desperately, Altar kicked at the dirt again.

Casca pitied the actions of a desperate man. Any standing he might have had with his tribe, or future leadership he might have imagined, disappeared in that instant. He had disgraced himself. A savage land it might have been, yet one did not go beyond its limits. Altar had lost.

Screaming out of control, Altar rushed at Khutulun with his hands stretched out in a final attempt to overrun her. The horrible ripping of flesh soon followed as Khutulun had sidestepped this rush and had dug the heel of her right foot against the side of Altar's knee. He crumpled in a giant pile of quivering flesh like a buffalo falling over the cliff during a hunt. With both hands trying to hold his knee together he tried keeping back a howl of pain. He had been struck harder and more viciously than any boulder or tree trunk ever could have. If fortunate, he was to walk again by next year, most likely with a severe limp. The leg would eventually heal, perhaps forever crippling his walk, however, the memory of his failed challenge and unforgivable strategy was never to be erased from all who had witnessed.

Just as abruptly as the challenge had been met, the Khan's attention turned to Niccolo and Maffeo. Altar had been dismissed. He had become once again irrelevant. Just another failed and disillusioned rival to the throne of the Mongols. Four of Altar's men rushed into the circle and retrieved their broken leader.

"Let the game continue." The proud voice of Khaidu Khan quieted the roaring crowds. "My champion is here for all challengers." The Khan looked toward Casca. Niccolo and Maffeo noted the Khan's wicked grin as he demanded a challenge while placing his hand on the golden necklace he had received.

"There is more?" Marco inquired, drained by the intensity of what he had witnessed. With one eye he watched Altar being helped away, quickly to disappear behind a wall of his men. Marco's gaze returned to fall upon the princess. She truly was a woman unlike any he thought could have existed in the world.

"My son is ready to defend the name. Bortey, he is, the eternal champion. Who will come and stand in his way?" Khaidu challenged.

A cloaked figure appeared from farther behind the Khan. Walking slowly and patiently he waited until a path had cleared in front of him, allowing him to enter the arena unobstructed.

"He has been champion for nearly ten years," Angor proudly informed Casca. "No one has been able to wager for years now. He has been unmatched."

Casca watched the man take slow steps to face his father, the Khan. Leaning forward slightly he paid his respects to his father and extended his hand to Khutulun, congratulating her

on her victory. Proudly she smiled and took her place alongside the Khan, just to his right.

"The tournament has been for two months," Angor continued. "Many tribes have sent their champions, bidding to reach
the finals and challenge Urechi." He smiled wickedly. "A few
have died during the competitions; the less fortunate had
lived." Angor pointed to a man sitting at the edge of the circle,
his head twisted obscenely to the left, beyond where its nat-
ural position seemed reasonable. Others, not unlike him,
watched from their broken bodies. Angor shook his head. "Petrok of the Buryats has emerged as the only worthy challenger. It is said he feels no pain."

Once again the beating of drums had settled down, allowing
everyone to focus on the confrontation. Petrok had also entered the circle, dressed in an immaculate cuirass. The leather
covering was new and unstained. Lustrous from the fires that
raged on into the night, it created a glow around the well-
oiled body of Petrok. It had been worn just for the Challenge.
Petrok was the youngest son of Blanar the Dark, Khan of the
great northern lake territory. He and his people were believed
to have vision like the creatures of the night. They prayed to
gods unmentionable by any not born of their tribe. Anyone
guilty of such oversight never lived long enough to tell their
tale.

Urechi and Petrok faced each other. They were monsters,
demons out of nightmares, huge and powerful men who had
dedicated themselves to the art of fighting. Petrok rubbed at
his arms and chest, moving the huge flanks of flesh around,
loosening and further oiling them in the process. A slippery
and elusive target he was going to be. His eyes boiled in the
fury and intensity only months of preparation and single-
minded dedication could have forged. He had waited years
for this fateful day. Just to compete in the challenge was
honor enough. Or so many insisted.

Urechi, son of Khaidu Khan, quietly stood as he removed
his robe. It was a sight not befitting a man. He was a creature
unlike any men. Marco and Vittorio gasped at the sight. No
woman could have spawned such a beast. His features were
curved and round, from his hairless domed head to his bowed
legs and hooked toes. A thing that resembled a nose, flattened
beyond description, protruded less than his thick and rounded

cheekbones. His squashed and sickle shaped nostrils let out a thin whistle every time he snorted in the night air. From years of fighting, of being held in the grasp of other powerful men, his ears had flattened and elongated, reaching backward, following the outline of the sides of his collapsed head. His eyes were narrow and deep set, the windows to his soul without expression.

A thick layer of oil and camel grease covered his bald head as well as the rest of his contorted body, giving him the appearance of a slithering bog beast or toad that had emerged from the mire. It was a difficult sight to behold, or to imagine being held in a close grasp by, face-to-face, with this creature.

Petrok swallowed hard as he stepped in and faced Urechi. He had heard of Urechi, yet seeing him was something that softened the strongest of men. Anxiously he surveyed his opponent. Moving to his left Petrok feigned and suddenly lunged at Urechi's legs. And it was over.

Urechi had pushed down on Petrok's back, throwing him off balance and spinning his own body, suddenly landing on Petrok's unsuspecting back, both of them crashing into the dirt. In an instant Petrok's head and shoulders were in an iron grip engulfed by Urechi's powerful arms. Mercilessly, Urechi pushed down on top of Petrok's head, driving Petrok's chin downward into his chest. Urechi had acted so quickly, not even a scream of pain or horror had escaped Petrok's lips.

No man could have resisted such pain and physical restraint. A few seconds later the blood stopped going to Petrok's head, forcing him to lose consciousness. Urechi held him awhile longer, pressing sideways until the screeching of bone on bone slowed him down, this last act making certain that, when Petrok awoke, the pain in his neck and headache to follow would never allow him to forget this day.

Urechi stood victorious, Petrok's near lifeless body at his feet. A roar of approval erupted from the crowd, hailing their champion. Petrok had lost honorably, unlike Altar who had disgraced himself in front of everyone.

A murmur of disappointed voices soon followed, displeased at the brevity of the fight, yet not dissatisfied with the overwhelming superiority of their champion. The description of the challenge was sure to be told and retold many times, eventually to become unrecognizable from the true events of this night.

Thousands of anxious faces watched the victor, for the moment the masses neglecting both food and drink. It had been a night of true champions. Urechi had gone on undefeated and unmatched while their princess, Khutulun, had thwarted another challenger while enriching herself with a thousand horses.

"My men are disappointed with the challenge." Khaidu Khan stood and welcomed his son with a grin. "You have outdone all expectations," he said, congratulating his champion. Urechi bowed his head accepting the praise.

"What do you think of our champion, honored guests?"

"He is more than we have heard," Maffeo graciously responded, unwilling to admit they had never heard of Urechi.

Subdued and unemotional, Urechi sat by his father, pulling a cloak over his shoulders. He rocked back and forth, sipping from a large cup of spring water, oblivious of all around. Looking out into nowhere he continued drinking the water. He was nothing but a child trapped within the body of a monster.

"What else have you brought for me?" Khaidu Khan suddenly addressed Niccolo and Maffeo.

Surprised by it, Maffeo tried gathering himself. "We have failed the Great Khan. Our trinket is unworthy." Maffeo looked at Niccolo and raised his eyebrows.

"It is of great value. It is enough for a dozen men to purchase land and horses. However, I have no such needs. I take what I like," Khaidu Khan continued while devouring the hind leg of a lamb. He paused while enjoyed the juicy and succulent piece of meat. Taking another mouthful of steaming flesh he mumbled, "Your gift does not come from the heart."

Stunned by the Khan's words, Marco and Vittorio cringed behind Maffeo, wondering what fate awaited them. Out of the corner of his eye, Marco noted Casca shaking his head.

"You do wield the paiza that is true, yet I require more. My cousin Khubilai is far from here. The old man and I have not spoken in decades. It may take a lifetime before I will ever meet up with him, maybe never. I will honor your passport, however—"

"I will take the challenge," Casca interrupted, wearied by

the Khan's roundabout ways. "I offer myself."

For what seemed an eternity, not a word was uttered after Casca's offer. Marco and Vittorio shook their heads, wondering if Casca had lost his mind. Khaidu Khan smiled. He had expected no less.

Casca stood and entered the circle to the cheer of thousands. This was a day to go down in history. Casca had wondered how and when the Khan would finally address him. The return or presence of Niccolo and Maffeo was of no consequence to the Khan. He had no interest in their journey or mission, only his allegiance to the empire and traditional observance of honoring the paiza made him tolerate this group of travelers. Casca was of the ultimate concern. If he proved himself to be what the Khan had expected, the empire would return to its glory.

Casca turned to the crowds and removed his tunic. Shouts of excitement rose from the perimeter. Any disappointment they might have held disappeared at the sight of an apparently worthy challenger. The beating of drums joined in the howl of thousands, shaking the mountainside.

Urechi rose and also entered the perimeter. The competitors faced each other and circled to the left. Their eyes locking into each other, the two searched deeply. It was clear to both of the formidable task ahead. Urechi smiled a contorted and disturbing grin at the prospects of a true challenge.

The thousands who had cheered wildly soon quieted, eventually realizing the monumental battle that was unfolding. Urechi, their champion, and this strange knotted and scarred man promised more. Many of them stared at Casca while searching within themselves, wondering if their thoughts were possible.

Casca slowly flexed his fingers while facing the obscene creature in front of him. With his shoulders hunched over and chin brought almost to his chest, he resembled nothing that Casca had ever seen. Urechi kept his head down while he peered through narrow slits at his adversary. Keeping on his toes he seemed to glide over the ground, his hooked bare feet not disturbing even a grain of dust.

It was clear to both that this was a fight not soon to end. They continued moving side to side, at times changing direction, yet never approaching each other. Casca weighed his adversary. This was not a man who was to fall to trickery or foolish feints. Almost reading his thoughts, Urechi nodded in agreement and slowly walked toward Casca with his hands raised.

They stood at a foot's distance, ready to test each other's strength and endurance. In the instant it took Casca to raise his hands and interlock his fingers against Urechi's, memories of another fight returned. It had been over fifty years, maybe much more. Genghis Khan had been just a boy named Temujin when Casca had last faced such an adversary. Dark times of misery and slavery they had been, once again freedom ripped from Casca, the feel of metal encircling his ankles and wrists his only company. Han, the giant man from Chingpao, had foolishly tried to crush Casca with his weight and size. Just like many others, Han had become another unwitting victim to prematurely fill the ground.

Casca had spent months dragging the chains of a slave between his feet, fighting beast and man alike for scraps of food and cupfuls of stagnant water just to satisfy Zhoutai, a slave owner with a penchant for bloody contests and an occasional hairless young boy. Zhoutai had foolishly treated Casca like the lowest of slaves, starving him, having him wear the dress of a woman, a ploy to underestimate his worth prior to wagering. Eventually Zhoutai faced death at the hands of Temujin, bringing pleasure to both Casca and Temujin, and to the young boys who were spared from Zhoutai's bloated and turgid weapon.

With their legs spread slightly and knees bent, Casca and Urechi clashed. They stood face-to-face, breathing the same foul air, their ears sickened by the screeching of teeth against teeth, bones popping in their joints, and muscles scraping against stretched tissues. With their backs arched and bodies pushed to the limit, they soon gasped for air.

The power that came from deep within men such as them flowed through both, straining and pulling, pushing with all they had, trying to gain an advantage, hopelessly attempting to find a moment of weakness or fear. There was none to be found. For what seemed like hours, the two giants stood face-to-face, their fingers interlocked, refusing to yield, unable to overcome the other's indefatigability.

The weight of two mountains leaned against each other,

unable to overcome the other, yet unwilling to crumble in defeat. Casca and Urechi peered into each other's eyes, trying to find something, anything that would help them gain an advantage. Sweat poured from their bodies, drenching them in the salty liquid, running down, eventually pooling by their feet, wetting the dirt. Only their blood could have made the land more fertile, bringing renewed growth the following season. They struggled, keeping the hold over each other's hands while also applying every bit of strength they held.

Casca's senses focused, forcing the whole of the world to disappear from around him, no sights or sounds penetrating the wall their conflict had created. Urechi gritted his teeth as he bent his left leg while straightening out the right.

The move had been subtle, but not unnoticed. A few minutes later Urechi repeated his actions, this time bending his right leg slightly and straightening out his left. Casca tightened his belly and smiled deep inside.

Men and women whispered to each other as they watched the two combatants. "How long can they hold out?" The words of one of Khaidu's wives could be heard. "Neither will yield," an old man suggested. "He must be the one," a voice whispered next to the Khan, bringing a small nod from Khaidu.

The princess Khutulun crouched by her father. Her eyes narrowed, appraising this unusual stranger.

Once again Urechi shifted his legs slightly, allowing himself a moment's rest, placing more of the strain on one leg, then eventually shifting to the other. His wide bare feet dug into the ground, allowing his toes that extended more like the fingers of a hand to grasp the dirt, anchoring him in his place. Casca's breathing had slowed, almost achieving a hypnotic state in which all his energy he directed toward enduring the assault and preparing for its end.

Casca patiently waited. The shift was soon to come. A gasp from the crowd followed as all realized the shrewdness of Casca's actions. He had waited until just the right time. As Urechi had done a dozen times before, there was the barely discernible shift in his stance, that became his undoing. Casca watched, waiting for the right instant. And then it happened. Sand flew around them, creating a cloud of dust the moment

Urechi had moved. Using the moment of instability the flexing of muscles had caused, Casca struck.

Stunned in disbelief, Urechi fell beneath Casca, his feet swept out from underneath himself by Casca's quick actions. The momentary shift of his center of balance had been sufficient to create an advantage. Now they both lay in the dirt, their arms and legs interlocked, trying to find an advantage that would make the other yield.

The crowd watched in awe, these two men writhing in the dirt, resembling serpents locked in mortal combat. Casca locked one arm around Urechi's neck and shoulder, trying to twist the man's body, stretching his neck while applying pressure to his ribs. Urechi turned within the hold, slithering his greased body from Casca's grasp, trying to find a way out. He locked his legs around Casca's, for the moment preventing Casca from gaining any advantage. They both gasped for the precious air that kept their lungs full and their minds clear.

Digging his own feet into the dirt, Casca lay against Urechi's body, holding him down while at the same time allowing the weight of his body to slowly drain his opponent. Urechi continued moving, doing all he could to twist from Casca's hold, hoping his endless stirring would find a way out of this shroud that enveloped him.

Pushing with all his reserves, Casca eventually found himself underneath Urechi's chin, his own elbow resting just beneath the lower edge of Urechi's breastplate. Casca strained his legs while twisting his body until it finally happened. A dozen centuries had tempered his mind and body sufficiently to overcome any man.

A barely audible breath of air unwillingly left Urechi's lungs. His chest was collapsing as he could no longer withstand the force of Casca's actions. The cartilage at the base of Urechi's breastplate was bending, ready to snap, approaching his lungs and liver. Had the pressure continued and the bone broken, Urechi would have met with an agonizing journey into death. The end was close as Urechi's body was finally giving up.

"He will have to end it." A whisper came to Casca's ears. He could not tell who had spoken it and was uncertain of its meaning.

"It is time." Someone else's voice sounded.

Casca and Urechi continued their titanic struggle, Urechi attempting to use every deception and last reserve of energy to withstand Casca's assault. His breathing became more shallow and labored.

A whimper caught Casca's attention as his eyes found Khutulun within the crowd of anxious faces. Her pleading face.

"My son will never yield." Khaidu was unable to veil his words from the emotion he was feeling. He stood, arms by his sides, shoulders fallen.

Casca was unable to see Urechi's eyes, yet he could feel the pain and anguish his opponent was likely feeling. Urechi could not and would not concede. He lived by rules that did not allow it. If death was the outcome to their battle he was willing to accept it. He was not about to allow anyone to come to his defense. Not unlike him, his father the Khan could not intervene. Dishonor it would have brought for generations. It was the way of the Mongols.

Casca continued exerting pressure for a moment longer until his eyes once again met Khutulun's. She bore the proud face of the warrior she was, but also one of the desperate sister who could not bear the thought of her brother's impending death.

Casca stood and extended his hand to Urechi. There was no need for death on this night. Urechi had lost nothing. His honor would remain and legend grow. Casca's gift to Khaidu Khan was greater than the precious stone-covered golden necklace he had been given, or anything else he could have received. Khaidu Khan knew who the man was who had defeated his son.

"Welcome back to our land, Old Young One," he declared while standing next to Casca. "The empire is at your feet. Lead us back to the way of the Genghis."

Casca faced Khaidu Khan, Urechi standing by his side, grasping his own chest, awaiting for his breath to return. Urechi bowed toward Casca while his eyes beggingly looked at his father. Khaidu received his son unflinchingly, without losing faith. It was the greatest gift. His son had lost to the Old Young One.

An immeasurable cheer rose from the crowd, for their own champion and Casca, the Old Young One who had returned to the empire of the Genghis.

Marco and Vittorio stood side by side, caught up in the emotion of the battle, overjoyed at Casca's victory and anxious to congratulate him. Mention of the old empire of the Genghis and of the Old Young One they did not care for at the moment. There was much they could not understand about Casca, yet at this time it did not seem to matter. Being in the Khan's favor was more than enough for now.

Casca faced Khaidu Khan, Casca's left hand anxiously wrapped around the handle of the largest cup of ayrag that could be found for the victor. In one gulp the contents of the cup were gone, much of the cold liquid splashing down Casca's neck and chest, the elixir also soothing and refreshing from within as it traveled down Casca's dried out throat.

Khaidu Khan joyously shook Casca's right hand and raised it overhead for all to see. Casca turned within the crowd of anxious and delirious men, men frenzied by the drink and the staggering events of the night. None had ever seen Khaidu Khan show such reverence to anyone, yet this time it was befitting. The Old Young One had returned.

Within all the commotion Casca caught Nomukh's eyes, pleased yet concerned. Casca had returned to the world of the Mongols, a beautiful yet cruel world, a land of honor and degradation. A world not unlike any other.

FOURTEEN

*C*asca returned to his tent much past midnight, the remnants of endless celebration, drinking, and music still reverberating throughout his body. He had proven himself a bottomless pit, nearly challenging the Khan with his appetite. Dozens of women had danced for him and offered themselves. Perhaps the Old Young One had returned looking for a mate, even if for a short while. It was the least they could do on this day.

Casca lay resting in his tent, the soft and deep rug comforting his aching body. He rolled his shoulders, enjoying this bed much more than the uneven rock on the outskirts of Hormuz nearly one year previous. A gentle breeze rustled the flap of the tent, cooling his sweaty and overheated chest. His body was sore from his clash with Urechi while his head still throbbed from the endless drink and deafening beat of the drums. The soft sounds of the morin khour, its curiously gentle melody coming from two vibrating strings, had been lost within the roar of a hundred drums and trumpets. The eerie undulations of the "desert's song" he had always welcomed; however, now only quiet and sleep could ease Casca's worn body.

No sooner than Casca had closed his eyes than the instincts of the eternal soldier stirred him. Someone was approaching his tent.

"You will not escape your punishment!" A voice came from outside the tent.

Casca sat up to face four huge men blocking the entryway to the tent. The four separated, allowing for their leader to step through and face Casca. "It is my duty to protect Urechi, after all."

Casca looked up at the stunning princess Khutulun. She stood proud, hands on her hips, head held up high, delivering an uncertain message. Women seldom came to Casca in order to protect their younger brothers. Without doubt that was not Khutulun's only reason.

The moon had slipped out from behind a large gray cloud, for now brightening the plateau, lighting the entrance to Casca's tent.

"Leave us!" she ordered abruptly.

Three of the men quickly left while the fourth hesitantly held his ground, his eyes wide with concern while his right hand reached for his beltline that held a short curved sword.

"Now!" she repeated her orders.

The man bit his lip while his right thumb nervously scratched at the hilt of the sword. Reluctantly he left the tent calling to the three guards that had departed a few seconds earlier.

"I offer my thanks, for the life of my brother. You are forgiven for defeating him," she strangely informed Casca.

Casca sat back, amused at her unusual approach. Her voice was firm, yet she did not seem to be able to make up her mind to thank him or to punish him.

Standing in front of him she drew the drawstring from the tunic that covered her chest. The stretched-out leather strings quickly gave way, freeing her beauty. If this was his punishment, Casca figured he could withstand losing sleep on this night. Dawn was not far away.

Casca looked up at Khutulun. *"She is a goddess!"* Casca remembered Vittorio's remark when first having seen the princess. She certainly was. God had not forgotten this land, seeding it with Aphrodite's likeness.

Khutulun stopped pulling on the drawstrings and reached for her hair. The wind blew softly, opening the flap of the tent, allowing the light of the moon to bathe the tent with the glow befitting a goddess. She loosened her tightly cropped black hair, allowing it to flow freely, the dark veil splashing down toward her waist and back. Khutulun shook her head, hypnotizing Casca.

He attempted to stand, but a quick look from her made him hold his place. There was no need for haste. She further loosened her tunic, allowing Casca a glimpse at her perfection. She smiled a bewitching smile. Sleep would be short on this night. If any.

Within moments she stood bare in front of Casca, nothing but her leggings and waist-long hair covering her. Her legs seemed even longer than before, smooth and oiled. Casca's eyes followed them from her soft instep to her gently rounded sheep-skin covered calves and muscular yet feminine thighs. Her hips arched leading to a thin waist, not a drop of unwanted flesh burdening her hard stomach. Khutulun moved her hands toward her chest, allowing her fingers to run over her perfect breasts, momentarily pausing as the motion of her fingers had nearly hypnotized Casca. She smiled once again, her eyes shining as if they were the rising sun. Lost in her magnificence, Casca began to return her smile.

In an instant she was on him, having a better and more controlling hold than Urechi had been able to achieve. This was a fight he did not need to win. Passionately she kissed him, wrapping her legs around him. He tried removing his shirt while their lips battled, trying to gain an advantage. She pushed Casca down on, then began disrobing him. Apparently not much of his help was needed on this night.

Casca reached for her, to be pushed back once again. Dark

hair ran down by her bosom and narrow waist, stroking
Casca's now bare chest. He sighed with the pleasure of her.
Suddenly her lips were on him again. The sickening sound of
teeth upon teeth, and blood flowing down his neck shocked
him as Khutulun's teeth ripped Casca's lower lip, the edges
of her sharp teeth meeting each other within his flesh. A wave
of hot and cold ran through his body as the pain of her actions
quickened his breathing and brought beads of sweat to his
brow. She also gasped deeply while her hungry lips drew
blood from him, nearly devouring him. Her tongue danced
over his neck and chest, flicking at the newly formed beads
of sweat, trailing a crimson line, leading toward his waist. If
the pain did not overwhelm, it was going to be a greatly
pleasurable night.

Within moments his clothes rested against the four corners
of the tent while Khutulun quickly mounted her prey. Passionately and without abandon, she forced her body upon his,
bringing herself over him and him within her.

Her legs closed tightly around Casca, trapping him tighter
than any beast that had ever been saddled. Faster and faster
she pounded herself against his willing body, pulling herself
down over him quicker and with more force than her weight
falling over him would have allowed. She shook from the
sensations within, her arms suddenly stiffening as she dug her
nails into his muscular arms. Casca opened his mouth trying
to protest, yet his words became silent as she leaned forward,
smothering his face with her bosom. Khutulun groaned from
the wetness and passion of his lips, intensifying her movements, her bosom melding with his chest and face. Her hair
flew violently from side to side, most of the time covering
her eyes, sometime allowing Casca a quick glimpse of her
contorted yet pleasured face. Anxiously and increasingly faster she forced herself against Casca, pulling him within her
in an attempt to make him yield.

Casca tasted his own blood again as she once more ravaged
his lips with her own. He shook, the pleasure and pain of her
mouth scorching him to his very essence. A look of anger
and frustration, almost panic, appeared on her face as she was
failing to make her prey submit. Gasping for air, she made
one last attempt to break him while still controlling her own
self. Drenched in sweat, she cried out passionately to the

keeper of the Eternal Blue Sky as she collapsed and buried her face in his chest. Underneath the cover of her wet hair Casca smiled. Somehow women always seemed to call out to powers unseen during such moments of passion.

Casca stroked her face, clearing an opening within her hair, trying to see her eyes. His fingers traced her wet and slightly parted lips. He ran his fingers along the edge of her lower teeth, feeling the sharpness of the weapon that had so raped his own lips. She sighed and held on tighter. With him deep inside her she had collapsed powerless and unconscious. Casca allowed her to rest for a short while. Dawn was not far away.

FIFTEEN

Before the first light of day the four guards returned. Quickly dressing her, the five of them disappeared, allowing Casca a while longer until he would need to wake. He turned within the cover of a thick blanket and rested. He licked at his wounded lip and smiled. The cold air that had entered the tent eased him, helping him drift off into much deserved rest. It would be long before Khutulun would leave his memory.

Morning seemed to come in an instant, the sound of people and animals waking him from a pleasurable slumber. A spirited young voice begged to be allowed to enter. She came in carrying a large pot of tea and bread. While Casca washed down the freshly baked bread with the hot tea while she quietly washed his face and neck with a warm washcloth. She looked down while washing away the trails of blood that had stained his neck and chest. The young girl bit her lip, hoping he would address her, yet fearing that she would have to respond. For an instant she looked up seeing Casca's recently embattled lip. It was best to ignore it and continue working she decided. She shortly finished her assignment, bowed and lifted the flap to the tent.

"Thank you," Casca called to her. The sound of her footsteps accelerated as she made a hasty retreat, away from his tent.

It was a cold morning on this spring day, the cool air coming off the mountain invigorating Casca with its bite. He inhaled and raised his hands over his head, allowing the morning sun to warm him.

The tent city was its usual busy self by the time the sun had completely broken over the horizon. The previous night's events had been more significant than most would ever experience, yet the everyday business of maintaining the run of the campsite took precedence. Casca was not unpleased, he had no desire at being mobbed or overwhelmed by questions and offers.

Pulling his shirt tightly over his chest Casca shook slightly from the chill of the morning. He yawned, still spent and already hungry. Somehow no feast could prevent the following day's hunger.

Casca touched his swollen lower lip with his right index finger. The exposed flesh had not quite closed, making him cringe. It would take a few days for it to overcome Khutulun's passionate kiss, eventually just another scar to add to his collection. Licking his lips gently he walked toward the Khan's yurt. From the outside it was the same as all the rest, Khaidu Khan insisting on no special treatment as Casca later found out.

Princess Khutulun was leaving, returning to her home village of Abrok, just north of the Shantai mountain range. She had one thousand horses to lead to new pastures. Forty men were at the ready to lead the charge through the mountain pass. Her personal guard stood by, making certain she was unharmed by overly anxious men who had been entranced by her beauty and her actions of the previous night.

Khaidu Khan stood by the side of his yurt, eyeing a large goblet of steamy hot tea that one of his wives held. Holding the misshapen cup with both hands he sipped the still steaming tea, almost grunting in pleasure from the nearly boiling hot beverage. Proudly he watched his daughter approach. Just as the previous night, Nomukh stood behind him, impassive and unemotional, merely observing the events of the day while he scratched at the hilt of his short sword.

Urechi bowed to his father the Khan, exchanged a few

words, and then mounted his horse. He was also returning to Abrok. His beaten-down eyes caught Casca's as he sat up in the saddle. Urechi smiled and lowered his head in reverence to the man that had beaten him. He owed his life to Casca.

Khutulun neared, walking between two guards, their helpful arms steadying her approach. Cupping his hands for her foot, one of them helped her onto her horse. She struggled trying to keep her balance, causing the other guard to steady her. With one hand the man held the stirrups, while with the other he stroked the horse's head and neck, assuring the uncertain beast. Within all the commotion and the attempt to keep her balance, her eyes searched for Casca. Momentarily she looked down, placing both hands on the saddle horn of her mount, shifting about in an attempt to find comfort. Still grimacing for an instant, she made eye contact with Casca. He returned a distant smile, clearly remembering what had happened the last time they had exchanged such pleasantries.

She grabbed the reins with her left hand, while she ran her upper teeth against her lower lip. Pleased with their nonverbal exchange, they made no further eye contact. Satisfied as never before, she rode off. Deep inside her she carried the seed of the Old Young One. It would be weeks before disappointment would meet with her.

"Come Old Teacher, Lao Shi, join me." Khaidu Khan invited Casca into his yurt.

Throughout the early morning they sat enjoying a meal served by one of Khaidu's youngest daughters while the two of them spoke. Khaidu continued devouring obscene mounds of flesh, as if he had missed out on the previous night's feast. He swirled warm fermented mare's milk in a huge goblet, taking sips from it when the oversized chunks of flesh refused to slip down his throat.

There was nothing subtle about Khaidu Khan or his intentions. He had waited for dozens of years for this day. As he had always expected, the Old Young One had returned to the land of the Mongols, a land Khaidu believed needed saving. Casca had made no attempt to deny his identity. If Khaidu was any indication of how he would be received, there was no reason to be concerned. Or so it seemed for now.

"The way of the empire, the proud empire of my grandfather Genghis Khan, is dying," Khaidu declared. "Khubilai

Khan, the grandson of the Genghis, has changed much over the last two decades. My cousin he may be, yet he is as distant from the old ways as the depth of hell is from the Eternal Blue sky." Khaidu looked up and touched his heart with the palm of his right hand.

Khaidu continued talking, at times his words muffled by the large chunks of flesh he ceaselessly devoured, causing Casca to welcome the foul-smelling swigs of mare's milk that allowed Khaidu's words once again to be intelligible. Once proud and ferocious, willing and able to conquer and lead, Khubilai had apparently softened in recent years. Campaigns continued to further the empire, yet the future was in doubt. Khubilai Khan had lost the old ways.

Khubilai Khan was living not in a yurt befitting a khan where the earth lay just beneath one's feet and a warhorse stood at the ready, but in palaces filled with marble floors, hot baths, and servants that cleaned and pampered their perfumed and grotesquely overweight leader. *"It is no way for a Mongol to live,"* Khaidu kept repeating to himself and to his guest.

"Khubilai is no longer the grandson of the Great Genghis, the father of the empire. You, Old Young One, will be greatly shamed by Khubilai. He has betrayed his heritage, he can no longer be trusted," Khaidu gravely concluded.

The empire of the Mongols had been nothing but a few dozen tribes living in the steppes, desperately craving for a leader, Casca recalled. Temujin had become such a leader two generations before, possessing the inherent ability and the willingness to learn to organize and unite people under one ruler. Casca had taught him well. Temujin had united all the tribes, and become the supreme Khan, Genghis Khan. But, now, Genghis Khan was long gone, the empire having survived decades of infighting and posturing between any and all brave or foolish enough to attempt to be next in line to the khanate.

Casca listened during the morning hours, seldom interrupting, realizing Khaidu needed to purge his thoughts. It quickly became obvious that Khaidu held little regard for his cousin. Khaidu's youngest daughter returned momentarily, bringing hot tea and honey, also a small vessel containing yak's milk. After being poured the steaming tea, Casca allowed two drops of the milk to fall into his goblet. It had been the only way Genghis Khan had drunk the beverage, to remember the old ways, when the empire was nothing but a dream. Khaidu smiled at Casca, and took his tea in the same manner.

"Chen-Chin," Khaidu continued after a momentary quiet, "Khubilai's oldest son is nothing, and nothing will become of him. He is learned in languages, manners of the court, and the arts of the Chinese, not in what a son of the Khan and the future ruler of the empire should be. Chen-Chin perfumes his body and cleanses after even the shortest rides on his horse." Khaidu shook his head, embarrassed and disgusted by his admittance of what the great grandson of Genghis Khan did. "He has been poisoned by the Chinese," he hissed, dejected by his own admissions.

"Khubilai has rejected the way of the khuriltai. He has mocked its significance and history. It is the law of the Jasagh. The Ghenghis has decreed the laws that enable us to select the khan to succeed Khubilai. Khubilai refuses to have the khans meet and choose a successor. He has cursed our people with his son as the next . . ."

Khaidu pounded his fist against his thigh in fury, the anger returning to his heart. "I hear his hands are soft and his eyes weak." He continued, further maddened by his thoughts of Chen-Chin. "He cannot string a bow without the greatest of effort and, once having done so, his aim is not true. Even those punished for the bow can outdo him." Khaidu quieted momentarily, not offering an explanation for his last few words.

"He does not even hold the name of a Mongol. Chen-Chin is a name befitting a Chinese woman, not a man who will rule the world." Khaidu continued with renewed vigor. "Khubilai has chosen his name to placate his subjects, his Chinese subjects. He has forgotten his roots." Khaidu shook his head and rubbed at his eyes and forehead with the heel of his hands. "He is a traitor," Khaidu hissed.

"Only Hulegu, the Il-Khan of Persia is still truly an ally of Khubilai. Hulegu, the last true blood brother of Khubilai however, can be dealt with. Not unlike his brother, he is weak. He has not even found a woman to give him a son. Only girls have been born of him. He has asked Khubilai to send him a bride that will change that. He is the last one to still believe in Khubilai. All others have rightfully deserted him. It is no way for a Mongol to live."

Casca came to learn much of the empire and its changes since last he had ridden with Genghis Khan. A lot had changed, especially according to Khaidu. Angered and depleted, Khaidu lowered his head in shame and despair.

Casca left Khaidu's yurt, burdened with thoughts of the empire and Khubilai Khan. It was difficult to believe that the grandson of the great Genghis, the man Niccolo and Maffeo had served and been the messengers of, could have been as Khaidu believed. It was true, Khubilai's message to the pope had not been one befitting a khan, he recalled, but the message of a man unlike Khaidu or Genghis Khan who had created an empire. Casca shook his head, trying to reason who Khubilai Khan was.

He did not see much of Marco and Vittorio on the days to follow. Both of them, probably lost in the endless sights and opportunities the tent city provided, were not anxious to leave. Casca was not displeased, contented to spend the following days alone, resting, and pondering what awaited all of them.

Khaidu Khan had been quite generous. The five of them left the tent city with fresh horses to serve as their mounts, and an additional five horses that could carry their wares. Well fed and watered, the fine animals would last until they made their way to Shang-tu. If not, they could have easily been replaced along the way at other Mongol camps. The golden paiza served many functions.

Pleased at the turn of events, Marco rode ahead of all of them, sometimes singing or whistling, desperately anxious to reach Shang-tu and the excitement it was to provide. For the first time in nearly two years, Maffeo and Niccolo smiled, at times even nodding to each other, realizing that their impossible return journey to the court of Khubilai Khan was becoming a reality. They knew nothing of Khaidu's fears about the next leader of the Mongols. Burdened with his own thoughts and the words of Khaidu Khan still sounding in his ears, Casca followed along, wondering what awaited in the new empire ruled over by Khubilai Khan.

• • •

They arrived in Shang-tu on a hot early summer day. Fifty men riding the sturdy horses of the steppes met them at the outskirts of the city. Wearing shiny cuirasses, bronze-tipped leather helmets, and flags dancing in the summer wind attached to stirrup brackets, the flamboyant group greeted the travelers. Most of them offered a serious face, enjoying their position as the Khan's welcome committee. A few showed signs of recognition toward Maffeo and Niccolo, surprised, nearly in awe at these remarkable men who had returned after all these years.

Maffeo held the golden paiza over his head for all to see, clearly an unnecessary act as they were immediately met with the personal greetings of Khubilai Khan. It had been six years since Niccolo and Maffeo had left for Venice. The two brothers gave each other a pleased look. Once more they had traveled half the length of the world. Casca smiled at the sight of the city, well suspecting the richness and luxury that most likely awaited them. News of his arrival had no doubt reached the ears of Khubilai Khan.

Shang-tu was a city unlike Marco and Vittorio had ever seen. K'ai-p'ing it had been called for years by the Ch'ing, however Khubilai Khan had renamed it. Shang-tu it had become, the Upper Capital as many Chinese now called it. To the Khan, it was his summer retreat, away from the blistering heat of the summer months. This place allowed him to take part in his favorite activity.

Located north of the Luan river, west of Dolon-nur, the largest of the Seven Lakes, it was a wonder of the world, easily rivaling many of the ancients. Just north of it, endless pasturelands were the home for tens of thousands of sturdy, short-legged Mongolian war mounts; in the south, fertile soil allowed for the tireless Chinese to grow their crops as they had done for thousands of years.

Divided into three sections, Shang-tu was a city that easily overwhelmed the senses. The outer city, in the shape of an immense square, was surrounded by an earthen wall the height of three men. Each side of the square housed well-defended gates, two each on the east and west sides, while one on the north and one on the south walls also protected this portion of the city. Observation posts dominated the walls with well-shielded turrets, allowing for dozens of watchmen and archers to stand guard day and night.

Khubilai Khan, officials, and men of the highest military rank lived within the inner city, another immeasurable, square-shaped area, itself surrounded by thick and well-guarded walls. Amongst rich and luxurious buildings stood the imperial palace, Ta-an ko as the Chinese called it. Situated in the northern section of the square, it dwarfed even the largest and most opulent of palaces, that merely laid insignificantly at its feet.

The Khan's marble palace was huge and foreboding. Endless towers reached for the sky, its walls glittery and wind-blown, while waterways bathed the ground-level walls of the palace, providing life for a variety of trees and flowers, creating a rich and striking scenery. A blanket of color enriched the immediate area surrounding the imperial palace. Not much had been left to irritate the eye of the Khan.

Situated north of the outer city sat a hunting preserve, made of endless meadowlands, lakes, streams, and heavily wooded forests. The Khan enjoyed many afternoons in the area, ridding his white stallion, following the wings of his gray gyr-falcon that hunted pigeons, pheasants, and rabbits. Lost in the peaceful meadows and forested areas, it allowed the Khan to escape the city and the politics of being the Khan. At such times, tales of the simple life, before there was an empire, made him long for stories he had heard from his grandfather, Genghis Khan.

The five travelers stared in awe at the immensity of the city. Maffeo and Niccolo had lived in Shang-tu before; however, that did not diminish its grandeur in their eyes. On the other hand, there was more to the world than Marco and Vittorio had ever dared imagine. In a world that most Europeans would have considered primitive and barbaric, a city and palace dominated. They followed along the broad avenue toward the imperial palace.

The city teemed with thousands of people and animals. Mongol and Chinese intermixed within the city walls, most of them scurrying along carrying their wares, leading their animals, or tending to their children. Shop owners and artisans lauded their merchandise, not unlike in any other part of the world. The sounds, smells, and sights of the Mongol empire permeated the air, hypnotizing the newcomers with their boundless diversity. The wonder of Ta-an ko awaited them.

Like a mountain, the walls of the marble palace faced them. Robed officials welcomed the travelers, leading them inside one of the huge portals, the shade the giant gates and walls had created cooling their anxious and fevered faces. Bowing generously, two men led Maffeo and Niccolo in one direction, while another two walked Casca toward his quarters. A few seconds later Casca noted Marco and Vittorio follow behind their guide.

It did not take very long for the filth of the road to be washed off his body, yet Casca was not about to hasten the three Chinese attendants in their duties. The scented hot bath was quite welcome, as was their eagerness. Wearing thin cotton tunics that stuck to their bodies from the water and steam, the three young girls were not hard on his eyes. Little had been left to his imagination as the clothes they wore followed every detail of their young beauty.

Nervously they went about their duties at the sight of his naked body, frightened yet excited. How much they knew about who he was did not matter for the moment. They had never seen such a man, and that was sufficient for now. Casca closed his eyes and exhaled. It had been many years since he had luxuriated such. Meticulously, they rescrubbed every part of his body, clearly knowing they had not overlooked anything, and taking pleasure at how their guest had enjoyed their adeptness.

Rested and dressed in fresh clothes, Casca was joined by Marco and Vittorio at the entrance to the banquet hall. They all wore colorful silk robes, each one worth ten times its weight in gold in a Venetian market. Pulling on the sleeves of his gold-lace red robe, Marco tried to get comfortable. He looked at Vittorio who could not stop touching the silk robe, or refrain from smelling the sleeves of his newly perfumed clothing. Casca smiled, amused at the discomfort the two felt, uneasy at being dressed as royalty after having spent the last two years in the wretchedness of the road. The last few hours had been different. He did not need to ask, it was clear the youngsters had enjoyed an afternoon similar to his own. The Khan's people knew how to treat important guests.

"This way, Marco." The three of them heard Maffeo's anxious voice. "You are meeting the Khan . . ." Maffeo's words trailed off, not knowing how to instruct his nephew at meeting the most powerful ruler the world knew. "You must be careful . . . do not speak unless you are spoken to . . . you have to—"

His forewarning was cut off by a portly official who led them into the banquet hall. "I am Hon-Pao." The little man smiled while pointing them through the doorway. His disfigured right hand hung limply by his side while he pointed with his left.

It was likely the largest room Marco and Vittorio had ever seen. The door had not done it justice. Marco's eyes widened while he searched for the walls or ceiling, his senses overwhelmed by this enclosed space that seemed to have no boundaries. He remembered visiting the old amphitheater in Rome, and wondered if it had been smaller than this place. Perhaps thousands of people crowded the room, their number and actions creating a city all its own. Mouth agape, Vittorio followed along.

They were led into the heart of the room, walking by hundreds of other guests, officials, and members of the Khan's personal guard. Taking turns, avoiding masses of men and women who seemed impenetrable at first, they eventually made their way to a guest table.

It was a table large enough for a dozen men; yet only five chairs had been placed on one side of it. Covered until it overflowed its sides, mounds of food and drink crowded the table. Steam rose from the roasted meat and heaps of honeyed or spiced vegetables, each looking more appetizing than the other. With a gleam in his eyes, Vittorio grinned while he shook his head. He licked his lips as he watched the grease run down the flank and leg of a roasted calf, then peaked at Marco. Marco smiled at his friend of childhood. After nearly three years on the hard road, Vittorio had lost a lot of himself from the blistering heat and the effort it had taken to make it this far. Finally he had become thin, his face almost showing indentations around his cheeks while his belly no longer overflowed his pants. That was likely to change soon if they were to come in the Khan's favor.

Rows upon rows of tables had been arranged in a rough

semicircle all around them, the angle of the tables facing a raised platform. Upon the platform a massive and thick table, seating perhaps ten, faced the room and the hundreds of tables. Behind the main platform a velvet curtain hid the access to the apparent outlet of this room.

At the foot of the platform, a dozen smaller tables were arranged also in a semicircle, with six tables on each side of a wide carpet-covered walkway. The carpet ended at the foot of the raised platform where steps led upward. Six lavishly dressed guards stood facing the crowd, their appearance and demeanor more ceremonial than functional. A lot of space had been left between these twelve tables and the raised pedestal. Food and entertainment was to take center stage.

Trumpets blared announcing the arrival of Khubilai Khan, quieting the room in an instant. The Khan of millions entered, walking side by side with his wife, Chabi, the empress. A roar erupted from the crowd, filling the room with sound that reverberated between the distant walls and high ceiling. They both wore imperial robes the likes of which the world had never seen. Made of the best silk the eastern world could provide and crafted by masters, the splendor of the land of Chin was well apparent. Brilliant colors had been sewn into the fabric of their robes, adding to the magnificence and pageantry of their clothes. Walking slowly, they made their way to the table and stood enjoying their welcome.

Khubilai Khan was a man perhaps in his sixties, broad and thick, his face rounded by age and a hedonistic life. Dark penetrating eyes, perhaps blunted by his years and plentiful drink, yet they still held more power than any other man. His well-trimmed beard reached down toward his chest, brushing against a silk scarf that he held with his left hand. In his right hand he uncomfortably held a short gold scepter, ornately tipped with the tamgha, the jade seal. Laced with gray, his hair and beard gave the appearance of a man much older. It did not take long for Casca to find the memory of Genghis Khan in his grandson's eyes.

The empress Chabi was not much younger than he, short, with a pleasant, almost benevolent look in her warm eyes. Chabi was the first wife, in truth the principal wife of the second ordos, the second house of Khubilai Khan; however, no one spoke of his first house or any previous wives. Now, she was the supreme empress, regardless of the past. She knew the Khan had others, wives and countless concubines, yet she held her position proudly, something she had worked hard at, and had earned beyond question. Chabi had become more than the mother of his children, she was his advisor and lifelong mate. She smiled proudly at her husband then shifted her eyes to a young man, perhaps thirty years of age, who stood on the Khan's right. It was the young prince, Chen-Chin, someone Casca had heard so much about.

Chen-Chin sat down alongside his father after bowing gracefully and kissing his father's hand and the hand of his mother. He was thin and clean looking. Narrow cheekbones, unlike the ones of most men of the steppes, his neck also thin, almost feminine, surprised Marco and Vittorio who had expected the son of Khubilai Khan, the future leader of the Mongol empire, to look much different. Chen-Chin's dark hair was long, yet neatly tied and held back behind his head. A red bow streamed with gold and black had been woven into his hair, holding it all back. He had no beard or mustache, unlike all the rest of his kind in this world. He sat quietly, looking at the Khan, awaiting his words.

More members of the Khan's immediate family sat to his right, Sando, a half brother of Khubilai, a man barely older than Chen-Chin, and two other men, both sons of the Khan. To the left of the Khan sat Chabi and one of their daughters. Also, Luhann, the only surviving sister of Chabi.

At the end of the table, sitting next to Luhann, a solemn looking man peered out over the crowd. It was Thogor-Pa, the arbitrator of the houses of Khubilai. Zhong Tsai Sze was the name the Chinese had given to the role of the conciliator. It was an unsavory job, having to mediate any and all disagreements or conflicts between the wives of the Khan. Thogor-Pa had held this undesired position longer than most could remember. It was a title that offered little reward, other than some strange self-satisfaction as the rivalry and conflict between the different ordos was as old as the custom of the houses themselves. Khubilai Khan had been pleased with Thogor-Pa and his handling of the conflicts. That satisfaction offered many rewards to Thogor-Pa. The sour smile on his face betrayed much about the man.

Standing by the twelve tables at the foot of the podium on

either side of the carpet, nearly a hundred dignitaries, officials, advisors, and high-ranking members of the military took their places. They were men of obviously different origin: Turks, Tibetan monks, Indian preceptors or Muslim traders, men the Khan had hired to serve. Clearly none of them was of Chinese ancestry, as the Khan believed it was best to engage only ones who would give him subservience for a price, as opposed to the conquered whose loyalties would always be under suspicion.

The gentle and subtle sounds of the mourin khour accompanied by the rhythmic beat of sheepskin drums eased everyone to their seats. Marco felt the hair rise on his back and neck from the intensity of being in the Khan's presence. Somehow simultaneously both he and Vittorio wondered why this experience was beyond what they had felt in the pontiff's presence back in Acre.

"I welcome you all." The Khan's penetrating voice stifled the sounds of the musicians, for the moment everyone awaiting his not-so-frequent words. Khubilai Khan raised a hand toward the table of newcomers.

Maffeo and Niccolo led Marco and Vittorio toward the red carpet that extended to the royal podium. The two youngsters followed, feeling the eyes of thousands upon them. A few faces smiled at Maffeo and Niccolo, welcoming them back, at the same time with inquisitive eyes looking at Casca who had remained at the table. Some shook their heads, disbelieving at their thoughts, others simply dismissing such foolish notions.

"Approach me, old friends." The Khan surprised everyone, allowing for his guests to face him without genuflecting in his presence. "Who have you brought with you after all these years?" Khubilai inquired. They stood until they reached the steps, where Maffeo and Niccolo fell to their knees. After all, it was the Khan of all Mongols, the ruler of the eastern world who had welcomed them.

Taking their lead, Vittorio also took his place behind them, the soft red carpet comforting his knees. Realizing where he was and who looked down upon him, he lowered his head. Lost in what was happening around him, Marco's eyes scanned all that he had not seen, eventually his eyes resting on Chen-Chin.

Gasps from the crowd awakened Marco from his momentary daze—however, not sufficiently enough as he continued standing. Instantly the six guards reached for their belts, ready to draw their weapons.

"Down, down," Maffeo's frenzied voice hissed at his nephew. "Do you want us dead?"

Finally, Marco went to his knees as Vittorio's strong grasp pulled him to the ground. Breathing in panicked exasperation, Marco bowed his head while still trying to get a look at the guards who had half drawn their short swords. Even with the fear of the Khan and his father's wrath, Marco's eyes lingered on the hand of one of the guards who had not resheathed his short sword completely. At last seeing the sword in its scabbard, Marco turned his head toward the royal family. Chen-Chin grinned at the sight of this newcomer, the two of them having made a momentary contact.

"We have been blessed to find our way back, mighty Khan; forgive our overdue return." Nicollo bowed even deeper as he addressed the Khan. "Our arrival would have been impossible without this man." Niccolo suddenly pointed to Casca, for the first time acknowledging Casca for all he had been to them, yet unknowing Casca's true significance. "He has been our guide and savior. Without him, we would have failed you, mighty one." Niccolo spoke while symbolically extending his hand toward Casca's table.

Khubilai Khan nodded his head. A silence that staggered the senses overtook the reception hall. No one had ever experienced a moment as such in the presence of the Khan. After all these years, the Old Young One had returned to the empire. Next to the Khan, the empress looked toward Casca, ignoring all else, trying to understand how the fortunes of the world had wound its threads, returning the messengers of the Khan along with the man who had sparked the birth of the empire. Her mind spun, trying to find an understanding of it all. Time passed in silence as the significance of what was happening demanded it. Chabi finally turned her head toward Khubilai Khan and smiled.

Casca stood and began to approach the Khan. Thousands milled around in uncertainty, excitement, and nerves. They were expected to understand and believe, discounting all that was reasonable. The Old Young One, the man of legend, walked amongst them. Casca took the path leading down the middle of the red carpet that separated the dozen tables in front of the podium. Without making it obvious, he attempted to see the reaction of all who stood and watched.

"We have brought a message from his Holiness Pope Gregory, pontiff of Rome, father of the church of Christ," Maffeo added, not realizing what Casca's arrival possibly meant to the Khan and his people. He was certain something unforeseen had happened, yet would not dare turn the back of his head toward the Khan. It would have been more disrespectful than standing in his presence. With his back to the crowd he continued, unaware of Casca's approach.

"Our pope's thoughts and prayers we have carried to you, along with this parchment detailing his reply," Maffeo continued. "Also, my nephew and his friend have come with us, long they have both traveled to be in your presence." Maffeo thought back at Pope Gregory and what had become of Acre and the latest of the Great Crusades. He nearly shook his head at the possibility that the land of Christ only held the dreaded Saracens. Perhaps Pope Gregory was no more after all.

Khubilai Khan rose to his feet, surprising members of his court. Raising a large goblet of ayrag he took a long drink. For the moment, he would allow Marco to live, forgiving his insolence, his actions having become irrelevant at this time.

"No one has ever shown me such loyalty. You, Maffeo and Niccolo, have become one with my family, one with the empire. What you wish to have, I will be joyous to part with. Your indiscretions will be forgiven in my house. Never will you need to ask for anything."

Hearing the Khan's overly generous words, Casca tried to read the thoughts in everyone's eyes who stood near the Khan, as he finally made his way toward the steps leading up to the podium. There was little doubt that Niccolo and Maffeo's favorable position with the Khan was to create instant jealousy and dangerous enemies, something Casca was certain the two men knew. With their heads bowed, Maffeo and Niccolo arose and stepped back, easing away from the platform that held the Khan's table. As they moved backward, they realized Casca had come up right behind them. Signaling for Marco and Vittorio also to rise and move back, they watched unfold the meeting of Khubilai Khan and Casca.

"It is true, you have also returned." His eyes focused on Casca. "I could not be certain." The Khan stood and extended his hands. "Is it possible?"

Even the air became still in the silence that Casca had created with his walk toward the podium. Holding their breath in utter amazement, most of the ones who stood on the edge of the walkway fixed their eyes on something they refused to believe.

Khubilai Khan stood by the edge of the podium, his feet nearing the steps that led up to it. Every person who held witness stood at the sight, the impossibility of it holding back even a gasp of disbelief. This stranger from their legends was about to face the Khan of Khans just as any two men would, unlike any other ever had. Holding and clasping each other's hands.

"I hope we have not disappointed," were the first words to be heard as Casca and Khubilai stood face-to-face.

"I had been told you would return."

Thousands cheered as Khubilai Khan welcomed the Old Young One. Trumpets blared and drums pounded, filling the room with the ear-shattering sounds of celebration.

"The teacher of the Genghis is among us," Khubilai declared. "Casca-Bahadur has returned. Lao-Shi he is, the old teacher of the Genghis. We will show him what the seeds had brought to bear." Khubilai faced thousands of his delirious subjects, in triumph holding the hand of Casca over his head.

"Enjoy the celebration," the Khan concluded. He and Casca would have their time to revisit the past, and plan the future.

The feast continued into the night, challenging the early morning, testing everyone's endurance, mental clarity, and waistline. Casca had decided to enjoy these precious hours and the hours to come in his quarters. There was much that he expected to speak of with the Khan. His improbable return to the empire was to bring great concern to some and joy to others.

The Khan's effort at the limits of excessiveness did not disappoint. It seemed that any and all creatures available and worthy of being eaten had been corralled and prepared. An endless stream of Chinese servants continued to fulfill their duties, feeding and watering the guests of the Khan. With impenetrable eyes they stole glances at Casca, unwilling to believe that this one unusual man had been the cause to all that had followed during the years.

Without any concerns, Marco and Vittorio enjoyed the food, drink, and the entertainment the Khan had provided. It was almost as if Casca's identity was of no consequence to them. Their lives had been preserved by this strange man more than once. To them that was sufficient.

Sleep finally arrived in the early morning for Casca. A filled belly and ayrag-drenched mind did not prevent him from restful sleep.

He was awakened in a not undesirable manner by the hushed voice of the three Chinese servants. Seeing movement within his bed they approached. Two of them used steaming wet cloths to wash and rouse him while the third brought the morning honeyed tea and fresh-baked bread. It was time to meet with the Khan.

The corridors leading to the Khan's quarters seemed to go on forever. Each passageway led farther into the marble palace, the hallways splitting into larger then smaller corridors, eventually ending with four identical doorways. Casca's guide Hon-Pao, an old man with a high-pitched voice and a trembling right hand, pointed to the door farthest to the right. Casca's eyes lingered on the elongated fingers of Hon-Pao as the man forced a smile from his lips. With the permission of two huge Mongol bodyguards that seemed to stifle the hallway with their size, Hon-Pao was allowed to knock on the door to the Khan's dwellings.

Casca looked inside as the gold lacquered heavy oak door swung on its hinges, allowing him in. The two guards grunted to each other as they also allowed Hon-Pao to enter.

Beyond a door that opened at the farthest portion of the room, the giggle of a young boy caught Casca's attention. The sound came from a chamber farther in, where underneath a golden silk bedsheeth Casca watched a round form squirm with laughter. The door to the room suddenly closed as Casca could hear the voice of the Khan. "I knew I would find you here, you little fox. Where is your father? Did he put you up to this?" The good-natured voice momentarily carried into a whisper.

"It is Temur, only son of Chen-Chin." Hon-Pao nodded to Casca as he stepped aside.

Thogor-Pa, the Zhong Tsai Zhe of the houses of Khubilai, also stood within the room, ready to kneel upon the appearance of the Khan. With his head down and pointed away from everyone, he awaited silently. He held a short dagger in its golden scabbard, gently stroking the ivory handle that extended from the rich cloth encircling the blade. Casca noted the man trying to catch a glimpse at the new arrivals. Clearly there was more to this man than a supervisor of the Khan's wives.

Casca turned his head away from Thogor-Pa and was surprised to find that Maffeo, Niccolo, Marco, and Vittorio were also next to him within this room. He had expected only the Khan to be present; however, their presence was not unwelcome.

Maffeo stood by Niccolo, speaking in hushed tones, while Marco with his hands by his temples peered over a large wooden table, scrutinizing a cloth map that overflowed its sides. From time to time he whispered to Vittorio while shaking his head.

It was a room worthy of no one. The splendor that enriched this room could have humbled most European princes or kings that fancied themselves as wealthy. A ceiling higher than three men topped off tapestry-covered walls and gold embroidered silk curtains. The sun brightly shone through the eastern window, illuminating the golden room. Heavy and thick furniture crowded the sides of the room, each one intricately, fastidiously worked. Within the wood, inlays of gold and precious stones further overwhelmed the senses. More chairs, tables, and statues than could have been possible, or reasonable, crowded the enclosure.

"My grandson, Temur, has had quite a busy morning." Khubilai Khan entered the room, Chabi trailing behind him as they came through the narrow doorway.

"I don't think the boy ever sleeps." She laughed while shaking her head.

Maffeo and Niccolo fell to their knees, soon to be followed by Marco and Vittorio at the sound of the Khan. Out of the corner of his eye Marco watched Hon-Pao anxiously pull at Casca's clothes, trying to bring him to his knees.

"Enough!" The Khan interrupted the early genuflection. "You are no longer required to kneel in my presence." Khubilai surprised all of them. "As long as no one else is present," he added, fatigued by the endless rituals. Millions had groveled at his feet, for now these men had been offered different.

"We are pleased you have all returned." Chabi smiled while she took her place by the Khan, both of them sitting down into a deep, richly clothed chair, supported with thick, splayed-out, black wooden legs the shape of tiger's paws. Nestling into comfort, the two smiled at the travelers.

Bowing out of habit, having realized the Khan was actually sitting while they were standing, Maffeo and Niccolo nearly panicked and looked up at them, unable to stand in their presence.

"It is all right," Khubilai Khan assured them as he stood and approached the table that held the map.

"Great Khan, we bring Pope Gregory's words to you," Maffeo indicated while holding out the rolled-up parchment toward the Khan. All these years Maffeo had kept it safe and dry, now only the breaking of the papal seal preventing it from being read.

"It is all coming together," the Khan mumbled to himself. "Just as I have hoped."

They all looked at the Khan, trying to figure what he was referring to.

"Does the Great Khan wish us to read the pope's message, or perhaps just to leave for now?" Niccolo inquired.

"Tell me of your journey, Casca-Bahadur. How did you come to be with these men on your return to the empire? My grandfather told me many unbelievable tales about you."

Marco, along with his father and uncle, stared at Casca, trying to understand. How could Casca have met the Khan's grandfather? Vittorio, still kneeling, was unable or unwilling even to look up at them. His mind refused to believe all they were speaking of. He anxiously scratched at his neck and chin, the habit returning to him in this moment of uncertainty.

"It is by chance occurrence that I met these men," Casca responded.

"It could not be that the world and its doings are so random," the Khan insisted. "It just could not. My grandfather, the Genghis, told me—"

"But it is true," Marco stepped in on the conversation. "Messer Casca saved me from certain death, ever since then, we have been together. He has been our savior and deliverer."

"Please forgive my son Marco, Great Khan. I have failed as a father. Forgive my failure. He is unable to keep quiet and realize whose presence he is in." Niccolo bowed even lower, trying to make up for Marco's disrespectful ways.

Maffeo and Niccolo cringed from Marco's foolish actions. They were not certain what was worse, interrupting the Khan or disagreeing with him. Either way, Marco had proven more insolent than anyone the Khan had likely ever dealt with.

Surprising them, the Khubilai smiled at Marco, amused at how little this young man knew of the world. Once again he would forgive the boy's impudence.

"So, tell me, young Marco, what do you think of my world? Is it what your pope believes it is? A world of thieves, murderers, and barbarians who overrun all who stand in their way?"

"Pope Gregory does not believe it is a world of thieves and murderers," Marco foolishly answered.

"I suppose you have been safe for now." Khubilai Khan quietly chuckled.

Numbed by Marco's answers, Maffeo and Niccolo were speechless. There was no return or redemption from Marco's comments. In so many words, he had not distinguished the Khan and his people from barbarians.

Undaunted by Marco's answers, the Khan continued. "Have you found your visit pleasurable?"

They all looked at the Khan, not understanding his good mood and unlikely questions. Marco was standing within ten feet of the most powerful man in the world, yet his words flowed as if without thought. Chabi allowed a smile to escape her lips, apparently having seen her husband practice such banter. Hon-Pao continued laying on the marble floor, his head turned sideways, looking away from all that was taking place. Thogor-Pa had been quiet all along, keeping to himself while secretly scrutinizing this strange scarred man who had been received with such glory by the Khan.

"I have been unworthy of the treatment." Marco's response finally showed some sense, though clearly not enough to erase his foolish diatribe of a few moments ago.

"Has anything displeased or perplexed you?" Khubilai

Khan continued, almost looking as if made unhappy by Marco's kind words.

"How could it, Great Khan? It is perfection that has met us in Shang-Tu and Ta-an ko, the royal palace," Niccolo tried answering for Marco.

"Your words are kind, Messer Niccolo," Chabi bowed her head in appreciation. "For certain Messer Marco had found it the same?" She smiled at Marco, knowing this brash young man had more on his mind.

"I wondered why the map of the Great Khan is so faulty?" Marco suddenly inquired, somehow once again not realizing how he was tempting fate.

Chabi stood within the wall of silence, herself amused by this young man who could not stifle his own thoughts. Frozen in panic, Maffeo and Niccolo were speechless, wondering if Marco had finally lost his mind.

"Tell me about the map," Khubilai inquired as he approached Marco and the table he stood by. The Khan took on a serious look, not one of anger, but of curiosity.

Maffeo and Niccolo had finally made it to their feet and stood alongside the table. Next to them, Marco flattened the map against the oak table, trying to expose as much of it as possible to the sunlight that shone through the opened curtains. Holding the short gold scepter in his right hand Khubilai Khan stood on one side of the table scrutinizing this unusually detailed map.

"It seems much of it is wrong." Marco did not stop talking for the next ten minutes, detailing all that he disagreed with. From the location of rivers in relation to other landmarks such as the sea or mountain ranges, to the relative distances between villages. Without limit, Marco detailed everything that he believed faulty or imperfect.

Casca watched all along, surprised at how he could not disagree with any of Marco's observations, and struck at how any one man, especially one as young and apparently unfocused, could have observed the world with such detail. He looked up at the Khan with agreement.

No one spoke a word, out of amazement and perhaps fear. All the while Khubilai watched and nodded his head. If this unusual young man was right, he could be of great value, the Khan pondered.

"Why have you not told me of your son?" Khubilai questioned Niccolo. "It is quite a gift he has."

"I have been blind myself of his abilities to . . ." Niccolo looked at his son and at the map at the same time, momentarily shaking his head at his inability to recollect all that Marco could.

"It is a day full of surprises." Khubilai laughed good naturedly. "It is a great day. All is as it should be, do you not think so Casca-Bahadur?"

"It is good to see the Khan of the world pleased as such. Only a great ruler could listen to a boy just as well as to his most trusted advisor. The blood of the Genghis does flow through your veins."

Khubilai Khan smiled, appreciating Casca's blatant flattery, and pleased to hear about his grandfather.

"It is always possible to learn," Niccolo added, trying to further soften Marco's disrespectful ways.

"Only fools and dead men are incapable of learning." Casca found himself recalling the words of his old friend Lao-tze at the same time as Chabi, the supreme empress, had decided to join into the conversation.

The Khan looked at Casca and the empress with amusement and surprise, hearing the words of the old sage quoted by both. It was true, only the dead and men too prideful and foolish could not learn.

"I will need to hear much more of what you have observed along the way, young Marco, much more." Khubilai Khan pointed his scepter at the young Venetian.

"It will by the utmost honor to be heard again," Marco spoke, finally having decided not to speak out of turn and inappropriately. He bowed his head to the Khan and took a step backward.

Turning away from Marco, Khubilai inquired, "What of your pope, does he know of me?"

"He does, Great Khan. We have told the pontiff of our mission and the great man that had sent us to complete it."

"What is his response?"

With trembling hands, Maffeo once again extended his hand toward the Khan, holding the rolled up parchment that held the papal seal.

"Read it for me," Khubilai ordered.

The dried seal crumbled beneath Maffeo's fingers as it was opened. It appeared to be a short message, hardly one that was worthy of guarding with one's life over years of travel.

Maffeo and Niccolo scrutinized the words of Pope Gregory as they turned toward the Khan.

"Pope Gregory sends his regards and admiration to the Khan. He regrets not being able to send any of his dignitaries along to teach of the word of Christ. He wishes more of the message of Christ had spread to the east to enlighten and to save ones needing of saving." Maffeo and Niccolo looked at the Khan, trying to gage if the endless words of faith and religion were displeasing him. "Pope Gregory," Maffeo continued, "hopes the common bond of the message of Christ can bring the world together."

"What else has he chosen to send along?"

"He did not choose to send any gifts, just a message of faith and friendship. The Pope wishes avenues of communication and understanding can be opened to allow our two people to meet," Maffeo concluded.

Casca nearly sneered, displeased how these men had carried so little along with them, braved all there was, to give a message wrapped in the supposed words of Christ. It was a foolish message for the pope to send, resting everything on the hope the Khan of all Mongols found faith sufficient on which to base the future.

"He is a man who speaks from the heart?"

"Yes, Great Khan. He believes that faith is the common bond that can bring our people and nations together."

"Your pope would be pleased to know that the word of Christ is not unknown to us," Chabi declared. "I myself have at times prayed to your God."

Casca caught Thogor-Pa's narrowing eyes at Chabi's last comments. The man had been unable to hide his displeasure at Chabi's response. It was clear his Budhist upbringing could not allow room for any false prophets to infect the Khan's heart. Thogor-Pa was clearly a man to be watched.

"Much of our beliefs are not dissimilar. It is enough for a beginning," the Khan added, apparently oblivious of Thogor-Pa's reaction.

"He is fearful of what the outside world can bring to the Holy Land," Niccolo offered, well knowing it was an issue the Khan had obviously considered. "Yet, he knows it is fear and ignorance that separate people. I am certain the pontiff would be pleased to know that the word of Christ has traveled around the world." Niccolo looked at Marco, remembering what his son had said to Pope Gregory back in Acre.

"So it is," Khubilai Khan agreed. "He fears my empire?" he questioned, without looking as if the answer was in any doubt.

"Yes," Niccolo admitted. "The pope hopes to have found an ally."

"He has not found an enemy," the Khan firmly stated. "Our worlds are far, yet, as time passes, the nations of the world cannot go on isolated. People of the world will eventually find a common bond."

Niccolo and Maffeo bowed, pleased at the Khan's response, yet knowing it would take years before Pope Gregory would ever receive an answer, or have to contend with any changes. Curious how the Khan spoke of other nations, Niccolo thought, when he was on a never-ending quest to conquer all that bordered on his lands. It did not seem like the words of a leader whose ancestors have also done just that.

"You are all guests of the empire. It is good to have the two of you back." The Khan looked at Niccolo and Maffeo quite pleased. "Your son, Marco, I find entertaining to listen to. He and his friend have also found a home in mine. From what the empress tells me, my son Chen-Chin is much like young Marco."

Marco smiled, pleased and honored at being likened to the son of the Khan. He bowed his head and stepped farther back. Vittorio watched Marco bite his lip, the young man trying to make certain not to speak out of turn or improperly yet again.

"Soon we will return to Khanbalic when the summer months have passed. Enjoy the fruits of life, my friends. Time in this world is fleeting." The Khan touched his thick graying beard with his left hand while the burden of his words weighed on him.

"We have been honored to be in the presence of the Great Khan. To serve will bring us joy." Niccolo bowed, nearly returning to his knees while he celebrated the Khan.

They all returned to their quarters. The days to follow were kind to them. Unquestionably being in the Khan's favor was something few have had the chance to revel in, while ones who had displeased him had found death something to look forward to. It was a place as any, where men ruled with power.

Niccolo and Maffeo reacquainted themselves with friends and merchants in Shang-Tu, while Marco and Vittorio roamed the four corners of this great city, almost refusing to sleep in the fear that they might miss out on something. There was much Shang-Tu had to offer.

Casca went about his way the following days and weeks, the distressed words of Khaidu Khan ringing in his ears while the hospitality of Khubilai Khan provided the pleasures that many years of the past had stolen from him. It was not long, Casca knew quite well, before strife would find him in this part of the world.

His days were undemanding, while the nights offered entertainment of all kinds. The Mongol people refused to allow even a single night to pass without a celebration of some sort. Life, as brief as it was, demanded not to be wasted. There was time without end in the Eternal Blue Sky for rest. For now, life was here to be savored.

Casca did not see much of Marco or Vittorio, who seemed to be on a tireless quest to see all there was to see in Shang-Tu and in the surrounding area. Chen-Chin, the Khan's oldest son and the future Khan of all Mongols, had formed a surprisingly strong bond with Marco and Vittorio. Perhaps it was the first time that the young prince had met someone like Marco who also saw the world with such wide-eyed excitement. Their paths led them in different directions, yet their friendship quickly grew. Both had been born to fathers who had given all their time to everyone but their sons. That in itself had been more than sufficient to draw them together.

Marco spent many days with Chen-Chin walking through the royal palace or riding the many trails in the forest just north of the city. Under the watchful eye of Sando, Khubilai Khan's young half brother, Marco and Chen-Chin went about undisturbed and unharmed. Sando was an unusually handsome young man. He was almost a head taller than Casca, with broad powerful shoulders. His hair was darker than a raven's feather, nearly glistening in the sun. He had the look of the Khan in his face, and something distant, likely a trait from his mother who had come from the land north of the Mongol steppes. Sando was unlike most of the royal family, never having shown any interest in ruling a people or leading campaigns. He had been satisfied being the head of the kesig, the Khan's personal bodyguards and protectors of the royal family. Proudly he served the Khan. That and the pleasures that the court life could bring was more than sufficient for Sando.

Sometimes amused, he watched the young prince Chen-Chin and Marco try and exchange words. The Afghan dialect Marco had picked up the previous year while crossing the Pamir had given him enough to communicate with Chen-Chin. It also seemed that within weeks, Marco had been able to learn much of what was needed to understand the twisted and unkind manners of the Mongol language. Chen-Chin at times would smile at Marco, appreciating how the young Venetian struggled with Mongolian, while at the same time amused to think what it was going to be like when Marco encountered the nearly impossible characters of the Chinese. As time quickly passed, their friendship grew, both of them realizing how different yet alike their lives had been. Their close friendship was not about to go unnoticed for long.

The summer days passed while Casca observed the empire of Khubilai Khan unfold itself in front of his eyes. The days when Temujin had been just a young man, dreaming of uniting all the people of the steppes, was far in the past. Khubilai Khan had taken his grandfather's dream and made it a reality. Not much had successfully stood in the Khan's way from achieving a united empire in the eastern world. From the frozen north to the burning jungles of Burma and Champa to the eastern edge of the land of Chin that bordered on the endless sea, to the western edge of the Pamir mountain range and the Arabian peninsula, the power of the Khan reigned supreme.

Khubilai Khan was the supreme Khan of all Mongols and the countless peoples they had conquered. Dozens of other Khans were subservient to Khubilai, with the right to govern their own land and people, but forever under the rule of the supreme Khan, their armies at the immediate disposal of Khubilai. From time to time Khans revolted, mostly never to be heard from again.

A few bordering nations had been left untouched, some by design while others by circumstance. The ones that had resisted had paid a great price as no one had been able to stand in the way of the Mongol horde. At times stubborn or foolish rulers had stood their ground, eventually to end up facing the consequences in death and tribute. The few lands that had escaped the Khan's armies eventually became an obsession that would bring about the Khan's downfall.

And now Khubilai had grown old and tired, his dream of a united empire with all of China at its knees nearly a reality. Only the people of the southern Sung empire had stood defiant, unwilling to yield to the mighty Khan. There were still other lands to conquer if one so desired, yet Khubilai's thoughts had turned to the future of the empire.

Chen-Chin would soon ascend to the throne of the eastern world. Although only in his early thirties, Chen-Chin had received an education that most would have taken many lifetimes to master. He was an unusually intelligent and introspective person who Khubilai had groomed well over the years to become what the emperor of all China needed. From his earliest years, Chen-Chin had spent his time mastering the teachings of Confucius, emphasizing the virtues and duties of a ruler. Tibetan Budhists and Taoists spent years teaching the young man of the human heart and the eternal soul.

Chen-Chin's education did not end with that. Khubilai insisted that his son needed to be instructed in the customs and etiquette necessary to lead all of the people of Chin. His son needed to know about the history and folklore of the people he was about to govern. The ways of an emperor who was to lead the whole eastern world needed to be unlike those of a Mongol khan. Chen-Chin needed to become civilized.

SIXTEEN

"Good morning Zhi-Zhe, I hope the sleep of the Khans has kept you in its arms last night." They were the same words Hon-Pao always greeted Casca with in the morning, yet this morning it felt different. Casca sat up in his oversized square bed and eyed Hon-Pao.

The little Chinese man tried standing tall, at once realizing Casca had sensed him well. Nervously he brought his deformed right hand to his mouth while with his left he waved for the two attendants to bring Casca the morning tea.

"Share the tea with me." Casca surprised Hon-Pao, who was nervous enough on this morning to begin with.

"Forgive me, my lord, I am not allowed to sit and take tea with the ones I serve. I am here to perform my duties and follow orders."

"Then I order you to sit with me and have tea," Casca responded.

Without seeming to realize Casca's attempt at lightening the mood, Hon-Pao sat and pulled his feet underneath himself. One of the servants looked at Hon-Pao in disbelief and fear. In all her years she had never seen one of their own sit with a guest, especially not with one who had stood face-to-face with the Khan.

"We will share the morning tea," Casca indicated to the young girl. While stumbling over her nervous feet, she was barely able to pour the tea without spilling it on herself or Casca. She stepped back and quickly left the room.

Hon-Pao held the cup with both hands, trying to steady his obviously shaking hands as he brought the rim to his lips.

Seeing him hesitate, Casca nodded and took a sip from his own cup. Casca peered into the old man's eyes, forcing him to speak.

"I never expected to sit for tea with you, Zhi-Zhe, Old Young One. If that is you. Could it be? My gung-gung, my grandfather, lived to be over one hundred years old, but he looked very old when he died. How could you be the same one the Genghis spoke of? You should have been dead a long time ago. It could not be . . ." His words trailed off after having spoken more to Casca within the last few moments than he had over the last two months.

Casca smiled at the little man who had shrunk down meekly while sitting next to him. "Who did this to your hand?" Casca startled Hon-Pao.

"It was an accident, a long time . . ." Hon-Pao stopped

speaking, seeing Casca shake his head. It was not the truth and Casca knew it.

"I was a foolish young man and had taken to the bow." Hon-Pao bit his lip while pulling his damaged hand within the robe. There was no reason for him to lie any further. "It was the last time I have touched one." The old man dropped his head to his chest and closed his eyes.

"And you were punished for it."

"Yes. I hung from the silk lines." Hon-Pao closed his left hand, protecting his fingers from the memories. "I had tried to hold back, but I could not. For hours they let me hang . . . the whole night I screamed into the darkness of the cell. I had been a humble servant for many years, ever since I was a young boy. For that, they allowed my left hand to go unpunished."

Hon-Pao pulled his right hand from within the robe and extended it. It was a horrid looking thing, elongated and knotted like the roots of a rotting tree. The nails that had fallen out many years before had been replaced by obscene black stumps. It was a reminder for all who dared to take up a weapon and resist the Mongol horde.

"And your family?"

A tear found its way down Hon-Pao's smiling face. The tear of joy and pain.

"Little there is left. Hardly any at all."

Hon-Pao smiled while quickly flicking the tear away from his cheek. "Ko, my granddaughter, is the only one. She is the flower of my life. The little heart of my heart." His face relaxed and his frown disappeared with the mention of her name.

"What of her parents?"

The frown instantly returned. "Her mother was found irresistible." Hon-Pao buried his face in his hands, the mention of her making him shed the tears of a grieving father. "My daughter was taken away from me. They killed her for refusing to satisfy. Her husband lived a few seconds longer until his neck was broken. His protestations were not tolerated." Hon-Pao offered little else and Casca did not need to know. This old man had given everything but his own life as a servant of the empire.

"Beware, Old Young One, there are many who wish you

well, but many who want your death." Hon-Pao's voice suddenly trembled in a whisper. "Your friends are in great peril also. The Great Khan is powerful, but he has grown old. There are few who he can truly trust. His enemies know it and it will not be long before they will take action on those who threaten their way." Hon-Pao nodded his head, his eyes wanting to share more with Casca. "Be weary, there are many in the Brotherhood who . . ."

Casca's mind raced back hundreds of years hearing of the Brotherhood. It could not have been the same, but the memories it reawakened shook him. His thoughts closed off, unable to hear for a moment what else Hon-Pao had chosen to say. Every wound and moment of pain the Brotherhood of the Lamb had punished him with came back to haunt him. He looked up at Hon-Pao, realizing the little man had stopped speaking.

"They have waited for you," Hon-Pao continued. "The Master had hoped your arrival would bring back the ways of the past. The way of the Genghis. If that is so, the land of my people will forever be enslaved by these barbarians." Hon-Pao bit his lip and covered his mouth realizing his dangerous words. He looked up at Casca awaiting his reaction. After all, the Old Young One had been the one responsible for the birth of the empire all those years past, and now here he was. Hon-Pao shuddered, hoping he had read Casca well. "The way of the Genghis will destroy the land of my people forever. You hold the future of all China in your hands." Once again Hon-Pao stopped, realizing what immeasurable burden rested on Casca.

Raising his head, Casca breathed deeply while emptying the cup of hot tea. For two months there has been nothing but rest and pleasure for him. As he had expected, once more his presence would change a nation.

"The Brotherhood—"

"Yes, they call themselves the Brotherhood of the Night," Hon-Pao interrupted. "There is one they call the Master; however, no one knows his true identity. It does not matter . . . he follows the words of Khaidu Khan and others who oppose Khubilai Khan. They live in the night, thousands, maybe tens of thousands. Death and darkness is their way. The cover of darkness has made them without fear and vicious beyond

comprehension. They are the scourge of my people's land."
Hon-Pao quieted momentarily while he touched his deformed
hand to his face.

Casca looked at this brave and unusual little man, who still
for reasons unknown had decided to warn him. He wondered
if Hon-Pao had come of his own volition. "The Brotherhood
wants to know of my loyalties. That is why you have come
to me?"

"You are the great Old Young One." Hon-Pao bowed toward Casca while still sitting cross-legged across from him.
"I have been sent by no one. I know you understand the truth.
The Brotherhood will want to know if they have found an
ally or an enemy." Hon-Pao breathed a sigh of relief. He had
taken it upon himself to warn Casca. Looking calmer than
before, he finally took a sip of tea, wetting his dry throat.

"The Brotherhood of the Night is powerful. They have
waited for a sign." Hon-Pao paused while looking up at
Casca. "Khubilai Khan is refusing a khurlitai, a meeting to
choose a successor. Chen-Chin will become Supreme Khan
by the will of his father. Everyone knows Chen-Chin to be
weak of body, not learned in the art of war. That will not be
allowed to happen, the Brotherhood will see to that."

Casca remembered Khaidu, the anger and disgust Khaidu
had so openly shown toward Khubilai and Chen-Chin. There
was great turmoil in the empire. Once again, as if by destiny,
Casca had found himself in this part of the world.

"They will send for you, Old Young One." Hon-Pao finally
concluded with a sigh, obviously nervous, yet relieved that he
had spoken such.

Hon-Pao's warning became a reality later in the day when a
young Mongol, burdened by a vacant look in his eyes, spoke
to Casca. Nodding his head, Casca followed the messenger
through many poorly lit passageways beneath the city of
Shang-Tu. For nearly half an hour they walked in silence, at
times passing by the same doorway, the practice an obvious
ploy to confuse Casca of the meeting place's whereabouts.

"We welcome you." A soft yet powerful voice spoke to
Casca from within the darkness. The passageway had led to
a small door that opened into a relatively large hall. By the
smell and looks of it, it was probably many feet underground,

definitely not part of the initial working of the royal palace, more likely a chamber that had been made by the Brotherhood. Two dozen men, hidden behind the dark robes and cloaks that men of religion often seemed to wear, looked upon Casca and the young messenger who still stood by him. They all stood within the darkness, only the light of a few candles brightening the enclosure.

"Come join us at the rebirth of the empire." The same unseen voice reached out toward Casca once more. An uncertain shadow slipped out from within the darkness at the opposite end of the room from where Casca was standing.

"For years we have waited for a sign, a sign that we must take action. We have never expected for the Old Young One to return, but here you stand amongst us." The voice quieted down further, still a certain sense of incredulity within the last words uttered.

"The empire as it is is dying. Not the swift sudden death dealt by battle, but one of slow agonizing death that only pestilence or weak men can bring about. Khubilai Khan wants to be the emperor of China. A feared but benevolent ruler he wants to be. Yet he forgets his roots. The Genghis, the Khan of all Khans, will never rest in the Eternal Blue Sky. Khubilai Khan has shamed and betrayed his people and the name of Genghis."

Casca remembered the same defiling words spoken by Khaidu months before. He looked at the figure in front of him who spoke with such hatred of Khubilai. There was abhorrence in every word the man spoke.

"The empire is dying in the hands of Khubilai. His son Chen-Chin is barely a man. His hands and mind are weak. His soul has been weakened by a crippled father and teachings fit for a monk, not the ruler of the world. He cannot be allowed to become Khan. As Khubilai will not allow a khurlitai, the throne will need to be taken."

There was little uncertainty in the word *taken* as the man had said it. An uprising was not far away.

"The Khan's friends who have returned are irrelevant. They will be dealt with. They have brought back nothing but weak words and poisoned thoughts. Join us in victory or stand aside. We do not wish to hurt the Old Young One. Yet if you stand against us, we will do what we must."

The man stopped momentarily, but not long enough to allow for a response. Steadfastly he continued. It was clear he held great concern regarding Casca's return. "Lead us, but do not stand in our way. The ones who have come from the land of the pope, we will allow them to live if they quickly disappear. The one known as Marco must be gone. He has brought the words of your weak God to infect Chen-Chin and the empire. He must be gone," the voice reiterated.

A light flickered from the many candles that illuminated the chamber. Directly above the head of the man who had spoken, Casca noted a sword and shield fastened against a wooden board that emerged from the back wall. A small golden crescent, like the shape of the early moon, rested on the handle of the sword. For an instant Casca's mind searched for something within the recent past. Memories of Nomukh, the man that had stood guard by Khaidu Khan came back to his thoughts.

"The ways of the old cannot rule the empire." Casca broke the silence as his thoughts returned to the present.

"It must. We as a Mongol people cannot live in the prisons that the Chinese cities have created. Their walls imprison our bodies and spirits. A Mongol lives in his tent with his warhorse by his side. It is the only way." The voice of the man softened, but the message of what he had said filled the room. It was the same as Khaidu had said. "The empire of the southern Sung must be crushed. Millions of horses will graze on what are now rice fields. The world will kneel at the foot of the Mongol empire."

Casca was led away from the chamber of the Brotherhood, thoughts of what the future would bring filling his mind as his guide took a different torturous path leading back to the outside. Perhaps not his own, but the lives of Marco and Vittorio were in peril. Even Niccolo and Maffeo were not safe upon their return, as the Brotherhood saw all of them as a threat to the empire.

The following weeks passed uneventfully, as if nothing had happened. Once in a while Casca noted scrutinizing eyes watching from a distance, the link of the Brotherhood obviously within them. Marco and Vittorio had not tired of their quest to enjoy all that Shang-Tu offered. They continued exploring every market or the tiniest of stores, purchasing items they did not need or making deals that would take a lifetime to complete. Vittorio had regained much of the weight he had lost over the past few years, while Marco's thin and youthful face seemed to have acquired a certain sense of maturity. The ever-watchful eyes of Khubilai's half brother Sando continued to keep them safe. It was clear the Khan also held concern for his new guests.

It was time for all of them to head south, toward Khanbalic. For all it had been, Shang-Tu was merely the temporary retreat from the scorching heat of the summer months. The adventure of a lifetime was nowhere near over for Marco and Vittorio. For now they had no knowledge of the dangers that lurked around them, and the secret order of the Brotherhood that wanted them to be no more. Marco and Chen-Chin, traveling side by side, joined the imperial procession that took the yearly journey to Khanbalic and the Forbidden City.

The enormity of Khanbalic dwarfed what they had thought the great city of Shang-Tu had been. Thousands upon thousand of men guarded the twelve gates that surrounded the city walls. The imposing walls seemed to go on forever, each time surprising them whenever they assumed there was no more. Casca smiled to himself remembering the insignificance of the city of Acre. This was a place beyond what the people of Europe could have imagined.

A giant gate opened for the Great Khan himself as he was carried through into the imperial courtyard. Priests and soldiers, concubines and artisans all stood side by side welcoming the returning Khan. Thousands cheered while waving multicolored flags and banners at the sight of the imperial guards. Music and celebration would continue into the early morning. Riding next to Maffeo, Casca exchanged unspoken words with the well-seasoned traveler. They had sensed it well. Amongst the tens of thousands of cheerful faces, danger awaited them.

It was a night of great celebration. Food and drink flowed endlessly, only taking a respite when the Khan's favorite entertainers took center stage. Magicians and soothsayers entertained the Khan and his guests, each attempting to outdo the other. Snake charmers and fire-eaters pushed their abilities to the limit, trying to have them be the ones the Khan remembered and spoke of in awe.

"What is that?" Marco remarked looking up into the night sky.

"They call it the burning powder. It was a gift from a monk living in the mountains of the southern empire. The monk insisted it was a gift from the gods to light the night sky, in brightness to celebrate the immortals themselves." Maffeo tried answering his nephew, struggling to overcome the cheers of the crowd that drowned out his words.

"Is it magic?"

"Only if you have never seen it before." Chen-Chin smiled to his friend Marco who stood dumbfounded by the burning air.

Streaks of fire emerged from the hollow shafts of bamboo shoots that were held by the magician's apprentices. Anxiously the fire shot skyward, until, as if depleted, it faded and died out with brilliant colors showering the dark background. Mouths agape, Marco and Vittorio applauded the unexpected entertainment.

Casca licked his lips and tasted the air. The smoke of the burning powder entered his nostrils and flooded his mind while it traveled into his lungs. He closed his eyes and for an instant enjoyed the bittersweet taste of the smoke that seemed to burrow itself into his brain. Not unlike the cold grip of steel that had been his companion for over a thousand years, the burning powder would never quite leave his side over the next millennia. It was the curse of the eternal mercenary.

Hundreds yelled out enthusiastically at the sight of the burning skies. It had been a show reserved only for celebrating the Khan. Just as loud as the cheers had been, complete nervous quiet overtook the enclosure where two young girls entered. Only the soft cry of the morin khour disturbed the silence.

"Who are they? Marco whispered to Chen-Chin.

"Just watch," his friend advised with a certain sense of amusement in his voice.

The two girls walked side by side, ignoring all around, as if they had eyes for no one but each other and were not aware of the hundreds of anxious faces. Moving slowly, they held each other's hands until they reached the middle of the enclosure.

The two girls began their dance while continually looking

into each other's eyes. They were the uncommon, nearly magical beauty that Marco and Vittorio had heard of for the last years from Maffeo. The sound of the morin khour was soon joined by the distant beat of a lone sheepskin drum. The sound slowly intensified, seeming to travel along the beating of the men's hearts.

Their long hair swept by their sides as the two girls faced each other. They swayed their arms and bodies around one other, turning their heads simultaneously, nearly touching, yet not allowing any other part of their bodies to meet. Thin silk veils covered their slight bodies, the cloth creating enough mystery to hide their nearly unclad beauty. No longer little girls, still they had not seen too many years as young women. At times the light from the nearby fires sent shadows between them, allowing the crowd shudders of excitement from the beauty in front of them. Within moments nothing could be heard as if they had all held their breath, bewitched by the dance. Casca smiled to himself watching Marco and Vittorio enjoy this most unusual of dances, knowing for certain how Marco's inner struggles tortured him. A slight stirring ran along Casca's lower lip, as if Khutulun's kiss beckoned him. His tongue scraped along his lower teeth, remembering that night.

The enchanted dance continued, hypnotizing even the strongest of will who would have preferred not to fall victim to the girls' wicked charms. They hypnotically wove their movements together, their actions becoming one, their arms stroking the air while their fingertips touched the silk robes they wore. Sweet perspiration ran down to one of the dancer's cheeks, creating a drop of water that hung from the middle of her upper lip. It rested momentarily until wetting her lips and the tip of her soft tongue. Marco's eyes widened as the other dancer shared the drop of water with her own lips.

He nervously looked at Chen-Chin while his shallow breathing further slowed. Anxiously shifting in his seat, Marco tried breaking the spell, yet he was unwilling or unable to look away for more than an instant. Chen-Chin returned a smile. He figured it was best if Marco did not know that the girls were sisters.

The early morning brought the end of the celebration, finally allowing Casca a return to his quarters where, if the

Khan's generosity was to continue, he would still not get any rest for a while longer. It was the sharp blade of the assassin that waited in the shadows on this day.

He could see nothing as he entered his quarters. The candles that would have lit the room were gone.

"Now, now!" The hushed voice of the assassin startled Casca the moment the thick war cloth was thrown over him. His senses, dulled by the endless cups of ayrag, had failed him, for the moment giving false hope to the would-be assassins. The cold blade entered his side while hands unseen tried pushing him against the wall. His blood boiled as the soldier within reawakened from the pain. Instead of yielding, he pushed forward and left his feet. The weight of his body surprised the wielder of the blade, the momentum of Casca's actions ripping the handle of the knife from the man's hands. Rolling within the darkness, Casca was back on his feet while pulling the short blade from his own body. The spurting blood and intensity of the pain shocked him, bringing back the instincts of the warrior. Only that and pain would remain eternal.

He stood within the darkness, with his left hand trying to close the door while his right hand held the blood-soaked blade. There was no need for light. The unseen edge flashed against warm flesh, draining blood and life from two of the men. They cried in horror and collapsed at Casca's feet. The third had been fortunate for now, escaping through the door before Casca had had the chance to close it.

"I am sorry." Hon-Pao's exasperated voice came down the hallway as the little man ran while holding a small oil lamp in front of him. "I should have been here with you, Old Young One. I am sorry."

Hon-Pao entered the room, the light of the lamp illuminating the grizzly remains. Casca's blade had been swift and precise. Beneath bloodied clothing lay two failed members of the Brotherhood. Casca stood within the room, his left hand holding his side, while his right hand held a short black sword.

"It was them, they made no secret about it. Are you all right?"

"I have seen that before." Casca opened the worn cuirass

of one of the men, exposing an ugly triangular scar on the man's chest.

"I will get some help."

"There is no need. They are the ones that needed help." Casca pointed at a scar on the other man's chest. Both scars were triangular, with the point facing up, while the base of the triangle faded away toward their bellies. It was the scar left by burning flesh. Casca looked at the tip of the blade he still held.

Hon-Pao watched Casca's side and shook his head. The trickle of blood had stopped completely. Casca removed his soaked shirt and wiped his left side with it. He looked at Hon-Pao who stood wide-eyed.

"You *are* the Old Young One." It was all that the little man could say. Unable to speak any further, Hon-Pao watched the normal fatal wound close up in front of his eyes, the final drop of blood caking against the torn skin.

Casca winced from the pain and cursed in a language Hon-Pao could not understand.

"The rest of them . . . ?"

"I have just come from their quarters. Marco and Vittorio are safe. They have done nothing but speak of the dancers. The prince has also gone to rest. He has an important day tomorrow."

Casca breathed deep and coughed. There was no blood in his lungs. The pain would last for a while. There was nothing new about that.

"Niccolo and Maffeo are still with Sando and the other imperial guards. They are all safe," Hon-Pao added, trying to quell Casca's concerns.

Morning came within a few hours. Casca opened his eyes to find Hon-Pao still standing by his bed, not a foot removed from where he had stood the previous night. The little man felt responsible, although it was doubtful he could have done much.

"I am all right. It is not the first time . . ." Casca figured there was no point in going on about his curse.

A slight figure entered the chamber carrying a bowl of water and a thick towel draped over her arm. Quietly she knelt by Casca's bed.

"Go ahead, Ko. The wound must be washed."

The young girl looked up while holding the wet towel, waiting for Casca to stand. She pulled the hood back over her shoulder exposing her face.

"I can trust no one else now. This is Ko, my granddaughter. She has no one else but me and her ya-ya, her other grandfather."

Casca looked down at the unusually beautiful girl. He could see why Hon-Pao spoke in such a way about her. She truly was a gift. Her long hair hung loosely by her sides, nearing her slight hips. Her face, looking unlike most other Chinese girls, mesmerized Casca for a moment. The darkest eyes he had ever seen looked into his, calling to him. Her long and curled eyelashes fluttered, then turned down. His lower lip burned as his tongue nearly traced the scar left by Khutulun's kiss. Her eyes met his for another moment then quickly lowered again. It was all that she dared on this day. Ko attempted a faint smile behind her shaking lips. Casca stood and pulled the bloodied shirt over his head. The expected gasp did not disappoint him.

Ko bit her lip and proceeded to wash the wound. The blood that had caked over the area was quickly soothed by the cloth and her soft touch. She continued washing the area, half expecting to have more blood gush out. Once again she gasped at the sight of a normally mortal wound that had healed down to a reddened jagged scar. It looked as if it had been healing for many weeks. Ko continued washing, hurrying along, wanting to leave the side of this unusual man who was making her feel so uneasy. Casca smiled watching a bead of perspiration run down her neck to quickly disappear within her bosom.

"Prince Nayan and Nasir al-Din have returned earlier this morning," Hon-Pao said, interrupting the moment. "They have turned back the great revolt of Durban in the north. Durban has been attacking the northern garrisons of the Khan, trying to gain land back his father had years ago lost to the empire . . ." Hon-Pao stopped for a moment, realizing, as he often did, that his thoughts had trailed off.

"Nayan is a grandson of one of the great Genghis's half brothers. He and general Nasir al-Din have been successful at defeating the opponents of Khubilai Khan." Hon-Pao continued, aware that Casca likely had no knowledge of them. "There will be a great feast welcoming them. Also, it is Chen-Chin's twenty-fifth birthday. The Great Khan will have a special celebration for his son—"

"Who else knows about last night?" Casca inquired while sitting up.

"I have told no one."

"The rest?"

"They are unharmed. The Brotherhood was brazen." Hon-Pao shook his head, almost in disbelief. "The Khan must be informed."

Casca nodded while still standing. He turned toward Hon-Pao, while putting on a new white shirt. Ko's breathing quickened watching Casca's knotted muscular body turn within the light of the morning sun. She stepped back and hid within her grandfather's one-armed embrace.

Just like the previous day, it was a day of feasting and celebration. By the time the sun was overhead, thousands had gathered within the Forbidden City to celebrate the return of heroes. Nayan and Nasir al-Din entered the broad gates to the cheer of thousands. They had defended the northern borders and returned with nearly five thousand horses, armaments, and bounty that such complete victory assured.

Kneeling in front of the Khan they waited until all voices settled. Few had been received as these men had on this day. The two of them stood with their heads bowed, paying their respects to the Khan. Nayan was short and bowlegged, as were many of his kind. He had spent most of his life on horseback, distorting his legs, nearly crippling himself. His eyes were dark, almost lost within the high cheekbones and bushy eyebrows. He bowed his head and extended his right hand toward the Khan in subservience.

Nasir al-Din was quite unlike Nayan. He was thin and clean shaven. His features, as his name, were from far in the west. For nearly two generations he and his family had served as the Khan's most trusted generals. Even from a distance Casca could read power and intelligence in the man's eyes.

"I welcome both of you. Few have served me as well and as long as you, Nasir al-Din my trusted friend, and you Nayan, my cousin." Both men broke into a slight grin, having been so recognized. It was seldom the Khan made such personal acknowledgments.

"Sit by me today. It is a great day," Khubilai concluded.

Any that would have thought the previous day's feast had exhausted the food and drink or the enthusiasm of the crowd would have been mistaken. With renewed vigor the feasting continued into the early evening until the first stars appeared overhead.

Marco and Vittorio sat by Casca, enjoying the feast, oblivious of Casca's injuries. The drink and food had made the injury more tolerable for certain. Casca smiled at Chen-Chin, the two of them amused at Marco and Vittorio who awaited the arrival of the dancing girls. Nearly one hundred tables had been set up in the middle of the courtyard, facing the entrance of one of the principal gates. As before, hundreds feasted while thousands served.

"It is the burning powder!" Vittorio enthusiastically exclaimed, both of them delighted at the spectacle that it had suddenly created. More and more flames shot up into the night sky, bursting, shattering the air with its multicolored flames, until, descending softly, extinguishing before reaching the ground. The smell of the smoke and the bright lights overcame the senses as Marco cried out with joy, "Over there, Vittorio, look there." Marco pointed to one of the turrets lit up by blue-green flames. Vittorio grinned and applauded.

Next to Casca, Sando, the Khan's half brother suddenly stiffened in his seat.

"Defend! Defend!" he yelled while jumping to his feet, upturning the table in front of him. Food and drink spilled everywhere, surprising the occupants of the table.

"Defend!" Sando yelled out once more while unsheathing his sword. Within the noise of the enthusiastic crowd, his voice was nearly lost to all except to the kesig and the imperial guard.

A cloud of arrows descended on them, impaling a dozen men who had stood to defend the Khan. From within the smoke and haze of the burning powder and the dark of night, the shriek of hundreds of horsemen broke through. Horns and drums sounded, further adding to the madness and confusion the sudden attack had created. Another volley of arrows rained down on them, ending the lives of many more. Drawing his own sword, Casca stood by Sando, while pushing Marco and Vittorio to the ground behind the upturned table.

Casca looked toward Khubilai who was lost behind a wall of the kesig's best trained and most trusted. They shielded his body with their own while another salvo of arrows sent many of them to the Eternal Blue Sky.

Chaos overtook the courtyard as most revelers were unable to defend themselves, many still not quite aware of what was taking place. Behind the cloud of dust the thundering hooves had created and the veil of darkness, the invaders pressed the attack.

Casca turned toward his right. Nayan's seat was empty. He had been received as a returning hero by the Khan, yet his allegiance lay elsewhere. He and his men had returned from the north to upturn the empire. It had been too easy to attack the unsuspecting Khan.

The previously frail-looking Nasir al-Din stood with his own sword in hand, ready to clash steel upon steel. He kicked at the table in front of him, knocking it into the path of the lead horse. His wait was not long. He slashed at the rider, ending his life before the man had even hit the ground. Impaled into the broken table, the horse thrashed around, crushing its master and anyone else in its path.

The salvo of arrows ended, to be replaced by the weight of hundreds of horses pressing upon the imperial guard that tried to shield the Khan. From all around, thousands rushed in to take part in this unexpected uprising.

Wincing from the pain in his side, Casca stood his ground. A slash of his sword split the neck of one of the charging horses, showering the area with blood as the beast stood on its hind legs, crushing everything beneath its hooves in its last seconds of life. Other horsemen took its place, ending with a similar fate, as it was not the first time Casca had warred with mounted warriors. Once unsaddled, most could not offer much resistance. The ones who did extended their lives by mere moments, until their soft bellies were pierced by the edge of Casca's sword.

In less than a minute Casca stood on top of fallen flesh, his feet sinking into the still throbbing entrails of warriors who had met their demise at the feet of the scarred stranger who defended the Khan. He fought on, swinging his blade endlessly, trying to stand up to the flood of invaders. The blood of man and beast alike overflowed in the courtyard, soaking the earth with its foul and salty stench. It was a mark on this day that would never leave.

Farther behind himself, Casca could hear Sando's voice order the loyal kesig warriors on their retreat into the palace. Caught in the mass of people, the Khan struggled to get to his own short sword and defend himself. His guards were not about to allow him. Their orders demanded that they do nothing but defend the Khan and the royal family. Still trying to unsheathe his sword, the Khan struggled to stay on his feet while protecting his wife Chabi with his own body.

More horsemen entered the now fully open gates, joining the battle. The urgency of their attack was certain as was Sando's anxiousness to get the Khan to safety. A hundred hooded men pounded their horses into the imperial guards, the hooves of the beasts pulverizing anyone who stood in their way. The invaders had little time. Even with their brazen and surprise attack they were greatly outnumbered. Their only chance was for a quick and precise strike.

Blood and death drenched the arena as the invaders were slowly turned back. The tangled flesh of man and beast became indistinguishable as the night wore on. Occasional arrows split the night sky, finding bodies, still piercing the dead and the living without prejudice. The few torches that had not been upturned during the attack now lit the arena of death. Cries of pain and horror reverberated within the walls of the courtyard, adding to the horror of the night.

In near darkness, Sando's men stood their ground, methodically defeating every pocket of resistance. Men and horses continued their battle, the cries of both shattering the ears of all who lived. Casca fought on, realizing none of these men was going to allow for an easy capture. A few of the invaders lived, not by choice but by their inability to end their own lives. They knew their own capture was not a desirable option.

At a distance, farther inside the palace, Khubilai Khan stood within the darkness, looking out at what his empire had brought upon itself. Perhaps his reign had done so. It was time for else. Hundreds had given their lives in their single-minded effort to destroy him, while hundreds more had died defending him and the empire. And here he stood, the Khan of the world, holding a clean sword in his right hand. It was a hollow victory.

Casca stood in the poorly lit room watching Khubilai pace back and forth. The Khan's hair hung loose, unkept, covering his angered face. He had been unharmed, yet he wished it could have been different. The attempt on his life had been foiled, but with a price. No one had ever attempted such an assault, and never had he felt so powerless and overly protected. He grunted in anger.

"You must rest Great Khan," Sando insisted.

"They all saw me cower away. It is no way for a Khan to act. It is no way for a Mongol," Khubilai yelled back.

"It was the only way. Chen-Chin is not yet ready to lead."

"He will be, of that I will make certain," Khubilai once again yelled back, well aware of Sando's concern.

"What of you?" Khubilai stopped his pacing.

Sando smiled a bloody smile. His face and neck were covered with blood, his left cheek collapsed by the hoof of one of the horses. Sando's broad, handsome face, the envy of many, had been reduced to a bloody grotesque form. He scraped some of the caked blood off his face and looked at the Khan.

"You live, my brother. That is what matters. The empire and your son need you."

"Chen-Chin, Sando is right. You will be emperor of all of China when the time is ready. It was not the kind of day you had hoped for on your twenty-fifth birthday, I know."

Chen-Chin looked up at his father, the thought of his birthday the farthest thought from his mind. He sat by his mother who tried to console him, unable to be less than the protective mother that she was. She stroked his face and smiled.

"You are safe, father. I do not need any more," Chen-Chin properly answered, yet Casca could feel the young prince was less than completely genuine.

"The white stallion I am sure you know about awaits you in my stable." Khubilai extended his hand toward Chen-Chin. "We will ride together."

Chen-Chin returned a smile and bowed at both his mother and father. Perhaps for once there would be no one but he and his father riding side by side. It would be a long while before he would feel so close to his father again.

"The Brotherhood must be punished." Sando broke the momentary silence. "They have waited and planned this attack for a long time. I can feel Khaidu's hand in all of this. Nayan would not dare on his own."

"Yes, they have grown strong. There has to be another way. I never expected them to be so brazen."

"They must be crushed. Completely!" Sando insisted.

"You cannot destroy an idea," Casca interrupted, surprising them. "You can kill all that you will find, but more will come."

Khubilai shook his head in acknowledgment. It was true. Sadly, Casca was right.

"Then I must be strong. They must know the Khan has not grown old and powerless." Khubilai pounded his fist against the wall. "I am still Khan."

"Long live Khubilai, long live the Great Khan," Sando yelled out, raising his sword over his head. Khubilai smiled, acknowledging the words of his brother. There had been few so loyal by his side.

The events of the day enraged Khubilai Khan. His subjects had found him to be weak and unworthy of the khanship. Many would pay for their insolence. The Brotherhood had been turned back for now, but not for long. They would not rest, regardless of the resistance.

The perception of weakness nearly maddened the Khan. Campaign upon campaign he ordered, unreasonably and foolishly demanding total submission by all who bordered his empire. Territories he had never shown interest in became his passion and undoing. His wife, his companion of nearly thirty years, no longer had his ear. Forsaking all advice and reason, Khubilai sent out expeditions to all corners of the empire, in a death race to conquer all who resisted him.

An angry and bitter man he was becoming, abandoning his family and reason, obsessed with expanding the empire, and strengthening the borders. Khubilai was forgetting his own words about stubbornness being one's undoing. Chen-Chin would eventually be ready to lead; until then, the empire would grow if the Khan's actions did not lead to its downfall.

The Brotherhood of the Night did not rest either. Their

attacks were merciless and increasingly frequent. At times lone men or women were sent to assassinate the Khan, in an attempt to rid the empire of an unworthy ruler or at least damage Khan's morale and have him question his own actions.

The years to follow were years of war and misery. Khubilai Khan looked upon the south, the immense Chinese empire of the Sung still defiant. The Khan had sent his best over the years, had used the tactics years of experience had taught him, yet the Sung had successfully resisted. It was a land of countless millions of people with seemingly endless resources. Its territory, which could provide unlimited taxes and could feed millions more, was irresistible to Khubilai. The famed port of Hangchow, through which a thousand ships passed each day, could add riches beyond belief. The south had to be conquered and made part of the Mongol empire. All of China needed to be under one ruler. Khubilai would have it no other way.

It was not until Chang Shi-Chen ruler of the Sung died unexpectedly that Khubilai was finally able to get a foothold in the south. Unprepared, the empress of the south, Ch'uan, with only her young son the child emperor Shih, as the crown prince, was forced to listen. She was not an unreasonable ruler, realizing that years of bloodshed resisting the mighty Mongol horde would bring death and hardship upon her people, possibly leading to oblivion. The Mongol threat to turn all of the Sung into a giant pasture land fit for thousands of the Khan's steeds to graze upon was sufficient to have her accept an unwanted truce. Death and hardship was replaced by a letter of submission that she reluctantly signed. She had no choice but to agree to taxes that drained the land, yet preserved their way of life and their own lives. The Khan of all China was no fool himself. Khubilai decided to receive the empress and her young son as guests of the new empire, assuring them comfort and safety in Khanbalic. It would have been ill advised to harm the symbol of Chinese royalty and culture. Eventually the Chinese people would be able to accept a benevolent ruler, even if not of Chinese birth.

Khubilai's decision not to destroy the Sung and bring total victory was not well received by the Brotherhood and others who opposed him; however, Khubilai knew there was no pleasing them. Only his death or the death of his son, Chen-Chin would have given them pleasure.

To the southeast, Wonjong, the King of Korea, soon came to form an alliance with the Khan, in essence becoming a vassal state. Wonjong anxiously sent lavish gifts to the Khan, demonstrating his loyalty and acceptance of Mongol law. Paying tribute was not as costly as the loss of life or his own removal from the throne. Further, Wonjong received help from Khubilai when his leadership was threatened. The Khan sent three thousand troops, reinstating King Wonjong to the throne, assuring continued loyalty and lack of hostility on his borders. On Cheju Island, off the coast of Korea, where the last of Wonjong's enemies were finally defeated, Khubilai converted much of the island into grazing area for horses and pasture land for sheep. It was a lesson to be learned for others who might have foolishly protected their land against the Mongol horde.

Further to the east, in a land beyond the ocean, which many Chinese called land of the rising sun, a nation of warriors had proudly resisted and succeeded at being unconquered. This, however, was a conflict that Khubilai would not win. Even nature had stood in his way, protecting the Japanese fleet and upturning his own.

"They will fall to my armies. There will be nowhere to run. Beyond the islands is the endless sea," Khubilai insisted.

"That weakness is their strength." Chabi tried reasoning with her husband, well knowing that his obsession was without remedy. There was no changing his mind.

"My army is strong. They will not fail their Khan!" Khubilai angrily snapped back.

"Never encircle an army without giving them a path to retreat. They will fight tenfold of their true abilities," said Chabi, quoting an old master.

"The words of Shiu-Lao Tze are distant. He had never met my armies," Khubilai stubbornly insisted.

Khubilai's men met with a horrible death. The ships the Korean king had supplied them with were sturdy and seaworthy. However, not on this day. The angry sea attacked the Mongol ships, turning hundreds of them into coffins, entombing men and horses alike in the depths of the ocean. Thousands of Mongols would forever lay on the ocean floor.

• • •

Niccolo and Maffeo's mission had become irrelevant. Their standing with the Khan had not diminished following the failed revolt allowing them to go about, for now, undisturbed. The Brotherhood had found them not worthy of their time. They, along with Marco and Vittorio, were assured by the Khan that their position and presence was important and had not changed. However, the Khan's interest in the west and any alliance with the leader of Christendom had become by no means unimportant at this time.

Maffeo and Niccolo went about as before, making contact with old acquaintances and forging new business relations. They were Venetian merchants whose lives did not change much during war or peace. They continued their trade for the exotic items of the mysterious east, always looking for new opportunities.

Casca remained in Khanbalic for years, at times not joining the royal procession to the north during the summer months. The sweltering heat that the Mongol's so hated was easily remedied by the cool breeze that seemed to blow through Khanbalic even during the hottest months. Hon-Pao had stayed with Casca at all times, having taken a liking to this unusual man of legend. Ko was not displeased with her grandfather's decision. She knew it was not very long before Casca would see her as a young woman.

At times Marco and Vittorio remained with Casca, or bravely even ventured farther south, into the jungles just north of Burma and Champa. The land of Chin had endless discoveries and opportunities for one like Marco who had such a thirst for knowledge. Most of the time, Marco traveled with Chen-Chin, learning all that the empire offered, and teaching the crown prince of the western world.

Temur mostly traveled with his father, Chen-Chin, which made Chen-Chin very happy. Unlike his own father, the Khan, he would get to know his own son. Young Temur was what all Mongol fathers would have wanted of their own, especially what the great-grandson of the Genghis should have been. Once having reached ten years of age the young prince was slowly becoming a full-fledged warrior. Looking unlike his father, the young man rode his horse as if he had been born in the saddle and had suckled attached underneath a mare since infancy. He could throw a lance or shoot an arrow without missing a beat, letting half a dozen arrows fly before the first would even find its mark. The blood of the Genghis clearly flowed through his veins.

Marco's life became richer and more satisfying, as long as he stayed within the protective land of the Khan, especially while under the watchful eye of Sando. He along with Vittorio had fallen into the young prince Chen-Chin's favor to enjoy the life of royalty. Strange as it was, their friendship was somehow unhindered by a different history, heritage, and future. They enjoyed each other's company, traveling through the empire and beyond, yet always under the watchful eye of Sando. He would have it no other way. If he was unable to personally oversee them, he made certain his most trusted men were at constant watch, preserving these sometime ungrateful men.

With Hon-Pao by his side, Casca entered the war room. After years of frustration, Casca's presence had been requested by the Khan. Now they all stood in a nearly empty four-walled room that had nothing but a table and a dozen chairs in it. No adornments of any sort had been allowed in this enclosure by the Khan since the revolt by Nayan.

"As it has been ordered." Meekly, Hon-Pao informed Thogor-Pa of their arrival. Thogor-Pa accepted the news without even looking at the Chinese servant. His distaste for the little man was not well cloaked.

Unceremoniously, Khubilai also entered the room with his clearly displeased wife by his side.

"Ungrateful beasts they are," Khubilai finally said. Next to him, Sando stood holding his short sword in his right hand, tapping the exposed tip of it with his left thumb. General Nasir al-Din also quietly stood, nearly mirroring Sando's actions. He was a man of few words who had learned long ago that listening brought more knowledge than speaking. Casca watched these two men while his brows furrowed, his mind searching into the near past.

Uncertain who the Khan had referred to, Casca nodded his head.

"I am very pleased that you are well, Old Young One.

Thogor-Pa has informed me of the many attempts on your life. I regret them." Khubilai spoke quietly yet it was clear he was enraged by the actions against Casca. "The Brotherhood has grown strong. It is unfortunate your return has been met with such displeasure by some."

"It is the greatest empire the world has even known. There is none without strife." Casca rested his hands on the hilt of his sword as he faced the Khan.

"And it will grow until all will bow to me. Chen-Chin will be a great leader to lead the empire into the next century. He will inherit the world."

Casca watched Chabi's sad eyes as the Khan spoke. It was difficult to know where her concerns lay, yet it was not unexpected.

"Chen-Chin will be returning soon from his studies. He will be ready when the time comes." Thogor-Pa bowed to the Khan, in his usual voice reaffirming the Khan's assertion. "Chen-Chin has taken his friends along as usual." Thogor-Pa flared his nostrils as he spoke of Marco and Vittorio. "Young prince Temur will also be returning with them. He has grown into a fine young man."

Khubilai smiled at the mention of his grandson. The sixteen-year-old Temur reminded him so much of himself, from the way he spoke, the way he looked, even the way he walked or turned his head. It was as if Temur were more his son than Chen-Chin, something that had not been lost on anyone.

"Where has Chen-Chin taken the boy?" Khubilai questioned.

"By the sea without end. Before returning from Korea he has chosen to visit the eastern shores of the Sung."

"So they have." Khubilai nodded without seeming to pay much attention.

"Word comes of Nayan's forces growing," Sando finally spoke, trying to return all of them to matters of greater concern. "He and Khaidu have been quiet for too long. It has been nearly three months since they have been heard from."

"Khaidu has been quite preoccupied with his grandson. The boy has grown extraordinarily. He is strong and wise beyond his years. By Khaidu's assertion, the young man has the blood of the Ghenghis." Sando looked at the Khan, trying to weigh if he was being heard.

"Yes, I know. His daughter Khutulun has given him quite a gift. The boy is unusual, not just by his actions but by his appearance."

Casca's mind raced back to his encounter with Khutulun. It had been over ten years. Was it possible? Could it be that the curse of Christ did not follow him into the mountains of China?

"The boy's eyes are light, nearly as blue as the Eternal Blue sky." Sando nodded while catching Casca's preoccupied frown. "Maybe it is a sign. No one knows the father of the child. It is as if he were a gift from above. That is what Khaidu has insisted."

"He is unimportant." Khubilai raised his tone. "The boy is just another boy. Maybe he will one day take Khaidu's throne, not mine," Khubilai angrily declared.

"Nayan has been spreading the words of the Brotherhood." Sando continued. "General Nasir al-Din has suggested an offensive against them. We have given Nayan too much time."

"Word is that he has amassed thousands to fight for him," Sando added.

Khubilai laughed. "Thousands? That is what concerns you? I have thousands of commanders who oversee thousands of soldiers. There is much flesh to protect me from the swords of Nayan."

"It is not just their number, Great Khan. It is the belief they have in their hearts that cannot be erased.

"No great emperor is without enemies. They will be dealt with," Khubilai insisted. "My concerns are not just with them. The king of Pagan in Burma is the one who is more of a threat. He commands millions and all his appetites are without boundary, from what I have been told."

It was not the first time Casca had heard Khubilai speak of Burma; mostly he spoke of it when he had no interest in what was being discussed. Once again, Casca's thoughts drifted to Khutulun and their encounter in the mountains. Could it be possible? And, if so, what could he . . . ?

"We will leave tomorrow, Great Khan." Nasir al-Din's voice returned him to matters at hand. "No matter what awaits us, Nayan must be dealt with."

• • •

Casca and Nasir al-Din rode side by side, heading east, supposedly to encounter the forces of Nayan. Nasir al-Din commanded a force of twenty thousand men, foot soldiers, and cavalry. Twelve thousand horses carried most of the men and supplies. It was an army large enough to occupy a small nation. Word had it that Nayan's forces were fewer in number. Casca thought of how Mongols would spill the blood of their own brothers. Nasir al-Din shook his head as he tried to look east, blocking the morning sun with his left hand.

"In two days we will reach the Ben-cho province, within it are a small group of villages that have been loyal to the Khan. There we can get new horses and supplies." Nasir al-Din shifted in his saddle as he addressed Casca.

"Loyal?"

"We can exchange a thousand of our horses for fresh ones," Nasir repeated without explaining what he had meant by loyalty.

Casca also shifted in his saddle allowing a huge scar on his right side to show. In one motion he adjusted his tunic and pulled a chunk of spiced meat from underneath the saddle. Its pungent aroma made Nasir smile.

"Are you truly the Old Young One of legend?" Nasir observed Casca's side, wondering how anyone could have survived a wound that left such a mark.

"Time and stories seem to exaggerate." Casca smiled while taking another bite of the rancid flesh between his teeth. It was a strange thing to eat, the knotted blend of meats and spices, yet it seemed to insist on a certain addiction Casca had recently found irresistible. Sometime warmed by the proximity to the horse's back, fermented by time, and the endless pounding of the saddle, it forced the rider to think back at the way the old Mongols had lived, on horseback nearly overrunning a petrified Europe.

The two of them rode on, Nasir also enjoying some of the spicy meat, the two of them having found a certain amity. The plain widened, allowing for their eyes to meet the distant horizon. Far ahead the blue sky met the ground. To the south, rice fields extended as far as the eye could see, while to the north, orchards dominated the landscape. Countless young women worked the fields as their ancestors had done for thousands of years, gathering the life-sustaining harvest while their eyes watched for cobras that never seemed to be too far off. Within the ankle-deep water, rats scurried around, many of them soon to become the meal of the poisonous serpents. The women would be safe as long as the rodents were in abundance.

"Some have suggested that I am the leader of the Brotherhood." Nasir spoke after nearly an hour of quiet.

"Doubtful. I believe I have met him," Casca answered in mild surprise.

"It is possible, but unlikely. I have heard many different descriptions of their master. Some even suggest he is really a woman, or that he does not exist."

"It is true that he does not need to exist. The fear of his name is sufficient."

"The Brotherhood speaks of honor and loyalty, yet they often have little of either. It is good to fear them. They are just as likely to strike with a poison dart as with a spiked mace. Not unlike a woman scorned, they will do whatever it takes." Nasir spoke as if recollecting a personal memory. His face took on a dark look as he turned toward Casca.

"It will be an ugly fight, no doubt." Casca looked ahead toward the horizon, figuring Nasir no longer wanted to speak of the Brotherhood.

They rode side by side for nearly an hour before Nasir spoke again.

"I have commanded thousands of men into countless battles, but this is the most unsavory of all." Nasir spit at the ground, obviously displeased by his mission. His anger did not rest with the actions of Nayan, his pain was something Casca figured was best left alone for now.

Casca was about to respond until he saw Nasir raise his head with a continued look of disgust. Three horsemen approached carrying news of the enemy.

"Ben-Cho, the villages—" One of the riders coughed violently as he tried gathering himself. "The villages have been burned . . . they killed everyone, worse than killed . . ." The leader was unable to finish his thoughts. Nasir nodded dismissing the rider.

Ben-Cho came into view in less than an hour. At the horizon smoke swirled from the burning straw and bamboo huts.

A familiar fog blanketed the skyline, the burning of human flesh poisoning the air unlike anything else. The wretched haunting cries of men who would have welcomed death traveled along the wind and burrowed into the ears of the newcomers. The ones who had lived existed on the edge of sanity, hoping for help or mercy.

Nasir and Casca slowed their horses as they came to the outskirts of the first village. Hundreds of men had been tied to bamboo stakes by the side of the road, clearly put on display for anyone who approached. Blood covered their bare hips and legs. It was a sight to nauseate the senses.

"Nayan . . ." It was all that Nasir al-Din was able to say, recognizing the rebel's handiwork.

Pools of thickened blood soiled the naked feet of these wretched souls, telling the tale of their torture. They hung by the ropes that held them up, their heads bowed, eyes lost in madness. Ropes had been tied to their privates in order to bring the greatest of pain in the most miserable fashion while the other end of the ropes had been tied to the saddles of horses. Had they been lucky, the ripping of their own flesh allowed for quick blood loss and the reward of death. The unlucky ones experienced the liquefying of their privates as the tightening noose forced their flesh to squeeze through an unnatural opening made by the knotted rope. Eventually the survivors' assaulted bodies would heal, forever to be crippled by the events of the day.

"There are no horses. Nayan has left little," one of Nasir al-Din's men reported while trying to hold back the heaving gurgles of a man ready to lose himself.

There was nothing and no one left in Ben-Cho or the immediate area. The rest of the villagers had been killed or presumably taken for the invader's pleasure or revenge. The remaining supplies, hundreds of barrels and sacks of food and drink were likely poisoned. Nasir al-Din had seen Nayan's handiwork before. Along with others, Nasir had well taught all the strategies of war; however, Nayan had taken it to new levels, finding ways to torture that never left the victim's thoughts.

They continued on, the cries of the butchered men ringing in their ears even after they were long out of ear shot. Nasir al-Din allowed a dozen of his men to remain in Ben-Cho and the surrounding villages and tend to the wounded. A not uncertain message had been sent to Khan.

"It won't be long." Nasir's forewarning came true the following night. The victims of Ben-Cho had been just a preview. A few hours before dawn, when men and horses slept deepest, hundreds of flaming arrows disturbed the night, raining onto the campsite. Horses whinnied from the flames that came from the sky and torched the tents, while men awoke in panic, trying to reason if the stars were falling or if the enemy had decided to attack at night.

The flaming arrows continued for three nights. It was more than enough to prevent sound sleep for the following nights when nothing but the eerie whisper of the northern wind disturbed the dark. The villages that Casca and Nasir came upon were barren, nothing but bodies of men and animals littering the ground. At times the sound of trumpets and gongs rang out through the night, disturbing the sleep and the sanity of Nasir's men. The flaming arrows returned a few nights later, in an attempt to further dishearten the campsite. It was clear that finding and destroying the rebels was not going to be an easy task. Casca and Nasir continued marching east, knowing that before long they would clash with Nayan.

"Nayan has decided to stand his ground on the eastern bank of the Kolau," Nasir was informed on an early morning. The young Mongol delivered his report, detailing what the advance party had found. It was an unusual positioning to take, yet Nayan had chosen well. The banks of the Kolau often shifted, hiding the best crossing location. The water was dark and murky, making it near impossible to gauge its depth. Obviously Nayan had mapped it out well, assuring the best strategy that could help his troops.

"He has sent three of his men to deliver a proposal," the young man said, completing his task and sitting up high on his horse, awaiting orders.

The three couriers, three undistinguished looking men wearing the same look of annoyance and disgust as Casca had seen Khaidu wear, approached slowly. Once within a few feet of Casca and Nasir al-Din they kicked at the sides of their horses, in a pathetic attempt to intimidate or assess their opponents.

"Nayan, Khan of the Mongols, wants to offer one last

chance to join him. His offer forgives all that has been done against him. A new beginning."

"The great Khubilai Khan does not recognize Nayan as the leader of all Mongols. Nayan's offer is rejected. Unreservedly rejected." Nasir sat motionless and looked out beyond the messengers, nearly ignoring them.

Not surprised by the response, the three turned and rode off. Their path took them toward the river where they quickly disappeared behind a thick group of trees and prickly bushes. Further beyond the trees the terrain appeared to change, providing a place for troops to stay hidden. There was little mystery regarding the whereabouts of Nayan's forces to Casca and Nasir al-Din.

Casca raised himself in the saddle and turned around. Behind him thousands of Mongols stood at the ready. This conflict was not going to be left to diplomacy. Next to him, Hon-Pao looked up. A blood soaked earth would be reflected against the clear blue sky on this day.

Within half an hour three new messengers appeared from behind the row of trees. They wore long dark robes that extended beneath their feet, while their faces were hidden behind dark red cloth, the color of thickened blood. Calmly they approached.

"Our Khan offers the territories of the northeast to you, honorable Nasir al-Din. With the troops at your disposal you can become Khan of your own land. Nayan has been generous. Allow the Mongol people to return to their roots." The messenger spoke softly, the tone reminding Casca of the Brotherhood.

"Nayan has nothing to offer me. Return to him with my message."

"We will leave. Our Khan will give you one hour for a response," the man answered, not seeming to have heard Nasir's reply. He tightly gripped the hilt of his sword as he looked beyond Casca and Nasir into the eyes of the Mongol warriors. The three rode off, following the same trail, quickly disappearing behind the line of trees.

Nasir gave orders to his commanders then turned toward Casca. "Nayan was a good student. He has learned his lessons well." Casca did not hear Nasir's last words, only the pounding of past battles thundered in his ears. He raised his sword and pointed toward the river. His nostrils flared awaiting the smell of future death.

Nasir al-Din was barely able to finish his words before the thunder of thousands of hooves shook the earth. From around the bend of the river the Mongol horde advanced at breakneck speed. Nasir's men shifted, quickly regrouping into an attack formation around their leader. A thousand horsemen appeared from behind the row of trees, heading straight for Casca. It was an old ploy Casca had seen dozens of times before, to attack the leader, hoping that a sudden strike could perhaps overwhelm Nasir, throwing his troops into disarray.

"No!" Nasir yelled out seeing his men begin to form a defensive wedge around him, trying to protect him from the onrushing cavalry. Nasir was not about to become a protected leader. He understood his importance quite well. However, he was not about to treat himself any different from any of his men. They were all soldiers with steel in their hands and hopefully courage in their hearts.

The sky darkened momentarily as thousands of Nayan's men had released their arrows. Not unlike a dragon out of a nightmare, the thousands of steel-tipped shafts traveled in the sky, changing shape, twisting, and turning until plummeting downward to ravage the men below with their barbed talons.

There was little time to waste and Casca knew that before the arrows were to hit their marks, at least three more salvos would be let loose. He watched another thousand arrows leave the string of the powerful Mongolian bows, these angled differently, almost as if to give Nasir and his men no way to escape. The whipping of thousands of feathered shafts into the sky sent ripples through the air. Another thousand arrows soon came to follow, yet in another direction again. Prepared as they had been, still many of Nasir's men fell within the first few moments of battle. The shields that they raised over their heads covered too little. Absorbing the loss from the deadly arrows, the rest stood their ground, keeping formation. The ones who had fallen would receive no tending to for hours. It was just the beginning.

Nasir's men answered with their own bows, the multitude of flying arrows meeting momentarily in the sky, reaching their summit, until crashing downward, digging deeply into the flesh of men and horses. By the time the two armies collided, great damage had been done and hundreds lay dead or dying. It was time for death to come in a more personal way, face-to-face, when Mongol brothers could watch the end in each other's eyes.

The sound of armies clashing, steel screeching, and men vanquished ruptured the day as Mongol brothers finally met. Nayan's attack had been sudden, yet not unexpected. In moments, blood and disjoined limbs that still twitched covered the ground, the hooves of horses and the edge of steel ripping flesh from bone. Casca viciously swung his blade, crashing it against shields, swords, and skulls. With his left hand holding a shield Casca maneuvered his horse around, only using his feet and legs. Becoming one with his obedient steed, he was the bringer of death on this day.

Next to him, wielding a much thinner and longer blade, Nasir commanded his men while also taking part in the battle. Quickly he swung the slight blade, slitting the necks of horses and piercing the sides of men where the leather cuirasses allowed a weakness. Avoiding the heavy war clubs of Nayan's men, he blinded them with quick thrusts of his pointy blade. Many fell at the feet of his horse, the lightning-quick blade having struck and found its mark before some of his opponents even realized that their lives were moments from being over. Death came quickly to them as their lifeblood drained from severed flesh.

The massacre of both sides continued as the future of the empire was being decided. Casca had discarded his blunted blade and continued with a newly found iron club. Its previous owner lay bleeding under his own horse, his back broken by the weight of the beast that had gone down from the slash of a sword. The man no longer had any use for the spiked club. From beneath his beast he would be forced to watch until death took him.

Casca's muscular arm, tempered by a thousand years of war, now wielded the death bringer. Unlike Nasir's quick thrusts of the blade, Casca struck down with the power of the blacksmith's hammer. Men were knocked off their saddles and horses collapsed from the impact of the iron club as the weapon had become an extension of Casca's arm. His bloodied chest heaved from the intensity as he nearly lost himself within the battle.

Trumpets blared in the distance as Casca watched another thousand horsemen appear on the eastern side of the river. Confidently they galloped toward the water, riding fifty abreast, ready to cross the Kolau. Just as Casca had suspected, Nayan had chosen and learned this area well, bringing troops from the other side of the river, rapidly crossing where the water was the shallowest.

They advanced straight toward where Casca and Nasir battled. The messengers had done nothing but determine where within the thousands of troops Nasir was located. It was a clear attempt to try to kill Nasir, hoping to break the morale of his men. However, Nasir had not been caught off guard.

Thousands of Mongols continued to battle, the warriors of the steppes killing each other, as it had been for as long as time itself. With the same fury and intensity that they had conquered half the world, they now battled against each other. From behind a mask of blood, Casca surveyed the place of death. His mind disjoined from the rest of himself, he watched as if from outside. With the fury of hell unleashed, he continued.

The thousand who had just joined the battle did not fare well. Within minutes nearly half of them had fallen, without having made any inroads toward Nasir al-Din. Casca and perhaps a hundred men around him welcomed them with steel clubs, spiked chains, and long spears. Hundreds of horses fell from the tips of the awaiting spears while their riders were butchered before they even hit the ground. A bloodbath this battle soon became, ripping away brothers, fathers, and sons.

The sound of bugles far off in the distance awakened Casca from the dreamlike trance in which he had found himself. He wiped his face clear of blood and sweat, yet the stupefying veil of battle remained. The bugles sounded again, this time even farther away. It was the call of retreat. Nayan had lost, and he was not about to sacrifice any more men. Their crusade would have to continue on another day. It was over for now.

The blood fever of the battle still raged inside Casca as he got off his horse. Suddenly his arms hung limply by his side, the fatigue of battle and the weight of his war club and shield finally taking their toll. He leaned against his trusted warhorse and pulled off the saddle. The beast deserved the rest. With its head down it anxiously awaited to be watered.

Hon-Pao stood in front of Casca, trying to determine if Casca's mind had returned. He reached out using a wet cloth and placed it against Casca's chest. Casca was covered with blood, some of it his own, while the rest was the blood of horses and perhaps dozens of men. Next to him, two Chinese servants tended to Nasir al-Din who did not look badly damaged. A few cuts on his arm and one larger gash that still pulsated blood from his left shoulder was all the damage Nasir had taken.

Seeing Hon-Pao's concern, Casca removed his own blood-ied cuirass. Some of the leather straps had been cut during the battle, while the rest were nearly imbedded into his tortured flesh. It was as if air had turned into blood on this day, stifling everything it encountered.

"I am fine," Casca tried answering Hon-Pao's questioning eyes. "Have been worse before."

Casca looked down toward a huge gash on his chest. Meat the size of his hand hung down from his chest toward his waistline. It spurted blood at every beating of his heart, further reddening the already soaked earth.

"I do not know what to do . . ." Hon-Pao's words were without end as he had never seen a man stand with such a wound. Casca could see in the little man's eyes the hope that he truly was the Old Young One, and that death would not come.

Nasir and his men turned toward Casca, mesmerized by this man of legend who stood his ground when his wounds should have brought him to his knees. They watched in horror as Casca reached with his right hand and pressed the hanging flesh back toward his chest. Hon-Pao placed a wide band of cloth against the shredded meat, his fingers digging into the bloodied mess as he tried to quell the bleeding. Wrapping it twice around Casca's chest and back he made a tight knot by his right shoulder.

Ignoring all who stared at him, Casca anxiously drank from a sheepskin bladder and took in the field of battle. Most of the wounded had been tended to while the dead would be returned to Khanbalic. These brave warriors would rest with their families before the long journey into the Eternal Blue Sky. It was the Mongol way. Their bodies needed to be prepared for the final passage into the afterlife. Without that, oblivion, a never-ending odyssey would not allow them rest.

Casca looked out over the wasted flesh that covered the ground. They were all Mongol, some brothers, yet of different beliefs. Perhaps in the afterlife they would be brothers again and find peace.

He stumbled momentarily. The fever of the battle having left him and allowed the loss of blood to finally weaken him. "You must rest," Hon-Pao anxiously insisted. "Even the Old Young One needs rest." Hon-Pao smiled, well knowing how Casca refused to show weakness.

The night of rest was welcomed by Casca who figured by morning his wound would be on its way to mending. The pain was always the worst the day after. If he could escape some of it by the cover of sleep, it would not be undesirable.

SEVENTEEN

*C*asca awoke the following morning feeling better than he had expected. Apparently none of the wounds had extended to his bones, which lessened the misery of the healing flesh. The second he awoke he met the smiling face of Hon-Pao.

"It is quite early." Hon-Pao extended a steaming cup of tea toward Casca. "Nayan has reportedly fled north toward the Mongol homeland. Undoubtedly he will return. Only death will crush his dreams."

"How far is the ocean to the east?" Casca surprised Hon-Pao with his question. The old man returned a pleased smile.

"We could be there in two days." Hon-Pao continued smiling as he spoke of heading east.

Taking an additional horse, Casca and Hon-Pao left by mid-morning. Casca sat in the saddle, trying to position himself in such a way as for his wound not to torture him from the pounding of the road. His blood had clotted during the night and all the flesh had started to close up. The curse of Christ had followed him even into this end of the world.

Nayan had lost badly from what Casca could tell. Most

likely it would be a long time before they could challenge Khubilai again; however, the Brotherhood would not rest. The hourglass would turn once more for Khubilai while the empire went on.

By nightfall the distant salty aroma of the ocean had caught Casca's nose. He inhaled, allowing his mind to drift into the recent past when they had all set sail for Acre nearly twenty years previous. Now he had traveled to the other end of the world, the curse of the eternal soldier giving him no rest.

"We should be there by tomorrow night." Hon-Pao pointed east, seeming to be hiding something about their destination. His emphasis on *there* was obvious, but not important enough for Casca to inquire.

The following day they reached their destination. They had seen few on the road the previous day, mostly farmers going about their lives the same way their forefathers had done for thousands of years. Empires rose and fell, but, for most, life went on undisturbed. If food and shelter were available it was sufficient.

Standing tall in the stirrups, Casca noted the outline of a solitary figure far ahead to the east. The endless blue sky blanketed the horizon, adding a perfect backdrop to the person standing by the house on the top of the hill. The figure appeared to stand by the side of a small house, tending to two farm animals, possibly goats. They rode for a few minutes longer until the figure came into focus, bringing a smile onto Hon-Pao's face.

He turned toward Casca. "It is my little butterfly. The little heart of my heart." Casca squinted his eyes while a smile also found its way onto his face. He had not seen Ko in years. They both kicked at the sides of their mounts. Hon-Pao was not the only one whose heart Ko had moved.

"You surprised me gung-gung. I thought my eyes were deceiving me. I see you did not come alone." Hon-Pao did not answer, allowing Casca and Ko's eyes to meet unhindered. He had known all along that it was inevitable.

"You are hurt." Ko's concern erased the smile from her face.

Casca reached for his chest while his eyes rested on Ko. She had certainly grown into a beautiful young woman. Curious, Casca thought, that she had not taken to a man yet. No doubt many had lusted after her. She was magnificent, likely melting the hearts and stupefying the thoughts of most men who gazed upon her. Her childhood years were not far behind, yet she had not been taken yet. She was perfection to Casca's eyes. He sat in the saddle, bewitched by her beauty. Her long black hair hung loosely by her sides, caressing her slight hips, outlining her flawless figure. Ko smiled while she reached out toward Casca, offering fresh water.

Still without speaking, he took the offering. Their hands met for an instant, almost forcing her tiny fingers to recoil from the contact from his skin. She smiled a nervous smile, her dark eyes sparkling while her lips parted slightly.

"You must be tired, grandfather. Let me take your horse," Ko offered, her mind swirling in an emotion she had not felt in years. Not since she had last seen Casca.

Casca and Hon-Pao entered the small wooden house. It rested high on a hilltop, overlooking the endless ocean. The high tide of late afternoon pounded the breakers against the rocky coastline, singing the eternal song of the sea and sending the salty aroma the fine mist always carried toward the sky. For a moment Casca had stood by the entrance to the house, looking out at the comforting sea and this place of solitude. The battlefield that had raged just two days away seemed very distant.

"Where are you OJIICHAN?"

Where are you grandfather? Ko walked ahead of them, pushing her way through a red-lace curtain. *Kokoro,* Casca mouthed the Japanese words that had been sewed into the cloth.

"Here my child." The voice came in from behind the house.

Ko turned toward them. "His name is Akiro, he is my ya-ya. My father's father." She smiled at Casca and offered her hand. Hon-Pao nodded his head. It had been nearly a dozen years since he had seen the old man.

The three of them walked through the back door into an unusual garden. "Welcome, old man," the soft voice of Akiro greeted them.

Hon-Pao laughed. "It has been a long time, old man. How have your eyes treated you?"

Akiro turned and faced them. His eyes were white and without sight. He returned a smile. "I have found new sight. With my hands and ears. Maybe it is better for me. I have seen too much for my lifetime."

"Maybe so. This is Casca. No doubt Ko has told you about him . . ." Hon-Pao did not finish his words; Akiro's nod assuring him that there was little that Ko did not share with both grandfathers.

Akiro was a slightly built man, who for reasons unknown to Casca had found his life away from Chingpao, the Land of the Rising Sun. Both Ko and Hon-Pao had spoken of Akiro before, yet they had never mentioned his name or the fact that he was Japanese. No doubt they had their reasons.

The old man walked slowly, yet did not need a cane or need to extend his hands to guide his way. In his world of darkness, Akiro had found sight in this tiny garden.

"He is a great man, Ojiichan. He knows more about the world than anyone I have ever heard of. Even my two grandfathers." Ko quieted down, realizing that perhaps her words of praise were disrespectful toward them.

"Your friends Marco and Vittorio should be back by sundown. I have never met anyone who asks as many questions as that young man Marco." Akiro laughed as he approached, bowed, and then shook hands with Hon-Pao and then Casca. "Welcome to my house, both of you." Akiro's vacant eyes faced Casca then turned toward Ko. The old man smiled as he turned his head back toward Casca. "It is time for tea. Ko, tea for our guests."

Unable to hide her embarrassment before turning her head, Ko walked ahead of them and disappeared inside one of the small side rooms.

The three followed in turn, leaving the small terrace that held Akiro's beautiful garden. It was an immaculately well-maintained place. The great Khan's gardens in Shang-Tu, cared for by hundreds of servants, paled by comparison. Perhaps two dozen trees, no higher than Akiro's knees, occupied the small enclosure. In between, multicolored flowers brought the whole garden to life, further adorning a setting befitting a royal mural. Each tree had been perfectly and patiently tended to. Akiro's hands had cleansed, watered, and preserved every trunk, branch, and leaf. The old man, blind as he was, could see as well into men's hearts as the garden that kept him company day after day.

Casca sat on the floor in front of a very low table. Next to him Hon-Pao and Akiro also sat, facing each other at opposite sides of the small square table. Casca shifted in his seat, trying to find comfort while his wounds still ached him terribly. His cough that had sent shivers of pain into his chest suddenly ceased at the sight of Ko entering the room.

Her long black hair had been tied and carefully placed behind her head, held down by a red bow. She wore the traditional clothes women of Chingpao wore at such ceremonies. Holding a small tray she stepped toward the three of them and kneeled. As she placed the tray onto the square table she kept her eyes down, unwilling to meet Casca's gaze. Meekly she poured the steaming tea into three small cups. Casca had come a long way from the yurt of Khaidu and his barbarian ways. It was always pleasurable to be so royally treated, especially when it was Ko, this magnificent creature, who so tried to please. The ceremonial offering continued for a while as the three men sat.

Marco and Vittorio returned later that evening to the home of Akiro. They were surprised yet quite pleased to find Casca and Hon-Pao waiting for them. It had been nearly two years since they had seen each other. Many years had passed since they had all come to China. Marco and Vittorio spoke the language of the land, wore the clothes, and ate the food of their new home. They had spent nearly as many years on the road and in China as back in Venice. The empire of Khubilai had become their home.

Marco had been able to grow a slight beard, finally giving him an older look than that of the young boy who had come from the other end of the world. Not much else had changed about Marco or Vittorio, they were still the best of friends, insisting on enjoying and discovering everything at the same time. Their friendship with Chen-Chin had also continued. Never did they spend more than a few months apart. It was an amity cherished by all three.

Just as they had done many times previously, Marco and Vittorio spent half the night hearing about Casca's adventures and sharing their own travels. News of the intensifying battles between Khubilai and the forces of Nayan and the Brotherhood shook Marco. He had been unharmed, thanks to good fortune and the presence of Sando's men who never quite let them out of their sights. However, his concern for his father and uncle immediately returned. Marco quietly sighed in relief hearing of Casca's assurance of their safety. Eventually the weight of the night wore on them, forcing an unwanted interruption to their story telling.

"We should go, Old Young One." Hon-Pao's voice awoke Casca shortly after sunup.

Still aching from the wounds, Casca made his way to the outside. Rest had been brief, but seeing Ko's smiling face quickly made Casca forget about sleep.

"Ko will lead the way," Vittorio anxiously informed all of them. "I will have to see it with my own eyes to believe it," he added.

The five of them took the awkward, torturous path down the side of the hill behind the house toward the sea. The morning sun rested over the ocean, shining straight at them, impeding their already difficult descent.

"This way." Ko led the way. "They have already started."

Within minutes they made their way down to the rocky shore where six young girls were hard at work.

"What are they doing?" Vittorio mumbled to himself. Both he and Marco gasped at the appearance of the six young girls.

Casca and Ko stood back, away from Marco and Vittorio who stood dumbfounded at this unusual group of young girls. With his arms crossed, Hon-Pao stared east into the endless ocean, his eyes seemingly focusing on nothing.

The six girls were diving for pearls. They wore little to impede their work. A narrow piece of cloth covered their waists while also holding a rope that was tied to a small basket. Inside the basket, the fruit of their labor clanged noisily as the girls emptied them.

"Over here, Ko!" One of the girls exclaimed seeing Casca and Ko approach.

Unable to help themselves, Marco and Vittorio also approached.

"How are they, Osugi? Blue or silver?" Ko addressed one of the girls.

"A little bit of both. Maybe you brought us luck." The girl giggled as she emptied the contents of her basket. Filling the basket with a few rocks she stepped toward the water. For a moment she looked back, amused by Marco and Vittorio's unexpected reaction. Seeing them stand as if hypnotized, she whipped her head backward, throwing her waist-long hair to-

ward her back. She took one more glance, then disappeared
beneath the soft waves of the cove.

Ko crouched down and quickly picked out two of the
shelled creatures Osugi had brought up from the ocean. Seemingly for no reason she shook them and brought them to her
ears. Pleased with her findings she stood up, still holding the
two shells.

"I've heard of this, but . . ." Marco was unable to finish his
words as his thoughts left him. No longer a boy, he had still
not been able to get used to seeing women appear as these
girls did.

"They are beautiful," he continued, unable to tear his eyes
away from the unclad little sirens. Next to him, Vittorio
watched one of the other girls place a few rocks into her
basket and quickly disappear beneath the waters of the cove.

"They have been doing this since they were little girls."
Ko smiled as she tried to bring Marco and Vittorio back to
their senses. "Watch what they do," she continued. "Try holding your breath as long as they do. Next to that big rock the
water is very deep and the shells abundant, that is where they
have been diving since yesterday. The rocks in their baskets
help them sink faster to where the shells are. Once they reach
the bottom, they discard the rocks and fill their baskets with
shells. That is all. The girls move from site to site, trying to
find the best spots."

Standing ankle deep in water, his feet sinking into the golden
sand, Vittorio took a deep breath as one of the girls disappeared
underneath the choppy waves of the ocean. The other girls also
followed suit, carrying their baskets filled with rocks. In seconds all the divers were gone, leaving Marco and Vittorio to
struggle holding their breath and wait for them to reappear. In
less than a minute they were both gasping for air.

Taking Casca by the hand, Ko turned and headed away from
the shore, toward the side of the cliff they had descended.
Reaching a large flat rock, she placed the two shells upon it.

"These two." She pointed to the shells and took Casca's
short sword. Her obviously well-practiced hands quickly
opened the shells, exposing the strange flesh that quivered
beneath the blade. She stood with both shells in her hands
and faced Casca. Looking up, holding his eyes with her own,
she smiled.

Casca extended his left hand and held the side of her face. Ko closed her eyes and leaned against his hand, cradling it between her face and shoulder. Casca stroked her soft cheek with his hand and brought his thumb by her lips. Just as the tip of his thumb touched the wetness of her mouth, his own lip felt a singe of fire. She smiled as she took the content of both shells into her mouth. Stepping closer to Casca she raised to her toes, offering her lips to him.

They kissed passionately, the content of her mouth finding its way into his. His tongue searched her mouth, brushing against her tiny teeth and suddenly something unusual. Their kiss and embrace continued for a while longer until she stepped back. At the tip of her tongue two large pearls sparkled in the morning light. She held the circular stones between her fingers and raised them into the air.

"They are like your eyes." She once again spoke as she raised the two pearls into the path of the sun's rays. The blue-gray pearls rolled between her delicate fingers as she held her hand up.

Casca reached out and held her by her waist. Flexing his arms he brought her up once more toward his lips. She gasped as her feet left the sand, her words lost within his kiss. There was not much to say for now. Without knowing, both of their thoughts drifted back to over ten years past when they had first met. It had been a worthwhile wait.

Forgetting about all else for now they walked toward the rock face they had descended earlier. Taking a different route, they climbed over the rocks that time, the wind, and the ocean had rounded off. Within moments they reached a small ledge that led into a small cavern. Casca smiled, remembering the Cave of Dolhan where Tazrack had met them in the mountains of Pamir. Pleasure and pain had followed him halfway around the world.

Lowering his head slightly, Casca entered the small enclosure. His feet were met by warmth and the softness of an unusual greenish rock. Casca looked up hearing the flutter of wings yielded by the escape of a large white bird. Up above, a small opening allowed the sun's rays to enter, shining down on them, brightening the cave.

"I have come here ever since I was a little girl," Ko whispered while she sat on the warm floor. They embraced as her lips came to his ear. "I wanted you to be the first." Bringing herself closer, her slight body soon became lost within his arms. Feeling the strength of his arms and the hardness of his chest, she moaned, anxiously gasping for her breath to return.

Her admission was not needed as Casca could easily tell by her uncertain actions. Other than her kiss, Casca would need to lead her. It was not an undesirable task. They spent the rest of the day together, lost in the pleasures their solitude provided.

Night came quickly, awakening Casca from an afternoon slumber.

"I have brought you some cool water." Ko extended a small oval cup. She stood at the entrance to the cave and smiled. There was little that covered her, the simplicity of the slight white silk dress allowing Casca not to be distracted and thus be able to appreciate her perfection. A gentle breeze entered the cave, fluttering her dress, caressing her slight features. Her coal-black hair hung loosely over her shoulders, cascading with its richness, hypnotizing Casca's eyes. She was the magical beauty that every thousand years the creator decides to send as a gift to the ones made in his image. Casca's eyes drifted over her glorious face, allowing a smile to quickly appear on his own.

Only the presence of the new moon and the blanket of stars brought light to brighten the entrance to the cave. Over her shoulder, Casca watched the sickle of the new moon grip the dark background of the stars. A thin dark cloud drifted from east to west, crossing over the yellow band in the sky. The soft winds drifting over the ocean sounded behind her, adding to the serenity of the moment.

Suddenly Casca's own eyes darkened as events of the last ten years crowded in his mind. He closed his eyes and brought both his hands to his face. The memory of Nomukh standing behind Khaidu all those years ago, the imperial guard that had stood by the first day he had met Khubilai Khan, Thogor-Pa, the Zhong Tsai Zhe of the ordos, and the men who had attempted to assassinate him in the palace of Khanbalic, they all rushed through his thoughts. Reflection of those events swirled in his mind as he tried to reason everything that the appearance of the moon had rekindled.

Breaking the spell the uncertain reminiscence had created, Casca extended his hand toward Ko. The water was cool and refreshing. "Thank you," he assured Ko, seeing her worried face. There was no reason to burden her with his concerns for now.

She kneeled by him, taking a wet cloth to his chest. The wound had miraculously healed, his flesh reattaching without the need for sutures to pull at his lacerated skin. Ko kissed at his chest and traced the edge of his newest wound with her wet lips. Casca shivered slightly, surprised how her soft touch had reawakened his skin, soothing him, making him forget about his injuries and concerns. Ko turned her head, allowing her cheek to brush up against his chest. The slight flutter of her eyelashes sent waves of pleasure throughout his body as they fanned against his chest. Casca looked down and touched her lithe skin just as she once again wet his chest with her lips. The night and passion held them company until they eventually fell asleep.

Casca awakened just as the first light of the morning found its way into the cavern. Laying face down on the soft ground, he shifted his head and was happy to find Ko lying next to him. Just enough of the sun's rays had entered to display Ko's unclad beauty.

Ko turned her head and smiled her bewitching smile. She held Casca's eyes with her own, speaking to him without even the slightest of movements. Casca's breath left him, his mind and body exhausted by her passion and the lack of sleep. He sighed, disappointed that fatigue still held him in its grasp. For once he preferred rest.

Refusing to show disappointment, Ko shifted and arched her back, raising her backside into the air. The morning sunlight entered the opening of the cave, creating a glow around her naked form as her breasts brushed against the warm floor. Her long black hair spilled over her sides, hanging down until touching the ground. The flowing hair caught the warm breeze that came in from the ocean, the salty air momentarily biting at Casca's eyes. With a devilish smile on her face, she grinned at Casca, tempting him with all her beauty. Unable to help himself, Casca extended a hand toward her. Perhaps he was not as tired as he had thought.

•   •   •

Their stay along the coast was brief. It was time to leave if they planned to meet up with Chen-Chin who was returning from Korea. Casca watched Ko's eyes moisten while she said good-bye to her grandfather Akiro. Casca had learned to like the little old man; in many ways, he reminded Casca of his long-gone friend, Shiu Lao-tze. Like many who were hindered by the loss of sight, Akiro had never lost his ability to see the world around him and read the hearts of humanity.

The return to Khanbalic was without much strife as they traveled unhindered. Marco looked forward to returning to Khanbalic. Life on the road was full of excitement and adventure, yet nothing could compare to the richness and the hedonistic lifestyle he had gotten accustomed to in the palace of Khubilai. An audience with the Khan awaited him when he would tell of all he had seen. For years he had been the Khan's eyes, noting everything and informing the Khan of all there was in the empire. This unusual gift had greatly aided the Khan over the years, ever since he had first come to Shang-Tu nearly fifteen years ago. Khubilai had always well received Marco's astuteness and ability to recall perfectly all that he encountered.

Marco and Chen-Chin clasped hands and embraced upon their reunion, pleased to see each other and share stories of their adventures. Casca watched Marco, Chen-Chin, and Vittorio interlock their thumbs and fingers. It was something the two Venetian friends had never parted with, eventually bringing their new friend to be part of the circle.

"Man nah boni bang gup ta!" Chen-Chin greeted them.

"What are you saying?" Marco inquired.

Chen-Chin smiled. "It is Korean. Just a greeting for old friends."

"You speak their language?" Vittorio questioned in surprise.

"That and a lot more," Chen-Chin cheerfully answered. "The language came easily to me. It surprised me, too. Along with that, I have learned about a new way of planting rice and other plants, new irrigation systems, a way to oversee tax collection—"

"All that in just a few months?" Marco interrupted with surprise in his voice.

"My father will be proud of me. The son of the Khan should know all that he can know." Chen-Chin looked at

Casca, Marco, and Vittorio, awaiting their nods of approval. "He will be very pleased." Chen-Chin continued smiling, yet unable to hide a slight hesitation in his last words.

"Any father would," Marco answered for all of them, disappointed in himself for not finding a better way to answer Chen-Chin's concern. Too many times he had seen Chen-Chin disappointed as the Khan's attention lay far from Chen-Chin's heart.

The three of them continued their banter, telling of the excitement the road had brought them. By nighttime, the morning of pearl diving had been retold nearly a dozen times. For those few hours, the worries of the world were far away.

Casca did not take part in their lightheartedness. He rode side by side with Hon-Pao, the two of them exchanging few words. The concerns Casca held did not allow him rest or time for telling tales. There was much uncertainty about the future of the empire. Thoughts of the Brotherhood haunted Casca, as images from the last few years contoured his thoughts as he tried to decipher them.

At times Hon-Pao looked up toward Casca, clearly sensing his troubled thoughts. Ko mostly rode her own horse behind them, at times stealing glances of Casca, at all times anticipating his passionate touch. She was not unaware of his troubled contemplation of the last few days, though she was not about to interefere either. After all, the Old Young One had returned to lead.

Passing by the province of Ben-Cho brought back to them the misery and death the villages had suffered. Most of the tortured men had died by now, while the ones that had lived would have likely preferred death. At least Nayan had not returned to further torture the tortured.

The undisturbed travel of the last few weeks was quickly broken by the news that awaited them in Khanbalic. Two days before reaching the outskirts of imperial city, four envoys met up with them.

"The Khan needs you." The leader of the four addressed Casca once within range. The man bowed toward Chen-Chin and quickly begged forgiveness for not having received the future Khan of all Mongols in the proper manner. Once having bowed to Chen-Chin, the man gasped for air in his hurried effort to inform Casca.

"The king of Pagan has lost his mind. He has refused the orders of submission and—"

"For years my father has spoken of them." Chen-Chin interrupted while kicking the sides of his horse. "I fear the Burmese army will be very dangerous. I have heard they lead tens of thousands of elephants into battle."

Marco looked toward Chen-Chin, the thought of tens of thousands of giant elephants charging down a slope in an open field overwhelming him. If true, it would be an unstoppable force, the kind most of the world had never seen. They had all seen the power of even one such animal. Thousands of them would be more powerful than the armies of whole nations.

Without much fanfare, Casca, Vittorio, and Marco were led toward the war room upon their arrival. About a dozen men crowded the room, speaking to each other in hushed tones. The Khan had often spoken of Burma and the Kingdom of Pagan in this room. Finally, action would need to be taken against the king. Ignoring them, Casca stood by the giant map, scrutinizing the road toward the south and the kingdom of Pagan. Two weeks travel to the southwest would bring them into the scorching hot jungles of Burma.

"I see your wound has healed well," Nasir al-Din nodded toward Casca. "We will lead the forces of the Khan into battle. I can feel the blood of the beasts awaiting us. . . ." Nasir did not finish his thoughts as Khubilai Khan entered the war room, flanked by the empress Chabi.

"Welcome home, Old Young One. I need your wisdom." Khubilai tried acting calmly, attempting not to show his obvious frustration in the newest developments. "Only one has returned," the Khan continued while approaching his half brother Sando. The two of them spoke for a few minutes, ignoring everyone else for the time being.

Maffeo and Niccolo also entered the war room, Maffeo trying to refrain from his usual broad grin, while Niccolo was obviously anxious to see Marco.

Marco and his father embraced and held each other for a few seconds while they exchanged a few words. The time when they merely shook hands or nodded their heads was far in the past. Letting go of the embrace, Niccolo stepped back and smiled at his son. "I see you have grown a fine beard, maybe even a few gray hairs."

Marco smiled in mild embarrassment and stepped toward his father, laughing softly as they again embraced. Vittorio clasped hands with Maffeo as the two of them also exchanged a few words.

Standing next to Marco, Chen-Chin anxiously awaited for his father the Khan to approach. Unable to completely turn away from Marco and Niccolo, he sighed. Marco tried reading his friend's lips as a dejected Chen-Chin lowered his head.

"Welcome home, my son." Chabi quickly approached Chen-Chin, well aware there was not much that she could do. Once again, the Khan was preoccupied, barely aware that his own son was present. Chen-Chin continued his sad smile and embraced his mother, the empress. She returned his smile and stroked his face. "You have become even more handsome," she tried cheering him.

"Help him in!" Sando's orders quickly focused everyone's attention on one of the war room doors.

A wretched looking thing entered, flanked by two huge kesig guards. Bloody and tattered clothing hung from the walking dead as the man was helped to a chair. In silence the man sat, holding his hands to his chest, trying to find comfort in this impossible situation. He moaned endlessly while pieces of blackened blood spurted from his torn lips. Clumps of dried blood hung from his battered and deformed face as the man suffered behind the mask of pain. His hands, wrapped in cloth, hid some horrible wounds as both appendages appeared to have been severely damaged.

Marco and Vittorio stood quietly, their minds requiring a few moments longer to be able to tolerate man's brutality. "What could have done that?" Vittorio whispered to no one in particular.

"This is the message King Narathithapate of Burma has sent," Sando informed everyone in the room.

It was obvious the man did not need to bring any written word. The wounds that had been inflicted upon him spoke more than any written message. Never had any of Khubilai's envoys been treated such.

"Why does he not speak?" Marco shook his head while he shivered at the thought of the agony the man must have endured.

"He cannot," Casca answered, pointing to his own mouth.

It was true. The man could never speak again. His tongue had been ripped out of his mouth to forever torture him.

"The king must be punished!" Khubilai Khan gritted his teeth, unable to hold back his anger.

"The new envoys left for the Kaungai border state two days ago. Once there, they will meet up with King Narathithapate's retinue. The king of Burma will need to show much understanding if he expects to live," Sando offered, in the same controlled manner in which Khubilai had spoken.

"You will leave tomorrow morning," Khubilai ordered Nasir. "You, Old Young One, I ask that you go along. My grandfather, the father of all Mongols, told me of your knowledge. There is nothing that you have not experienced."

"He has told you of Hannibal."

"Yes, Old Young One. I remember as a young child hearing of the great general, Hannibal, crossing the mountains of the western world, nearly overtaking the Roman Empire. With his few elephants he was all but victorious, I . . ." Khubilai stopped his words realizing his voice had betrayed him. He had shown weakness and fear. The threat of the Burmese army had brought him great concern.

"It will be good to add some of the elephants to my forces," Khubilai continued, in a feeble attempt to undo his previously weak words.

"I will be honored to join the forces of the great Khubilai," Casca insisted, attempting to erase any weakness that might have been perceived.

"The empire will be victorious." Khubilai was not about to say any more. It was clear that the challenge had been made, a great challenge that could lead to the downfall of the Mongol empire. This was more than Nayan's revolt or the constant harassment of the Brotherhood. The king of Burma needed to be punished in a very decisive manner.

It was as if the earth had moved. The ground shook underneath the hooves of twenty thousand horses. Nasir al-Din and Casca rode side by side, leading the forces of Khubilai toward the south, toward certain confrontation. The faces of thousands of warriors did not hide what they all knew. Many, likely thousands of them, would never return to Khanbalic. If fortunate, the Eternal Blue Sky would receive them for their final resting place.

The southern heat soon met up with them, slowing down man and horse alike. Water was abundant, which helped, yet each step became a burden with the suffocating breath of the jungle air. Hunting for food had been quite easy, providing plenty of flesh for the Mongol army to feed on. Less lively and consuming not quite the usual amount of ayrag and beer, the feasts were not about to be left out. It was the only way for true Mongol warriors to exist.

Riding side by side, Casca and Nasir al-Din made their way up a hillside overlooking a vast plain. Waist-deep elephant grass extended to the horizon until disappearing in the dense forest.

"Two more days to Kaungai." Nasir al-Din extended his hand toward the southwest as he addressed one of his sub-commanders.

Casca and Nasir al-Din kicked at the sides of their horses as they entered the tall grass. Behind them, the unstoppable forces of Khubilai followed.

Casca reached for his forehead and wiped the sweat off his brow. Hesitating for a moment, he inhaled deeply. While tasting the air, his eyes narrowed. He turned toward Nasir who had slowed the pace of his horse. Their eyes met for an instant, which proved to be more than sufficient. Nasir had sensed the same. He nodded his head once as they both picked up the pace and rode ahead of the rest.

"What happened?" Marco questioned Vittorio and Hon-Pao. The two shook their heads.

Unsatisfied with the lack of an answer, Marco kicked at the sides of his horse and followed Casca and Nasir, forcing Vittorio and Hon-Pao to do the same. They all reached the edge of the forest at the same time and dismounted.

Casca took the reins of his warhorse and advanced slowly. Nodding his head just once, he signaled Nasir who also dismounted. They both gritted their teeth as they inhaled the sweetened air. A bead of sweat ran down between Nasir's eyes, forcing him to angrily shake his head.

"Up ahead, in that clearing." Casca pointed with his left hand.

Marco and Vittorio also dismounted and quietly followed.

Ahead of them, white smoke swirled among the trees, disappearing within the thick verdant leaves. Within the clearing, white rocks had been arranged in a circle, protecting the fire that had nearly died down.

Once again Casca and Nasir looked at each other. There was no mistaking what the feast had been. Long thick bones lay side by side, almost as if arranged in a particular fashion for anyone who would come upon them to see. The ends of the bones had been gnawed off and the marrow sucked out.

"Cannibals," Vittorio whispered.

Hon-Pao shook his head, suddenly realizing what they were witnessing.

Casca reached down and picked up a burned piece of a leather stirrup. He held it in his hands and faced Nasir whose face was covered with sour perspiration. Nasir had not been born of Mongol blood; yet having lived all his life amongst them had instilled within him what was forbidden. The Burmese had eaten the envoy's horses. It was an unforgivable sin. A Mongol would eat his own flesh before eating the flesh of his horse. The Burmese had committed the ultimate insult from which there was no redemption. As Khubilai had said: The king must be punished.

The five of them left the forest and rejoined the rest of the troops. Heading farther south, they paralleled the edge of the forest. Slowly the trees thinned out, allowing all of Nasir's men to work their way toward a certain clash of forces. They did not travel more than an hour before Casca stiffened in his saddle and stood up in his stirrups. Once more he tasted the air.

Imperceptible at first, a queasy feeling overtook both he and Nasir as they advanced. Nasir took ever-quickening breaths, once more the taste of the air making his thoughts spin. It was not long before it showed itself.

A horrid stench soon battered their senses as they continued moving. It clung to the ground, like an entity in itself traveling over it, anxious to burrow itself into everyone's mind. The putrid smell of death engulfed them as they continued farther into Burmese territory. It was as if the air had been poisoned, suffocating them, preventing even a moment's rest. Rubbing at their burning eyes, Marco and Vittorio moved on, hoping their next breath would be a reprieve.

They could see nothing but a few small trees and bushes that interrupted the even flow of the land. Casca reached down and picked up a stained yellow flower. Its white petals held the blood of war. Farther ahead, flesh separated from its owner hung within the prickly jagged edges of a yenser bush. With the tip of his sword, Nasir lifted the rotting flesh from the bark of a tree. As they continued, pieces of Khubilai's doomed envoys littered the land.

"They must have dragged them through the thorns until they all perished." Vittorio shook his head, sickened by the sight and smell that hovered over them.

"Couldn't be," was all Marco could say, witnessing the trail of blood. He looked around, trying to make sense of the way these men had died. There were no obvious hoof marks or signs pointing where the men had been dragged to their deaths.

"Maybe tigers devoured them." Marco tried finding an answer that would satisfy.

Casca and Nasir continued riding, at times stopping to point out more signs of death.

"They were hacked with iron hammers," Vittorio concluded, seeing bent and crushed bones on a flat rock. The ends of arm and leg bones had been forced open, their contents allowed to spill over the rock. The vermin that followed had been summoned by the stain and stench of human debris. Next to this sight that demanded of nightmares, Marco and Vittorio cringed while they looked at other pieces of flesh that were covered by hungry and noisy flies.

They continued riding amongst the pieces of rotting meat and shards of bone. Soon they came upon half a dozen waist-high bushes, which held more decaying debris. Strips of flesh and sinew had been ripped and displayed as an obvious message.

Once again Casca and Nasir exchanged glances.

"How did they die?" Vittorio questioned, realizing the bushes covered with the flesh of the envoys had no thorns.

"Best not to know." Nasir shook his head, trying to hold the truth from Marco and Vittorio.

Casca reached down and picked up a piece of rotting skin. Holding it on the tip of his long sword he looked at Nasir. "They were not killed with weapons."

"I knew it; tigers must have ambushed them all," Marco once again suggested.

"No, Marco, they were killed by men." Nasir reasoned there was no sense in withholding the truth.

Marco lifted his hands while still holding the reins and shook his head. A tear came to his eye that he quickly wiped away. "How?"

"They were ripped to shreds, torn apart piece by piece. Their bones were used to disembowel and crush every part of their own bodies. No weapons had been used. Only hands." Casca concluded.

Marco and Vittorio cringed in horror. They had seen enough death for a dozen lifetimes, yet they could have never imagined the horrible cruelty and obscenity of using one's own hands to kill and shred a man's body to pieces. Marco let go of the reins and looked at his own hands. "They will never reach the Eternal Blue Sky," he mumbled.

It was the first time Vittorio had heard his friend speak of the Eternal Blue Sky as something other than pagan foolishness and obscenity. Even he understood. The Burmese had made certain that the envoys were so punished as never to be able to reach their final resting place. Their torn pieces lay spread out across the plains and forests, their souls lost forever in a hostile land.

"We are very close." Nasir kicked at the sides of his horse and moved ahead of them. The manner by which the envoys had been killed was inexcusable. It was best for now to continue moving.

They rode for two more hours before anyone spoke. Casca reached for his neck and wiped the perspiration away. It was not the suffocating heat of the previous days that had brought the fever. The battle was near. He held his fingertips against his neck, feeling the pounding of his blood. It was going to be a battle unlike any. The memory of a hundred wars rushed through his mind and the thousands, perhaps millions, he had seen perish.

Pulling back on the reins of their horses, both Nasir and Casca looked ahead. A wide plain opened up ahead of them beyond which lay the Mekong River. Farther southeast, the northern portion of Burma signaled the end of their journey.

There the giant armies of King Narathithapate and Khubilai Khan would clash.

By late afternoon they had easily traversed the region and crossed the Mekong. It had been quiet, without any signs of a Burmese resistance or advance scouts.

"Beyond that valley." Nasir pointed south toward an immense bamboo forest that formed the northern border of the probable field of battle. Khubilai's twenty thousand men made their way down the slight incline, finally setting camp within the forest. A broad valley plain opened up beyond the forest, gradually elevating to the east and west, finally flattening out to the south. The arena awaited them.

The heavily wooded forest eventually thinned out, allowing Nasir's men enough room to feed and maneuver their horses. The deep grass that covered the plain was thinner and shorter within the forest where the shade created by the trees stifled its growth. It was a good place to rest before battle.

By nightfall it became apparent that the enemy awaited them beyond the great plain. The trumpeting of elephants and many campfires did not at all help hide their location. It was also unlikely it had been their desire to do so. The Burmese knew quite well that none had ever warred against an army such as theirs. If the sound of the elephants sent fear to their enemies, the greater their advantage would be.

Casca and Nasir al-Din sat by their own campfire, enjoying the cool water that washed down their meal. Quietly sitting next to them, Marco and Vittorio gritted their teeth in near panic and fear, questioning why they had so foolishly decided to come along. Marco wondered if they would ever see Chen-Chin again. By orders of Khubilai, Chen-Chin and his son Temur had stayed within the safety of Khanbalic.

Sensing their disquiet, Nasir caught Marco's wide-eyed stare. "The great Khan would be disappointed if you do not return to Khanbalic."

"Will anyone of us return?" Marco finally spoke.

"You and your friend should not take part in this," Nasir suggested. "I will have you positioned toward the rear. I do not want to upset the Khan."

"We will stay," Marco answered for both himself and Vittorio. "The Great Khan will want my report as usual. I do not want to disappoint."

"Neither do I. You will stay here, within the forest, or head toward the eastern higher ground where the elephants are certain not to go," Nasir ordered, certain that Marco and Vittorio would not be displeased. If all went well, they could observe the whole field of battle without risking their lives. This battle was not for the weak. Meekly, Marco and Vittorio quieted, not at all discontented.

They all sat, attempting to ignore the strident sounds of thousands of elephants that seemed to be not far off. Looking toward the edge of the forest, Casca held his long blade and tapped the side of a bamboo sapling. Thousands of the saplings, not much thicker than Casca's wrist, made up much of the forest. Farther within the forest, older and thicker trees dominated, darkening the area. Beyond them to the south, the elephant grass covered the ground for thousands of feet.

"We will need to draw them into the forest, where the charge of the beasts will not aid them," Nasir addressed Casca. Not getting any response, Nasir stood and looked out toward the grass-covered plain. Casca also stood next to Nasir and watched the waist-deep grass that bent in the evening breeze.

"I will have a thousand archers within these trees. From that height their arrows will reach much farther than these Burmese savages expect. I also have a little surprise for the elephants." Nasir grinned at his last comment. "It should be enough to give us an advantage." Nasir nodded his head, apparently pleased at his own design. He furrowed his brow seeing Casca shake his head.

"The elephants will need to enter the forest, yet not know it," Casca answered while touching the side of his blade with his left thumb.

"They will never charge their animals into the forest. All we can hope for is to slow them down." Nasir turned his head toward Casca, trying to reason what this battle-scared man was thinking.

Casca continued shaking his head. "It is doubtful they will charge if we are not in the clear. I will need a thousand men."

They worked through the night preparing for battle. Time was fleeting. It was unlikely that much diplomacy would be employed the following day. The charge of the elephants needed to be met with force and cunning.

"Over there." Casca pointed south toward the Burmese camp while sitting on his horses at the edge of the forest. Morning had come swiftly with barely a few hours of rest.

"I see." Nasir sat high in the saddle, watching a lone rider approach. It was difficult to see who the rider was, and it did not much matter. Khubilai and the king of Burma did not mobilize an army of tens of thousands just to discuss peace. If anything, it was a last attempt to disconcert and infuriate the army of Khubilai.

A lone figure appeared beyond the sea of grass. He moved slowly and awkwardly, weaving through the high grass as he made his way toward Casca and Nasir. The face of death approached. Nasir quickly recognized the man. It was one of the envoys sent by Khubilai, presumably the last one still alive.

The man's face had been savaged. Not just by the brutal hands of the Burmese, but by what they had allowed it to become. Flies swarmed around the unclad body of the man while maggots ate the flesh of the nearly dead man. His eyes were empty and his face ripped free of skin as nothing but the filthy vermin that ate away the flesh of the dead occupied it. His chest and neck had been slashed and opened to these beasts that ate away at this tortured man prematurely. He had not been allowed to die before the disciples of the afterworld started their foul work.

Nasir unsheathed his sword and ended the man's agony. No one deserved to suffer so. The Burmese had guaranteed themselves a horrible journey into death. Nasir signaled to two of his men. The ropes that had held the wretched soul tied to the saddle fell beneath Nasir's blade as the man was taken off his horse. The fallen envoy would be returned to Khanbalic for a proper burial. Unlike all his brethren that had been killed and bodies spread over the land, he would be rewarded with a burial and a journey into the Eternal Blue Sky.

The earth shook beneath the pounding of thousands of feet. It had begun. Casca raised his head and looked toward the south. Far away, at the edge of the grass plain, the great beasts had started their charge. Thousands of elephants had begun their march, spanning nearly the whole width of the field. The Burmese commanders had expanded their ranks to the sides, making certain no one could escape the wave of his forces. Unless the Khan's armies fled north into the woods, they would be decimated to the last man and horse.

Nasir turned and allowed a slight smile to appear on his face. He held the grip of his sword and waited. Within minutes the sound of drums, gongs, and the trumpeting of the elephants traveled along the field of battle, assaulting the ears and minds of the Mongol army. Ten thousand of Khubilai's best calmly stood their ground in the open field, awaiting orders.

The headlong charge of the Burmese accelerated as they approached the forces of Khubilai. The tusks of the beasts had been covered with sheets of shiny metal that bounced the rays of the sun, creating the image of thousands of swords slashing through the high grass. Hanging on either side of the animals, long handled spikes and maces swayed with every movement.

Casca could see half a dozen men standing on top of each elephant, anxiously waiting for the moment when they could launch their arrows. With their elbows resting on the wooden tower each elephant carried, they added to the intensity of the moment with their own war cries. Their faces painted in the colors of war distorted from their howls as they cheered on the behemoths. Many of them laughed with delight at the sight of the soldiers ready to stand up to them, ignorantly standing completely unprotected in front of the forest. Sitting on top of the howdah, the leather and brass saddle each beast carried, the mahouts ordered the elephants into a full gallop, anxious to quickly crush the foolish Mongols. It was their undoing.

The charge of thousands of monstrous elephants entered what had been the forest five hundred feet before they ever reached the forces of Khubilai. During the night, following Casca's orders, the area of the forest adjacent to the grass-covered field had been cleared, as thousands of bamboo trees and saplings had been cut down to within two feet of the ground, leaving a sea of sharp spikes that hid within the grass. Although thinner than in the open field, sufficient grass was present to hide the swords of death. Rolling out of control like an avalanche in winter, the charging elephants met their demise.

A scream out of nightmares shook the valley as the first wave of charging beasts reached the field of sharpened spikes.

By hundreds they collapsed as the pointed bamboo trunks ripped at the unprotected soles of their feet, sending them to the ground, impaling the riders and the bellies of the elephants themselves. The ones behind them collapsed over their own kind as the momentum of the charge prevented them from slowing their attack.

The moment the first beasts reached the hidden forest of spikes, Nasir's men released their arrows. Thousands of shafts whistled through the air, carrying more than just barbed arrows. The morning sky darkened momentarily before the arrows found their marks. Nasir had learned from the Chinese about the burning powder.

The flaming arrows carried more than just fire. Falling to the ground, the little packets of powder that had been carefully tied to each arrow burst into flames, engulfing the dried elephant grass. The eastern and western portion of the valley sprung up walls of fire, clearly maddening the charging beasts, forcing many of them to turn. The few that had been able to halt their advance turned to be swallowed up by the burning grass, or retreated where they trampled upon their own cavalry and foot soldiers.

Insanity overtook the thousands of panicked beasts. What the Burmese commanders had expected to be an easy victory became the beginning of a horrible defeat within minutes. The sound of all living things filled the valley, drowning out any orders anyone would have given. Nasir's men needed no commands while the Burmese forces could have followed none.

The flesh of men, horses, and elephants intermixed within the sea of sharpened spikes, all creatures writhing in pain and insanity. The ones not pierced by the razor-sharp spikes were trampled by the crush of the charging elephants. Stumbling and collapsing they were impaled and disemboweled, draining their life juices into the pit of death. Time seemed to stand still as the avalanche of the falling continued until the mountain of flesh prevented the further advance of any more men or beasts. Hungrily the earth soaked up the life that had been spilled.

Finally able to turn within this chaos, a portion of the Burmese army attempted to regroup. With fire on two sides and a mountain of flesh behind them, they formed pockets of resistance, ready to defend or lead a new charge. Defiantly they fashioned a defensive posture, ready to repel the Mongol horde. But not for long. It was time for Nasir's men to attack. The Burmese commander would need to learn a lesson never to be forgotten. Taking five thousand men each around the pool of death, Casca and Nasir led their attack on the remaining Burmese forces. For now the elephants would be of no concern.

The nearly overwhelmed Burmese forces tried standing their ground one last time. However, they had lost all expected advantage. Still greatly outnumbering the Khan's troops, they attempted to seize an uncertain victory, more likely to save themselves. It was not to be. Cavalry and foot soldiers met the forces of Khubilai on this day of madness.

Leading the attack, Casca led his men down the incline of the land, outflanking the startled soldiers. At the same time, Nasir's men joined the battle from the west, forcing a fight to the death as most of the Burmese army had been trapped. Casca's arm wielded his long sword, hacking through the opposition, leading a clear path through for the rest of the men to follow. Bodies of men and horses fell by the wayside as the two armies battled. Separated from the thousands of elephants, the Burmese foot soldiers and cavalry were quickly outmatched.

Groups of them tried holding their ground, using their long spears to hold off horses, yet without much success. Slowly they fell to the swords of the Mongol horde, while a few fortunate ones were able to retreat. Thousands battled on into the afternoon, unknowing of their fate as all communication had been lost. The strong survived while the weak would be no more. It was as old as time itself.

By nightfall, only the cries of the wounded broke the silence. Marco and Vittorio quietly sat by the campfire watching Casca and Nasir tend to their wounds. It had been a great victory, yet much blood had been spilled on both sides. For now hostilities would not continue; however, it was unlikely that peace could ever be. Revenge ruled the human soul here as well as anyplace else.

EIGHTEEN

The return to Khanbalic was long as the wounded hindered the pace they were able to take. Behind them, hundreds of elephants were led north to the court of Khubilai. It was a bounty as few others. Khubilai had been right all along about the Burmese threat. It was a country of millions that could assemble a formidable army. Good fortune had been on their side with the help of Casca. Once again the history of a nation turned as Casca had found himself within another conflict. The future of Burma and the Mongol empire was uncertain, yet for now the threat had been turned back. As great of a defeat as it had been, their conflict was likely not over.

As they progressed north, they left behind the stifling heat of the jungle, allowing them a reprieve. Nights were filled with celebration, food, and drink as any nights that the Mongol army enjoyed. It was a joyous return to Khanbalic, the victorious forces having decisively beaten back the Mongol empire's greatest threat.

Casca and Nasir returned to a city darkened by sadness. The usual song and celebration that always awaited a returning army were absent. Chen-Chin, the crown prince, was dying. He had fallen ill two nights previous, the grip of fever and convulsions overtaking his body.

Khubilai Khan, the Khan of the world, quietly stood within the shadows of Chen-Chin's room. Hunched over and head hanging down he listened to his son's labored breathing. Khubilai appeared much older than his years, the hard living and now the agony of impending loss draining and testing him to his limits. Overtaken by his son's impending death had left him nearly paralyzed. With hollow and depleted eyes he watched the saddest of moments.

Next to Khubilai, Thogor-Pa held a tray with a pitcher of cold water. Clearly aware of the Khan's sorrow, he kept silent, only speaking in hushed tones when spoken to. At times he extended a wet cloth to the empress to soothe the fever that seemed to be torturing Chen-Chin's head.

"Get that pillow away from him," Chabi angrily demanded, seeing her son gasp for air. His fevered head could not find comfort within the gold-tasseled silk pillows. "Cold water, he is burning up. Someone get him some water!" Chabi insisted with obvious terror in her voice. Listening to her panicked request, Thogor-Pa once again handed a new piece of wet cloth.

Beneath golden silk sheets, Chen-Chin clung to life, at times shaking uncontrollably, at other times vacantly looking into nothingness. The darkness of his eyes, becoming more vacant by the minute, did not bode well for him. He shook his head as if wanting to escape the clutches of death.

At the foot of Chen-Chin's bed, Temur kneeled, his head buried in his hands. At times he looked up toward his father, desperately hoping to see a sign of recovery. He groaned and shook seeing his father suffer such.

Casca watched everyone's saddened eyes as they all stood by. Chabi and Temur kneeled by Chen-Chin's bed, hoping for a miracle. Farther behind them, Sando gripped at the handle of his sword, clenching his teeth, snorting the hot air of the room. He shook his head seeing Casca.

"I just don't know. It can't be," Sando repeated endlessly.

"How long?" Casca whispered.

"Two days ago Chen-Chin and I went riding. The same as we have done hundreds of times." Sando whispered to Casca, trying not to disturb the quiet of the room.

"He rode his white stallion as always. Just as he jumped a small brook by the willow trees, he unexpectedly fell hard. It didn't seem to be that bad, just a few scratches on his face and neck, nothing else. Maybe a little embarrassment." Sando tried controlling his emotions. "Nothing more. We continued riding until dusk. By the time . . ."

Hon-Pao and Ko entered the room, quietly waiting in case the empress needed anything. Draped in her grandfather's embrace, Ko quietly sobbed watching all the suffering.

"By nightfall he had taken ill," Sando continued. "That was two nights ago. Ever since then he has been gripped by fever and convulsions. No one knows what had overtaken his body."

Casca stepped closer to the bed and looked down on Chen-Chin. The young prince tried a faint smile.

"You were victorious. The Old Young One truly has returned to the empire. The empire will forever be strong for . . ." Chen-Chin coughed and rubbed at his neck. "It tastes so bitter," he complained.

"Don't talk, save your strength." The teary voice of Chabi tried helping her dying son.

"My friends, come closer. Don't be worried, I do not carry any sickness." Chen-Chin raised his head and spoke to Marco and Vittorio who had been quietly standing a few feet away.

"There is a lot more you need to teach me Chen-Chin." Marco smiled as he extended his hand toward the bed.

Vittorio also reached out as the three of them clasped their fingers, forming the ring of friendship. All was not well, yet it was the closest bond the three of them had with each other. Exhausted by the effort, Chen-Chin's head fell back into the pillow while his arm hung down by the side of the bed. Dragging his hand under the cover, Chen-Chin once again rubbed at his neck.

Casca's eyes narrowed as he searched for something he had hoped would not be true. The words of Nasir came back to haunt him as he remembered what the commander of Khubilai's forces had told him about the Brotherhood.

Casca stood as his eyes caught those of Sando. An eerie quiet settled in on Chen-Chin's room. They all stood motionless, awaiting for Casca to speak. Casca reached for his own neck as he stood in silence.

"The tea that you love, maybe that will help the bitter taste." Vittorio attempted to help, somehow oblivious to what was happening. Hearing the suggestion, Ko quickly left the room to bring the honeyed tea that she had often seen the young prince enjoy.

"Treachery! That is what I see," Casca said, surprising everyone. He reached for Chen-Chin's neck. "Amongst these scrapes I see the hand of sedition." Casca reached for his own neck, his fingers tracing the two tiny scars left by a snake's fangs over a millennium ago. The bitter taste of the poison returned to his lips. He looked out at anyone who would make eye contact. It was clear, yet he needed to wait.

Casca could hear Khubilai's shallow breathing begin to intensify. Sando took a step forward and looked down on Chen-Chin's perspiration covered neck. "Treachery!" he whispered as he looked up at Casca. Behind Chen-Chin's left ear, a perfectly round pinhole was hidden within the scrapes. The mark of a poison dart.

They both turned and faced everyone else who stood within the room.

"I got it, right here. Plenty of spice and honey in it, just—" Ko was unable to complete her words as Thogor-Pa's left hand and forearm engulfed her neck.

The merciless blade of the assassin blended into the poorly lit room as Thogor-Pa had drawn the black sword. The tray of tea spilled by her feet as Ko was slammed against the doorway. Unable to cry for help she tried pushing her assailant away. Her tiny hands were able to do little, yet enough. Fighting for her life she grabbed for Thogor-Pa's chest and pulled on his clothes.

A dark triangular scar showed itself on Thogor-Pa's chest. It was not the first time Casca had seen the mark. The mark of the Brotherhood, hidden all these years from the Khan and everyone around him, had been exposed. Treachery came from within the empire.

"You will let her go," Casca barked at Thogor-Pa. He stepped forward, within just a few feet of the traitor.

The instant that followed horrified and left its mark in Casca's mind and heart for the next century. The black blade, veiled by the shadow and light of Chen-Chin's candlelit room, slashed at Ko. In an instant she fell to the ground, frantically holding her blood covered neck. Thogor-Pa's actions had been sufficient for him to flee. He ran through the doorway and disappeared into the night. There would be no way of finding him. Undoubtedly the myriad dark passageways that crisscrossed beneath the palace of Khubilai would give him safe haven, for now. She would be avenged.

Casca crouched by Ko's fallen body. He desperately tried holding back the flow of blood, yet without success. Within moments his hands and arms were covered by the red stain of death. Just as countless times before, someone Casca had cared for would leave him, the pain of her death to scar him forever, worse than the ripping of his own flesh.

"Kokoro, my little heart, don't leave me. Please don't, I

have no one left." Hon-Pao cried on his knees as he watched life drain from Ko's face.

"I am sorry gung-gung. I love you . . ." Ko's words to her grandfather became indistinguishable as blood flooded her throat.

Casca tried holding back the blood, pushing harder against her neck, clearly realizing that her wounds could not be remedied. Within his hands he found a thin leather strap that held an object.

"I will miss you, I will always love . . ." There were no more words that came from Ko, yet her thoughts and wishes would forever leave their mark in the hearts of those who stood present.

Seeing the end, Casca embraced Ko, allowing her still bleeding body to overflow his. He softly kissed her bloodied lips, making her part of himself. Holding her with his left arm he felt something clinging to his right hand. Twisted within his fingers he found a small leather pouch that had been nestled against Ko's slight neck. It held the two blue-gray pearls.

The room fell silent. Nothing could be heard but Hon-Pao's cries of the grieving grandfather. Hon-Pao had outlived all his family. There was no one left. The worst possible punishment would torture him to his last days.

Casca stood and looked at his hands. None dared make eye contact with him in this moment of misery. *"Good-bye my love . . ."* He heard Ko's voice once again as a warm wave rose from her fallen body and clouded his mind. Casca shook his head from the uncertain feeling, trying to return to the reality of this day. Hearing Chen-Chin's cough, his mind resharpened. With a heavy heart he approached the fallen prince's bed.

"I will join her on her journey." Chen-Chin grimly stated while attempting a weak smile.

"My son. You cannot." Khubilai Khan finally spoke, suddenly realizing that death had found its way into this room. The harvester of souls was also about to take his son. He kneeled by Chen-Chin's bed. Next to him Chabi sobbed while resting her head next to Chen-Chin's face. Her cheek felt the burning of her son's pain.

"I want to ride the white horse with you," Chen-Chin whispered to his father. Khubilai closed his eyes and shuddered, his son's words flooding his mind from the past. His whole world collapsed in on him as everything that he had been about became unimportant. Thoughts of the empire disappeared as he held his son's trembling hands.

"I want to ride with you, father." It was the last words Chen-Chin spoke. The desire to be with his father would never be fulfilled. A single tear to be followed by many found its way from Khubilai's saddened eye, trailing into his white beard.

Nothing more was spoken. Even the sun joined in on this day, almost as if the sky darkened without even a single cloud. The Eternal Blue Sky received another soul.

NINETEEN

Dark days followed in the capital of the Mongol empire. Chen-Chin, the victim of a cowardly act, would be buried. The empire suddenly had no successor. A single dart had found its mark, changing the future of the world.

Shrouded in the darkness that only a wounded heart could bring, Khubilai mourned his son. No one, including Chabi, had spoken to him since the previous day. No one had dared. Hidden from the world, he sat facing the polished metal mirror in front of him. An old man looked back from the reflection, a frustrated and saddened man. He had lost something that had been so obvious and clear all these years, yet he had been blind to it. Khubilai had lost the love of his son. Strangely, the pain of his loss had found a certain calmness that would eventually turn into the death of thousands.

There was but one thing that would ever so slightly remedy the horror of what had so punished Khubilai. Nasir reported the only news Khubilai was willing to hear. Nayan and the forces of the Brotherhood were amassing their armies. The great Khan of the Mongol's was ready to fall. Or so they thought.

No one could have recognized the man that took the reins to the Khan's white horse the following day. It was as if time had turned back nearly half a lifetime, giving renewed strength and vigor to Khubilai. The blood of his ancestors flowed through his body, awakening every reserve of strength.

Quietly he rode along, his face impassive, all the rage of the world buried deep within him. The immensity of his wrath boiled inside, tempered by something no one could understand, or want to have let loose on them. The thousands of warriors who followed along, usually loud and boisterous, men whose voices raged and weapons banged endlessly against each other, had strangely taken their leader's quiet somberness as their own. As if a wave had spread through the troops, the Khan's demeanor had hypnotized all of them, their own quiet allowing them an understanding of the empire's fortunes. The Great Khan had been challenged, the future of the world was about to be decided in the field of battle.

Next to the Khan, Casca existed in his own hell, relentlessly reliving Ko's bloody death, and angered for allowing himself to open his heart. A dozen centuries had not been enough to teach him a lesson. Every time he had given of himself, his curse had returned, ripping another loved one from his heart. Casca looked at his reddened hands, the stain of Ko's death reminding him of her untimely departure from this world. Much blood would join it before it was all over. Only the cold blood of his enemies would help wash away the wretchedness of that fateful day.

The army of Khubilai flowed north, following the path toward the Mongol homeland. Nayan had returned north toward Kharakorum, hoping to find reinforcements and recruit new men for his cause.

"At least one hundred men are about six hours ahead of us, heading in the same direction," one of Nasir al-Din's advance scouts informed the Khan.

Khubilai nodded and returned to his own musing. Thogor-Pa, the Khan's most trusted, the Zhong Tsai Zhe who had mediated and settled hundreds of disputes for the ordos, was fleeing north, trying to escape the wrath of Khubilai. The world was not large enough for this traitor. Khubilai would see to that.

Riding behind Nasir al-Din, Marco whispered, "I am sure we are heading into a trap. Nayan will no doubt know the Khan has mobilized thousands of his troops."

"It will not matter," Nasir simply answered.

Hearing Nasir's answer Marco looked at the Great Khan. The quiet intensity of Khubilai told of the same. Other than the gods themselves, all would fall at the feet of the Khan's army.

Marco had been right. Ten day's journey north brought them to their destination. Nayan had dug in defensive positions all along a wide plain and had rested his troops. He patiently awaited the Khan's forces. There would be no surprise over anyone's actions.

With Khubilai Khan leading the attack, the infernal battle pitting Mongol brother against brother, and father against son, was about to commence. No messengers were sent as there was nothing to debate. The empire was at the crossroads.

Khubilai sat high in the saddle, his right hand holding a sword while with his left he signaled for his troops to advance. He was not the old broken man of a few days ago, bent and decrepit, only anxious for his next meal or afternoon of rest. Khubilai had returned to his youth of fifty years past when riding all day to reach a battlefield was no more of an effort than breathing the air.

The Great Khan screamed into battle, his eyes ablaze, the pain of his broken heart leading him forward. Nothing was going to stand in his way as a lifetime of dreams had been upturned by the poisoned tip of an assassin's dart. The loss of his son could never be remedied no matter how many would soil the land with their blood, yet it was the only way for the Khan of Khans.

Countless thousands roared into the middle of the field, the sound of their voices drowning out the thunder of drums, gongs, and whistles that always accompanied the charge of a Mongolian army. Blood would run like the streams of spring.

The Khan's blade was the first one to meet steel as he had spurred his white horse ahead of all his men, anxious to clash with the enemy. With three quick thrusts of his own sword, Casca felled the first three men who had dared challenge him. Whether it was three or three thousand men trying to contain them, he would find Thogor-Pa amongst Nayan's forces. There was nowhere to hide on this day.

In a matter of seconds the Khan's horse was no longer white, the blood of a dozen men having painted it the color of death. Khubilai wielded his blade like the sickle of the autumn harvest. Relentlessly he surged forward, felling men by his wayside as he and Casca created a wedge within Nayan's defending forces.

"Ahead, by the trees!" Casca warned Khubilai as the two of them continued to reach deeper and deeper into Nayan's defenses. Leading his horse by the pressure on the stirrups and the tightening of his calves, Khubilai turned and faced the direction of Nayan's tent. Many stood in his way, hoping that the shear weight of their defense could contain the attack. It was a futile effort on their part.

Ignoring his own kesig guards, Khubilai pushed on with Casca fighting side by side. Sando followed along, trying to do all that he could to preserve the Khan's safety. It was an impossible task, yet he was not about to attempt to reason with the Khan. Khubilai's long white hair had become loose, flowing down toward his shoulders, whipping side to side with every swing of his blade. Not unlike a demon out of hell, this maddened pallid creature descended on its prey, bringing the fury of unrelenting revenge as its ally.

It was not long before Nayan's men fell to their heels, overwhelmed by the intensity and savageness of Khubilai's attack. Seeing their own leader fighting with such ferocity, the Khan's troops accelerated their own attack, further pushing and dismantling Nayan's ranks.

"Ahead!" Casca's voice focused Khubilai's sight about fifty feet behind Nayan's tent. A group of forty or fifty warriors shielded Nayan and apparently a few of his closest advisors. Casca's heart pounded with greater intensity as Thogor-Pa's location became a certainty. A bitter smile found its way onto Casca's lips.

Leading the charge, Casca and Khubilai made certain they were the first to reach Nayan's last remaining pocket of resistance. Wiping the splattered blood of his most recent victim from his face, Sando followed along. Standing defiant, Nayan still stood cowardly behind the last five of his men. His few remaining guards softened the earth with their life juices as they bled into the ground, foolishly having attempted to turn back Casca's blade. Swords crossed momentarily followed by cries of help as the five outmatched defenders crashed as if their bones had been pulled from within their legs. Like sacks of meat thrown off a wagon they rolled haphazardly at their commander's feet. Stripped of all his defense, Nayan tried holding Khubilai at bay.

"You cannot kill me, cousin. You cannot spill the blood of your own family," Nayan protested as he stood next to Thogor-Pa.

Casca met Thogor-Pa's venomous eyes. They looked fiercely into each other's souls, instantly to be horrified by what they saw. Thogor-Pa was about to die in a horrible manner.

"You have betrayed the name of the Genghis. You are no longer a Mongol." Nayan foolishly protested, somehow hoping to save his own miserable skin.

"Chen-Chin is dead." Casca knew Khubilai would speak no more. The Khan ordered for his men to approach. Nayan's eyes widened in disbelief seeing three of the Khan's men carrying a large rectangular carpet.

"Your traitorous blood will not soil the land of the Khan." Nasir al-Din stared down at Nayan as he directed his men.

Nayan's arms fell by his sides, finally realizing that the end was near. He stepped forward, allowing himself to be placed in the middle of the black and red carpet. In moments he had been imprisoned in the ceremonial shackles of his forbearers. Khubilai would not spill the blood of his ancestors that reached all the way back to the father of the empire, Genghis Khan.

Quickly Nayan was lost within the rolled-up carpet, only the tip of his head showing itself on one end. Khubilai bowed his head, signaling for his men to proceed. Death came quickly and without mercy as Sando led a dozen of Khubilai's riders, trampling the body of Nayan beneath the hooves of their horses' feet. Nayan needed to be forgotten as he had brought enough misery to the empire.

All the while Casca held Thogor-Pa with his eyes. Nayan's quick death had been expected. Thogor-Pa would enjoy no such luxury. The last four of Thogor-Pa's men, cloaked men dressed in the garb of the brotherhood, stood with drawn swords. Signaling a dozen of his men, Nasir called for the execution of the four.

"No." Casca raised his sword.

The four defenders were no match for Casca's fury. Sweeping their cloaks, trying to hide their blade, or disorient their adversary, they attempted to turn back Casca's attack. Within seconds their bodies littered the blood-soaked dirt at Casca's feet.

"You cannot kill . . ." Thogor-Pa was unable to complete his predictable words. It mattered not that he could become a martyr, a symbol for the Mongol army to revolt and return to a past way of being.

Thogor-Pa's neck lay engulfed within Casca's left hand. The two searched each other's eyes, trying to find something unforeseen. It was a simple matter of revenge and death. Thogor-Pa's life would end in short order.

Casca calmly stood in front of Thogor-Pa and raised his long blade to the traitor's neck. This was no time for hesitation, yet Casca lowered his blood-covered sword. A curious and pleased look appeared on Thogor-Pa's face as he misread Casca's intent.

"Too easy to die," Casca hissed, realizing that bleeding Thogor-Pa's filthy blood would not satisfy. The vise around Thogor-Pa's tightened, causing him to cough then hold his breath. Within seconds no more blood flowed to his brain, making him writhe in agony.

The sound of his broken neck signaled the end of his miserable existence as Casca allowed the lifeless body to fall and soil the ground. Thogor-Pa would rot in this field, to be forgotten.

The return to Khanbalic was without celebration. It was perhaps the first time ever that a victorious Mongol army did not rejoice and celebrate. It had been a hollow and unsatisfying reprisal. Nayan and Thogor-Pa had been punished, yet neither Chen-Chin nor Ko could ever be avenged. Their death could not be remedied. Chen-Chin would be mourned for years, every one of Khubilai's waking moments to be tortured by his own blind foolishness. The one thing that did not require an army to conquer, the love of his son, he had lost and would never be able to regain. For that he would never be able to absolve himself.

"Now? How can you ask me of such a thing?" Niccolo and Maffeo faced Khubilai Khan while kneeling on a marble step.

They knew their request would never be welcomed or even tolerated. Khubilai was greatly displeased hearing of their wishes. Behind them, Casca stood by the doorway, watching Khubilai further age in front of him.

"You are my friends. My only true friends. The only ones who have never asked or expected anything of me. Does your stay at my court not please you?"

In a near pathetic manner, Khubilai attempted to change their minds. It was foolish to offer wealth to such men; true they were merchants, yet they had never shown the uncontrollable thirst for gain and profit that many of their kind were known for. Khubilai coughed into his trembling hands, anxious to find a way to remedy this unforeseen situation. The Great Khan had aged terribly in the recent weeks, the death of his son finally draining him of all reserves.

"No one had ever been so well received and so royally treated. It would be impossible." Maffeo bowed even further, hoping not to overly anger the Khan. "We have been treated like kings."

"You have promised never to ask me this," Khubilai insisted.

"It has been long, Great Khan." Niccolo raised his eyes. "I have become an old man. If not now, I will never be able to return. The road is long and hard." Niccolo lowered his shoulders, realizing he did not look or act the role of an old man. Years had been kind to both him and Maffeo, preserving much of their strength and endurance.

Khubilai shook his head and smiled. "You are not as old as I. Why must you go?"

"We have also made a promise to another great man. Pope Gregory has entrusted us with his letter. We must return to Rome with an answer." The message of nearly twenty years seemed insignificant at the time, yet Khubilai had always respected Niccolo and Maffeo's righteousness.

"Your son, Marco. Surely he will stay. He is my eyes to the empire."

"He is also ready to leave," Niccolo answered.

"I will miss him greatly, he has . . ." Khubilai's words trailed off slowly. Maffeo and Niccolo watched this old man age even further. Crestfallen, Khubilai nodded.

"Will you ever return?"

"We cannot promise, Great Khan."

"Then you must do one more service to the empire," Khubilai insisted. "I need someone I can trust."

Anxious and wide-eyed, Maffeo and Niccolo tried guessing the Khan's wishes.

"Only girls have been born to my brother Hulegu, the Il-Khan of Persia. I need you to escort a bride to his court. The second daughter of Sando, Kochicin is her name. She will be Hulegu's new bride. It will help bring the empire together. Other than Sando, Hulegu is the only one of my blood who has never challenged for the throne."

"We will be honored." Niccolo and Maffeo retreated, pleased yet disappointed of the Khan. Khubilai had grown old. All the fight that he had been famous for had died along with the loss of Chen-Chin. Yet, perhaps Khubilai had found a way to allow them to go, without losing the last bit of himself.

It was a sad sight to see the Khan of the world nearly grovel. No one had ever refused his request before. At least they could do one more service to the empire.

"And you, Old Young One. You truly have been the Lao Shi, the old teacher as many of my subjects call you."

"I will help escort Kochicin. It is also my time to go. Perhaps one day I will return to the empire, the empire of Temur Khan."

For the first time in a long while, Khubilai Khan allowed a smile to escape his lips.

"Yes, Temur. My grandson." Khubilai's smile broadened.

Khubilai had been quite generous. A dozen of the Khan's best horses had been prepared, half of them carrying wealth that could purchase a kingdom. It was a long journey ahead, filled with peril and excitement.

Princess Kochicin, the beautiful and shy bride-to-be, anxiously awaited their departure. She would greatly miss her father, Sando, and the luxury of Khanbalic, yet, she would be queen of Persia, the principal wife of Khan Hulegu. For nearly two years she had known of her fortune, and now it was going to become a reality. Flashing a pleased smile, she watched the final preparations.

"I cannot believe we are finally going to leave." Vittorio

shook his head while he fastened the saddle of his horse. The thought of returning to Venice, and once again crossing most of the known world, was a daunting task.

"I will miss the Khan and . . . I will miss everything." Marco laughed, realizing it would take hours to list all the wonders of the East they had experienced.

"What was his name again? Carvo? Oh, yeah. Carvo Donatello. I doubt if he is still alive." Maffeo laughed at his recollection of nearly twenty years past.

"Bitter men seem to live forever, Maffeo. Don't be surprised if he hasn't change a bit. I wonder if it is safe to return, Marco." Niccolo looked at his son and smiled.

Marco returned the smile and continued overseeing the preparation for their departure. They were all saddened by their parting, yet it was time. Marco held the message Khubilai Khan was sending to Pope Gregory in his hands and placed it against his heart. It was a mission that had taken nearly twenty years. Marco wondered what great changes could have taken place back in Venice and the Holy Land.

One hundred of Sando's most trusted stood at the ready to escort the princes. Casca watched the rugged warriors of the steppes sitting high in the saddle, patiently waiting. Most of them had taken part in turning back Nayan's rebellious attack. The empire was once again secure.

Casca raised his eyes to meet Khubilai's solemn face. The Khan of Khans needed to be strong to lead his people. Chabi, his companion of nearly forty years, stood quietly by his side, aware of her husband's age and recent losses. He would need her strength in the years to come.

"I am ready, grandfather." Temur's youthful voice startled Casca for an instant.

Kicking the sides of the horse, Prince Temur approached. Khubilai Khan smiled and saddled up. The two white mounts whinnied as Temur and Khubilai led them toward the willow forest. Khubilai extended his left arm and placed it on his grandson's shoulder as they rode off, side by side.

TWENTY

The return to Venice was no easy undertaking. It carried the same danger and adventure their voyage of nearly twenty years previous had demanded of them. The road was long and provided plenty of opportunity for peril. Better planned and lucky enough not to encounter pirates of land and sea, they returned to the noisy port of Venice within two years. They had been fortunate to have the company of the scarred man the Mongols had called the Old Young One. For twenty years they had traveled along with this mystery, reaping the rewards of his company. There was no use in questioning his existence, as too many times they had experienced the unnatural and unbelievable.

The future of the Mongol empire would play itself out. In his few remaining years Khubilai Khan needed to do what he had failed to do over the previous two decades. Having refused a khurlitai, he had been forced to provide the next ruler of the Mongol empire. Temur Khan, the great-grandson of the Genghis, would hold the future of the empire in his hands for rest of the world to see.

Once again Casca journeyed down the dark alleyway of the western canal. Not much had changed over the last twenty years since he had last walked these paths. A cloudy night hid the stars overhead, while even the full moon struggled to shine through. The sound of water splashing and gondolas bouncing against each other were the only noise that disturbed the night. It was a late summer night in Venice.

Cries of distress broke the calm, awakening Casca from his thoughtful reminiscence. His hand reached for his sword beneath his robe while he began to pick up the pace. Veiled figures ran ahead of Casca, chasing someone unseen to him. He pushed the sword back in its scabbard. Thoughts of over twenty years past rushed back at him, remembering that fateful night when he had saved Marco. Perhaps that had changed the world, perhaps not. He would probably never know. It was just one man after all. A merchant that unlike many of his craft, had made it back from distant lands.

Casca sighed, contemplating his existence and purpose. Would interfering once more change the world or would inaction allow it to turn for the better? After all, how important could any one man be? The uncertainty made him shake his head. His thoughts returned to that fateful day on Golgotha when he, a young and brash foot soldier had changed heaven and earth for the rest of history. It was too much for one man to comprehend.

Time had come to leave this part of the world for now. The last twenty years had left memories that would not soon leave him. Casca reached for his neck where a small leather talisman held the blue-gray pearl. Bitterly he smiled while continuing to walk in near darkness.

Leaving Venice, Casca headed toward the cool air of the northern mountain range. Inside the saddle of his horse he carried a handful of precious stones—rubies, emeralds and a dozen pea-sized diamonds. Khubilai Khan's gifts would no doubt be of help over the years to come. Casca did not need wealth or power, he needed to find the solitude that always seemed to elude him.

He wondered what would ever become of Marco and the rest of them. Would history remember them? Or were they to be eventually lost in the anonymity most of humanity disappeared in? Eventually the last twenty years would meld in his memories to be replaced by war, death, and, worst of all, possibly the love for another woman. It was the greatest pain he had ever encountered.

Kicking at the sides of his horse, Casca made his way up a trail adjacent to a noisy stream. The sun's rays watered his eyes, forcing him to dismount and rest beneath the shade of a large willow tree. Holding his sword with his right hand beneath his robe, Casca rested.

He awoke to the sound of two boys laughing. They chased each other while also trying to capture a few yellow butterflies. Noticing this unusual man so close to them, they quieted down and cowered away for a moment. Deciding to take a chance, the older of the two bravely addressed Casca.

"Our village is just around the bend of the river. Would

you like to see?" They anxiously looked toward this giant man. "Our mother makes the best bread ever," the boy said, trying to coax Casca.

Casca stood and followed the two boys. They were about eight and ten years old, filthy, and reeking from the stench of goat cheese. The two laughed and skipped ahead of Casca as the three walked the few hundred feet to the village. There was not much there, a few dozen huts built next to the stream that snaked down the mountainside. An anxious woman met up with them hearing their boisterous laughter.

"The two of you need to wash right . . ."

Her voice was cut off at the sight of Casca leading his horse about fifty feet behind them. She brought the palm of her hand to her forehead, trying to block the glare coming off the water. Suddenly, without any obvious reason, her fear seemed to dissipate. Casca was strange looking, but he was just one man, after all, and his eyes did not carry the iniquity that she had too often seen.

Casca walked into the village without much notice from anyone. Strange and frightening he may have appeared, yet, very much like the boys' mother, the people of this village did not seem to be concerned. The villagers went about their tasks, milking their goats, bringing pails of water from farther upstream, or just playing with their children. It was going to take more than one stranger to disturb their way of life.

"Welcome. Are you hungry?" the woman welcomed Casca.

"Thank you." Casca extended the reigns of his horse to the older of the two boys who gladly led the beast to a drinking trough by the side of the hut.

"Will you stay for a meal?"

Casca sat and enjoyed the hospitality of these people. The two boys giggled and nudged each other while they sat with their mother, watching Casca eat.

The day blended into the next, then the next. Casca awoke every morning undisturbed, without the weight of the world's troubles on his shoulders. He gathered firewood, helped hunt for food, or just sat by the stream looking out over the valley. The villagers accepted and appreciated his efforts, while at the same time respected his quiet musing. There was not much to do, which pleased Casca for the time being. In this tiny village he had quickly found the solitude that had eluded him for so long.

Weeks and months followed until Casca realized he had been in this village for years. No one questioned who he was and where he had come from. The two young boys grew into strong young men, while their mother willingly accepted his presence without showing any disquiet. He soon became the boys' teacher and friend, finding himself in the same position he had often taken over the centuries.

Whoever had been their father had also become unimportant. Seeing time pass so quickly Casca sometimes wondered when he would need to leave this place. Eventually the lack of change in his appearance would be scrutinized and possibly even feared. Sometimes late at night he thought of taking his belongings and leaving under the cover of darkness, yet he could not get himself to do so. Life was simple and pleasant. Nothing better awaited him elsewhere.

Just as the hourglass seemed to turn for Casca, the curse of his existence found him even within these tranquil mountains. It came in the form of an old trader of peppercorn who had made his way into their small village. Barking loudly, a scraggly dog raced around a broken-down burrow the old man led by a leather strap. The three pathetic creatures arrived on a hot summer day, unknowingly bringing death with them. The scourge of the black death once more found Casca, almost as if having followed him.

Within days the first victims of the blight fell into a bloody oblivion. In two weeks most of the villagers had been afflicted or had been buried. Their breath was ripped from their lungs, torturing them to the end. The last two to die were the young men who seemingly just days before had found Casca underneath the willow tree.

Two days previous they had buried their mother. Now it was their turn. Casca threw dirt over their remains, covering the last two victims of the black reaper, who he had laid thousands to rest over the years. Casca looked around, once again left alone, punished to outlive the ages.

Cursing into the heavens, he left the village by the stream. Eventually the heat of summer and the frigid air of winter would cleanse this place of death. Casca looked down on the three small mounds of dirt that hid the bodies of the ones he had grown to care for. There was no justice.

He followed the trail heading north, anxious to distance himself from this place. Casca wondered if there was anyplace on earth death would not pursue him. It was as if the plague had followed him halfway around the world to upend his every moment of peace. The punishment to watch all he cared for perish in front of his eyes was the eternal torment. The curse of Christ would leave him no rest.

Years passed as Casca traveled the roads of Europe, at times staying in places for a while, until circumstances demanded his departure, yet most often keeping to himself waiting for His return. What was it going to take? The darkest days of humanity, of death, degradation, and despair held most of the land. Was that going to bring the creator out of His hiding? Or was there no return, only an eternity of misery and waiting? The fearful and apocalyptic words of the church brought no resolve, or hope either. In their eyes, all roads led to hell unless there was blind following of their preaching. The age of reason was beyond the horizon.

However, within the wretchedness of disease poverty, and despair, mankind could still battle for power and land. The apocalyptic words of the church were of little use, as nothing could stifle man's thirst for control of each other. There was no escaping the only truth Casca had ever encountered. War and death were the only certainties in this world.

The English and French continued their centuries-long conflict, ensuring every generation would leave its dead to rot in the fields of battle. Time did not seem to have changed the way the two felt about each other. The two decades that Casca had spent in the East had brought little change in the Christian world. The sometime noble and brave words of the crusades had fallen on deaf ears, bringing nothing but greed and impiety to most of the land.

Weighed down by dulled thought, pathetic leadership, and the weight of their armor, the French forces waddled in to the field of battle where the long bows of the English army cut them down, flooding the land with their lives. The French, more stubborn than a pack of old mules, had learned nothing about warfare over the last few decades.

Feeling confident and superior as usual, the French charged

into battle. They became oversized targets for the English longbowmen who cut them down at their leisure. By the time the French had realized all was lost in the battle of Crecy, thousands of them had been impaled by the arrows of the English. It was an embarrassment that would remain in history forever, while their conflict would continue for decades. Nameless battlefields littered the ground with the stiffened corpses of the French and English, while they tried to vanquish each other and become the major power of Europe.

Sickened by the endless bloodletting, Casca headed north toward the fjords that he had not seen in centuries. The time to find serenity had returned once again after decades of war. Casca Ruffio Longinus was tired of it all. No matter the disgust he had developed over the dozen centuries, war always seemed to bring him back into the curse he would carry forever. The eternal soldier. Once again he needed a reprieve.

The decades spent in the frozen northern seas allowed him to find solace for a while. Learning to build strong and hardy boats quickly became his obsession. Casca spent many years whaling and exploring the north seas with his friend Feyodor. Talk of lands farther to the west amused and sometimes frightened most that Casca spoke to, as the thought of worlds beyond the water seemed unimaginable. To most of them, the ocean eventually extended into the eternal winter. Beyond that, there was nothing.

The frigid air weakened even the strongest, but the peacefulness and serenity of the land still pleased him. Decades passed and friends died, once again leaving Casca to bury them and mourn their loss. Old and crippled by hard life, Feyodor succumbed to age and the only certainty of life. Casca stood alone next to the burial ground where his friend rested for eternity. The cutting wind stabbed at Casca's face, forcing him to cover up and turn away from the wintry blast of ice and snow. There was no one left for him here either.

Gathering his belongings, Casca headed south, once again heading toward the land of the French and English. Their struggles had continued undaunted, wasting each other's lives over the generations. Little had changed. Heading east he regrettably passed through the city of Koblenz. It was a city of Great Dying as nearly half perished at the hands of the Black

Plague. Nothing else took both rich and poor without prejudice.

Eventually Casca found his way to the Mediterranean where the edge of the land met the Pillars of Hercules. The warmth of the air and softness of the land brought comfort as Casca made his way into the town of Lagos, next to Sagres, on the southwestern tip of the peninsula.

It was a peaceful town of a few hundred people, most of them shipbuilders, map makers, and instrument designers. The massive plateau of Sagres Point looked out over the ocean and the endless sheer cliffs to the south. Toward the north, an old lighthouse that had been rebuilt following an earlier Muslim assault warned incoming ships of shallow waters. In recent years, Sagres had become the town of Vila do Infante, the prince's town.

Few noticed the scarred man that walked down by the edge of the water. He breathed in the air and allowed the scent and sounds of the ocean to fill his mind. Casca stopped and looked at a somewhat unusual looking boat that was being completed along the quay.

"We could use another strong arm," a small clean-shaven man addressed Casca.

Casca turned and faced the young man.

"How are you at handling ropes and sails?" the man inquired once more with a bright smile on his face.

"Fair." It was all Casca would say for now.

The work was hard, but it allowed Casca to lose himself in something he had learned to love over the years. Unusual in design, the ships fascinated Casca. He had seen thousands of them over the centuries, many of them in battle or commerce. Just like those, these seemed to have been designed with a purpose.

"We can sail into the wind with these sails." Henry, the young man that had hired Casca, spoke with excitement in his voice.

Casca raised his head and looked up at the sails. The sixty-foot boat held up two lateen-rigged square masts that seemed curiously oversized for the ship. It held no beakhead or stern castle, just a simple curved stem, something Casca had not seen in years. The oversized masts seemed impractical for long ocean voyages, almost as if the design was missing something, possibly an additional mizzen or a fore-and-aft sail. Casca looked at its broad base and obviously extensive cargo hold, reminding him somewhat of the Chinese junks he had seen over one hundred years previous in the port of Hangchow.

"It will do well in shallow waters." Casca nodded, at the same time wondering about its maneuverability in rough waters.

Henry smiled, appreciating Casca's knowledge of seagoing ships. The two of them developed an easy friendship as Casca was willing to listen to Henry speak of his obsession with shipbuilding and the plan to travel along the western coast of the dark continent to find new lands and new opportunities. Henry did not need to say it, but Casca clearly knew that the forced conversion of all people met through Henry's travels was a major reason for their urgency and perseverance in building these boats. The church's agenda was not unfamiliar.

It was also clear Henry was no ordinary shipbuilder. Henry's hands may have had scars, but they were not the hands of a man who had been born into poverty. Neither was the way Henry spoke or walked. The royal blood clearly flowed through his veins. Casca did not seem to care, which allowed Henry a certain sense of comfort.

Weeks passed during which Casca found that working through the hot day allowed his bones to warm after the many years spent in the frozen north. The cold winters that had nearly frostbitten his fingers and toes were slowly returning to life. The cool evening breeze also soothed him, bringing fond memories of time spent in Acre with his father. Tazrack's gift from over a hundred years past had remained with Casca, something he would forever be indebted for, yet would never be able to repay. Somehow the simple life and lack of demands on his sword allowed a brief reprieve for the eternal soldier.

Casca watched Henry sit on a wooden bench with his back to the west, reading a haphazardly arranged handful of papers. By the end of the night when most workers had given up the day's work and headed for rest, Henry often read by the light of the setting sun. Quickly he would become lost in the words the papers offered.

Seeing Casca approach, Henry folded the papers together and tied them up with a blackened leather strap.

"The sun has surely been hot over the last two days," Henry said, attempting some idle chatter. Seeing Casca not respond, Henry smiled. "Your hands weren't made for the building of ships."

Casca sat on the wooden rail and faced Henry. He looked at his thick calloused hands and brought them to his neck. A frown appeared on his face. His fingers traced the leather pouch hanging from an old strap.

"Soon this ship will sail south. I know there has to be a way . . ."

Casca sat listening to Henry, realizing that this was no ordinary shipbuilder. There was an unusual intensity in his eyes. Henry may have been of royal blood, but he seemed to take no interest in the usual rewards such positions offered. The desire to learn and explore was his obsession.

"It is just the first of many. The design has been changed a dozen times to fit . . ." Henry stopped speaking, realizing that Casca had suddenly become quiet and contemplative.

"I don't know how that thing will ever take to water." Henry raised his head and pointed to the large and cumbersome looking boat docked adjacent to the caravel.

Casca had earlier thought the same. The "thing" Henry was referring to hardly seemed fit to survive the angry waters of the Atlantic, although Casca had sailed on many that had not looked much better. This one creaked within the grasp of the waters and sounded like it was going to sink every time it bounced against the wharf. Casca turned away and looked west toward the setting sun.

"Enough of these ships for a while." Henry laughed. "I know I have spoken to you of my little sister before. My fair-haired Isabella may be young, but she has been promised to the prince of Aragon. It will be a great joining of our two nations. Have I mentioned . . . ?"

Casca stood by the newly completed rail of the caravel, looking beyond Henry who just sat and spoke of alliances, kings and the continual struggle for power amongst the nations of Europe. Just as preoccupied as Henry was with the building of ships, he continuously returned to the endless dealings between his father, King Joao of Portugal, his two older brothers, and the arranged marriage of his little sister. It was just another joining of a prince and princess. The world would go on as always. The balance of power was not about to shift over their union. Intriguing and relevant as it may have been, Casca was unable to hear any of it on this night. His thoughts had slipped into the past.

Casca continued nodding while looking west, nearly oblivious of Henry's voice. For some reason he was hearing less and less of what Henry was saying. Henry had been his usual talkative self, but Casca's thoughts had become preoccupied by something even he could not determine. Suddenly he looked toward Henry's waist as the young man had placed the bundle of papers into a leather purse.

"They are stories of travel and adventure," Henry remarked, seeing Casca look down at the stack of papers he had been reading ever since they had met.

Casca raised his eyes and nodded in mild surprise. He had expected Henry to be looking at drawings of ships or something alike to it, not reading about someone's travels.

"These stories were written by a prisoner of war over one hundred years ago," Henry offered. Seeing Casca unwilling to speak, he continued.

"Strange as it may seem, this man Rustichiello wrote about things that happened in lands far away. In places almost beyond our imagination. His tales are of places at the end of the world where great mysteries and riches await. For years the road has been filled with obstacles, mountains, endless deserts, and fields of battle—however, I believe it will take . . ."

Casca continued nodding, having lost all interest in what Henry was saying. After all, how could a prisoner be writing about travel and adventure? Perhaps they were the stories of a mad man. Being imprisoned had a way of bringing words of the insane to anyone.

Seeing Casca have no interest in what he was saying, Henry continued undaunted.

"Rustichiello did not write about his own travels, but of a young man named Captain Polo, Marco Polo and his father and uncle."

Casca's breathing stopped. His mind swirled as he looked at Henry.

"Marco?"

"Yes, Marco Polo," Henry happily answered, pleased that he had gotten Casca's attention.

"Marco Polo had traveled all the way to the court of the legendary Khubilai Khan over one hundred years ago. There are many things, I should say endless things, that seem unbelievable in his stories. First of all, this man who he does not name who had saved his life and traveled along with them . . ."

Henry stopped talking for a moment not quite certain himself for the reason of it. Casca had been looking at him without blinking since he had mentioned the name of Marco. Looking down at the bundle of papers by his waist, Henry shook his head and raised his eyes toward Casca. He smiled at his foolish thoughts and sat down.

Casca reached toward his neck and held the small leather pouch that contained the single blue-gray pearl. He looked up at the blanket of stars and smiled bitterly. Overhead, the Seven Sisters pointed to the west, leading foolish men toward the open seas. Farther north, the Great Dipper led the true way to the North Star. His thoughts returned to over a century past, to Hormuz, where they had buried Octavio far from his hometown of Alexandria and his seven sisters that he had loved so much. Pain of the past always seemed to revisit. For Casca it was the only constant in this world.

"I have never seen one so beautiful." By the light of the moon, the pearl sparkled as Casca held it between his fingers.

"Where . . . ?" Henry's words ended seeing Casca suddenly palm the pearl. "I will check the rigging one more time."

Henry walked away, leaving Casca alone with his thoughts. Once again Casca held the blue-gray pearl between his fingers, rolling it, remembering the day Ko had been buried with the pearl clenched tightly between her lifeless fingers. His thoughts held prisoner by the past tortured him once more.

Henry returned perhaps an hour later to find Casca standing by the rail, still looking out toward the ocean.

"Look at those imbeciles." Henry pointed to the dilapidated ship moored next to them. Drunken men ran and fought on deck, cursing at each other in strange languages, while others likely less intoxicated tried to keep them from killing each other. The melee continued for a while, while more cargo was brought on board, making Casca and Henry wonder if they were actually witnessing some celebration of sorts.

"I hear they are heading out to sea in a few days. Good riddance. They are nothing but a bunch of mercenaries and pirates, foolish men looking for adventure and bounty." Henry scoffed at them.

Casca's eyes narrowed as he breathed in the salty air. He held his breath for a few seconds as if trying to recall something distant. Dissatisfied by what he could not understand, Casca shook his head.

"Maybe it is time for me to get some sleep. Tomorrow is a big day. I guess they all are." Henry laughed at his own cheerful words. "One step closer to finishing the boat and a day closer to peace, at least in this part of the world." Henry continued for a while longer, talking of his sister Isabella, as usual, and her impending joining with the prince of Aragon. Casca could hear nothing but the sounds of the ocean and voices from the distant past.

Casca awoke early, just as the sun was peaking over the eastern cliffs. His sleep had been restless and unsatisfying. He walked on the wharf, still lost in thought and pained by memories.

"We could use another hand on deck." The voice of a bearded man startled him.

Casca looked up at the man and the filthy hand extended toward him. The large cumbersome boat bobbed on the waves, unsettling Casca about possibly joining the crew of this vessel. Four robed men kneeled on the squalid deck behind their bald-headed leader, chanting in unison. They all faced east for the first prayer of the day.

"You've got nothing to do but stay alert and have your sword ready. Looks like you can do that." The man laughed while eyeing Casca's sword. "One hour."

Casca looked toward Henry's new sailing ship, then shifted his eyes toward this pathetic looking thing in front of him. The merchant ship looked broad and cumbersome making Casca wonder how it would take to the sea. He sighed at the thought of returning to the mainland where he had seen nothing but war and pestilence for the last one hundred years.

It was time to leave this land once more and distance himself from the memories Henry had unknowingly reawakened. A better fate likely awaited him sailing the open seas. The majesty of the ocean had often brought tranquility to Casca's tortured soul. While straightening the sword in its sheath, Casca boarded the *Kuta*. . . .